THE HOUSESHARE

Fiona O'Brien left an award-winning career in advertising to write her first novel in 2002 and has now published several bestsellers, including *The Love Book*, *The Summer Visitors* and *The Summer We Were Friends*. She lives in Sandymount, Dublin.

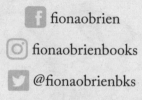

 fionaobrien

 fionaobrienbooks

 @fionaobrienbks

ALSO BY FIONA O'BRIEN

None of My Affair
No Reservations
Without Him
The Love Book
The Summer Visitors
The Summer We Were Friends

Fiona O'Brien

The Houseshare

HACHETTE
BOOKS
IRELAND

Copyright © 2022 Fiona O'Brien

The right of Fiona O'Brien to be identified as the author of
the work has been asserted by her in accordance with the
Copyright, Designs and Patents Act 1988.

First published in Ireland in 2022 by HACHETTE BOOKS IRELAND

First published in paperback in 2023

1

Cataloguing in Publication Data is available from the British Library.

ISBN 9781529354614

Typeset in Adobe Caslon Pro by Bookends Publishing Services, Dublin
Printed and bound in Great Britain by Clays, Elcograf S.p.A.

Hachette Books Ireland policy is to use papers that are natural, renewable
and recyclable products and made from wood grown in sustainable forests.
The logging and manufacturing processes are expected to conform to
the environmental regulations of the country of origin.

Hachette Books Ireland
8 Castlecourt Centre
Castleknock
Dublin 15, Ireland

A division of Hachette UK Ltd
Carmelite House, 50 Victoria Embankment, EC4Y 0DZ

www.hachettebooksireland.ie

For
Jennifer O'Brien (1986–2019)
Forever passionate about justice, Shakespeare,
Harry Potter, pink, animals and Lululemon –
not necessarily in that order.
In our hearts always.

Prologue

Five years earlier . . .

Morah thought of the house as her own. And in a way it was. It was her home, certainly – the only happy one she had ever known. That alone made it precious to her. And if caring for somewhere tenderly, tending to every nook and cranny with studious affection, knowing every curve and groove of the place like the surface of her own skin counted for anything at all, then surely each attentive stroke and loving caress she had bestowed on it over the years had *made* it hers. After all, she reasoned – you didn't have to own something for it to belong to you.

Morah had read somewhere that houses were affected by the people who passed through them, the lives that unfolded beneath their roofs, the stories they contained – which made her all the more vigilant in her duties as caretaker, or *concierge*, as she preferred to think of herself. Today a new tenant was moving in to 24 Ulysses Crescent, bringing the number in the house back up to six, so Morah was doubly eager that her meticulous care of the shared areas was visible for all to see. She plumped and stroked cushions as if they were beloved pets, threw open windows as if greeting a long-lost friend, and had dusted and hoovered within an inch of her life. Now the house was even more pristine than usual. She had surpassed herself – Morah was her own harshest critic in this respect – its beautiful Georgian proportions reflected in the light that streamed through generous and symmetrical windows.

Even though it was Doctor Ed (who owned the house) who had helped her, had supported her in her time of need, it was the house itself – Morah felt deep down – which had truly helped her to recover. So much so, that everything that had gone before often seemed to her like the memory of a rather dark, disturbing film she had been forced to watch – and had long since consigned to a closed recess of her mind marked *do not revisit*.

The people who shared the house were important too, and with the arrival of this latest tenant, all six flats would be occupied. The tenants in general certainly didn't escape Morah's discreet but watchful supervision. It wasn't that she vetted them, as such. But she felt confident that should she need to voice a reservation about any of them, Doctor Ed would listen to her and take her advice into serious consideration.

As it was, they were a happy lot who had passed through the house since she had come to live here almost ten years ago – young, most of them, apart from herself and Doctor Ed, who lived in his small flat in the garden, even though number 24 had formerly been his family home. But he had been a widower for the last twelve years, and now, at seventy-three, the tenants in the house had become his substitute family.

The newest tenant was due to arrive any minute. And for once Morah knew nothing about her – it had all happened very quickly. Doctor Ed had met this woman – a widow – at a gathering, and when she'd heard he owned a house in flats on Ulysses Crescent, and that one was currently vacant, she had begged to be shown it and had fallen in love with flat 3 at first sight. And why wouldn't she? Morah reasoned. All six of the flats were beautiful in their own way. She would have liked to meet this woman first, to size her up – but Morah had been down the country on a few days off at the time when the flat had been shown. From the corner of her eye now, she noticed an elegant dark-green van pulling up outside, *G.A. Stevens and Son Removals* was written on the side – and at that moment the doorbell sounded, making her jump. Morah took a quick look in the mirror, straightened her white overall, and patted her hair, fixed a pleasant but business-like expression on her face, and went to answer the door.

'Hello!' the glamorous older woman said brightly as she rushed past Morah. 'I'm moving into number 3 today!' She waved at Morah as she started up the stairs. 'The guys are right outside with my furniture – must dash! I'm Evelyn, by the way.' She looked back briefly. 'Evelyn Malone.'

She hadn't even waited for Morah to introduce herself. And why would she? Women like Evelyn Malone didn't stop for the little people. She was acting as if she owned the place already. She had dismissed Morah without so much as a second glance before she barged past her. Which was just as well, really. Because if she had paused to interact with her for just a moment, she might have noticed Morah's face paling. She might have thought the sharp intake of breath, as

Morah gasped, rather odd. She might even have noticed the flare of recognition in Morah's eyes, as they widened in horror.

Because although Evelyn clearly didn't recognise Morah, Morah knew *exactly* who Evelyn Malone was. She just never, in her wildest nightmares, thought she would have to share a house with her.

Chapter One

Present day

The best thing about her apartment – Evelyn didn't like referring to it as a flat – was its proximity to the sea. 24 Ulysses Crescent not only overlooked the undulating spread of Dublin Bay from its elegant perch on the sought-after terrace, but was conveniently located just across the road from Mariner's Cove, a favourite bathing spot, one which Evelyn – long before she came to live there – frequented. She was heading there now for her early-morning swim. She pulled on her red one-piece and tied up her shoulder-length hair with a favourite paisley headband. Her hair was no longer the glossy black mane of her youth (she had been referred to as a raven-haired beauty in those days), but neither was it grey. When she'd begun to resent the tyranny of covering her roots, Evelyn had consulted with her then hairdresser – a rather dashing man of Viennese and Polish extraction – who, despite his preference for his own sex, had both appreciated and understood the exact nature of Evelyn's beauty and her dilemma. She had allowed him to persuade her to strip out the last of her faded colour and put in a platinum rinse. The result had been sensational. The dramatic flaxen white hair set off her olive skin and dark eyes to striking effect, and even now, twenty-five years later, she was maintaining the ritual. These days she frequented a local salon – not nearly as much fun as visiting dear Valerio, who had eventually moved abroad – but a similar effect was achieved, and the local salon was cheaper. Now that she was into 'the third act' as she referred to her stage in life, she was more prudent with money. After all, it didn't grow on trees. Poor Lenny, her late husband, had had every intention of leaving her comfortably off – but as his financial portfolio was heavily invested in property, he had lost his shirt in the crash of 2008 and, unbeknown to Evelyn, had re-mortgaged the house in an effort to get back on track. When he'd died of a heart attack seven years later, the banks had swiftly announced they would repossess the house if Evelyn failed to pay her mortgage arrears, which was when she was alerted to the situation for the first time. The amount was quite impossible for her to come up with. But it would take a lot more than an implosion of the global economy to curtail Evelyn Malone – she had risen to the unforeseen occasion with aplomb. For the following two years she had continued to live in the house, stalling the banks with false promises and keeping herself afloat by the skin of her teeth. She'd sold the sleek Mercedes, the expensive jewellery, her late husband's collection of modern art, which she had never shared his enthusiasm for. Money wasn't everything: she had long ago left behind any attachment to things purely material (age was very liberating in that respect), and status symbols – whether designer handbags or flashy cars – no longer held any appeal. She had style, and no amount of money could buy that. Evelyn always looked terrific – back in her fashion-icon days and equally now, at seventy-six. A lot she put down to genetics: she had been lucky with her tall, lithe figure and looks – the former she maintained with swimming, yoga, and a careful diet, the latter with taste, attitude, and a penchant for flamboyance. Her surroundings, on the other hand, mattered greatly to her. That was why her apartment had been such a find.

In fact, her financial misfortune (the exasperated bank was by this time threatening a humiliating eviction) was how she had found number 3 – which just went to prove her motto: *It's an ill wind that blows no good*. It was at a support group she had attended at the suggestion of a friend – for people who had lost their savings – that she had met retired doctor Ed Hamilton. He had been in a similar position previously, having lost his private pension in property speculation – and when they were chatting (she had naturally gravitated towards the most attractive man in the room to engage him in conversation) he'd mentioned that he'd had his old family home in Ulysses Crescent turned into flats. He himself had moved into the granny flat at the end of the garden and was surviving these days on his modest state pension and rent from his tenants. Evelyn had thought this both inventive and brave, and enquired whether he found strangers taking over his house upsetting – she also deduced there was no longer a living *Mrs* Hamilton. At seventy-eight years of age, Ed was two years her senior, and still a rather attractive and distinguished-looking man. But Doctor Ed had said his garden was far more important to him than any house, and this way he got to keep it, and his familiar address and neighbours – and into the bargain had made some wonderful new friends. 'We're like a big happy family,' he had said, smiling. 'In fact, one of the flats is just about to become vacant – I'm looking for a new tenant.'

When Evelyn had subsequently been given the guided tour, and seen the beautifully converted interior of number 24, with its wonderful period details, high ceilings and generous windows, she had immediately decided she had to live there, and begged Ed to give her number 3, on the first floor. It wasn't terribly big, but the view over Dublin Bay was perfect, and the rent, although steep, was manageable. It would have to be, Evelyn had decided then, because the only alternative was to live with her daughter, Pauline, in London – and she didn't know which of them would be more horrified at the prospect. Her artist son, Tristan – her golden boy, so different from his sister – was in New York, but living in America with him wasn't on the cards either. He was an indigent artist and had already been a significant drain on her own finances as it was – not that she had begrudged it to him at the time, but things were different now.

So she had sold her antique furniture, and for good measure all the Georgian fixtures and fittings, including the many fireplaces, original plasterwork and floorboards – left the gutted remains of the house to the banks, and moved in to apartment number 3 at 24 Ulysses Crescent and embraced her new life. There was still one significant problem, however. She could only afford to pay for three months of this new life. After that her funds would run out. She needed to figure out a way to pay the rent for the rest of her life. It was while she had been swimming in the sea one freezing March morning that she'd had her lightbulb moment. There was someone she knew who could *easily* afford to help her out – and he owed her big time. She wondered why she hadn't thought of it before. Bobby Radcliffe had let her down badly when it counted, and her whole life had pivoted on the repercussions. Despite her sworn assurances all those years ago – had it really been forty-odd? – that he would never hear from her again, it had been easy enough to track him down through his Dublin office. And he had been more than happy to help her. In fact he'd insisted upon it – especially when she had shared with him her revelation. He had been surprised and thrilled to hear from her, he'd told her – interrupting his precious time on the Portuguese golf course to take her call. More importantly, he was deeply grateful to her for keeping her secret to herself all this time. So the rent for her apartment in 24 Ulysses Crescent had been quickly taken care of, and the ongoing arrangement – such as it was – had been working perfectly well ever since. Evelyn had always been a survivor – she saw no reason to let some foolish decisions of her deceased husband get in the way of her having a pleasant lifestyle, even if it did mean bending the truth a little.

Now, she belted her white towelling robe tightly to show off her waist, slipped her feet into flip-flops and paused to consider herself in the full-length mirror before heading out. 'Evelyn Malone,' she said firmly, tilting her head to her reflection, 'you are some woman for one woman!'

Outside, the terrace was bathed in early-morning light.

The traffic on the main road hadn't yet gained momentum, though the odd early starter whizzed by. Although a pedestrian traffic light had been erected to facilitate people crossing the road to Mariner's Cove, Evelyn rarely needed to wait for it. She checked for oncoming cars – they tended to drive at high speed at this time of the morning, having the road mostly to themselves – but only a sports car was heading towards her. She put one foot on the road (she loved playing this game of chicken) and, sure enough, the driver slowed down and came to a considered halt – gallantly waving her across the road. She smiled her appreciation and waved back, jauntily making her way to the other side. The driver grinned and shook his head. It was a man, of course; a woman would have sped on by. As dear Bobby had always said to her: 'Evie, if a woman has it at seventeen, she'll have it at seventy-seven – and you've got it.' Well, she had only another year to go to prove him right, and she certainly liked to think she would.

She passed the Martello round tower on her right and made her way down the steps to the cove. Already a group of regulars were in the water or towelling themselves down, a few enjoying a hot drink from the flask they'd brought with them for their après-swim chat. Although it was late May now, and the days were getting warmer, the early mornings were still cold – especially when just out of the water.

'Morning, Evelyn.' An older man was making his way out of the water. 'It's beautiful in there today.'

'Morning, Peter. I've been looking forward to this since last night.' She waded in and slipped under, the briskly cool water enveloping her like silk as she swam over to a circle of women treading water and chatting.

'Here's Evelyn now, you can ask her yourself!' One of them nodded in her direction.

'Ask Evelyn what?' She lay back, floating, and tipped up her toes, chin tucked towards her chest.

'How do you look so amazing?' the girl asked wonderingly. 'You're in such good shape . . .'

'For an oldie, you mean?'

'No! By any standards. Your figure – it's unbelievable.'

'She's always looked like that. Haven't you, Evelyn?' An older woman with a creased face smiled.

'I've been lucky, I won't deny it. But swimming definitely helps – and so did smoking until everyone got all goody-goody about it and made us give up. I put on a few pounds then, I can tell you.'

'And I bet you lost all three of them a week later too.' A large woman with broken veins on her face laughed.

'You know me, Sally – I'm always running around doing something. I can't sit still at all.'

'Grandad says you used to be a real heartbreaker in your day.' Sally's daughter Carole eyed her speculatively.

'Tell your grandad it still *is* my day.'

The girl laughed.

'You don't have a mean bone in your body, do you, Evelyn?' Sally said to the group in general. 'Evelyn's probably the most idolised person in Abbottsville! We all aspire to being Evelyn one day. What I wouldn't give for your energy – I don't know how you do it. Swimming, painting, yoga – and she still finds time to help out Nessa with the castle fair.'

The young girl looked suitably chastened. 'I didn't mean—'

'Of course you didn't – I know *that*.' Evelyn grinned, splashing water towards her. 'But less of the *used to be* . . . Both Goldie Hawn and Joanna Lumley are seventy-six too, you know – and you don't see them slowing down.'

'Who?' Carole looked blank as the older women laughed.

'See what you're up against?' Sally said.

'That's my cue to move on, I think. See you later, girls!' Evelyn stretched away from them and kicked off, before turning onto her back and executing a strong, graceful back-stroke out into the bay.

When she got out of the water twenty minutes later, and reached for her towel robe on the railing, she caught sight of two of the other tenants in the house – Nessa, the girl who ran the local vegan café, organised the fair, and did tarot card readings on the side, was chatting to Mike, from flat number 1, who was their resident sculptor.

'Hi, Evelyn.' Nessa greeted her warmly. 'It's warmed up quite a bit, hasn't it?' She was referring to the water temperature, which had finally reached double digits.

'It's divine!' Evelyn sat down on a low wall to pat her feet dry. 'Isn't this a bit early for you, Mike?' Evelyn lifted her eyebrows at the tall dark-haired guy who was pulling on a sweatshirt.

'He's been trying to beat you to it recently, Evelyn.' Nessa grinned. 'Ever since I told him you were always the first one down in the mornings.'

'I thought you were one of the mid-day brigade,' Evelyn said to him.

'I am, usually.' He shrugged. 'I just thought I'd change up my routine now that the sculpture is at the foundry.'

'That's so exciting,' Nessa said. 'I can't wait to see it. When's it going up?'

'About another month. Give or take . . . I'm expecting to hear from the council any day now with a date.'

'Well, I hope he's good-looking, your sculpture, if he's going to be a permanent fixture,' Evelyn said. 'Either way, I think a bronze embodiment of a man looking out to sea, refusing to give up hope for the return of his wife lost in a shipwreck, is both romantic and a very timely reminder to all of you men not to take us women for granted.'

'I'm not sure that's the intention of the council in com-memorating the tragedy of the 1807 shipwreck, Evelyn.' Mike grinned. 'But I'll bear it in mind.'

'Any chance of a sneak preview?' Evelyn asked.

'Nice try.' Mike grinned. 'Afraid it's strictly under wraps – but I'm happy with it.'

'Well, I'm sure it will be worth the wait.' Evelyn waved as she headed off. 'Have a wonderful day, guys!' She ran up the steps.

'Evelyn, be careful!' Nessa called after her, shaking her blonde curls. 'I don't know how she doesn't kill herself,' she said to Mike. 'Those flip-flops are lethal if you hit a wet patch. I've seen younger people than her come a cropper.'

'I don't think caution has found its way into Evelyn's vocabulary,' Mike said, looking after her as she disappeared.

'She's amazing, really. I've never known anyone her age – no, make that anyone of any age – who's so . . . engaged with life. She puts us all to shame. I think we need a support group to cope with living under the same roof as her.'

'Well, I just hope I have her appetite for life when I'm at that stage.'

✧

Evelyn was smiling to herself as she crossed the road and made her way around the corner and into Ulysses Crescent, waving at more friends who were on their way down. The first swim of the day always made her feel incredible, gave her a high that lasted all day. With a bit of luck she might fit another one in later – although she'd promised to meet Dana, who was revamping her small art gallery in the town, and go over her colour scheme with her. Thinking of the gallery brought Evelyn's thoughts back to Mike. That body of his was quite a work of art itself . . . if she were forty years younger, thirty even! He was tall – six two or three, easily – she saw that when she stood beside him, being five foot nine herself. And Nessa was clearly smitten by him. Evelyn couldn't say she blamed her. Despite being perfectly polite and friendly, Mike had an intriguing, rather introverted manner, Evelyn had observed. One that suggested an intensely private character – there was an invisible barrier underneath the affable exterior which would make women insanely keen to get past.

Nessa, for all her pretty liveliness and flirtatious manner, didn't stand a chance with him. Evelyn saw that right away. All her life Evelyn had been able to read men with an invisible radar. As a younger woman she had known at the exchange of a first glance whether or not a man could be hers – and she never bothered, much less worried, about ones that wouldn't. It had saved her a lifetime of heartaches and wasted emotions and probably accounted for her reputation as a heartbreaker. She hadn't been, though – Evelyn didn't break hearts: she just made very sure no one got to break hers, which was an entirely different kettle of fish. She only wished more women followed her example. But in the end heartache had sought her out and found her anyway. If she had been a more reflective woman she might have reasoned that she deserved it. But Evelyn didn't do regrets or wishful thinking – that way disaster lay. Instead she ploughed relentlessly forward; it was the only way she knew how.

She reached for her front-door key and let herself in to the impressive hall with its sea-green walls and diagonally laid large black and white marble tiles. The tall gilt-framed mirror that hung on the opposite wall reflected her image in the flattering early sunlight filtered through the stained-glass fanlight over the front door. Inside it was still quiet, most of the other residents yet to go about their day. From upstairs, the aroma of freshly brewed coffee floated in the air. She wandered over to the antique hall desk, where she noticed that her online order of books had arrived in yesterday's post – she must have missed them. Picking the package up, she continued up the first flight of stairs which ran along the right of the house before sweeping across to the left on the return, and then up again along the far wall towards the first floor, when Stella from number 4, her neighbour across the way who was an estate agent, flew past her and headed downstairs to her first showing of the day. 'Morning, Evelyn!'

'Morning, darling!' Evelyn waved at Stella's retreating back without turning around and began to tear her package open as the young woman ran down the stairs and out the door – and that was when it happened. Evelyn's flip-flop caught on the stair tread – she staggered, then lost her balance, grasping wildly for the banister before tumbling back the four steps to the landing. For a terribly long moment, all she could do was try to catch her breath, before severe pain radiated sharply from her groin on her left side. Struggling to push herself up on her forearms, she looked back at her left leg which remained twisted outwards at an unnatural angle. For the first time in her life, Evelyn Malone couldn't move. She was unable to get up. 'Oh, shit,' she whispered.

Chapter Two

The rain-wet slates of Hackney rooftops sparkled below her in the evening sunlight as Pauline Malone glanced out the window of her tiny kitchen, idly rubbing the top of the oven with a scouring sponge, phone to the ear in her other hand. It had been a wet spring, but according to the latest forecasts, the rest of May would be warm and dry.

'You really should go over, Pauline – I would if I didn't have this exhibition coming up. Hopefully I'll be able to shift a couple of my bigger paintings . . .' She listened to her half-brother Tristan's laboured sigh, feeling the habitual detachment. It was easy to issue orders from across the Atlantic – easy to list the reasons why – when your most pressing concern was making everyone understand what a misunderstood artist you were. She pictured him pushing a hand through his golden hair. The American twang was stronger than the last time they had spoken.

'I can't just drop everything,' she said. The sponge moved more urgently now across the hob – exasperation always made her edgy. 'I'm needed here, you know.' Her voice rose and she swallowed, hating the defensive tone that crept in. There was no contest, of course. There never had been.

Tristan always came out on top. He won because he was the much younger child, the golden boy. He won because he was an artist, not a dull, boring social worker. He won because he wasn't her. Pauline had inherited the features that made women consider her late father ruggedly handsome – while Tristan had inherited his own father's height and looks along with a twist of Evelyn's fine-boned, graceful beauty. Pauline had been Lacey to his Cagney. More Frances McDormand than Frances Farmer.

People who got to know her over the years – friends, acquaintances, work colleagues – gathered reasonably quickly that Pauline's relationship with her mother was a 'difficult' one. That was, if they discovered she had a mother at all. Pauline – if at all possible – avoided mentioning her. It was easier not to. Talking about Evelyn made her real – and it was hard enough to keep her looming shadow out of mind. Pauline had managed the out of sight bit, but it didn't lessen the acute sense of humiliation that clung like a second skin – of knowing she was and always had been a disappointment to her mother. In the early days she had subconsciously sought attention by rebelling – until it had become apparent that Evelyn had neither the insight nor the inclination to discover what, if anything, was at the root of her daughter's contrariness. Eventually, the rebellion had escalated to the level at which Pauline was happy to acknowledge she was a distinct embarrassment to her mother, and over the years both had mutually if tacitly agreed not to burden the other with their presence unless absolutely necessary. Birthday and Christmas cards were exchanged and that was about it. Pauline assumed – correctly it turned out – that the arrangement had resulted in a certain relief for Evelyn. As for herself, she had become exhausted – and the estrangement, which continued to the present day, was easier than admitting that her mother had no interest whatsoever in, or affection for, her only daughter.

'She wouldn't want me there, Tristan. I'm sure she'd much rather depend on her wonderful circle of friends who love her so much.'

'Pauline, she's your *mother*, for heaven's sake. That's the bottom line.'

Pauline knew her relationship with their mother was totally confusing to Tristan, who continued to be exasperated by their estrangement.

'This is a chance for you to finally bond with her, Pauline. You could look after her while she recuperates.'

Pauline almost laughed out loud at the idea. 'I don't think so.'

'It would be an opportunity, Pauline . . . she's seventy-six. She won't be here forever. She'd like to at least hear from you – I know she would.'

'You mean *you'd* like her to hear from me.'

There was a pause then, during which Pauline guessed Tristan was biting back his next comment and rolling his eyes . . . while she grudgingly reminded herself she wasn't fifteen anymore and something would have to be done about the matter. Also, she didn't want to alienate her only sibling. It wasn't Tristan's fault, any of this.

'Look, leave it with me and I'll think about visiting her,' she said. 'They're not letting her out of hospital just yet, are they?'

'No . . . no – another week or so, her surgeon said.'

She could hear the relief in his voice that she hadn't outright refused. He sounded tired. She had to remember that he had his own worries too. A career that had never got off the ground, and possibly a growing suspicion was dawning that he wasn't really the golden boy their mother had always led him to believe he was.

'Let's talk in a few days,' she said.

She put her phone down on the countertop – only noticing then that the fingers on her other hand had been rubbed raw by her furious scouring.

Chapter Three

'So,' Truth had said to her without preamble on the phone the following day, 'I'll be free next week, and I've booked us into a lovely country house hotel in Oxfordshire for this weekend – and you're coming with me. We need to catch up, Mum, it's been ages – it'll be a belated birthday present as well.'

'You already sent me a birthday present, Tru.' Pauline had glanced at the wonderful flower arrangement her daughter had sent her, which took up almost the entire hall. Her council flat in the tower block was tiny, but she finally owned it outright, and the address was in the now trendy part of Hackney. Looking out over the rooftops below her, lit by early-morning or evening sun, and wondering about the lives going on underneath them was one of her favourite things to do. It reminded her of *Mary Poppins* for some bizarre reason.

'Well, you deserve another one.' Pauline had heard the grin in her daughter's voice. 'Just take Friday and Monday off.'

What was it with her brother, and now her daughter, assuming she could just demand time off? 'I can't just take off whenever I feel like it, Tru. I'll have to clear it with Sheila.' Pauline had frowned, thinking about the compassionate leave she was already in the process of working out with her colleagues in the women's shelter. Tristan had texted her that Evelyn was coming out of hospital the following week. Pauline still couldn't quite get her head around it – she suspected she was in denial. Facing anything to do with her mother had that effect on her – never mind the thought of going back to Dublin after over thirty years.

'I'll have to check with work.' Pauline had sighed, then added hurriedly, 'But that sounds absolutely lovely, Tru, thank you.'

In the event, her boss, Sheila, had insisted she take the long weekend. 'Of course you must, Pauline! You never take time off. It'll be lovely for you spending time with Tru – especially facing into the other thing . . .' Sheila knew the toll the prospective trip to Dublin was taking on Pauline.

And now, here she was, sitting in a fluffy bathrobe by a heated swimming pool admiring her newly painted finger nails and toenails, watching her daughter clock up seemingly effortless lengths of the pool.

An hour later, after an elegant and delicious afternoon tea of the tiniest and most delicate sandwiches Pauline had ever seen, and scones with cream and jam that melted in her mouth, they went back to their suite for a rest before dinner.

'I can hardly keep my eyes open.' Pauline smiled sleepily at her daughter who was propped up by cushions on the other bed, looking at her laptop.

'You're not supposed to – this is a rest for you, remember?'

'Fine one to talk, you are.' Pauline frowned at the laptop. 'We agreed, no work – remember?'

'It's not work, I'm just checking email.'

Pauline worried about her daughter although she was intensely proud of her. She thought she worked too hard, and she looked more drawn and tired since she had last seen her. Truth had always been driven. She was a gifted student who had seemed to take exams and scholarships in her stride – only Pauline knew the intense work and study that had gone into her seemingly meteoric rise up the career ladder. After obtaining a double first in law from Oxford, and completing her bar training, Truth had been accepted to a sought-after chambers for pupillage and was the youngest barrister called to the bar that year. Now part of a successful and thriving practice, Truth represented victims of sexual assault or women who had been sexually harassed or excluded in the workplace – and her prosecuting skills and reputation brought frowns of concern and displeasure from opposing lawyers who were informed they would be coming up against her.

Pauline studied her now, while Truth was immersed in her screen, quietly marvelling yet again at the miracle of nature and favourable genetic arrangements that had somehow been responsible for bringing this gorgeous creature into the world. She remembered holding her in the hospital, that very first time, looking into those big dark eyes that had seemed to see right through her, that were at once so wise and unperturbed – and the names she had been so undecided about, had dithered over to distraction, and had driven Tony mad with over the preceding nine months had all faded to nothing as she'd gazed in wonder at her infant daughter. She had named her Truth, there and then. Later she had decided she had named her after Sojourner Truth, the famous abolitionist and women's rights activist, and partly that was the case – somewhere in her memory, she figured that had probably been where she had heard the name – but Pauline knew deep down that when she had looked at Truth, gazed at her, wondered at her, she knew above all else that she wanted this perfect girl child to be untarnished by all the false, manipulative narratives she had been fed by her own mother. And so she'd named her daughter Truth. Although secretly she believed the child had named herself. The name had come to Pauline so suddenly and so insistently as she had held her that anything else had seemed laughably inappropriate.

In the dining room later that evening, Pauline sipped a glass of red wine while she waited for Truth – who had been held up on a phone call – to join her. She was looking at the few other diners dotted around, and wondering if sitting in the formal room with its huge windows, silk drapes and mirrored over-mantels was as much an unexpected treat for them as for her – or was dining in places where waiters hovered solicitously second nature to them? She fingered the pristine cutlery mindlessly, fiddled with the starched napkin and then reminded herself sternly to keep still. She was so accustomed to fixing and straightening and polishing things around her, she found it almost impossible to just sit and be waited on. She wondered was it obvious . . . but sneaking another glance around the room she saw that no one was taking any undue notice of her. On the contrary, their collective glances seemed to be drawn in the opposite direction towards the main doors, which had swung open and were now being held by two members of staff. Through them walked Truth, all five foot ten inches of her, in Converse trainers, skinny jeans, and a long white silk shirt. Looking at her daughter – as a stranger might – Pauline could see why heads turned when she passed by. She had Tony's height and easy, long-limbed gait, his olive-skinned colouring, dark hair and arresting eyes framed by unfairly thick lashes and naturally full, striking brows. Her nose, which still had the slight bump from when she fell out of her buggy as a toddler, curved slightly downwards at its tip, but managed to per- fectly balance her rather large mouth, which – grinning now, as she caught sight of Pauline – revealed her perfectly aligned white teeth. Watching her, Pauline decided there was something different about Truth since the last time she had seen her, which was just over a month ago – but she couldn't pinpoint exactly what. Her hair was pretty much the same, still long and straight, a few layers added maybe, but there was something a little guarded in her expression, and she seemed to be a bit on edge.

'That was Dad, I couldn't get him off the phone.' Truth sat down breathlessly. Truth and her father, Tony, had recon- nected six years ago and maintained a sporadic, if reasonably affectionate, and mostly, as far as Pauline could tell, online relationship.

'How is he?' Pauline made an ongoing effort to be neutral when she enquired about her erstwhile partner.

'Still shacked up with the German broad.' Truth shrugged.

Tony's ongoing liaisons with successive women over the years had become a source of either mild amusement or grudging disbelief – depending on Pauline's humour. The same devil-may-care attitude and irresponsible habits that she had found so beguiling and attractive in her youth (how had she ever found living in a squat empowering?) were, not surprisingly, the death knell to their brief relationship. As a permanently out-of-work musician, reluctant to pursue any kind of real job, Tony and his charms had lasted only long enough for him to stay around for Truth's first eighteen months. Pauline assumed the women who had taken her place over the years had been equally charmed initially, until either they, or he, had been unable to tolerate the tedium and requirements of normal domesticity.

'This one's lasting longer than most,' Truth observed, pouring some water.

'He's getting old, that's why.'

'Sixty-five isn't old!' Truth's eyebrows lifted.

'In your father's case, you're probably right,' Pauline said. 'I'm pretty sure he's just as incapable of acting his age now as when we were together.'

'People do grow up, you know.' Truth looked at her pointedly. 'You guys were only together for just over two years, remember.'

'I knew all I needed to know – believe me.'

'He might have changed, that's all. It was a long time ago.'

It was, but it didn't feel like it – not when Pauline thought about it. The years had passed in a blink.

She remembered doing her Leaving Certificate in the Dublin technical college after being kicked out of yet another private school for doing drugs and refusing to abandon her punk hair and clothes. Then she had gone to London, had finally got away. She'd hooked up with friends of friends, all doing pretty much what she did: going to gigs, flashing their punk credentials, getting out of it, getting the dole – and crashing in the squat where she'd wake shivering and bleary-eyed and do it all over again. She shuddered now at the thought. Tony, nine years her senior, of British African-Caribbean heritage, all long limbs and leather, with his piercing green eyes and guitar-strumming, had seemed so exotic to her then – dangerous, anarchic, exciting. When she'd discovered she was pregnant she was shocked, and unexpectedly confused, totally unprepared for Tony's reaction – which had been to tell her to relax, that it would be fun to have a kid around. And it *was* fun, in the very beginning – until the social worker found them a flat and encouraged Tony to get a job. Then it hadn't been fun at all . . .

But having Truth had saved her – Pauline was sure of it. Without her, she didn't like to think how her self-destructive tendencies might have played out. When Tony had left them – without a forwarding address – Pauline had straightened herself out, and with the help of her social worker had traced confirmation of her exam results in Dublin (she'd been surprised to see how well she had done) and been admitted to the training scheme which led to a part-time university degree course and her subsequent career in social work.

'Maybe,' Pauline conceded.

It wasn't her intention to belittle Truth's father to her, but she wanted her to be vigilant about the tendency to addiction in the family and to protect Truth from any possible let-downs. Truth had eventually tracked Tony down when she was ready to – on Facebook – and he had been eager to re-establish contact, delighted and relieved, Pauline suspected, that not only was his abandoned daughter now a highly respected lawyer but a high-earning one, who would not be burdening her father with requests for financial support. Truth had visited Tony once or twice, met his two other children – a brother and sister both a lot younger than her and with different mothers – and Truth now seemed to be tolerantly affectionate towards her father. As for any addictive tendencies, Pauline needn't have worried – apart from working too hard, Truth didn't smoke, take drugs, or drink to excess. She was independent to a fault and under no illusions about ever relying on a man to complete her life. In fact, sometimes Pauline wondered if she had gone too far in that respect, indoctrinating her daughter as she had while she was growing up – but she was so intent on keeping her safe and free from unhealthy relationships with either substances or men that she hadn't been able to hold back.

'How's Josh?' Pauline changed the subject.

'He's good – last time I saw him.'

Pauline looked at her. 'Meaning?'

'We decided to consciously uncouple,' Truth said, looking innocent.

'Really?' Pauline was taken aback. She had rather liked Josh, even if he had been a bit buttoned-up and posh – he had always been nice to Pauline on the few occasions they had met and was obviously mad about Truth. 'Why?'

Truth shrugged. 'We just sort of ran out of road, I guess. Not enough in common. I didn't really see a future together.'

'You could've fooled me.' Pauline didn't push it. She recognised the evasive tone – there would be no point in enquiring further.

'So,' Truth said after they had finished dinner and were

having coffee, 'you're still stressed about Grandma Evelyn, yeah?' She eyed Pauline. 'I can tell.'

Pauline knew there was no point protesting. But before she could speak, Truth went on.

'I've been thinking . . .'

'What?'

'Well, I know this might sound like a random idea, but . . . I'm on a natural break after this last case, and chambers are giving me some time off to recharge my batteries. I want to go off-grid for a while as well, social media-wise. Ireland would be a nice place to relax – I think I should go over and stay with Grandma Evelyn in Dublin, instead of you feeling like you have to just because Tristan wants you to. We can phone and text to keep you in the loop.'

'You!'

'Yeah. What's the problem with that? I've never been to Dublin, and I can't remember the last time I met Grandma Evelyn—'

'You were seven years old.' Pauline remembered the awkward First Holy Communion lunch acutely.

'Exactly. I'd like to get to know her before she, like, dies or something – and I'd like to go to Dublin, have a look around. I don't have any history with her, like you do – and then you won't have to get stressed about anything.'

For just a second, Pauline considered the possibility and had an unconscious intake of breath. The thought wasn't just freeing, it was . . . glorious! She must have hesitated just an instant too long because Truth pressed on.

'See! I knew you were stressed about it. You know,' she pressed, 'you've never really told me why you and Grandma

Evelyn don't get along. What exactly happened between you to cause this rift?'

Pauline chose her words carefully. 'Nothing specific happened as such. Sometimes I just think children are born to the wrong parents. Evelyn was the wrong mother for me and I certainly seemed to have been the wrong daughter for her. We just didn't understand each other. We're both a lot happier without each other in our respective lives,' she said. 'But that's no reason that you shouldn't get along like a house on fire with her. Most people think she's wonderful. She's certainly very charming, when she wants to be.'

'Well that settles it. There's absolutely no point, Mum, in putting yourself through that kind of stress when you don't have to. I'll go. Okay?'

'But you—'

'But I what? I don't know how to look after someone? You're not exactly a nurse yourself – and I'm good with people, you've often said so. I'm young, agile and willing.' She wiggled her eyebrows. 'Besides, Uncle Tris said there's some sort of community nurse who'll be coming in. And it won't be a drag for me the way it obviously is for you. It might even be fun . . .'

'Ah,' said Pauline, realising Truth and Tristan had already discussed the viability of Truth going to Dublin instead of her. Not that Pauline minded, it was just that she wondered at her daughter's sudden enthusiasm and interest in going to stay with her grandmother. What Pauline had been about to say was, *But you don't know what she's like*, and Truth didn't, how could she? But then, what Truth said made a lot of sense. She had a right to get to know her grandmother, while she still could. And Truth was well able to handle herself – she wouldn't be swayed or intimidated by Evelyn. But it was the more insidious thought that bothered her: Evelyn could be so manipulative . . . what if she got inside Truth's head? What if she tried to change her, if it affected their own relationship? Pauline couldn't bear to think of that.

'I'm not sure . . .'

'Well, I'm sure. So that's settled then.'

After they'd retired to their room, Truth flung herself down on her bed and back against the mountain of pillows – reaching for the remote control to turn on the TV. An advertisement for the Irish tourist board immediately filled the screen with beautiful scenery and people strolling through ancient sites and socialising happily on pub benches.

'See? It's a sign.' Truth was pleased. 'Six weeks in Dublin will be cool.'

'Six weeks? That long? I thought you meant a short visit.'

'No, six weeks – it's not a biggie . . .'

'Tru, really – I don't think—'

'I *want* to do this, okay?'

Pauline recognised the stubborn set of her chin, and held her hands up. 'Alright . . . but don't say I didn't warn you.' Pauline assumed Truth wanted or needed to get away after breaking up with Josh. It was the only explanation for this extraordinary decision. 'And Truth?'

'What?'

'If it gets difficult, I can come over.'

'Difficult?' Truth laughed. 'Mum, I argue for a living! Relax, will you? I can do this. And anyway, I want to check out my Irish roots – it's half my ancestry, after all.'

'Well, it certainly is that,' Pauline agreed.

And that's when it hit her – it wasn't that her daughter looked different, it was that Pauline, caught off-guard, had allowed herself to see her objectively as she had walked into the dining room earlier. Truth hadn't changed . . . it was Pauline who had been refusing to acknowledge the evidence before her that was as plain as the nose on her face – that her beloved daughter had turned into the living image of her grandmother. She could see it now, from old photographs, and it almost took her breath away. Truth Malone was like a carbon copy of Evelyn as a young woman in her heyday. But in every other respect – as far as Pauline was concerned – Truth couldn't be more *unlike* Evelyn. And that's the way Pauline intended things to remain. She had put a lot of work into raising Truth to be an independent, modern, empathetic young woman. She just hoped going to Dublin to stay with Evelyn wouldn't mess with Truth's head. Tristan would no doubt have painted a much sunnier version of Evelyn when talking to Truth. Nevertheless, Truth had a right to get to know her grandmother – it remained to be seen just what she would make of her . . . and there was nothing whatsoever Pauline could do to influence the outcome, without betraying her own values and sense of fair play.

Chapter Four

Morah turned the key in the lock and slowly pushed open the door. For a moment she remained on the threshold, savouring the anticipation of finally being able to inspect Evelyn's flat in detail. Or rather – Morah reminded herself – her *apartment*, as Evelyn referred to it. Well, she would, wouldn't she? Apartment sounded more glamorous than just plain old flat – and Evelyn was all about image.

The place didn't disappoint. Walking in through the short hallway (which was as far as she had ever been able to see before) with its darkly polished floors and scattered rugs, she closed the door softly behind her, resisting the urge to tip-toe. The bedroom was to the left, and a small cloakroom to the right. Beyond these, the reason Evelyn had fallen in love with the flat became apparent. The proportions of the main room, with its tall picture windows, were magnificent. There was a view out to sea at the front and onto the communal garden at the back – and beyond that to the Dublin mountains. The small kitchen made up in character for what it lacked in space. Morah walked around slowly, noting every detail. She had to hand it to the woman – Evelyn had taste. No one else would have dared to decorate so boldly.

The walls at first glance appeared to be almost black, but on closer inspection were a deep grey. They glittered with gilt-framed paintings of every size whose jewelled colours were accentuated by the dark background. There were framed photographs too – she would examine those later. Over the marble fireplace a huge ornate mirror hung, reflecting the light from the windows. One had the impression of entering a kind of secret place . . . an Aladdin's cave of treasures. The windows were draped with deep pink silk similar to the sumptuously upholstered and cushioned sofas, with a scattering of individual, smaller novelty cushions, some with witty sayings. The whole effect was both daring and immaculately tasteful. Morah tried to recall what it reminded her of – she knew she had seen something similar, somewhere. And then it came to her – Blakes Hotel in London, which had caused such a stir when it opened its doors in 1978. Morah had never been there, but she knew it had been a hotspot in its time from the many society magazines she had assiduously bought and hoarded over the years – and she remembered how daring the dark, exotic interior décor had been considered by the gossip columns. She went back to the bedroom, where the colours were reversed – here the walls were deep pink and the drapes were grey silk. The bedroom also looked out to sea, and the large bed was dressed in plain white, with a grey silk spread turned back and matching smaller silk cushions resting against the larger pillows. A silk Chinese robe hung limply from a hook on the back of the door. Another large mirror took up almost the entire space of the far wall, and Morah was caught momentarily in its reflection. A small, tidy woman of a certain age in a white overall looked back at her. Her figure was still trim, and her tinted yellow hair with the fringe that stopped just over her heavily pencilled brows was curled and held back with two tortoiseshell combs in a style that had remained unchanged in twenty-odd years. Her lip colour and nails always matched, and she still wore full make-up, giving her apple-cheeked complexion a rather doll-like, powdery appearance. Despite the lines she had acquired over the years – the dimples her father had always loved were still there when she smiled, when he used to call her his 'little peach blossom' – genuine smiles were rare these days. It hadn't always been like that, though. That was just how things had turned out. Life could be cruel like that. Way back when, Morah Finlay, like so many others, had been a girl with dreams. Hers had just got trampled on. The face in the mirror tightened. She turned away, opening the wardrobe behind her, set into the wall, running her hands along the rail of clothes ranging from casual to flamboyant, before pulling out a colourful kaftan-style dress. Holding it up to her neck, she studied her reflection in the mirror, regarding the effect. She didn't have Evelyn's height, of course, wouldn't have got away with any of the styles Evelyn favoured – but most of them wouldn't have been to Morah's taste anyway. She put the garment back. There was no time for dawdling. She didn't have to rush, she would have plenty of opportunities over the next week or so while Evelyn was in hospital, but she couldn't take an inordinately long time in the flat either – and there was something she was hoping to find. First she would do what she had been instructed to by Doctor Ed.

The others – Evelyn's fan club, as Morah privately referred

to them – had got such a shock when they had heard what happened to her. Evelyn of all people – so fit and agile, even if she was in her seventies. It had been Nessa, returning from her own morning swim, who had found Evelyn and called the ambulance. Doctor Ed had driven to the hospital the minute he heard about it, and stayed with Evelyn until she had been stabilised and the course of treatment decided upon. That had been a week ago. In the meantime, Morah had been entrusted to keep an eye on the apartment in Evelyn's absence and to make any necessary arrangements. She already kept a key, of course, to all the other flats – in case of lockouts or emergencies – that was part of her duties. But until now she had never had one to Evelyn's flat – only Doctor Ed was allowed that privilege. He had given it to Morah this morning, along with the instructions to make up the bed in the spare room. And Morah would do anything for Doctor Ed. As far as she was concerned, he had helped her put her life back together, and she was eternally grateful to him.

At the time – almost ten years ago now – Morah had hardly been able to believe her ears when Doctor Ed had suggested the arrangement. She had attended his practice as a patient over the years, ever since she had returned to Dublin after her depressive episode. She had been horribly nervous and fragile on her return, even if it was to a different part of the city from where she had previously lived with the family whose children she had cared for so lovingly. Dear Susan and little Joey, they'd be all grown up now – she often thought of them, still kept a photo of them on her dresser. Doctor Ed had been so kind to her then, as she had gradually confided in him – told him about how she had been sent home to her elderly parents in the midlands in disgrace, her good name ruined. She had been so upset at having to leave her charges – especially little Joey, who would have been too young to understand where or why she had gone. That had been the hardest part. Telling her parents had been gruelling in a different way – explaining why being fired from the job she loved so much, up in the big city, hadn't been her fault. It was enough that a child coming to harm could have happened on her watch – she who loved him so devotedly. Then, of course, the rumours had found their nasty, insinuating way back to Morah's home town, and eventually reached her parents – who although trusting, were naïve and easily swayed by the majority. And the majority had been of the opinion that Morah Finley had always had ideas about herself, ideas of grandeur, had been too big for her small-town boots. Had considered herself too cosmopolitan for a place like Lurganbarry. Episodes from long ago were resurrected, aired for reinspection – like the time she was suspended from school for being caught smoking and drinking beer with a local lad behind the bicycle sheds. Or that she had been the first to sport short shorts in the middle of winter, albeit over dark tights. The undeniable fact that the lads had called her a 'goer'. No mention was made of the love she had for children, how they loved her in return, her willingness to babysit for little or no recompense at the drop of a hat, or the way she had selflessly and without griping dedicated herself to caring for and bathing her paralysed grandmother until her death, or helped her own mother dutifully in the house and on the small farm holding while her brother and father went drinking and carousing at the local fairs. None of that was recalled at all.

Lying low at home had been even more hellish than she had anticipated. The depression had set in quickly, followed by the breakdown, and once she had escaped incarceration at the local mental health institution, she had fled back to Dublin to survive any way she knew how. Then she had, by the grace of God, been directed to Doctor Ed, who had listened to her, adjusted and sorted her medication, directed her to a support group and eventually helped her get on the training course so she could become a proper healthcare assistant, a companion to the elderly and vulnerable. When the second of her long-term clients who she had lived with passed away, it was Doctor Ed who told her of his scheme to turn his house into flats and how he would need a caretaker on site – and that a small flat would go with the position. It was the second time in her life that he had saved her. She had thought then that it was too good to be true. She loved the house, her duties and her fellow tenants. But then one of the tenants had left. And Morah had found, to her enormous shock, that Evelyn Malone – the woman responsible for ruining her life – would be the new arrival.

Despite her shock, Morah certainly wasn't going to allow anyone – let alone the woman she detested above all others – get in the way of the perfect job and position for her golden years and the dear little studio flat that went with it. Evelyn Malone had caused far too much damage already in the short time Morah's life had intersected with hers. She wasn't going to let it happen again. When Evelyn had arrived that day and buzzed her way back into Morah's life through the impatient pressing of the intercom, she had been far too concerned with directing the entire moving operation to realise the effect she'd had on Morah, who was seeing her again after all these years. And in that same instant, Morah understood that Evelyn had no idea who had just opened the door to her. She didn't recognise Morah. And why would she? Apart from the passage of years, Morah's own appearance had changed utterly. Her hair was now tinted blonde, and she wore a neat overall. New lines and wrinkles had appeared that told of her inner struggles in the intervening time, and her formally plump face was now hollowed. Understanding that she was in the category of 'household staff', Evelyn had barely glanced at her. And in the days that followed, she had been charmingly dismissive of her, concentrating her efforts on impressing and beguiling the new neighbours who would be of *real* interest and importance. It gave Morah untold delight then – as it did now – that Evelyn Malone had no idea who she was, or what – more to the point – Morah knew about her.

Initially Morah hadn't been happy about the news of Evelyn's granddaughter coming over to stay with her for the duration of her post-hip-replacement rehabilitation. She had envisaged herself assuming the role. It was the obvious solution. That would have given her plenty of time to look around – though on the other hand it might have been more awkward, not to mention irritating. This way – although her time was limited – at least she was in the flat alone and unsupervised, and could go about her business uninterrupted. Morah had been waiting patiently for five years – since Evelyn had moved into flat 3 – to have just such an opportunity, and she wasn't going to waste it now. She was determined to find something, *anything*, that might help her get back at Evelyn for the monstrously unfair injustice done to her all those years ago, and more specifically, the part Evelyn had played in it.

This granddaughter, according to Doctor Ed, was a girl whom Evelyn hadn't even laid eyes on since she was a child. What if they didn't hit it off? Evelyn would be trapped – stuck in her beautiful (if rather small) apartment, unable to go out or drive, or even to swim – with what could very well turn out to be a sullen, unobliging thirty-something. Evelyn would be at the girl's mercy. Morah had a moment of deep satisfaction at the prospect, taking out the fresh sheets from the airing cupboard to make up the spare bed in Evelyn's office, as the small second room was referred to. This was where the unknown granddaughter would sleep while she was here. And her name! Doctor Ed had told them when he'd sent the WhatsApp message to their small group to keep them all in the loop as to how Evelyn was doing. 'Truth', he'd told them, was the name of the young woman who would be coming to stay with Evelyn. Morah had almost laughed out loud when she'd read it. Not because she thought it was silly – sure all the young ones had daft names these days, many named after fruit, or even the weather: Apple and Storm sprang to mind. No, it was the outrageous irony of it. That the biggest, most brazen lying *bitch* she had ever encountered should have a granddaughter named Truth almost took Morah's breath away. Of course no one knew the real story. Evelyn was far too clever to let anyone see that side of her. And even if people did know, they would probably say Evelyn had mellowed with time – developed a conscience, perhaps. The accumulation of years did that to a person. Morah's mouth curled derisively. Not in Evelyn's case. Leopards like Evelyn Malone didn't change their spots – they just got better at hiding them.

Now, patting the cover down and satisfied that the bed was properly made, Morah opened the windows so the flat could have its airing and got down to the real business which occupied her intention. First, she examined carefully the photographs that stood on various occasional tables – the usual family ones, Evelyn as a young woman with dark hair and big eyes, with a man, her husband she assumed, on beaches and on the ski slopes. More gatherings, social events, one or two with a baby held by her or her husband. A young man with a wife and child – her son, presumably – but none she could see of the impending granddaughter. It was the same on the walls and on the cork board hanging in the tiny kitchen. Morah began to open drawers then, one after the other, and rifled through them impatiently. She found the usual stuff: bank account details and financial folders which she put in her bag to look over at her leisure back in her own flat. Finally she headed back to the bedroom, starting at the bedside locker nearest her. There was a passport, trinkets, but no photographs. She tried the locker on the other side, clearly the side Evelyn slept on, opening the drawer roughly. Nail files, hand cream, a card or two . . . and then she hit pay dirt! The battered airmail envelope from which she took the three faded colour photographs fell from her hand as she hungrily stared at its contents, taking in every centimetre of each shot. There was Evelyn, back in

1982, young, beautiful and clearly in love. She must have been in her mid-thirties in the photograph. And Robert Radcliffe . . . Morah had been so happy working for the Radcliffes back then . . . she had forgotten how handsome Mrs Radcliffe's husband had been. He and Evelyn made a stunning couple. But it was the one of Evelyn smiling with young Susan looking bored and little Joey on her lap that made Morah want to rip the photo apart with her teeth. The nerve of the bloody woman! As if those children would ever have been happy with *her* as a stepmother. But it didn't stop Evelyn bulldozing her way in there – even though their own mother had been depressed and convalescing in hospital a lot of the time. Morah quickly took out her phone and snapped each of the photos, then put them back. There were letters too, from Robert, which she also photographed. Then, hearing voices on the stairs outside, she closed the drawer, grabbed her bag, and took a deep breath. One last glance around the flat and she went out, locking the door behind her.

Chapter Five

'Look, I get it, I really do.' Josh was pacing now, up and down the open-plan living room of Truth's flat in Islington.

'Actually, I don't think you do.' Truth folded her arms.

'Darling.' Josh fixed her with his most earnest expression, his gaze steely with intent – a look his opponents in the courtroom recognised meant a battle. 'I do – I know how scary it is. Okay, I admit I might have reacted a little too hastily when you first told me about it.'

Not just hastily, Truth thought. The word *dismissive* sprang to mind – callous, even.

'I've had death threats myself – it goes with the territory in our business – we deal with low-lifes a lot of the time. Make that most of the time – even if they're togged out in designer gear and worth millions. Once people feel threatened, they'll do anything they can to get you off their case. Literally. They're almost always empty threats. But these people who are targeting you aren't even *proper* criminals, Truth. And even if they were, you have security on the door here and we can get you more – you know your firm will cover that. But running away to Ireland? Truth . . . it's just – just – well, it's not you. You're *fierce*, babe, you're a fighter, that's what I love about you – you've never run away from anything.'

'First of all,' Truth said mildly, 'I am not running away – I am taking a break which my partners agreed I am due and think is a good idea under the circumstances. Second of all,' she looked at him meaningfully, 'I don't see that your opinion is relevant since we are no longer a couple.'

Josh lifted his eyebrows. 'I'm going to ignore the latter part of that statement, darling – it's simply inadmissible! You know we're great together – I love you! This whole thing has just freaked you out, you're not thinking straight. I mean, Ireland . . .' He shook his head imperceptibly, frowning, as if the thought of the place was not alone bizarre, but distasteful.

'My grandmother needs me. I might not get another chance to get to know her.'

'Darling, I will take you to meet this elusive grandmother myself – as often and as regularly as you like – but right now you need to stay *here*. You're needed here.' Josh pointed to the ground in front of him as if there might be any confusion. 'I need you. And Turnbull and Lennox most certainly need you.'

'I am not a dog to be called to heel, Josh.' Truth looked at him, amused. 'I need to do this – it's not about you. I've made up my mind. I'm going to Ireland and that's all there is to it.'

'Fine.' Josh held up his hands in defeat. 'Go if you must. I'll come and see you there – maybe after a week or two you'll be feeling differently.'

'I'm going to be off social media and I'd prefer if you

didn't contact me. I really need some space, Josh. I've told my friends and they understand.' Her friends were the easy part – most of Truth's contemporaries were as hard-working and driven as she was, and they hardly ever met up these days. 'You need to leave now, Josh.'

Truth smiled at him wearily. She had known he wouldn't back down without a significant protest, and she knew he cared about her. But this was about her – not Josh. She was done trying to explain how the online abuse and threats were having such a negative effect on her. Josh's answer to everything was, *What does it matter what anyone else thinks about you – I love you.* Like that was all the affirmation she needed in life. Josh loved her, Josh thought she was clever, Josh thought she was beautiful – more importantly, perhaps, Josh thought she had as bright a future as his own was shaping up to be in the world of prosecuting counsels. But when the hideous torrent of abuse erupted out of nowhere, Josh had almost laughed at her when he heard the reason. Then when he saw her genuine distress develop over the days and weeks that followed, he had advised her as if she were a client – not a lover.

He meant well, of course he did. Truth knew that. But she also knew instinctively that it was not the response she needed. Not that any response would have lessened the ghastliness of what she was going through, but apart from anything else, the situation had revealed Josh's conviction that his own advice and feelings on any subject overrode any and all deviations to the contrary that Truth might be experiencing. Unfortunately, Josh's answer to everything was, *Do as I say, and think how I think*, and it simply didn't work for Truth. As far as she was concerned they were over. She had broken up with him gently over a week ago. He had given her space for the following week and then the charm offensive had begun. She had agreed after a multitude of texts and emails to meet him briefly this evening at her place, and was wearily beginning to understand that failing to comply with Josh's suggestions – entreaties, even – was unfortunately making him even more persistent in his efforts to win her back.

'Please, Josh?' She held the door open for him.

He walked reluctantly towards her and stopped to take her in his arms, where she tolerated a brief hug, but then pulled away. 'You're the best thing that's ever happened to me, Truth – you know that.' It was a statement, not a question. 'I'm not going to let this . . . this *craziness* come between us. I won't let it get the better of us.'

'Goodnight, Josh.' She pushed him gently out the door and closed it behind him. Then she went into the kitchen and poured herself a glass of water, took a long drink, and leaned back against the wall. Breathe, she reminded herself. Deep, slow breaths.

On her bed, the open suitcase lay half packed for her prospective trip to Dublin. It was true what she had said to Josh, her grandmother did need her – or someone who could fit the bill, and it might as well be her. But that wasn't the real reason she was going. Josh was right, she was running away – and once she had made the decision, she couldn't do it fast enough. Living on her nerves and three hours' sleep a night wasn't helping her deal with the situation, and her senior partners had urged her to take some time out – to get away. Although Truth knew there was no getting away from the abuse, not as long as she went online anyway.

There was a time when the most stressful episode of her career life was when she was threatened at knifepoint by the insanely irate husband of an abused wife she was representing. But terrifying though the ordeal had been, it was over relatively quickly and the guilty party arrested – it didn't begin to compare to the ongoing and escalating fear she was experiencing now, which didn't show any signs of letting up. Every day she found herself looking over her shoulder, or averting her eyes from curious glances on the Tube – innocent or otherwise – and every night she checked and double-checked her locks, especially the security lock she had installed on her bedroom door. And still she didn't sleep. She had been tempted to confide in her mother during their weekend away, but she didn't want to worry Pauline – who would have been both outraged on her behalf and frantically worried about her. That's when the trip to Dublin began to seem like an opportunity to lie low for a while. It made obvious sense, and the more Truth thought about it, the more she realised she was curious to meet this enigmatic grandmother she had heard so little about. Hopefully helping out Evelyn in her flat would be a welcome distraction from her current troubles.

It was the arbitrary nature of how the whole thing took off that still made her shake her head in bewilderment and despair. She, who had spent her entire career defending the rights of women in the workplace and out of it. After lunch with a girlfriend one day, she had noticed some unusual activity on Twitter. On closer inspection it became clear she was being accused of hypocrisy, anti-feminism, and betraying the very women she claimed to represent. 'One rule for us . . . and another for the elite barrister,' one comment read.

That was one of the nicer ones. Then the tone and count escalated until the mob had whipped up fury and outrage. The whole thing had happened so suddenly and out of the blue, it had taken her and the firm's Human Resources department most of the following day to work out what had started it. The offending comment she was accused of could be traced back to an interview she had given to a well-known women's fashion magazine a few months earlier. 'You're not going to like this . . .' one of the legal team told her. 'Here it is.' Tim indicated the article on screen, where there was a photo of Truth and a number of other glamorous career women discussing their personal style both in the office and out of it.

'So what?' Truth said. 'It's a fashion piece – where's the problem?'

'Here.' Tim pointed to a piece of text as Truth bent closer to read it. In an off-the-cuff remark about how a lot of her day was spent running from one hearing or courtroom to another, she had remarked, 'I mostly wear flats when I'm working. I learned the hard way what trouble high heels can get women into . . .' Truth had gone on to relate an amusing account of when she had been running for a cab and went over on her ankle, twisting it badly and ending up in A&E. But the interviewer hadn't included that part of the story and the latter part of the sentence had been deliberately taken out of context. *I learned the hard way what trouble high heels can get women into* had been presented online as if Truth had uttered it as a standalone comment – inferring that women shouldn't wear high heels unless they were asking for unwanted attention, or worse.

'But that's insane,' Truth protested. 'It was a simple anec-
dote about me running for a taxi and falling over.'

'Welcome to the world of online abuse, Truth. A sentence can be construed to mean whatever the trolls want it
to, I'm afraid.' Tim frowned. 'And no one is likely to check
the source of the comment for verification – that's our job.
And even if they did, they wouldn't care. I'm afraid the
mob's intent is to simply make you and the comment sound
as bad as possible. If I were you I'd stay off social media for
the foreseeable – this could get pretty ugly.'

He hadn't been exaggerating. Over the following weeks
everything from character slurs to suggestions she kill herself and death threats poured in. While she tried initially to
ignore it, to tough it out, eventually the abuse took its toll.
She had to cut short dinner in a restaurant one evening when
she felt certain a woman was staring at her. Charities she
had represented ceased to seek out her services, and speaking events dried up for no reason.

In the beginning Josh had tried to jolly her out of it. Then
when even he saw the severity of the hounding, he did his best
to be patient with her. But Josh was someone who liked action
and confrontation, which was why he did so well at the bar.
And fighting back wasn't an option in this case, not without
months of tracking down the trolls and taking relevant people
to court. Truth understood that Josh had been attracted to her
because she was unlike any other woman he knew. When
they had first met over a case that he had been called in on to
consult with, Josh had thought she was joking when she told
him her name. Truth was used to people thinking she had
invented her name as an attention-seeking ploy – particularly

given her profession. But over lunch she had made it clear to him that she was as determined and unstoppable as the woman she'd been named after, Sojourner Truth. From that moment he had become first intrigued by her, and soon after besotted with her. But once the abuse got a grip, Josh became frustrated by the fact that he, especially, was helpless to do anything, except tell her to ignore it and that it would go away eventually. So far there was no sign of this happening. Because of how stories fly around the world in seconds, Truth's story was hijacked – and a horribly false narrative became the defining truth about her. The irony wasn't lost on her: the woman who for a living had taken on, exposed and convicted some of society's most violent men, and spent her career defending the women they abused, now found her nemesis was a fashion blogger called Billie Bubbles.

Chapter Six

Evelyn didn't like hospitals. The last time she had been admitted as a patient was to have her tonsils removed at the age of ten, and as far as she was concerned the intervening years and technical advances had done nothing to improve the general experience. She couldn't believe her bad luck in falling down the stairs and breaking her hip. Being dispatched in the ambulance was an upsettingly disjointed memory now, and since her operation three days ago she was feeling dopey on painkillers when she needed to have her wits about her. If only they would give her time to think, but it was one constant intrusion after another in the step-down unit.

Although outwardly Evelyn was being relentlessly charming to all the hospital staff, she just wanted to be left in peace for a few hours. She had seen her young surgeon with the brisk manner briefly, who assured her he was pleased with how the surgery had gone. She was having physio twice a day. There seemed to be an ever-changing rota of nursing staff all asking her the same questions over and over, and on top of all that she had been instructed to have someone collect anything that needed washing and have it taken home – as hospitals no longer provided a laundry facility. Doctor Ed was being marvellous and was dropping by later – she would have to give the bag to him. She would ask him to give it to Nessa to look after, otherwise it would be that weird Morah going through her things and she simply couldn't bear the thought of that. The woman gave her the creeps. She had caught Morah on more than one occasion since she had moved into number 24 looking at her with a strangely speculative expression on her face – as if she were contemplating something decidedly nasty.

From behind the privacy of her drawn cubicle curtain, Evelyn reached for her hand-held magnifying mirror and studied her face carefully. She didn't like the slightly grey tinge her complexion was taking on, and her hair would need retouching soon. If only she could go swimming . . . but the surgeon had told her sea swimming was out of the question for the foreseeable – even if she could get out of bed unaided. No wonder she felt disoriented . . . her early-morning dip was the drug that set her up for the day. But that wasn't the real reason she was feeling out of kilter – nor was it her recent surgery. What was eating Evelyn *really* was that, for the first time she could remember, she wasn't in control. Decisions were being made on her behalf without her being consulted. Tristan had rung – several times now – and during the latest conversation had informed her that her granddaughter Truth, Pauline's girl, would be coming over to stay with her for the duration of her recuperation in the apartment, to help her out around the place. For a moment, Evelyn had been about to refuse the suggestion and tell him she would organise her own home help if needed, thank you very much – but then had realised just how much effort that would take and how Doctor Ed and the others in number 24 (possibly even Morah) might wish to become involved. So she had settled for what she considered the lesser of two evils. This didn't mean she had to like the arrangement.

She hadn't seen her granddaughter since the child's First Holy Communion, which had been both an awkward and dull affair twenty-five years ago. The child had been a strange little thing then – all gangly arms and legs and big, watchful eyes. Pauline had been civil but there was a distinct coolness towards her mother, which Evelyn happily ignored. Apparently Truth had asked for her grandmother to attend the small ceremony and lunch afterwards, which was the only reason Evelyn had been invited. She had no idea what the girl would be like now. Tristan had told her as much as he could, which was that she was a very clever lawyer, but that hardly helped. Evelyn frowned. She would be stuck with this girl, reliant on her, but it seemed to be the most sensible option she could avail of – she would just have to make the best of it. She put on some bright lipstick and smiled. Things could always be worse. It could have been Pauline who was coming over.

'Glad to see somebody's happy to see me,' the physiotherapist said, coming over to Evelyn's bed.

Evelyn gave her her best smile. 'Oh, there's always something to be cheerful about. I learned that trick a long time ago.'

'I only wish more patients had your wonderful attitude,' the physiotherapist replied.

Chapter Seven

'I need a reading!'

Nessa jumped out of her skin as Stella grabbed her urgently by the arm, causing the wet towel she was wrapped in after swimming to almost fall off her in the hall of number 24 as she rifled through the morning post.

'Now! *Please?*' Stella said. 'It's an emergency.'

'Sorry, yes. Yes, of course, if it's an emergency!' Nessa hastily tucked her towel back under her arm. In her hand she clutched a damp letter, an unwelcome bill from her telephone company. Bills seemed to be the only post she received these days. Her towel, Nessa noticed now, was very wet and was dripping onto the hall table, where the remaining letters and flyers were spotted with water. Nessa could tell as she moved away from the table towards Stella, and the towel dripped steadily onto the floor, that the agitated woman was staring at her, trying not very hard to hide her obvious irritation at Nessa's sloppiness.

It always struck Nessa as strange when Stella wanted a reading. The woman was so organised, so neat, so . . . well, *obsessive*, that it was difficult to understand why she would be interested in something as intuitive and heart-centred as a tarot reading. 'Can you give me half an hour?' Nessa said.

'I'll have to get dressed and ask Theresa to open up the café for me.'

'Okay, if I have to. But I need to pick Freddy up from pre-school at one . . .' Stella seemed even more stressed than usual. In her medium-heeled tan pumps, which matched her handbag, which matched her tightly pulled leather belt, she was practically quivering with tension.

'Everything okay?' Nessa asked, feeling increasingly concerned.

'So far as I can tell,' Stella said, giving her a tight little smile. 'We'll know more later, won't we?' She manoeuvred around Nessa so she could spread the post out on the table, allowing it to dry in neatly ordered columns.

'You should have a swim while you're waiting for me,' Nessa said. 'The water's perfect today – it's very healing.'

'I'm sure.' Stella made for the stairs. She lived on the first floor, opposite Evelyn. 'But I need to check my email,' she said briskly. 'I'll see you in half an hour.'

Nessa shook her head watching Stella go upstairs. The woman was becoming more OCD every time she met her. If the vibes Nessa had picked up from her in their brief exchange were anything to go by, she wouldn't be looking forward to the reading. Of all the people she'd met through living in number 24, Stella Montgomery's aura was by far the murkiest.

Fortunately she couldn't complain about the other tenants: they were lovely, as was Doctor Ed himself. Rory who ran the basement gym was a pet; Bruce was a nice guy; and Mike, who also lived on the ground floor, had become a really good mate. She could have done with more female friends – Stella wasn't exactly the sympathetic type, and Morah scurried around the place with her head down most of the time. But Evelyn was a wonderful neighbour, and according to Doctor Ed her granddaughter was coming to stay with her to help her after her operation. She might be fun.

✧

Nessa Gilmore's flat was rather like a pop-up shop. The décor evolved according to her current and ever-changing whims. There were several constant features, though, such as her yoga mat, her small table filled with crystals, and the little corner which she referred to as her meditation spot, where she would sit cross-legged to connect with her inner source of divine guidance. Her bedroom – which just about fitted her double bed – was currently painted in ochre, draped with shawls and throws inspired by her recent trip to India. The small living room, whose walls were a deep azure, resembled a charming coastal cottage, strewn with cotton rugs, a wooden coffee table and a sofa, which was covered in a cheery blue and white linen stripe. Pale blue and white linen curtains billowed in the breeze from the open window and a small TV was largely hidden on the cupboard shelf in the alcove. Two large seascapes (painted by artist friends) reinforced the nautical theme. A row of multicoloured beaded curtains acted as a divider to the tiny kitchen from where the smell of fresh coffee floated. Nessa preferred a chai latte, which she had picked up earlier, but Stella, when she came for her reading, would want black coffee – she never drank anything else.

Nessa sat down for a moment, smoothing her floaty white cotton dress, and took deep, measured breaths to centre her energy. Her swim earlier had given her a natural high, but some clients – and Stella was one – brought their own very distinct energy with them into her space. And when that energy was negative, Nessa found doing the reading particularly draining. She lit an incense stick, picked up a piece of obsidian crystal (to ward off negative energy), and drew an imaginary circle around her to protect her own aura. Then she asked the spirit world for guidance during the reading for the highest good of all concerned. Exactly half an hour after she'd met Stella in the hall, the doorbell buzzed, rousing Nessa from her breathing exercise.

'Coffee?' Nessa asked Stella, leading her into the small second bedroom which served as her office and where she held her readings. She indicated the seat for Stella to take on one side of the table, where her tarot stack sat in a corner beside a trio of fat candles.

'Yes, black, please.' Stella sat down.

When Nessa returned with the coffee, Stella was looking expectant.

'Is there anything in particular you'd like me to focus on?' Nessa asked her.

She wanted to know first whether there *was* something she needed to be concerned about – if the cards would pick it up.

'Not really.'

Clearly there was something bothering Stella, but equally clearly she wasn't going to say.

'I thought you said it was an emergency . . .' Nessa's brows lifted.

'I might have been hasty. Let's see what the cards say, shall we?'

Nessa took a deep breath and held her tongue. She didn't need any cards to tell her it was going to be a difficult reading. She realised suddenly, in the way things often came to her out of nowhere, that Stella's emergency was about Bruce and the very attractive blonde woman that Nessa had glimpsed coming down the stairs with him. What Stella really wanted to know was, *Who was that woman I saw leaving Bruce's flat this morning?*

Most of Doctor Ed's tenants had been impressed when a recently divorced couple took the two newly vacated flats in number 24 so they could co-parent their little boy, Freddy.

Bruce was an easy-going guy, but Stella . . . well, she struck Nessa from the outset as someone who needed always to be in control, both of herself and the world around her, which included her three-year-old son and her former husband.

The tarot cards began with simple messages, with the usual stuff: Stella was stressed. She was feeling some lower back pain – a session with a massage therapist might be an idea. Work was going well and a promotion was on the cards. Yet Stella looked blank and uninterested – clearly she was waiting for other news.

Nessa reshuffled the cards and asked Stella to choose another ten, which she then arranged on the table and looked at.

Loss . . . danger . . . Nessa frowned. Too unclear to be useful and too dark to hint at.

'Does it say anything about family?' Stella asked.

Nessa shook her head. 'I'm not getting anything out of the ordinary. Everything seems good. Why? Is there a family member you're worried about?'

'No . . .' Stella was vague. 'I was just wondering if there was anything there about Bruce? You know . . . that I need to be aware of?'

'That's not how it works, Stella, you know that.' Nessa looked her in the eye. 'That would only come up if Bruce were here himself, for a reading – or if you were here for a joint couples reading. If you're looking for information about Bruce, you'd be better off asking him yourself.'

Stella's eyes narrowed. 'I just worry about him sometimes. He *is* the father of my child, after all.'

But Nessa just smiled and went on talking about Stella's career and a possible trip abroad. Finally she asked, 'Any other questions?'

'No, thank you.'

Stella didn't press her for anything more, so Nessa wrapped up the reading. 'See you later in the garden for a drink, maybe?' she said, taking the cash Stella held out.

'Maybe.'

When Stella had gone, Nessa curled her feet underneath her on the sofa and sipped a glass of water. Stella clearly felt Bruce was slipping beyond her control. Even if she hadn't seen his mystery overnight guest, she must have noticed that her ex-husband, whom she treated like her personal babysitter, grocery shopper and general gofer, was actually a very attractive man. Clearly it was finally dawning on Stella that there were other women out there who would be more than happy to treat him with the kindness and respect he was entitled to.

Nessa grinned to herself.

Evelyn, as usual, had been absolutely right. She had spotted and evaluated the relationship dynamic between Stella and her ex-husband soon after they had moved in to number 24. Evelyn had felt very sorry for Bruce, so clearly still in love with his wife and utterly bewildered and at a loss as to how or why his marriage had ended. Over drinks one evening in the garden, about six months after he and his ex-wife had moved in, Bruce had confided to Evelyn and Nessa and Doctor Ed how miserable he was. Evelyn had looked at him speculatively and asked him straight out. 'Do you want your wife back?'

Bruce had blinked. 'She wouldn't even entertain the idea. I consider myself lucky she's allowing me to live under the same roof as her – well, you know what I mean.'

'That's because she's making things easy for herself,' Evelyn had said crisply. 'But you didn't answer my question.'

'Yes – yes, I'd love to get her back. I just want to be a family again, a proper one.' He'd looked as if he might cry.

'Well, I can help you do that.'

'Evelyn—' Doctor Ed had intervened. He was shaking his head and laughing. 'Really . . . you shouldn't.'

'Shouldn't what?' She'd grinned at him challengingly. 'Give a young man some well-intentioned advice?'

'I was going to say interfere in other people's relationships – tenants in particular.'

'Could you, though? Really?' Bruce had pressed her.

'The answer to that is yes,' Evelyn had said. 'But you'd have to do everything I tell you, and I must warn you . . .'

'What?' Bruce was desperate. 'I know it might not work –
but anything's worth a try.'

'Oh, it'll work alright. I can pretty much guarantee you
that. What I have to warn you about is that by the time I've
finished with you, you may not *want* her back.'

Bruce had looked disbelieving.

'You see,' Evelyn had gone on, 'behind that miserable
hangdog expression lurks a very good-looking man. You're a
good height, you have nice, broad shoulders, olive skin,
lovely eyes – and good teeth.'

'You make it sound like he's a horse.' Nessa had giggled.

'The point is, the raw material is there. If it wasn't, I
wouldn't be suggesting this. If I can get you to adopt the
right attitude, too, so much the better. But you have to follow my advice to the letter – or I won't play.'

Bruce had swigged back the last of his drink. 'It's a deal,'
he'd said, with the beginnings of a happy slur.

'Good. Think it over, by all means, and if you want to go
ahead, we'll meet once a week. And it's going to require
hard work on your part, I have to warn you – not least of
which will be a regular gym session.' Evelyn had assessed
him. 'You could do with beefing up a bit, and physical exercise is a great confidence booster. But I assure you it will be
very rewarding hard work.'

Nessa remembered the night well. She had thought it
hilarious at the time, convinced Evelyn was joking, but both
Bruce and Evelyn were as good as their word. And Nessa
had to admit – Bruce's transformation had been a sight to
behold. And if his lovely seeming new girlfriend was anything to go by, Evelyn's coaching had not been in vain. Nessa

smiled. Bruce deserved a break – he was such a nice guy and he'd been working really hard. Rory in the gym had been impressed by his dedication. Nessa had wondered how long it would be before Stella started taking note. She'd found the reading more difficult than usual, quite apart from knowing that Stella was fishing for information about her ex-husband. She had seen the prediction of loss, which may well have indicated that Bruce would settle with someone new, but she had also seen the danger card come up.

Nessa shivered. She always warned clients to take care and be vigilant about the usual things – driving, health and general safety – but she never indicated danger. There was no point alarming people, and it might never come to pass – or at least not in any way that she could accurately decipher.

Idly she shuffled and turned over the cards for herself, noting with a wry smile that romance was on the horizon. Goodness! Who could that possibly be concerning?

Last year she had been dumped yet again by her long-time on-off boyfriend Ryan, and she doubted she'd find anyone else until she got over him. Part of her didn't want to. Maybe he was coming back? Then she remembered the very attractive man she'd seen earlier running up the steps of the house next door, which after over a year of extensive and occasionally very noisy refurbishment finally seemed to have a new inhabitant. Maybe she would bump into him one of these days . . .

Chapter Eight

The traffic was slow – even now at lunchtime – thanks to the good weather and more people than usual making their way to Mariner's Cove. As her car crawled along the coast road, Stella tried to distract herself from gut-twisting impatience by watching groups of friends and families clutching beach bags and swimming paraphernalia. Through her open window, the gentle breeze carried their shrieks of fun and carefree laughter as they made their way down to the popular bathing spot. It was ironic – swimming and the prospect of a more casual lifestyle, she remembered, had been one of the reasons she'd moved to Ulysses Crescent. She had intended becoming one of the daily regulars who swam come hail, rain or snow – year in and year out – except it hadn't turned out that way. Stella could count on one hand the number of times she'd been in the sea in the eighteen months since they had moved here.

She glanced at the dashboard clock – ten to one – she had to make it in time. She absolutely hated being late, and although Sophie at Les Petits Enfants claimed to be flexible about pick-up times, Sella had noted her very French disdain towards parents who allowed tardiness to become a pattern. Nothing was said, of course – but disapproval was evident in the slight flare of her nostrils and an incline of her elegant head.

For some reason Stella could not fathom, she had begun to crave Sophie's approval of late. This may have come about after witnessing Sophie's obvious pleasure at seeing Bruce turn up to collect Freddy some weeks ago when Stella had got her days muddled, thinking it was her turn. As Stella watched from her car outside, Sophie had practically fawned over him.

What was going on with Bruce? Throughout their relationship, even after they'd divorced, it was Stella who chose his clothes and encouraged him to watch his diet – especially when he had started to put on a few pounds. And now? Well . . .

Stella had been so tempted to ask Nessa if there were any romantic prospects on the horizon for Bruce – although what she really wanted know was: was it possible to get her ex-husband back, before it was too late? But no, she wasn't going to let Nessa Gilmore know how she was thinking. She didn't want her telling the other tenants, she didn't want to be laughed at, she didn't want to appear as though her life was spiralling out of control, that she might have made a terrible, stupid mistake . . .

She remembered the exact minute the idea of Ulysses Crescent had presented itself to her, when a colleague in rentals had mentioned in passing the two lovely flats that had become vacant at the same time in the beautifully refurbished Georgian house on the elegant terrace. 'They'll be snapped up, of course,' the girl had said. 'Flats hardly ever come up in that terrace – I can think of two clients already who'd jump at them.' She had reached for her phone.

'Wait.' Stella had interrupted her. 'Just a minute – can you give me the details before you make any calls?'

'Sure.' The girl emailed her the rough draft she had drawn up for the intended advertisement. 'But the commission's still mine if they take it,' she'd said. 'I can only give you an hour at most – is it for a friend?'

'Hmm, what?' Stella had hardly looked up, already engrossed in the photos on her screen. 'No, nothing like that.'

It was fate, Stella had been sure of it. She and Bruce had accepted the offer on their small townhouse and Bruce was already depressed at the few apartments he had looked at for himself. Living back at home with his parents was taking its toll too. With the sale due to close in the next month, Stella still hadn't found anywhere for her and Freddy either. *Maybe you don't want to*, the small voice prompted her, the one that kept her awake at night as she tossed and turned, unable to sleep. The one she didn't want to listen to. She still couldn't believe it had come to this. Bruce and her splitting up after just eighteen months of married life. How had it happened? They had been happy together for five years as a couple, then Stella had found she was pregnant. It had been unexpected, sure, but they'd been thrilled at the same time. Getting married had seemed like the next natural step in their already solid relationship. They had been happy for those six months – really happy. Looking forward to being a real little family. And then Freddy had arrived, and despite the initial joy and excitement of getting to know her new baby, Stella had found herself unravelling – there was no other word for it. Every little thing Bruce did began to drive her mad. If he wasn't getting on her nerves, he was getting under her feet. She knew he was trying to help, but she didn't need help – she had her routine down to a fine art. If Bruce would just leave her and Freddy alone, everything would be fine. He was sitting on the couch every evening while she was preparing for the day to come – leaving things where they should be – until Bruce would scatter everything again looking for the remote control he was usually sitting on. It drove her – quite literally – to distraction. It got to the point where she was hardly able to look at him, never mind talk to him – and suggestions of date nights brought her out in a rash. The only one-on-one quality time Stella wanted was with Freddy – he was the new man in her life, the sole centre of her universe. She simply didn't remember or want to contemplate a life before him. Any memory of her pre-Freddy existence, including – or possibly *especially* – her relationship with his father, was as interesting to her as watching football – which she loathed.

Eventually, it was Bruce who'd offered to move out for a while – so she could get her head together. Counselling was suggested – he was hurt and bewildered by the changes in her and in their hitherto happy relationship. But the emerging evidence of the trial separation for Stella was that the longer she had the house to herself, the happier she became. She was genuinely quite astonished at how easy it had been to adapt to a home without Bruce. There was order, finally. Followed swiftly by an unanticipated sense of peace that had previously eluded her. Her routine ran like clockwork, and Freddy, sensing the new tranquil atmosphere, slept long and soundly. She could go to her couch, with a cup of hot choc-olate, and not find crumbs, or trip over discarded shoes – and watch whatever shows took her fancy, without hearing snores from the other end of the sofa. When she expressed the wish to make the situation permanent – Bruce had been requesting readmittance – he was so heartbroken and shocked she almost relented. There then followed an awk-ward few months when he'd agreed to put the house up for sale and look for an apartment. And then Ulysses Crescent had fallen into Stella's lap. It was a heaven-sent solution (her mother had been praying).

She'd put the suggestion to Bruce over a drink in the old pub where they'd first met. 'What do you think?' Her eyes were bright. 'It's the perfect solution, it makes so much sense. And we can co-parent so much more easily this way.'

Bruce was as surprised as he was doubtful. He looked at the shots on her laptop. 'They're beautiful flats alright . . . but I thought you wanted to get away from me?' His big dark eyes, that had become somewhat lost in the recent puffiness of his face, were confused.

'Not get *away*, Brucie, just be . . . apart . . . separate – you know, have my own space again. Since Freddy—'

'Yes, I know – I get it. You've said so often enough at this stage.' He was downcast.

'We'd be on separate floors, but in the same house. It's perfect! Freddy could see us both whenever he wanted.' She played her trump card. 'You know it makes sense.'

'Maybe.' He seemed unsure. 'What happens if you decide I'm still too near? I'm not going to be moved on again, you know.'

'Don't be silly! Of course I wouldn't think that. We'll have completely independent lives – just be near each other for our little boy. Please, Brucie . . .? I know we're not a couple anymore, but I want us always to be friends. I'd miss seeing you if you were too far away.'

She watched his face work as he struggled with the prospect and then gave in – powerless, as he had always been, to refuse her.

'Alright. But I'm warning you – if you change your mind, it'll be too bad. I won't be unsettled again – this has already been too much of an upheaval for me.' He scowled. 'But I need to get out from under Mam and Dad's feet – my moving back in hasn't been fair on them.'

'Exactly.' Stella squeezed his hand. 'This makes so much sense for all of us. I just know it's going to be great.' She beamed.

And it had been great in the eighteen months since they'd moved in – was still going great. The flats were perfect, the other tenants were lovely (well, except for Morah, who was an acquired taste, but she was alright once you learned to work your way around her) and everyone adored little Freddy.

Stella and Bruce were certainly never short of babysitters or childminders if they both had to be out at the same time.

Bruce seemed relieved and happy to be near his little boy and ex-wife. They still, in a strange way, felt like a little family – just that Daddy lived upstairs. Stella had even helped him settle in and furnish his flat. She had wanted a new look for her own living arrangement, so Bruce had been welcome to the big old sofa from their townhouse and the few bits he wanted or needed. She had even set the couch up right in front of his huge smart TV – the only new item he had treated himself to – just the way he liked it.

Even parenting Freddy had been a breeze. They had worried he might be confused and upset – but he seemed to accept the whole thing as the adventure they had pitched it as. And staying with Mummy or Daddy on their allocated nights or weekends seemed just like an extended babysitting episode while the other parent was on time off.

But then something unexpected happened. Stella couldn't put her finger on exactly when it had started – or perhaps she had been too preoccupied with her own life and work to notice. First it was the weight Bruce had always been prone to and had accumulated over the last five years . . . it began to drop off him. He just said he couldn't be bothered to cook for himself – his daily menu was porridge for breakfast, no time for lunch or maybe a salad or wrap on the run, and in the evening he whipped up an omelette before settling down to TV and a couple of beers, without the crisps and chocolate Stella used to stock in the treats cupboard – Bruce found he didn't really miss them. Then, Stella noticed, he began going to Rory's Gym in the basement of the house, becoming friendly with Rory and a few of the regular guys. Throughout winter, when everyone was wrapped up in woollies and Bruce was still wearing his old suits to work, it hadn't been so obvious. But once summer came around there was no missing the new, improved, fit Bruce. The transformation was quite astonishing. Her ex-husband had abs.

Bruce had never looked this good even when she had first met him. The bone structure and the lovely brown, well-meaning eyes she had found so attractive seemed clearer now. He was more purposeful and he seemed . . . well, happy and brimming with confidence. More intriguing to Stella, some sort of style makeover had clearly taken place, one which had not required her consultation or input. Gone were the baggy weekend jeans and oversized rugby shirts – replaced by slimmer versions and a variety of on-trend fitted jumpers and tops which clung to Bruce's broad shoulders and his newly V-shaped torso. He had taken up daily running and swimming as well, so he had a good base tan, and the few stringy bits of hair he had been so anxious to hold onto during their marriage had been shaved, and he now rocked a new, well-oiled, sallow-skinned scalp – which gave him an edge that Stella would never in a million years have imagined. Perhaps the most astonishing development of all had been the tattoo on his right (now sculpted) bicep. Bruce! Getting inked up! Stella almost fainted with shock. Worse, she discovered she liked it. A lot. Although she hadn't as yet been able to get close enough to see what it said, or represented. Either way, Stella had to admit – much to her chagrin – that her former physical and sartorial slob of a husband now looked, well, hot.

There was no getting away from it. And when she wasn't discreetly checking him out each time she caught sight of him or had to hand Freddy over to him, she was busy noticing *other* women check him out. This had been alarming enough to her, but manageable – after all, he was still her Brucie, they were still a team, of sorts. It was just that lately she had noticed he had stopped asking her if she needed anything picked up when he was doing his own weekly shop – or more concerning still, had given up asking her advice about matters when previously he had always relied so heavily on her opinion. Now Stella knew the reason why. Bruce had found another woman.

It had been such a shock, she couldn't quite process it. Stella had been leaving for work ten minutes later than usual – Freddy had been fussing because he couldn't find the wildflower that Doctor Ed had given him from the garden the evening before. Stella had found the wilted plant on his pillow when she had gone in to check on him, sound asleep, and promptly binned it. But Freddy was set on bringing the flower to nursery to tell his friend Jilly about it. It had meant Stella being nine minutes behind schedule, one of those precious minutes spent retrieving the worse-for-wear flower from the bin and running it under the tap to clean it. She'd been double-locking her front door when she'd heard soft laughter and voices floating up from below – one of which was Bruce's. She'd looked over the bannisters towards the ground floor and had caught a glimpse of blonde hair, and the back of a slim, white shirt, where her ex-husband's hand was placed protectively on the small of the woman's back. For a moment Stella had been rooted to the spot, until she'd been forced to lunge for Freddy who was headed for the stairs.

'Shhh!' She'd put her finger to her lips instinctively. If Freddy had caught sight of his dad he'd have shrieked at him and her cover would have been blown.

He had looked up at her then, and said crossly, 'But you said *hurry*, Mummy! Hurry! We're late.'

Chapter Nine

'I'm not having a go.' His ex-wife was smiling. 'Really. I just think we owe it to each other to be honest. I mean, this morning me and Freddy could have run slap bang into you and this new friend of yours. I realise I was running behind schedule, but it would have been very unsettling for Freddy. We have to be careful, Bruce – for his sake.'

'Yeah, of course.' Bruce had been on his way upstairs from work when he'd run into Stella on her way down. Now he felt panicky, exposed. When had she turned from the woman he'd married into this tense, brittle character?

But panicked or not, he was determined to stand firm. 'Goes without saying. I'm glad you brought it up, actually.' He took a deep breath, might as well be hung for a sheep as a lamb. 'I was thinking it would be a good idea to introduce Freddy to Annika one of these days. She's dying to meet him.'

'*Annika.*' Stella somehow managed to make the name sound ridiculous while keeping her smile fixed in place. 'Really? Let's just see if Annika is going to be around for long. I don't want to confuse him just yet – it's way too soon.'

'Um, me and Annika have been seeing each other for' – he frowned, doing the mental calculations – 'almost three months now. I would have brought her back here sooner or later – usually we stay at her place – but last night her neighbours were having a party, it was going to be a late one. Anyway, I want to introduce her to everyone here. So Freddy's going to meet her one way or another – be better if he meets her with me first.'

Stella was momentarily speechless. 'Three months?' Her voice rose. 'Almost three whole months, and you never thought to mention it to me?'

Bruce squared his shoulders and remembered Evelyn's advice. Stand firm!

'Didn't know you'd care, to be honest.' He checked his watch. 'Right, well, I need to get a move on – tide's on the way out. I'm going for a quick dip and then I'll pick Freddy up from you. Where is he, by the way?' Bruce frowned.

'In the garden, with Doctor Ed,' Stella said. 'He's watching him for me – I need to answer some emails.'

'Great – well, I'll see you in twenty or so.' And he raced up to his flat, taking the stairs two at a time.

✧

Stella made her way downstairs in a sort of trance. Bruce, whose only previous association with water had been the shower he used to hog for far too long – leaving the bathroom in a mess of damp towels, strewn clothes and steamed-up mirrors in the process – was swimming twice a day. He had acquired a new girlfriend whom he intended introducing to their son and the world at large – even the tenants of this house. All without consulting her at any stage – even now.

Stella could barely take it in. He had simply announced what he would be doing as matter-of-factly as if he had been telling her about a commercial property lease he had negotiated. How had this happened? How had she not noticed the signs? Exactly when had she lost his undivided attention?

Chapter Ten

'**G**arden's looking good, Ed.' Mike lowered himself down in the little sunken outdoor seating area he had built for the doctor, which consisted of a trio of wooden benches around a small pond at the end of the main garden. It was where Doctor Ed relaxed at the end of the day and almost any other time as well, either to read the paper, check the racing results, or have a nice G&T while contemplating his handiwork. The June roses were coming into bloom now, and their delicate fragrance hung in the air.

Doctor Ed was delighted to have Mike join him. Since he didn't have children himself, he felt paternal towards all his younger tenants – Mike, Bruce, Nessa. Perhaps Stella not so much, there was something rather prickly about her – she was trickier to warm to. But he had a particular soft spot for Mike.

'I've never seen such a growth spurt as the last few weeks.' The doctor stroked his neatly trimmed beard. 'All that rain and now the fine weather – there's something new to notice every day. How's your chap coming along?' He was almost as interested in Mike's sculpture as he was in his own garden – which was saying something.

'Good, good. If the foundry guys are happy, so am I.'

'How long more?'

'Another month, give or take. They're putting down the foundations on the pier next week.'

'Fantastic! I'll be going down to see that.'

'See what?' Nessa appeared in her floaty dress and sat down beside Doctor Ed, a cup of homemade lemonade in hand.

'They're putting down the foundations for Mike's *Waiting Man* next week, on the pier.'

'Cool. How long will that take?'

'Three to four weeks – it won't be particularly interesting,' Mike pointed out. 'Just like the foundations for any building going down.' He shrugged.

'Ah, but it's not just any building, is it?' Nessa tilted her head. 'This foundation is the first step in making our local ghost man a physical reality we can all finally lay eyes on. I for one can't wait to meet him.'

'Flower, Nessa!' Three-year-old Freddy was solemn as he held out the dandelion. 'For you.' His little hands were grubby from digging.

'Oh, thank you, Freddy! That's so lovely of you to give me a flower. I love it.' Nessa clasped it to her chest and then put it behind her ear. 'How about that?'

'Pretty!' Freddy laughed, doubling over and clutching his knees.

Nessa shook her head and laughed with him. 'You are the cutest thing I have ever seen.' She looked up at the two men. 'I'd run away with him.'

'He is a particularly entrancing specimen, Nessa, I'll give you that.' Doctor Ed grinned. 'Though I'll bet even Freddy has his moments. They all do, you know. Mind you, he's always been perfectly behaved with me – a pleasure to look after, aren't you, Freddy?' But Freddy was absorbed back at the flower bed.

'Oh, what are you *doing*, Freddy?'

The others looked around to see Stella making her way over to him.

'Mummy!' He scrambled to his feet and hurtled towards her – leaving small clay handprints on her pale yellow skirt as he clutched her legs. 'Making flowers. Come and see.'

He grabbed her hand, which she pulled away and looked at with distaste, pulling a tissue from her pocket and wiping it. 'You're filthy.' She sounded unusually angry.

'Hey, Buddy!' Bruce called, fresh from his swim. Running down the garden behind Stella, he raced over to Freddy and swung him up in the air.

'Daddy!' Freddy shrieked.

'I'm so sorry, Stella.' Doctor Ed stood up. 'That was my fault – I didn't think . . .'

Stella glared at him. 'Come on, Freddy, bath time. You can see Daddy later.'

'It's fine – I can take him now,' Bruce said over his shoulder. 'It's my night anyway, you go ahead.'

'But his routine—'

'I know the drill.' Bruce raised his eyes. 'I can give him his bath, Stella.' He shook his head and laughed, not entirely pleasantly. 'You can get as dirty as you like, pal.' Bruce squatted down by the flower bed beside his son. 'Go ahead,' he said rather pointedly, looking up at Stella. 'You're officially off duty.'

For a couple of awkward seconds, Stella stood there, until

Doctor Ed said quickly, 'I have a better idea. Why not join me in a G&T, Stella? All of you? I'll just pop inside and top up supplies.'

Once inside his small garden flat – or the bunker, as he referred to it – Ed rested his hands on the kitchen counter, feeling rather perplexed. What was the matter with Stella? She was becoming more confrontational than ever. She had never seemed to have a particularly warm personality . . . Bruce had mentioned once that she'd changed after Freddy was born. Ed wondered if perhaps that might be significant. Could he be missing something important here? Or was he just becoming an old busybody – he was a retired GP, not a mental health expert, he reminded himself. All the same, he might have a word with his friend Harry Beecham, who was a psychiatrist. Ed hated any kind of tension in the house. He went over to his cupboards and took down a bottle of gin.

'You can put a slug in this, for sure.' Nessa held up her cup of lemonade as soon as he re-emerged.

'That's what I like to hear!'

'I'd have brought more lemonade down if I'd known.'

'No need, I have plenty of tonic.' He put down a few plastic cups and dispensed some gin into each. 'Excuse the lack of crystal, chaps – but the dishwasher's on.'

'Never stopped us before.' Mike grinned. He picked up the tonic bottle and topped up the cups, handing one to Stella, who took it gratefully.

'To Evelyn's return.' Doctor Ed held up his mug. 'They're letting her out next week –Friday.'

'Oh, that's great news,' Nessa said. 'I was wondering when she was coming home. It hasn't been the same without her.'

'Morah's been getting the flat ready for both her and her granddaughter. We'll have to have one of our communal barbecues to introduce her to everyone.'

Nessa clapped her hands. 'Good idea! How about I get some grub together? The guys can sort the booze, and we can set it up to welcome Evelyn home and introduce her granddaughter to everyone at the same time.'

Doctor Ed smiled. He loved when his tenants were gathered all around him – his surrogates, as he referred to them. He'd also been missing Evelyn badly, more than he expected, and he was counting the days until her return. 'In that case, I'll be in charge of cocktails and Bruce and Mike can take care of the beer.'

'Good that's settled,' said Nessa. 'You all around for, say, 7 p.m.? That shouldn't be too late for Evelyn.'

'When has anything ever been too late for Evelyn?' Ed said.

'Good point. But she'll be tired.'

'Or raring to go.'

'Sounds great,' Bruce said. Then added rather hesitantly, to no one in particular, 'Em, would it be alright if I asked a friend along?'

'Sure, the more the merrier,' said Nessa – a little too breezily, flicking a mischievous glance at Doctor Ed.

But he was watching Stella, who had drained her gin and was striding back towards the house. He shook his head imperceptibly when he met Nessa's eyes. He was feeling increasingly uneasy about the whole Stella and Bruce situation.

Chapter Eleven

'So, are you still bringing a friend to the barbecue tonight?' Nessa was sitting on the rocks after her early swim, wrapped in a towel and sipping the herbal tea she had brought in a flask. It was 6.30, and the sun was an hour old in a clear blue sky. Bruce had climbed out of the water to join her while he dried off.

'Yes, I am.' He was resolute. 'I wasn't sure if I should have cleared it with Stella first, but Annika wants to meet my friends and stuff, and she's so . . . easy and straightforward with me – never playing any games, I always know where I stand with her. It just seemed unfair not to treat her the same way. Freddy wants to meet her too – he's very excited.' Bruce's face softened. 'I just told him I had a new friend who'd be coming to the barbecue.'

'Annika's a lovely name – where'd you meet?'

'Work. She's an architect on one of the new commercial developments in the financial centre – my team were in charge of one of the leases. We got chatting at a breakfast meeting after the media launch. Her mum's Swedish . . .'

'Well, I look forward to meeting her. How's Stella taking it?'

He shrugged. 'She was a bit put out. Apparently she heard me and Annika leaving for work one morning last week and confronted me about it. I don't see why she'd care one way or the other at this stage. But I just sort of blurted it out about inviting Annika to the barbecue that night in the garden while you guys were there, 'cos it was easier. I haven't seen her since then. I doubt we'll be staying long – like I said, I've got Freddy this weekend, so we'll just grab something to eat and then I'll put Fred to bed.'

Nessa was pleased for Bruce. It was clear now to anyone who knew him – including presumably his ex-wife, Stella – that Bruce had left behind any notions of winning her back and was instead intent on enjoying his new, healthier life-style, which now included a new girlfriend. Nessa had never seen him looking or seeming this happy.

'Want some tea?' Nessa waved her flask at him.

'Not if it's that herbal muck.' Bruce grinned. 'I'll see you in The Friendly Plate in a bit if you're there. I need a proper coffee before I hit the road.'

'I'll walk back with you – I need to make tracks too.' Nessa gathered up her stuff. 'I'm there for breakfast because that's the busiest time, but then I'm leaving Theresa to run the show. I've got a barbecue to organise and the fair is only four weeks away. I need to talk to the food stall people and double check with the Portaloo company.'

✧

Breakfast was busy as usual at Nessa's café – The Friendly Plate had gathered quite a regular clientele since she had opened two years ago, especially with office workers looking for a healthy start to their working day. Nessa always did a top-up coffee run – she liked to go around tables with the filter jug, offering top-ups at breakfast. Most clients didn't take advantage, and as a goodwill gesture it was paying off. It also gave her a chance to chat to customers and find out more about them – it was surprising what people would reveal in answer to 'What kind of a day are you facing?' Nessa had already lured people away from the other two cafés in the town. After checking stock, and having a look at her delivery list for the day, she left the ever-capable Theresa to manage the lunchtime paninis, packed her notepad and pen in her canvas bag with the two hens' faces painted on it, and headed for the castle.

It was almost eleven o'clock now, and most of the premises along the main street were open. She dropped in to Baubles, the modern jewellery store, to admire some of the new stackable bangles with different words elegantly scripted on them so you could wear a particular slogan for the day, discreetly arranged along your arms, and laughed when Jilly, who ran the shop, jangled her chosen bangles reading *Can't you see I'm busy* at her. Both Jilly and Dana – the latter ran the small art gallery and had popped in for a chat – would be having stalls at the fair. 'How's Evelyn doing? Any news?' They were eager for an update.

'She's coming home later today,' Nessa said. 'And her granddaughter's getting in too from London – she'll be staying with her for a few weeks.'

'Oh, that's good – it was such bad luck, her tripping on the stairs like that. So fortunate you found her so quickly.'

'Not that quickly. Half an hour, and she was in awful

pain. It was just so unfortunate that Morah was hoovering in one of the flats above and didn't hear her.'

Down by the seafront, Nessa had a quick look in Wax Lyrical for some new scented candles. Along the boardwalk, people strolled contentedly, enjoying the sudden spell of hot weather. Youngsters whizzed by on scooters and bikes, and a local ice cream van positioned itself for maximum sales exposure by the pier. The sea was as blue and calm as Nessa had ever seen it. Turning right, she climbed the road leading to the castle, whose crumbling ruins looked down over the town and out to sea from its elevated, if decaying, position. Paddy – the self-appointed gatekeeper who sat by the gap in the wall and relied on tips from kind-hearted tourists – had been stationed at the remains of the entrance for as long as anyone could remember, or care. Today he was stretched out in a deckchair enjoying the sun. He opened an eye at Nessa. 'Howya. Any word on the duchess?' He always referred to Evelyn as Duchess.

'She's getting out today.'

'Ah, that's good. You'd miss her. Tell her I'll take her for an ice cream when she's up for it.'

'I'll pass that on. I'm just going to take a look around up above. I need to double check how many stalls we'll be able to accommodate this year.'

'Be my guest.' Paddy waved her on.

It was a polite ritual. Paddy's title was as fictitious as the gate he presumed to keep guard over, the castle long ago having reverted to the state, and what was left of it was nowadays under the auspices of the local council. But Paddy held his position in great regard, and since no one had ever had cause to object to him, the hours he kept on duty at his makeshift table and couple of chairs – where he chatted with like-minded individuals – filled his day and sense of purpose admirably. 'Busy today.' He inclined his head towards the path ahead of her. 'Some fella claiming to be a descendant of the Fitzgeralds – there's always one.' He laughed. 'Wanting to look around what's left of the family seat.'

'Don't get sunburnt.' Nessa cracked their running joke. Paddy was generally the colour of a walnut table by this stage of exposition to the elements, irrespective of the weather. Nessa assumed it was an accumulation of summers.

'Ah, we live in hope.' Paddy grinned. 'Who needs the Riviera, wha'?'

Nessa made her way up along the path until she reached the remains of the first tower – and turned to admire the view over the coast. Below her a flotilla of white sails weaved jerkily in and out at capricious angles – it was the time of year the local yacht club held its summer sailing courses. To the left of them, by the pier, she could see builders at work and realised they must be preparing to put down the foundations Mike had been talking about for his sculpture. A shiver ran down her spine. Mike's sculpture was an interpretation of *The Waiting Man*, the local legend which held that the ghost of a man whose wife had been lost in the great shipwreck of 1807 could be seen standing at the end of the pier – just where the sculpture would be – waiting, with his child in his arms, unable to accept that his spouse had been lost. The legend had been almost forgotten at this stage, had become a part of sentimental folklore – until Mike discovered it during his research into local history, and the council had commissioned the sculpture. No one alive could remember exactly when the ghost had last been seen – although there was always the odd spurious claim. What wasn't spoken about so often, though, was the fact that he was only supposed to appear to warn of a looming tragedy.

Nessa paused for a moment to breathe in the stillness. She hadn't been able to shake the vague feeling of unease she'd had since doing Stella's reading, and in the grounds of the castle Nessa had always found peace – it was where she came to re-centre herself when she felt out of kilter spiritually. The castle had been the centre of Abbottsville since its beginnings in medieval times. In 1539, it had been granted by Henry V lll to a branch of Cistercian monks, from which the general area drew its name. When the abbey had been dissolved the castle was inhabited by a succession of families in various stages of favour with the crown, the most enduring of whom had been the Fitzgerald clan. Although it had been a large castle by local standards, with a number of buildings, all that remained today was the original gatehouse with its high vault overhead and the sloping ruins of two of the large three-storey towers that formed one side of the main hall. The interior buildings had long since disappeared, making it an ideal space for the local fair, which was held annually, and other various enterprises – most recently a murder mystery night and an outdoor movie event.

'It's quite a view, isn't it?' Nessa turned at the sound of a man's American accent behind her.

'Yes, it is – we tend to take it for granted. Oh, aren't you—?' Nessa was pretty sure she had seen this man running up the steps to the house next door the day before.

'My name is Ari.' He smiled. 'Forgive me, I didn't mean to creep up on you. It's my first time in Dublin. I'm here for a while with work.' He held out his hand.

'I'm Nessa, I run the vegan café on the main street. But if I'm not mistaken, I think we're neighbours.'

'We are? Cool.' He lifted his eyebrows.

'Yeah, I live in number 24 Ulysses Crescent – was that you I saw running up the steps to number 23 yesterday?'

'Yes, that would have been me.' He nodded, smiling. 'Glad to make your acquaintance, Nessa.'

'You've done an incredible job on the house. From what I can see,' she added hurriedly.

'Thank you. Although I can't claim I had much to do with it – we use the same firm for all our residential properties. But it's a fine house and the Crescent is a wonderful example of Georgian architecture.'

'Are you in the building business?'

'Reconstruction, you could say.' He looked around him. 'I'd like to have seen this place in its heyday. Pretty impressive, huh?'

'It would have been. Nowadays it just makes for a pretty backdrop – we get a lot of painters up here.'

'Do you paint?'

'Me? No . . . I'm just here to check on a few details – we're having our annual fair here in the grounds at the end of July. It's mostly food stalls and crafts, with a play area for kids. It's a kind of local tradition.'

'Sounds like fun. I'll try and get to it if I can – hopefully I'll still be here – it'd be good to meet some of the locals. See you around!' He began to walk on.

'In that case—'

He turned back, curious.

'Well, it's short notice, I know, but we're having a barbecue this evening. Around seven? It'd be great if you could make it, and feel free to bring anyone along . . . wife, kids . . . significant other . . .'

'That's very kind of you – I'd like that. I won't be bringing anyone. But it'd be great to get to know some of my neighbours.'

'Well, it'll mostly just be us.'

'Your family?'

'No . . . well, yes . . . our house – that is, Doctor Ed's house, number 24 – it's in flats . . . apartments. During the summer we often have get-togethers in the communal garden. We're kind of like a family.'

'Okay, cool. Well, I look forward to meeting Doctor Ed and whoever else is on the list.'

'Great – see you at seven, Ari? Was that what you said your name was?'

'That's me! Aristes Fitzgerald Christopoulos.' He grinned. 'My friends call me Ari. My father's family are Greek,' he explained. 'My mother is half Irish, half Argentinian. Hence the Fitzgerald part. I live in Boston these days – mostly. I believe we have links on my mother's side to the Fitzgeralds of Abbottsville Castle. I was just checking the old place out for her.'

'Wow! Okay . . . well, we'll look forward to seeing you later, Ari.'

'Likewise.' He waved as he walked away.

Checking the time, Nessa wondered if Evelyn might be

home already – and there was also the granddaughter to meet. It'd be good to have another girl around the place, maybe make a new friend. Stella didn't exactly fit the bill.

She did a quick recce, noted any unwieldy tree roots or other new obstacles that might prove problematic for stall-holders, took some shots on her phone, then headed back. She still had to pick up the food for this evening – she could grab everything else she needed back at the café.

She couldn't wait to tell the others. Evelyn in particular would be delighted. A dark, handsome and rather exotic new neighbour coming along to her welcome-home barbe-cue. That would be right up her street.

Chapter Twelve

She was so delighted, she could have broken into song. Although it had been under four weeks since the accident, it felt like a veritable eternity since Evelyn had been in her cherished apartment. She was seated now, in a supportive armchair loaned to her by Doctor Ed, with an attractive shawl draped over her legs. Her luxurious sink-into sofas would be of no use to her for now – she'd never be able to get up from them, crutches or no crutches. The walking frame – provided by Morah with a certain amount of satisfaction (she had borrowed it from a friend who worked in a retirement home, apparently) – had been banished to Evelyn's wardrobe. Morah had not been happy about this, although Evelyn had assured her she could manage perfectly well on two crutches, thank you, and would be down to one after another week. Even so, Morah had refused to remove the walker. Evelyn suspected that even though Morah's efforts to have her avail of it had been thwarted, she remained determined it would sit in broad view as a reminder to anyone who entered the flat of how close they all were to the indignities of old age. It had almost come to a row.

Evelyn had always thought the little woman odd and rather disagreeable – watchful, especially – but Doctor Ed set such store by her, and all the other tenants relied on her for various cleaning or babysitting duties or letting in workmen and the like, that it would have been a very poor strategy for Evelyn to fall out with her. All the same, she had to admit Morah had done a good job keeping her apartment fresh and well aired, although it pained her to think that the woman had finally had unfettered access to her living quarters. Up until now she had never allowed anyone but Doctor Ed to hold a key – and that was the way she liked it. If it hadn't been for that stupid accident . . . but there was no point dwelling on it, the worst was behind her now.

The whole experience had been exhausting. She had spent two weeks in the step-down unit, while poor Tristan had been so worried about her he had insisted on someone coming to stay with her to supervise and help out while she recovered at home. That had alarmed her almost more than anything. He'd even suggested at one stage that Pauline come over! As if he didn't know they were as good as permanently estranged. Imagine having to introduce Pauline to the rest of the tenants! They knew she had a daughter, of course, but only that she lived in London and had a very busy career – that much was true. Otherwise, Evelyn was vague. As far as she was concerned, her real family was here. Anyway, apart from Doctor Ed and Morah, the others were all young and too busy in their own lives to notice if anything were amiss in hers. Her daughter had been unpredictable, to say the least, when she was young . . . nothing but trouble, in fact, as far as Evelyn remembered – which was something she avoided doing if at all possible . . .

Evelyn had never been entirely sure whether Pauline

had been a honeymoon baby or the result of their then increasingly risqué – and on Chris's part, rather demanding – amorous escapades. Although she and Christopher, Pauline's father, were officially a dating couple at the time, the consequences of pre-marital sexual encounters in 1960s Ireland were risky at best, and downright disastrous at worst. Whatever the case, Evelyn had been so frightened by the possibility she might have been pregnant at the time, in 1966, that when she told Chris this might be the case, and also pointed out the only acceptable solution to the situation, which was a speedy wedding, they both acted promptly. Either way, Pauline had arrived early, and inopportunely, as far as Evelyn was concerned. Once the wedding was over, and the baby was born in due course, things had settled into the usual marital routine, and Evelyn found herself saddled with a colicky baby who rarely slept and who interfered hugely with her social life. She insisted Chris hire a full-time nurse for the child, and when the baby and nurse bonded happily, Evelyn had felt a sense of relief and escape that bordered on intoxicating. From then on she decided to avoid any more children, and Christopher, pleased to have his wife in better spirits and back to her old self now that she could throw herself into the full-time social life their set indulged in, was happy to go along with her wishes. Pauline, who inherited her father's ruggedly handsome looks, was not a pretty child, which did nothing to endear her further to Evelyn as she grew older. Evelyn simply wasn't the maternal type. As far as she was concerned, she'd had the child and done her duty.

And Pauline duly progressed from being a lonely child to

a sullen and rebellious teen. As far as Evelyn was concerned, her daughter had simply been impossible – and she refused to admit or even contemplate that she had played any part whatsoever in how their relationship had turned out. Which was why she avoided thinking about it, if at all possible. The idea of Pauline coming back to Dublin after over thirty years to look after her while she recuperated was quite out of the question. Evelyn shuddered just contemplating it.

Of the available options, Truth coming over was a far better idea. Evelyn sat up a little straighter in her chair and rearranged the shawl. She just hoped Truth didn't take after her mother. If she did, Evelyn would send her packing.

'Would you be a dear and bring me my hand mirror, Morah – it's on the dressing table. And any of my lipsticks, please – a pink one would do nicely.'

There had been a small welcoming committee in the hall when Evelyn had arrived home. Doctor Ed had picked her up from the convalescent wing in his car, and Nessa, Mike and Morah, and Rory from the basement gym, had been waiting at the house to greet her. The others were out at work, of course. When she reached her apartment – Rory and Doctor Ed had supported her on either side as she went painstakingly up the stairs – there had been a wonderful arrangement of flowers waiting for her on the table in the bay window. It was all very touching. Morah had suggested then that she should stay and wait with Evelyn until Truth arrived. Evelyn hadn't been thrilled by the idea, but seeing as someone would have to let Truth in to her apartment, she'd had to graciously acquiesce. The subsequent, rather terse forty-five minutes or so that had passed between Evelyn and Morah had been the longest time they had spent in each other's company, despite living under the same roof for the past five years. Evelyn flicked a glance now at Morah out of the corner of her eye, as she touched up her lipstick and straightened the colourful necklace of modern stones she was wearing. The woman appeared to be staring at her with barely disguised distaste.

'Are you alright, Morah?' Evelyn paused, lipstick midair. 'Is there a problem?'

'None at all.' She gave a tight smile. 'Why would there be?'

'You don't have to stay, you know – I'm quite alright here in my chair. It's not as if I'm going to be leaping up and running around. My granddaughter should be here any minute – I'm sure you've got better things to be doing.'

'I told Doctor Ed I'd stay until the girl arrived,' Morah said, with a stubborn tilt to her chin.

She was giving Evelyn the creeps. It also irritated Evelyn hugely that Morah kept referring to Truth as 'the girl' – not even your granddaughter. But Evelyn bit her lip rather than remind her that her granddaughter had a name. There was no point in giving Morah the satisfaction of knowing she had succeeded in annoying her.

Chapter Thirteen

It was mid-afternoon as Truth strolled along the seafront towards her grandmother's address, but before getting there she stopped for a coffee at The Friendly Plate café, set in a row of arty shops, and sat down to check her messages. There was one from Pauline, wishing her luck and telling her to call her when she could. Another from a girlfriend and colleague, and one from Josh:

> *You're probably in Ireland by now, if my calculations are correct – so have a lovely time and look after yourself. I'm here 24/7 if you need me. Tell Granny I look forward to meeting her* ☺ *x*

Truth knew Josh meant well and was trying to be amusing – or at least she gave him the benefit of the doubt – but the tone of the text made her feel irritated. She had asked him not to contact her, and although he claimed to be worried about her, it was all too clear to Truth that her breaking up with him had presented him with a challenge, rather than a *fait accompli*. Josh simply wasn't going to accept that they were no longer a couple. That's what annoyed her. Well, she wasn't going to play along – Josh could indulge whatever fantasies he wanted to make himself feel better about things, but as far as she was concerned they were over. And if he kept on texting her or emailing her as if nothing had changed, they wouldn't even be able to remain friends – which she very much wanted to do. Josh was clever, highly entertaining, and a terrific lawyer – they'd had some great times together – but recent events had thrown light on a more disappointing side of his character, and Truth realised he wasn't quite the man she had thought he was. This latest text proved her right. If Josh had even a glimmer of sympathy – never mind empathy – for the terrible toll the online abuse had taken on her, he wouldn't be sending her a text message when she'd specifically asked him not to. As for the 'meeting Granny' line – well, she could hardly claim to be surprised. Josh was persistent – it had been one of the things she'd admired about him. But what worked in haranguing or cross-examining a witness in the courtroom didn't work in relationships. And Truth wasn't going to be bullied by anyone – however nicely. She had a mob of angry trolls on her case. A disgruntled ex-boyfriend was just more grist to the mill. Besides, Josh was such a charmer, she suspected he would probably wrap Evelyn around his little finger at first sight. That was one meeting she was going to make sure *didn't* take place. Even her mother had been captivated by him – and Pauline wasn't noted for giving men any kind of easy credit.

She suddenly felt claustrophobic in the small shop, and asked for the remains of her coffee to be transferred to a carry-out mug. She continued her walk towards Evelyn's – although she still felt unsettled. *Relax*, she told herself. This was just typical Josh – he was never going to give up easily.

He was a gentleman at heart – it wasn't as if he was going to become a stalker; she was just letting the crazy online stuff of the last six weeks make her overreact.

The sound of water lapping against stone made her look up, and she saw a slipway ahead which led to a small pier. In spite of everything she had just been thinking about, her heart lifted at the sight of the pretty harbour and the beach beyond. It was so different to the landscape she had left behind in London mere hours ago – she felt transported to a completely different world. A few gulls circled above while another sidled towards her, hopeful, presumably, of some food. The wall of the pier divided the harbour from the open ocean, and she found a small gap in it to slip through and sit on the rocks looking out to sea, cradling her coffee, letting the breeze and the warm sun and the sounds of children shrieking with delight in the distance remind her she was officially off duty. It felt good to be off social media too. Let the trolls write what they liked about her – she didn't have to look at it. She saw most of her 'friends' these days on Instagram – there was something shallow and hollow about that. Right now, Truth just wanted to relish being in the moment. Maybe here she might meet and make some new friends – people who lived in the real world and not online.

She took a deep breath, reminding herself there was no case to fret over, no witness to worry about, no judge to win over – she just had to stay here, look after her grandmother, and try to forget that there were people out there who thought she deserved to die, who knew where she lived, and who enjoyed making vile threats against her. She remembered the first note she had found in her letterbox at home, and held in her hands, which read simply:

You deserve to be dead you stupid bitch and we'll decide when.

For Josh the solution had been simple: 'Move in with me, darling – you know it makes sense.' Even then, he had been working the situation to his advantage.

A shout, and a splash of warm coffee on her leg, brought her back to the present – her hands were shaking. The shout – which had made her jump – was followed by a loud clank, and Truth scrambled to her feet; whatever brief peace she had been enjoying had been rudely interrupted. On the other side of the gap in the wall, the source of the noise was clear to see – a group of workmen were unloading materials from a large truck and cordoning off the area in front. One of them was about to start drilling.

Truth's curiosity got the better of her. 'What's going up here?' she asked the one who seemed to be in charge.

'No idea, love, I'm just following instructions from the council engineer.' He had a strong accent she found difficult to make out.

It was such a lovely spot, she felt a pang of regret. It was a shame to spoil it with – more than likely, she guessed – a coffee stand or bicycles to rent. She was about to head back when another, altogether different sound made her stop in her tracks. The sound was sweet and soulful – and the melody familiar – although she couldn't place it. Turning around, she saw a guy standing by the wall – not far from where she'd been on the other side – playing a brass instrument. He was lost in the moment, his eyes closed as he swayed to the music. Something about him made her stop and stare – his colouring was sallow, although his skin was pale, contrasting against the dark hair that reached his shoulders, lifting now in the sudden breeze. His lips pressed against the mouthpiece in utter concentration. Then his eyes opened, and for a second he looked right at her, holding her gaze, and she had the strangest sensation he was playing just to her. Flustered, she looked away, and was reassured to see she wasn't the only one affected in this way. Around her, the workmen had downed tools to a man, and stood smiling wistfully, or perhaps just in admiration, as he played. A few passers-by strolled over to listen too, until after a few moments the spell came to an end, and he gave a mock bow and nodded as people clapped.

'What *is* that tune? It's so familiar . . .' Truth said to no one in particular.

'"The Swan",' a woman beside her said, smiling as she picked up her shopping to go on her way. 'Gets me every time.'

'Of course,' Truth murmured. She knew it was familiar. All the times she had watched – mesmerised – as a little girl while the beautiful ballerina danced as the tragic swan, fluttering to her graceful death.

'Okay to crack on, Mike?' a man in a hard hat called to the musician as he passed by.

'Sure, go for it!' He clapped the man on the shoulder. And right on cue the drilling started.

On impulse, Truth followed the musician, a discreet space behind, as he strolled back to a bench by the wall where a case lay open flat and he bent down to pack the instrument away.

Intrigued, she decided she had to speak to him. 'Um, is that a trombone – I was just wondering?'

He straightened and looked around. Up close his eyes were green under dark brows. His mouth curved in a half smile as he answered her. 'It's a euphonium.'

She looked blank.

'Like a tuba,' he explained, 'but smaller.'

'Oh. Well, that . . . that was beautiful, I just wanted to say.'

'Thanks. That's what the name euphonium means – *beautiful sound.*'

'It was a shame those workmen had to start up – I think people would have liked to hear you play more.'

'I always play just the one piece – it's a kind of tradition.' He sat down against the wall and leaned back, stretching his legs and folding his arms as he looked up at her.

'Oh.' She wasn't sure what to say to that. 'Like a practice?'

She had the feeling he was weighing up whether or not she was worth talking to.

'No, I have a project going up here.' He indicated the workmen. 'A sculpture – it's become a kind of ritual for me to play this piece before the foundations go down, just for luck, I guess. The guy who wrote the composition, Saint-Saens, wrote the whole thing, *The Carnival of the Animals*, for a joke. 'Le Cygne' was the only movement from it he allowed to be published in his lifetime – and it became a huge success.' He shrugged. 'Any kind of art is subjective, people can love it or hate it – particularly when it's going up in such a public space. I'd rather they loved mine, obviously.'

'So you serenade it . . .' Truth found the idea charming. 'And you always play this piece?'

'Like I said, it's a ritual.' His eyes squinted as he looked up at her. 'Trust me – you don't want to hear me sing.' He stood up, grinned at her, and swung the case off the wall. 'See you.' And he walked away.

A sculptor who serenaded his work . . . and she hadn't even asked him what the sculpture was – now she wouldn't get another chance to talk to him. The realisation left her strangely deflated.

As she checked directions to Ulysses Crescent on her phone, she failed to notice the elderly gentleman with the white moustache and neatly shaped beard sitting behind his paper, wearing a linen suit and straw boater, who had noted the exchange between her and the euphonium player with interest.

✧

Truth made her way to the house in a few minutes, pressing the bell to flat number 3 and hearing the front door buzz open. A tinny female voice came through the intercom telling her to come up to the first floor, and clicked off before she could reply or venture her identity or greeting. As she climbed up the two flights of stairs covered in soft, silver carpet, Truth took in the spacious hall, high ceilings, and elaborate cornicing and proportions of the beautiful Georgian house. For a moment, she wondered just what she was letting herself in for. She didn't have long to speculate. As she reached the landing a small figure stood imperiously at the open door to the flat. 'You're very welcome, I'm sure,' the woman said, looking up at her. 'I'm Morah. I live on the top floor and I also act as the concierge. You must be Truth.' She held out her hand stiffly.

'Yes, I am.' Truth smiled at her. 'I'm very pleased to meet you and thank you so much for taking care of Granny's flat while she was in hospital. Mum and I are very grateful to you.'

Morah inclined her head and visibly softened. 'It was no trouble. I was glad to be of help.' She studied Truth intently and seemed reluctant to let her in to the flat. For an awkward moment, Truth hovered uncertainly, as Morah stood in the doorway. She wondered who the woman reminded her of – and then stifled a grin as it struck her: Morah could have given Bette Davis a good run for her money vying for her role in *What Ever Happened to Baby Jane?*

'Morah?' another woman's voice called. 'What on earth are you doing out there? Where is my granddaughter?'

'You'd better go in,' Morah said, waving Truth ahead of her.

Truth did as she was told and walked along a short corridor and into a splendid room where a beautiful (there was no other way to describe her) older woman with platinum hair tied back from her face in a bright red headband regarded her with interest from an armchair.

'Let me guess.' Truth grinned. 'You must be Grandma Evelyn.' She bent to kiss her on the cheek. 'It's been a while, right?'

'It certainly has.' Evelyn seemed delighted. 'The crutches are a bit of a giveaway.' She waved one.

Truth disentangled her backpack and dumped it on the

floor. 'I was just telling Morah how appreciative we are of her looking after the flat while you were in hospital. Mum sends her love.'

'That's very kind of her. I'm looking forward to hearing all the news,' Evelyn said, then added to Morah, who was still listening, 'Don't let us detain you a minute longer, Morah.' The dismissal was playful – but the intention was clear. She turned back to Truth. 'Morah's been kind enough to wait with me so someone could let you in. But now you're here . . .' Again, she smiled pointedly at Morah, who looked as if she didn't want to budge – on the contrary, she seemed fascinated by Truth. 'Just pull the door behind you, Morah.' Evelyn nodded, willing her to go.

Truth watched the exchange with interest.

'Well,' Morah left the room reluctantly, 'if you need anything, let me know.'

'Thank you, Morah.'

When she had gone, Evelyn rolled her eyes. 'Weird little woman – I'll tell you about her later.' She sat back and looked at Truth. 'But first, would you like to make yourself a coffee or tea?'

'I've just had one – but can I make one for you?'

'Not at all. Sit down there. I want to hear all about you! Every little detail.'

Truth flung herself onto a sofa. 'This is a lovely room.'

'And that' – her grandmother noted the soft leather designer bag – 'is a very lovely piece of workmanship. I'll bet it cost a pretty penny, but good quality is an investment, and you wear it well.'

'I work hard. Being able to afford nice things is one of the perks of the job.' Truth decided she liked Evelyn. Judging from the flat, and her manner – her grandmother clearly had attitude.

Evelyn was leaning forward, looking at her closely. 'I thought you would look more like your mother, but . . .'

'I'm more like my dad, I think.'

'Has anyone ever told you you're a dead ringer for *me*?'

'Really?' Truth's eyebrows lifted – this was news to her. 'How flattering.'

Evelyn smiled as she studied Truth from her chair. 'Really – look over there, if you don't believe me.' She pointed to a table of photographs, where her younger self featured in a series of glamorous outfits and parties from the 1960s and '70s.

Truth went over to check them out. She thought maybe she could see the resemblance. 'Those are great photographs . . . and cool gear,' she said. 'Well, we clearly have a love of clothes in common – that's a good start. Did you keep any of them?'

'Some of the more useful items might be lurking in my wardrobe.' Evelyn considered the possibility. 'But I'm pretty sure the glamorous stuff you'd be interested in is long gone – more's the pity. I've learned to travel light in my latter years. Makes life a lot easier.'

'Speaking of making things easier . . .' Truth wandered back. 'What is it you're going to need me to do? How can I be of help? Can I get you anything now?'

'Not at all. You're terribly good to come over – I do appreciate it. It's such a bore all this. But the doctor was very specific about the routine I'm to follow. I'm on two crutches now – after this week I can go down to one. I'm going to need assistance getting in and out of the shower and bed. And you'll have to help me get these awful compression stockings on and off.' She lifted a trouser leg to reveal the elasticated support bandage. 'Otherwise, it's really just getting meals together – I don't eat much – and helping fetch and carry. And it would be great if you could help Nessa out a bit if she needs it – you'll meet her, she lives on the ground floor. She organises the castle fair day, which is at the end of July, and I usually give her a hand. And please don't worry,' she looked serious, 'I won't expect you to sit in here with me, you know. I'm very independent. Once I'm set up with a drink and my iPad, I'll be quite happy in front of the TV. You'll find plenty to do, and the other tenants are a lovely lot – a few seem to be about your age, I'd imagine. If you look out the windows, you'll see we're only minutes from the town centre and across the road from a wonderful swimming spot. Do you swim?'

'Yeah, but usually in warmer water than I'm guessing that is.' Truth admired the view from the front window.

'Wait until you try it, you'll be hooked – everyone is. The cold is the best thing about it – it's what gives you the high.'

'Mmm . . .' Truth was doubtful.

Evelyn laughed. 'Well, go and have a look at your room and get settled in, then tell me what you'd like to do. There's plenty of hot water if you'd like a bath or shower. Oh, and did I mention there's a barbecue this evening?'

'A barbecue?'

'Yes, to welcome me home – the other tenants have organised it for me – isn't that sweet of them? It's right here in the garden – so we don't have to actually go anywhere.'

'Well, I guess that's dinner taken care of.'

'Exactly.'

'I really like your decorating style.' Truth came back from the bedroom after a few minutes and looked about her. She studied some of the smaller paintings up close. 'It's bold.'

'Yes, well, I was never the sort of person to do things by halves. And this apartment – let's just say I was determined to be happy here. I'd had a bit of a tricky time after Lenny died and finding he'd re-mortgaged the house to the hilt after the crash.'

'I never knew that.' Truth was taken aback.

'Why would you? It wasn't your problem. And I like solving my own. I made an exception in allowing you to come over because I was curious to see you again.' Evelyn smiled. 'But when I found this place I wanted it to be a constant reminder of some really happy times – so I decorated with that in mind.' She looked faraway for a second. 'If it seems to remind you of an upmarket nightclub,' she grinned, 'I won't be offended. That may not altogether be an accident.'

Truth laughed. 'I'm not sure what it reminds me of – it's kind of unique. Although grey is terribly popular still.'

'It wasn't when I did my place up – people thought I was mad.'

'And the cerise curtains and sofas really work with it.'

'I like to think so.'

'So which nightclub was it you wanted to be reminded of?'

'Ah,' said Evelyn dreamily. 'One or two favourites . . . Although of course you're too young to have known Annabel's in its heyday. But there's plenty of time to hear my stories – and I want to hear all about you.'

'I know you've been married twice, right? To my mum's father first, obviously, Christopher. And I can see why you were considered a beauty – Tristan told me that, anyway.'

'Did he now?' Evelyn seemed amused. 'Well, I married Chris, your grandfather, when I was very young. I'd just turned twenty. Then your mother came along, as you know.' She smiled. 'Chris was killed in a car crash four years later and I was left a young widow. I met Lenny, then, Tristan's father, in 1972, and we were very happy together. Tristan coming along ten years later was rather a surprise – I hadn't intended on having more children – but these things happen, don't they?'

'That explains the age gap between my mum and Uncle Tris. It's good they have each other, though,' Truth said. 'They're close despite their difference in age.'

'Yes, I'm glad about that.' Evelyn studied her. 'It's good for Pauline to have someone in her life she can talk to and depend upon – your mother can be quite . . . defensive. That can put people off. I'm sure you know we've had our own relationship problems over the years . . . that's why I'm so happy she has Tristan. Everyone needs family support. She has you, obviously, but one never wants to burden one's children . . .'

'I'd really like to hear about you and Mum sometime,' Truth said. 'If you'd like to talk about it? Mum doesn't really say much . . .'

'Perhaps . . .' Evelyn said. 'But not today – I don't believe in dwelling on the past. Suffice to say you're very wise to be an independent career woman. I wish I had been. Both men and children can let you down when you least expect it, I find.'

Truth laughed. 'Well, we've got lots of time to get to know each other. I think I will have a shower now, if that's alright. I could do with a hair wash before this barbecue – is there anything you need before I go to unpack?'

'Not a thing. I have my iPad beside me so I'll just catch up on my messages.'

'I won't be long, twenty minutes, maybe? Yell if you need me – I'll leave the door open.'

'Take as long as you like.' Evelyn waved her off.

✧

As the shower pelted to life and the muffled sound of some-one singing about never getting back together drifted out from the bathroom, Evelyn leaned back in her chair and smiled. Truth had turned out to be even better than she had dared to hope. Her granddaughter was smart, beautiful, and clearly had a sense of humour. She certainly hadn't got that from her mother.

Evelyn was perturbed, however, that Truth was so keen to delve into Evelyn and Pauline's lack of relationship. Evelyn wasn't keen on that at all. She preferred the past to remain in the past. That was where it belonged. She hadn't been joking when she'd told Truth she wished she had been an independent woman. If she'd had the courage to remain on her own and not to marry Lenny . . . then who knows what might have become of her? Instead she had met Robert Radcliffe, Lenny's business associate, and that whole lethal attraction thing between them had been unleashed. She had been sailing very close to the wind back then. She'd been lucky to escape with her reputation relatively unscathed from the whole business. It had all been so long ago . . . but Bobby had been the one . . . there was no denying that. They had both fallen madly for each other. Evelyn had been willing and ready to run away with him, except then he had bottled out. At least he was paying for it now, in a manner of speaking. If it wasn't for Bobby, she wouldn't be sitting here now in her beautiful apartment in number 24. And she had a clever and interesting granddaughter to get to know.

Evelyn's rehabilitation was going to be much more entertaining than she had expected. Just as she always maintained – *it's an ill wind that blows no good*. Having Truth around the place was going to be fun, she just knew it. She was like a breath of fresh air. As the effect of her daily painkillers kicked in and made her drowsy, her eyelids became heavy, and she allowed them to close. For the duration of her brief snooze, Evelyn dreamed of mini-skirts, a shag haircut, and a pair of white wet-look over-the-knee boots that had been the envy of all her friends when she had been the first to sport them.

✧

Rory was in the grip of emotion as he sat on the wooden pub bench in the garden of number 24. Nessa had asked if he would help her set things up, and Rory had more than willingly obliged. He had procured and delivered the tables and chairs from a mate of his who ran a corporate entertainment business, and now the garden was all set for the barbecue later that evening.

It was half past four now, and the garden was looking particularly peaceful in the June sunlight. Under Doctor Ed's loving supervision, the magnolias, rock roses and poppies had all come into bloom, and in the pond the pristine white water lily unfurled its petals, reminding Rory of Nessa when she wore her white swimsuit in the sea, her golden curls caught up in a matching white scrunchie, bobbing in the water. He watched her now, fetching them both a drink after their hard work. The food was safely stored in the kitchen, the beer table set up, the drinks chilling and the barbecue primed and ready for action.

Rory sighed. He had never felt like this – as if everything beautiful he laid his eyes on was only a pale imitation of the loveliness that was Nessa. He couldn't take his eyes off her. Her grace, her softness, the way she moved – everything about her filled him with delight. He loved her with every fibre of his being and she had absolutely no idea. And he had no idea how to go about telling her. Every time he tried to ask her out on a date, the words failed him. He wanted it to be perfect. Nothing was too good for her. She was a goddess worthy of adoration. If only he'd lived in medieval times he could have gone off to war for her . . . if he were a man of words he would write poetry to her . . . if—

'Earth to Rory?' Nessa put a beer in front of him and slipped onto the other side of the bench, a faint sheen of perspiration glowing on the crest of her cheekbones. Rory ached to reach over and brush her cheek gently with his thumb – like they did in the movies – only knowing his luck, he'd end up sticking his finger in her eye.

'Sorry?'

'I was just asking you if you fancied a swim? I'm roasting after lugging all this stuff around. I could do with cooling off before the barbecue.'

Rory had already rescheduled two clients in order to spend time with Nessa, he couldn't afford to cancel a third. His face fell. 'I'd really like to, but—'

'Oh, no worries – you've been so good to do all this for me . . .' She fished for her phone as it rang, reaching into her back jean pocket.

Rory scowled at the injustice of missing another opportunity to spend time with Nessa – semi-undressed time, especially.

Nessa seemed taken aback by the phone call. 'Oh, hi, right . . . yes, well, that's great, I guess . . .' She chewed her lip and brushed her curls back distractedly. 'Look, I don't know, I'll have to check my diary for July, I'm going to be really busy with the fair and everything . . . Yes, probably . . .'

Rory watched her carefully, while he sipped his beer.

'Yes, well, maybe,' Nessa went on. 'I know it would be great . . . but just let me think about it, okay? Yeah, you too.' She finished the call, looking sheepish.

'What was that all about?' Rory hated the suspicious tone in his voice but he was incapable of dissembling, and he could tell Nessa was flustered.

'That was Ryan.' She was trying to sound disinterested, but her face was flushed and she was clearly trying to supress a whole cluster of emotions. 'He – he's going to be working for a year in Berlin . . . he just needs somewhere to stay for a week or so before he leaves . . .'

Rory groaned. 'Please tell me you're not going to let that plonker take advantage of you again, Nessa!'

'That's not fair, Rory!' Nessa protested weakly. 'He's invited me over to Berlin.'

'Sure he has.' Rory's eyes narrowed. 'Free rent and sex before he buggers off and leaves you again – I won't be holding my breath.'

'Oh, don't be mean.' Nessa looked as if she might cry. 'Ryan and I go back a long way.'

'You're too trusting, Ness, too kind – he's taking advantage. The guy's a complete dickhead.' Rory shook his head in despair. 'But if you want to let him back into your life again, that's your call.'

The previous glow of contentment Rory had been relishing was replaced by a crushing frustration, as any hopes he harboured of possibly winning over Nessa's affection at the barbecue later were cruelly dashed. He would just have to go on doing what he had done since the day he had set eyes on her – love her hopelessly from afar.

Chapter Fourteen

Truth's first official duty, she knew, would be to assist and accompany her grandmother to the welcome-home barbecue that evening. Evelyn decided that although she could get around on two crutches, for the duration of the barbecue she would use the wheelchair the health service had provided, which was kept downstairs in the hall. That way she could get comfortable, she said, and Truth could move her around outside without her having to sit down and get up all the time – it also meant she wouldn't get stuck with someone she didn't want to. This didn't mean, however, that she wasn't going to dress up. 'It's these horrid compression stockings I hate,' she said, making a face. 'So unattractive. I think I'll wear my green linen trousers' – she indicated the wardrobe Truth would find them in – 'and the Pucci kaftan. That's it – the emerald green and lavender one.'

Truth took out the silk garment and held it up. 'This is Pucci?'

'Certainly is. No one did kaftan's like Emilio.'

'It's beautiful.'

'Also very comfortable. I'm afraid you'll have to help me pull the trousers up and get the kaftan over my head.' Evelyn stood by her bed. 'What are *you* going to wear?'

'Jeans? It's not like I packed any resort wear.' Truth raised an eyebrow. 'I have a nice white silk shirt – that'll have to do. I didn't think this thing would be dressy?'

'It won't, I can assure you. But I have never dressed to other people's expectations and I'm not going to start now. Tell me more about your work.' Evelyn held her arms obediently as Truth arranged the kaftan.

'Well, I think Tristan told you that I'm a barrister?'

'Yes. How exciting!'

'And I represent women who've been sexually or otherwise abused. Increasingly my clients are women who have been compromised in the workplace.'

'Oh.' Evelyn sounded disappointed. 'That sounds depressing.'

'Depends on the case.'

'Do you have a boyfriend? Is he a barrister too?'

'I used to. He's an ex-boyfriend now. But yes, he's a barrister – and a very good one.'

'Did he finish with you?'

'No, I broke up with him – we kind of came to a point of no return.'

'So you're not upset about it?' Evelyn looked at her keenly.

'No-o-o. Not exactly.' Truth wondered where this was going.

'Then you're free and single!'

'Well, I'm not exactly looking for romance, if that's what you mean.'

'That's usually when it finds you – don't you think?'

'I'm here to look after *you* and see that you don't fall over again.'

'You make it sound as if it was my fault I fell over in the first place.'

'I didn't say that. But it doesn't hurt to be careful.'

'I've always been a risk-taker – I'm not about to change now. This is just an unfortunate setback.' Evelyn was amused.

'Risk-taking's all very well, but there are always consequences.'

'Oh, please don't tell me you're going to be all po-faced about everything. Haven't you ever taken any risks? Life's much too short to live it timidly. I was just unlucky, that's all. I still don't know what I tripped on. I wouldn't put it past Morah to have soaped the stairs deliberately – she doesn't like me at all, you know.'

'Why not?'

'How would I know? That's her problem.' Evelyn frowned. 'Right, you can deposit me over there in front of my mirror and I'll do my make-up. You go and get yourself ready and then we'll make our grand entrance. I'm sure they're all dying to meet you.'

The mouth-watering aroma of barbecuing meat floated up from the garden well before Truth had wheeled Evelyn down the wooden ramp someone had thoughtfully built over the steps that led down to the lower area. A cheer went up from an older man Truth guessed must be Doctor Ed, which made the others look up and rush to greet Evelyn as if she were a returning champion.

'Thank you!' She beamed. 'You've all been so kind! And this . . .' Evelyn waved a hand towards Truth '. . . is my gorgeous grand-daughter, Truth – who has dropped everything to come and look after me. Isn't that sweet of her? She's a very high-powered lawyer, you know.'

'Okay, Evelyn – dial it down a notch, hmm?' Truth leaned in to murmur as she pushed the chair.

'Now, why don't you come over here, Evelyn.' Doctor Ed indicated a spot he'd cleared beside the stone table. 'Then you can set up camp and be comfortable and we can all wait on you hand and foot. You'll be like Scarlett O'Hara.' He took over the chair from Truth. 'Truth, I suggest you take this opportunity to mingle while I monopolise your grandmother.'

The girl who seemed to be in charge of the grill was Nessa. She hurried over to welcome Truth and introduce her to the others. Nessa was lovely, Truth thought, with her sweet face and welcoming manner. Rory, who was clearly a body-builder type, shook her hand and said she would be welcome at the gym any time if she needed to work out or fancied a few training sessions. Bruce was in commercial property leasing and seemed interested that she was a lawyer. His blonde and rather serious girlfriend Annika was an architect. The adorable little three-year-old boy, Freddy, who was tearing around, was Bruce's son, but it was Stella, Bruce indicated – an attractive brunette with severely pulled back hair, presently talking with Morah – who was the boy's mother.

'It's such a convenient arrangement Bruce and Stella have, I think,' Annika said, looking up at Bruce. 'Isn't it great they can both make it work like this?' She smiled at Truth.

'It certainly must be great for Freddy,' Truth agreed, although privately she could think of nothing worse than living in the same house as your ex-partner – flats or no flats.

Nessa, hovering over the grill, was looking back towards the door from time to time. 'We're just expecting one other guest,' she told Truth. 'He's Greek-American. He's just moved in next door for a while. They've done an amazing job on the house – I'd give anything to see inside. Must have taken most of the year – and no expense spared, if you know what I mean.' She rubbed her fingers together indicating no shortage of money. 'In fact, I must go and tell Evelyn, I forgot to earlier – she'll be delighted. We've all been wondering what was going to happen with the house, or who was doing it up.' She put down her spatula and hurried over to Evelyn to bring her up to date. 'Keep an eye on the steaks, would you, Truth? I'll just be a sec.'

'Sure.' Truth was glad to have something to do to make her feel useful. She took the opportunity to quietly observe how things were going. Evelyn and Doctor Ed were deep in conversation – presumably discussing the arrival of the new guest, as Nessa was making her way back. Rory was throwing Freddy into the air and swinging him around, to shrieks of delight, but his gaze was following Nessa. To her left, Truth noticed Morah, still talking to Stella – both looked disapproving.

'Any idea when Mike will be getting here with those beers?' Rory called to Nessa.

'Shouldn't be long – any minute, I'd imagine.'

Truth supposed Mike must be the final tenant due back – everyone else seemed to be here already.

Out of the corner of her eye, Truth saw Stella walking over to Bruce and Annika. Stella put her hand on Bruce's arm and said something to him.

'He's fine, Stella.' Bruce looked over at Freddy, still clambering over Rory.

'If you can't be bothered to watch him, Bruce – then I will,' Stella said. 'I realise having Freddy may be interfering with your *date night*,' she smiled pointedly at Annika, 'but we already agreed the timetable. He really should go to bed, he's getting way too over-stimulated.'

'It's seven fifteen, Stella – I'll take him up at eight.'

'Fine,' she said. 'I'll watch him while you two eat. It's nice to know where your priorities lie.'

Annika looked extremely uncomfortable. 'I don't mind if—'

'Frankly, this is none of your business,' Stella said to her, leaving Bruce open-mouthed.

The scene that might have followed was narrowly avoided as Nessa waved and called out, 'Hi Ari!' and a dark, good-looking guy wearing an open-necked shirt and jeans strolled into the garden, with the bearing and easy manner of someone entirely confident of a welcoming reception.

'Good evening, everybody!' He gave the slightest of continental bows. 'It's so kind of you to invite me to your gathering – I've been looking forward to it all day. Allow me to introduce myself – Aristes Fitzgerald Christopoulos. My friends call me Ari – I hope you will too.'

Nessa was not the only one to be pleased by Ari's appearance, Truth noted. As introductions were made and two bottles of wine handed over to Doctor Ed (who proclaimed them a wonderful vintage), Ari worked his way around the small group with relentless charm.

'Nessa tells us you're in reconstruction,' Doctor Ed said.

'That was a little vague of me,' Ari replied. 'I'm actually a reconstructive surgeon.'

'Really?' Doctor Ed looked pleased. 'Well, I used to be in general practice myself. What brings you to Dublin, apart from your spectacular new house?'

'I'm here to give a course on the finer points of anthropometric analysis regarding cleft palate in particular, facial reconstruction in general. I do a lot of paediatric work in India, and I've made some interesting observations.'

'How fascinating.' Doctor Ed was clearly impressed.

'I'm so sorry to hear about your recent mishap.' He directed his earnest attention now to Evelyn, who was studying him with interest. 'Nessa was telling me you tripped on the stairs.'

'Yes, I did. It was just after my morning swim. I swim every day, and I can't wait to get back to it, I can tell you. I'm not very good at sitting still. Isn't that true, Ed?'

'None of us can keep up with her.' Doctor Ed shook his head.

'But my granddaughter' – Evelyn indicated Truth, who was helping Nessa at the grill – 'has come over from London to help me while I recover.' Ari's gaze swivelled appreciatively in her direction.

'Truth!' Evelyn called. 'Come over and meet our new neighbour!'

Truth brought a plate of food for Evelyn with her.

'Truth . . . what an interesting name,' Ari said. 'So you're new in town too?'

'Yes, I just got here today.'

'Ari's a reconstructive surgeon,' said Evelyn.

'Really?'

'Do you do facelifts?' Evelyn looked interested.

'Yes, I do a lot of cosmetic work – but traumatic recon-structive surgery is my passion. Facial deformity, injury – I do a lot of pro bono work in underprivileged parts of the world.' He smiled. 'The cosmetic work back home pays the bills.'

The rest of the group had drifted over now, interested to hear him. 'It's scarily common here, all that cosmetic work stuff, I see it in the gym all the time,' Rory said. 'And that's just the guys.' Everyone laughed.

'Well, people are taking more care of themselves these days, I guess, and if they don't like the way they look, they have the option to change that.'

'Hey, Mike!' Rory called back towards the house to a shadowy figure moving about the kitchen. 'You took your time, mate! Let's be having those beers out here, please!'

✧

It took Truth a second, because he looked different, somehow. Or perhaps it was the shock of seeing him again and out of context. As he strolled down to the garden carrying a crate of beer, and pausing to joke with Rory – handing him a bottle while he grabbed a plate for himself – his expression had lost the earlier intensity she recalled from their brief meeting on the pier. When he turned towards Truth and saw her, a flicker of recognition registered before his features rearranged in a polite mask of curiosity. For some inexplicable reason, during that seemingly longer than normal second, the unflappable composure Truth relied upon – both in court and out of it – deserted her. Ridiculous though her rational mind appeared to find it, she suddenly felt as exposed as if she were standing there naked.

Her grandmother's voice broke the rather uncomfortable spell. 'Mike,' Evelyn waved to him, 'put those beers in the cooler and come and say hello – tell me all the news I've missed. You haven't met my granddaughter.'

Mike did as he was told, then made his way over. 'It's good to see you back, Evelyn, how are you?'

'All the better for being back on home turf. Truth, this is Mike, our resident sculptor.' Evelyn waved her granddaughter over. 'Truth's a very high-powered lawyer, and she's come over especially to look after me – isn't that kind of her?'

'Hi.' Truth chewed her lip.

'Hello.' Mike made no reference to their earlier meeting. 'Good to meet you.' He was polite.

Truth wasn't sure how to respond. She wasn't used to being unacknowledged, and Mike not referring to their earlier meeting on the pier made her suddenly feel wrong-footed. To her annoyance she felt herself blushing.

'Can't you see the family resemblance, Mike? Truth's a carbon copy of me when I was young and beautiful.' Evelyn looked expectantly from one to the other.

Mike considered the question, but Truth felt sure it was only for the sake of good manners. Her blush deepened.

'There's certainly a strong resemblance,' he conceded. 'It's your bone structure.'

'Meet our new neighbour, Mike!' Rory grinned. 'Ari's moved in next door. Mike's in your line of work, Ari.'

'Good to meet you, Mike,' Ari said, shaking hands. 'You're in medicine too?'

'What's he been telling you?' Mike shook his head, laughing. 'No, I'm a sculptor.'

'Ah – I see. A real artist. Rory and I merely attempt to fix the outside – but you reveal the true beauty *within* to the outside world, right?'

'What a charming way to put it.' Evelyn was impressed.

Ari went on. 'Wasn't it Michelangelo who said – if I'm not mistaken – *I saw the angel in the marble, and I carved to set him free.*'

'You're not mistaken – that's quite right,' Mike said.

'It's not a dissimilar process in my own work,' Ari reflected. 'I can see the possibilities that lie beneath the facial obstructions – the trouble is, with surgery you have nerves and blood vessels to worry about.' He made a wry face. 'Perfection doesn't exist,' he glanced at Truth, 'but we do our best, with whatever tools we have at our disposal, right?'

'Is that how you work, Mike?' Evelyn asked. 'Can you see beneath the exterior of marble?'

'I work with the lost wax method,' Mike said. 'It's a process of building up, initially, followed by a series of positives and negatives – too technical to explain just now – but there's a lot of anatomical work involved. That's mostly what I studied in Florence.'

'Ari, come and get some food!' Nessa called.

'Excuse me for a moment,' Ari said, 'while I get something to eat. This spread looks delicious.'

Just then Truth's phone rang, and she fished it out of her

bag. 'Back in a sec,' she said to Evelyn. 'I need to take this inside.'

She didn't – the call was from her gas supplier back home in London – but it gave her as good an excuse as any to slip away for a few minutes, and she was suddenly feeling inexplicably on edge. It had been a long day, and meeting her grandmother for the first time in so many years had been rather overwhelming. No wonder she was feeling a bit flustered. She just needed to take a few slow, deep breaths and she'd be fine. Except that a few deep breaths later she wasn't feeling any more calm. Quite the contrary. Meeting Mike again so unexpectedly had startled her – but not as much as her response to him ignoring their earlier meeting. What did it matter? Why should it rattle her? He was just some random guy . . . an artist . . . not her type at all.

Chapter Fifteen

'Hey, man!' Rory waved from the treadmill as Mike shouldered open the door of the basement gym. 'Wasn't expecting you down here at seven in the morning.'

Mike dumped his gym bag. 'I was finding it hard to sleep – thought I might as well get the workout over.'

'When I heard feet on the stairs I assumed it was Bruce, but I guess he has company. I'd trade a workout for some extra time in bed with a warm blonde. Kind of weird, though, with your ex-wife on the floor below you.' He shook his head. 'Modern family, eh?' Rory upped his pace. 'Speaking of which, what'd you think of Evelyn's granddaughter?'

'The lawyer? Wasn't really talking to her.'

'Oh yeah?' Rory didn't seem convinced. 'Weird name, *Truth* – I mean, what's that about?'

Mike settled in on the rower. 'Why don't you ask her?'

'I don't think so. Nessa told me she prosecutes for women in sexual assault and discrimination cases and the like. You wouldn't want to offend a woman like that. Knowing me, I'd put my size thirteens in it. Plus, she's too tall for me. Now Nessa . . . Nessa's got that softness thing going on, hasn't she? She's always talking about losing weight but I think she's just *perfect*. And, man, I just love her hair, those curls – it's amazing right after a swim.' He hardly paused for breath. 'And have you tasted her Guinness bread?' Rory kissed his fingers. 'Heaven – and it's not even bad for you.'

Mike smiled. 'It's good bread alright.'

'Can you believe that plonker Ryan, her ex-boyfriend, is trying to get her to let him stay with her before he leaves for Berlin?' Rory said. 'I heard her on the phone when he rang her before the barbecue last week.'

'Have you not told her you're in love with her yet?' Mike said.

'Ah, stop, man, will you? My heart is broken enough already. She doesn't know I exist, except as a friend. That plastic surgeon fella was chatting her up as well.' Rory scowled. 'Now he's a *real* babe magnet. And he's *loaded*. Nessa said his family have property all over . . .'

'I'm sure that wouldn't matter to Nessa.'

'On the positive side,' Rory made the thumbs-up sign as he ran, 'he's only here for three months – lives in Boston, but always off to India and the like, fixing kids' faces for free.'

'He might fix your nose.' Mike grinned.

'What's wrong with my nose? That break is my badge of honour – Champions Cup, Thomond Park, 2015, I'll have you know.'

'Yeah, yeah – you and Conor Murray . . .'

'Anyway,' Rory was clearly on a roll, 'I don't think Aristotle's the type to settle down. Nessa's a keeper, and something tells me he's not looking for one of those.'

'So you're safe then,' said Mike. 'And by the way, I think his name's Aristes.'

'Whatever. Now Truth, though – I'd say he'd like her alright. I saw him watching her.'

'Really?' Mike sounded disinterested.

Realising he'd lost his audience, Rory sped up. 'Right, 'nuff of the chat. Time to get Shreddy Krueger.'

Chapter Sixteen

It was Morah's day for cleaning Doctor Ed's flat, and she was scrubbing the sink with a vigour that bordered on controlled fury when he came in from the garden to get a drink.

'How are you, Morah?' He smiled at her.

'I'm fine, doctor – how are you?'

'Good, good, thanks. I've just come in to go through my post and maybe have a cup of tea – will you join me?' Doctor Ed put his straw gardening hat on the counter.

'I'll put the kettle on.'

Doctor Ed sat down at the table he used as a desk and sorted through some papers, taking a pen discreetly from his shirt pocket. 'Did you enjoy the barbecue last week? I saw you were chatting to Stella.'

'I'm not really an outdoor person, as you know.' Morah patted her hair. 'I prefer to eat at a table *indoors*. But it was pleasant enough – these things are for young people, really.'

'Quite a few new faces, weren't there?' Doctor Ed scratched his forehead. 'Bruce's new friend—'

'*Partner*, apparently – they're an item. For the moment anyway.'

'Yes, yes, Annika – that's her name. She seemed very

nice – I was only speaking to her briefly. Wonderfully modern arrangement . . .'

Morah snorted. 'It's immoral – that's what it is. Stella may be making out she's alright with her husband bringing a new woman in under the same roof as her and the child – but she's as rattled as a pair of castanets. Can you blame her?'

'Ex-husband,' Doctor Ed pointed out, taking the mug of tea Morah handed him. 'And they do live in separate flats, and floors – although, I grant you, the situation is not without prospective complications.'

'She has no one but herself to blame.' Morah sniffed. 'I told her that. What's the child going to make of it? She should take her husband back and send that woman packing before—'

'Before what?' The question was put mildly but Doctor Ed was clearly curious.

'Before something worse happens.'

Doctor Ed jotted down a note or two, then murmured something about the roses. 'And Evelyn's granddaughter, Truth – beautiful girl! Such an extraordinary resemblance! Very interesting to talk to.'

'Hmm.'

'Was I imagining it, Morah, or do I sense a certain *froideur* between you and Evelyn?' The pen paused. 'I've sometimes had the feeling you don't like her very much?'

Morah took a plate from the cupboard and cut a generous slice of Nessa's carrot cake for the doctor. 'I don't have any feelings one way or the other about Evelyn, as you well know, doctor. I'm glad she's out of hospital, of course.'

'Evelyn tends to be flamboyant. She can . . . overlook

things at times – people, even. It's just her nature – she doesn't mean anything by it.' Doctor Ed smiled at her. 'You've been so marvellous, Morah, looking after the apartment for her and everything. She does appreciate it, you know. We all do.'

I don't give a feck whether or not she appreciates it – I found what I needed to find. Morah thought briefly of the photos and documents as she put the plate in front of him. 'I'm certainly not looking for any gratitude, doctor. Evelyn thanked me in her own way.'

'It's just that I wouldn't want you to have your feelings hurt, Morah – I know how sensitive you are. Evelyn may seem to be . . . well . . . *taken up* with her granddaughter and so forth at the moment. You know what she's like . . . with Evelyn it's always the next shiny object.'

'Like that plastic surgeon – she clearly found him *mesmerising*. She was fairly quizzing him.'

Doctor Ed laughed. 'He was very entertaining. I liked him immensely. He's very good at what he does too – I looked him up. World class.'

'He told me I had very good skin,' Morah said, sitting down primly.

'And so you do, Morah. So you do.'

Morah thought men were really very stupid – no matter how many degrees they had. Imagine Doctor Ed assuming she'd be hurt by Evelyn ignoring her. Sure when had the woman ever done anything else? She knew he was just keeping an eye on her in his own way – making sure nothing upset her unduly. What was interesting to Morah though was that Doctor Ed clearly had no idea how much she actually hated Evelyn Malone. Things didn't often go Morah's way in life, but Evelyn falling down the stairs couldn't have happened to a nicer person, as far as she was concerned. She had heard her calls for help that fateful day – it had been Morah's day to clean Bruce's flat. She had been dusting on the landing and heard Evelyn's shouts from below. She had peered over the bannisters and seen the woman prostrate on the floor. Then she had simply continued into Bruce's flat, closed the door behind her, and turned on the hoover full blast. Not that she wished bad luck on anyone – but some people had their just deserts coming to them. And Evelyn Malone was one of them.

'Have another slice of cake, doctor.'

Chapter Seventeen

'But you *must* go for a swim!' Evelyn said to Truth. 'It's a crime *not to* on a day like this. Besides, my friends will be wanting to know how I am, how I'm doing. They'll be concerned about me.'

'Surely all the other regulars will have kept them up to speed.'

'But that's not the same as hearing from *you* – and I want them all to meet you.'

'So you want me to be your personal envoy in a bathing suit.'

'Exactly! I couldn't have put it better myself! Nessa usually goes at this time too – I'm sure she'd love you to join her.'

'I don't have a bathing suit.'

'Take one of mine – I must have hundreds. I kept all my bikinis.' Evelyn pointed. 'Third drawer in the wardrobe – have a rummage. Several of them should fit you.' She looked at Truth, critically assessing her. 'Although I might have been a teensy bit smaller in the hips.'

Truth lifted her eyebrows. 'Right. I'll see what I can find.'

✦

'You can't be serious.' Truth squealed, holding on to the railing and dipping a toe in. 'It's *Baltic*!

'It's gorgeous once you're in, I promise!' Nessa came down to join her. 'Best to do it quickly when you're not used to it. When you are – you'll find this is lukewarm.' She pressed under in a ripple of water, her blonde curls straining from a hastily fastened topknot. 'It's February and March that really are cold.'

'I think you're all lunatics.' Truth was up to her knees now. 'You're just prolonging the agony.'

A group of teenage boys ran in past her, splashing wildly in their wake. Truth glared at them.

'C'mon,' Nessa called. 'Just get under.'

So she did. She pushed off from the small jetty beginning a breast stroke and thought she was going to die of shock. 'I – can't – b-b-breathe.'

Nessa laughed at the look on her face and swam back towards her. 'Keep going, just twenty seconds and you won't feel a thing.'

There was nothing for it but to power through it – Truth struck out in a front crawl and kept going. Gradually, the swell of sea became a rhythm, the water grew warmer, and the buoyancy of the salt water energised her. When she stopped for a breather, she was surprised to see how far out she had come. She floated for a bit, looking back at the coastal skyline, dominated by the castle on the hill, and the hotchpotch of seafront houses, some large and Georgian, others villa types, and some pretty cottages. She swam back at a more leisurely rate, where Nessa was waiting for her by the pier.

'So . . . you can swim!' Nessa laughed. 'Evelyn will be delighted.'

'I can't believe she swims here every day.'

'Never misses it. Regular as clockwork – she must be hating not being able to get into the water. When will she be able to swim again?'

'I think she told me she could swim in a pool at four weeks – but was advised not to get in the sea for about three months. Not because of the water – more of a safety issue with the currents and that she wouldn't have the strength necessary.'

'Wow. Well, maybe she can get in if two strong men hold on to her.'

'I think she'd enjoy that.'

✧

'Well, how was it? Are you a convert?' Evelyn was sitting on the bench in the garden where Doctor Ed had set her up with a gin and tonic. 'You both look wonderful – I can't tell you what I'd give to get in the sea right now.'

'Well, as soon as you can, we'll arrange it.'

'That surgeon was ridiculous saying I had to wait three months – I mean, I can drive at six weeks.'

'You don't have a car.'

'That's not the point.' Evelyn frowned. 'If I can get in the water at four weeks and drive at six – why can't I get in the sea?'

'In case you get swept away, *Grandma*!' Truth teased Evelyn. 'But Nessa here has the solution.'

'Yes, I was just saying we can have two strong men for you to hold on to!'

'Now you're talking. But seriously, as long as I wasn't on my own – and I wouldn't be – I wouldn't get swept out to sea, would I? Anyway, it would be a wonderful way to go.' Evelyn took a sip of her drink. 'Speaking of strong men, what did you think of our new neighbour, girls?'

'He's lovely, isn't he?' Nessa said. 'So easy to talk to and so . . . chivalrous.'

'That's a word you don't hear very often these days. Handsome chap, isn't he? And he's free and single.' Evelyn looked at them meaningfully.

'Divorced,' said Truth.

'Same thing.'

'He told me he has two children,' Nessa said. 'A boy and a girl – they're in Greece on holidays with their mum's family – she's an heiress to a shipping dynasty, apparently.'

'Then he won't have to worry too much about alimony,' said Evelyn. 'Very eligible.'

'Maybe.' Truth shrugged. 'It's unlikely he's looking to settle down right now if his divorce is recent? I come across those types a lot in London – they always marry their own tribe. Super rich, or aristocrats, or both.'

'Don't be so negative, Truth,' Evelyn said. 'People fall in love all the time, you know, and then the rules go out the window.'

'Do you think?' Nessa sounded anxious.

'I know they do.'

'No one seems to fall in love with me.' Nessa chewed her lip.

'Then you're choosing the wrong men – or worse, allowing them to choose *you*. *And* waste your time.'

'Evelyn!' Truth was horrified.

'Well, it's true, isn't it? Men will always waste your time if you allow them to. It's up to the woman to decide which way she wants things to go. Or as you're so fond of saying these days – you need to decide and implement your boundaries.'

'How do you mean?' Nessa was intrigued.

Evelyn sighed. 'Don't they teach you anything about reeling in a man anymore?'

'Clearly I was missing for the lesson if they did,' Nessa said.

Truth shook her head in disbelief at what she was hearing.

'Put simply,' Evelyn said, 'you decide what you're willing to put up with and what you're not – and if the chap isn't coming up to scratch, then you must ditch him immediately.'

'This is the *softly, softly* approach, I'm assuming?' Truth was sarcastic.

Nessa looked stricken. 'But what if you're in love with him?'

'Oh, phooey.' Evelyn waved a dismissive hand. 'The point is, you have to *make* a man decide whether he wants you or not, before he wastes your best years. If he does want you, then fall in love with him by all means – but if being in love obscures your instincts to look out for yourself and your best interests, well then it's a handicap – and one with serious long-term consequences.'

'Such as?'

'Being left alone.'

Nessa looked worried.

'With respect, Evelyn,' Truth said, 'I think things might have moved on a bit since your dating days.'

'Perhaps, but the essentials remain the same. Look at Bruce – he took my advice and has a lovely new girlfriend to show for it, one who's far more suited to him than that awful Stella.'

'Evelyn! Keep your voice down! You can't go around interfering in people's relationships and making sweeping statements like that!' Truth was horrified.

'She is very good at this stuff,' Nessa admitted. 'Do you think I need to lose weight?' This was directed at Evelyn.

'No, I don't, and I'd tell you if I thought you did. You're gorgeous and curvy and—'

'My thighs are *huge*.'

'I was going to say, you are *luscious*.' Evelyn was firm. 'Any man will think you are perfect. Which you are. And you're a divine cook.'

'What about you, Truth?' Nessa perked up. 'Any man in your life?'

'Not at the moment. There was one . . . but we broke up.'

'Oh, I'm sorry.'

'It's alright, we weren't right for each other.'

'What do you think of our local men? Any of them take your fancy?' Nessa asked.

'I'm really not looking to hook up with anyone just now.'

'If I were you, I'd be looking over the wall.' Evelyn indicated Ari's house next door.

'She doesn't listen to a word I say.' Truth shook her head at Nessa.

'I'll bet a girl could have a very nice time with that Ari.' Evelyn smiled. 'It would be very handy to have a surgeon in the family – and right next door too.'

'You've got a doctor right here, Grandma.'

'Very funny. Ed's more of a gardener these days than a doctor, although it is handy having him on call, I must say.'

'Did I hear my name mentioned?' Doctor Ed appeared. 'I was having a snooze in the bunker.'

'We were just singing your praises,' said Evelyn. 'Now, Truth, if you wouldn't mind helping me upstairs.' Evelyn stood up slowly. 'Ed, feel free to drop in later for a drinkie. Just text me to let me know when you're on your way.'

'Super.' Doctor Ed perked up. 'We can try some of that Château Latour Ari brought. I've been looking forward to opening it.'

'She has a better social life than all of us,' said Nessa, shaking her head.

'If you're not doing anything later,' Truth said to Nessa out of earshot as Doctor Ed helped Evelyn to her feet, 'fancy going out for something to eat? I could do with getting out of the flat.'

'Great idea. Do you like Italian?'

'Love it.'

'I'll book us in to our local – it's just around the corner.'

✦

Truth took the opportunity to make a quick call to Pauline before meeting Nessa for dinner. But it went straight to voicemail. 'Hi, Mum,' she said. 'It's me. Just thought I'd try and catch you for a quick chat. It's nothing important, I'm just settling in, you know, finding my feet a bit. Everyone's being really kind to me—'

Pauline called back almost immediately, sounding breathless. 'Tru!' she said. 'How's it going?'

'Hi, Mum! I'm just on my way out to dinner with Nessa, one of the tenants here. I'm having a really nice time, just getting to know everyone, you know . . .'

'And how are you finding your grandmother?'

'She's doing really well – she's, ah, interesting . . . I'm beginning to understand where you were coming from . . . But never mind her, how are you?'

'I'm fine! Well, just you remember to look after yourself while you're there. And I'm glad you're having a nice time. Enjoy your dinner – I'll try and call you tomorrow. I'm helping out at the church coffee morning at twelve, I'll call you after that – then we can talk properly.'

'Great. I'll make sure I can chat then. Love you.'

'Love you too, Tru.'

Chapter Eighteen

At seven thirty, Truth got a text from Nessa to say she'd meet her downstairs in the hall.

'Are you alright if I go out now, Evelyn? I won't be late.'

'I'm absolutely fine.' Evelyn was sitting in her chair after a light microwaved dinner. 'Ed's coming up for a nightcap or two, he has a key – and he can help me to bed before he goes if you're not back yet. Don't look so shocked – he is a retired doctor, you know – and I promise I won't lead him astray.' Evelyn looked mischievous. '*Botched* is on – we love watching that. Ari was very impressed, when we were chatting at the barbecue, at how up to date I was with the latest cosmetic techniques.'

'Right. Well, see you later, then.'

✦

'I love your dress,' Truth said, as they strolled towards the main shopping street. Truth was wearing a pair of relaxed dungarees over a cutaway white T-shirt but Nessa was in lime-green floaty linen, with a matching headband artfully tying up some of her curls. She wore dangly earrings in the shape of lemons, and a lot of bangles jangled as she walked along.

'Oh, thanks,' Nessa said. 'I made it myself.'

'You look beautiful. And you can make your own clothes as well?'

'I've always been handy with a sewing machine. I'd give anything for your height, though – dungarees would look ridiculous on me. But we work with what we've got, right?'

Nessa pointed out a few favourite boutiques and Dana's art gallery on the way.

The restaurant was down a small street leading towards the seafront, and since it was such a warm evening they sat outside in the small cobbled courtyard. Although it was still bright, fairy lights twinkled along the awnings and threaded through the potted trees that surrounded them. In the small, intimate space, people laughed and sipped wine while waiting staff weaved in and out of tables exclaiming to each other in urgent Italian.

'So, how are you finding Dublin so far?' Nessa asked. She glanced at the menu.

'It's not how I expected it to be – although I'm not sure what I expected, if that makes sense.'

'To be fair, Abbottsville isn't exactly typical city centre Dublin,' Nessa said. 'But the DART will take you into the city in about twenty minutes.' The local electric commuter rail stop was down the road.

'It's a beautiful town, and I haven't even seen it properly. I'd like to go up to the castle, have more of a look around. I'll do the tourist stuff as well, but there's plenty of time for that.' They paused while a waiter took their order.

'What's it like getting to know Evelyn?'

'Honestly? She seems really great.' Truth paused, wondering how much to share with Nessa. 'But there's been this kind of falling out between her and my mum for, like, years. They're estranged, really. It started way before I was born. I'd like to get to the bottom of it if I can while I'm here, but obviously it's a very delicate subject to broach – I'll have to bide my time and hope Evelyn might open up to me.'

'Seriously?' Nessa was surprised. 'I can't imagine anyone falling out with Evelyn – did your mum tell you why?'

'No, it's not something she likes talking about – and mostly there's never time. She brought me up on her own, as a single mum. She works in a women's shelter. I went away to college when I was seventeen, I'm thirty-two now, and after that we never seemed to get enough time to talk about stuff. I guess I was busy building my legal career – when we did get to spend time together I hated pushing her to talk about stuff that obviously upset her.'

Nessa was intrigued.

'I have an uncle, Mum's only brother . . . well, half-brother. He lives in New York. He's much younger than her, though – there's quite an age gap. I asked him about it once or twice but he just said Mum and Evelyn never got along. It's just one of those family things, I guess.'

The waitress came with their order just then, depositing a plate of squid ink pasta in front of Truth and a large grilled ribeye steak for Nessa. 'Don't let any of your customers see you eating that!' Truth said.

'Just because I run a vegan restaurant doesn't mean I am one.' She grinned. 'I trained as a cook, but when I was working in my last place I noticed there was a gap in the market for a good vegan café – so I opened one. I don't eat much meat – but sometimes I just crave a good steak, you know?'

'You won't hear any argument from me.'

'So tell me about you – and your name – is it really your birth name?'

'Yep, it really is.' Truth trotted out the well-worn story. 'I was named after Sojourner Truth.' Nessa looked blank. 'An abolitionist and women's rights activist,' Truth explained. 'My mum and dad split when I was about eighteen months. Mum brought me up. We were pretty poor, really, looking back. I grew up in a series of council flats – but somehow Mum always kept things together.'

Nessa was taken aback. 'Didn't anyone help her?'

'Oh, Mum was adamant about doing things on her own. We were welfare-dependent a lot, then Mum got better qualified, got a better job, and I got scholarships and went to college – and, well, here I am.'

'Wow, that's impressive. Scholarships, plural. You must be seriously brainy. What about your dad?'

'I made contact with him a few years ago, and we reconnected. We're good. He's a musician, works as a sound engineer now, he lives in Germany. He has two other kids, a lot younger than me – by two different women. He's living with the current one. He was happy to hear from me – I think he's sorry about how he behaved back then.'

'Your mum sounds like she's incredible.'

'Yeah.' Truth smiled. 'She totally is. Pretty invincible too.'

'I would expect nothing less from a daughter of Evelyn's,' said Nessa. 'Maybe that's why they clashed?'

'Maybe.' Truth shrugged. 'But I'm beginning to see that Evelyn wouldn't be the easiest mother to have. She's quite an intimidating personality . . . What about you?'

Nessa made a dismissive sound. 'Not nearly as impressive as your story. I'm really pretty boring. Average home, average family, four siblings – well, that's pretty average for Ireland. I always knew I wanted to cook, to be around food. I wasn't any good at school much, but I loved home economics. I did a full-time catering course, my parents helped me set up my first café and the rest is history.'

Truth was mindful of Nessa's earlier remark to Evelyn, so she didn't probe about her romantic life. But Nessa seemed happy to bring the conversation around to it herself.

'I was in an on–off relationship for a long time with someone before I realised he was never going to love me.' Nessa's eyes filled. 'At first I thought I could make him see how good we were together – and we were, you know, we really were, it wasn't just wishful thinking on my part.' She bit her lip. 'But every time, after a year or so, he'd break up with me. I'd be heartbroken, and sometime later – when his latest girlfriend hadn't worked out – he'd come back to me. We'd be happy again, until the next time. I'd like to say I was strong enough to tell him to get lost, but the truth is he left me again. We'd been renting a place together, so that made it kind of final this time, when he moved out. I couldn't afford the rent on my own, and I didn't want to stay there anyway after . . . well . . .' She stopped.

'You don't have to—'

'No, I do.' She took a breath. 'It's good for me to say it. Because sometimes . . . I know this sounds really stupid, but sometimes I feel like it never really happened, the break-up. That he just, I dunno . . . went out somewhere and he'll be back. Does that sound crazy?'

Truth shook her head. 'Not at all.' She'd listened to similar accounts from hundreds of women she represented.

Nessa took a gulp of her wine. 'I think it's because we'd been together for so long. He's the only person I've been in a proper relationship with ever. Funnily enough he rang me the day of our barbecue, but for once I didn't beg him to come back.' She looked rueful. 'Anyway, that's how I ended up in number 24, and really it's been the best thing that could have happened to me. I've made new friends – we're like a little family there. Then I opened the café . . . I'm starting to feel stronger now.' She smiled. 'When I do eventually grow up, I want to be just like Evelyn.'

'I'm really sorry you had to go through all that. And I'm sure there are loads of lovely men out there who'd be dying to go out with you.'

'I used to have a real crush on Mike when he moved in first,' Nessa admitted.

'The sculptor? Yeah, I saw him on the pier before I knew he lived at our place. He was playing a piece of music for some work of his he said was going up.'

'I can't believe I missed that. I was all set to be there and a client needed an emergency meeting. Imagine an artist who serenades his work! Isn't that just so romantic?'

'I guess.'

Privately, Truth thought it was more egocentric than romantic. 'You don't still have a crush on him, do you?'

'Oh, no, no. And he certainly doesn't have any interest in

me – not *that* way. I mean, he's been lovely to me and every-thing, but we're just mates. He's quite a complex guy, Mike, he can seem quite withdrawn sometimes, I guess it's his art-istic side . . . but he's so talented. Wait 'til you see his wooden sculptures – the ones he does for fun – they're just amazing. He and Doctor Ed are great buddies too, which is nice. Mike built the bench set-up at the end of the garden for him – and he did the ramp for Evelyn's wheelchair as well.'

'That was good of him.' Truth was pleasantly surprised. So Mike was introverted, and not stand-offish, as she'd assumed. She'd passed him in the hall the other day, and he'd smiled at her before disappearing in to his flat, but she was damned if she was going to engage him in conversation again. It clearly hadn't endeared her to him the first time around.

'That's what I love about number 24 – it's like we're all just one big family really. Well, except for Stella and Bruce.' Nessa made an awkward face. 'That's a whole other story.'

They chatted for a while longer, shared a sinful dessert, then Truth checked her watch.

'I'd better be getting back. I don't want to leave Evelyn for too long – although Doctor Ed was dropping by for a nightcap. She said he could help her to bed.'

'Better make sure you knock before you go in.'

'Surely it's not like that, is it?'

'Who knows?' Nessa laughed. 'That woman is a law unto herself.'

Chapter Nineteen

Sometimes, on waking, Mike had to take a minute to work out if he was in his studio or his flat. The black-out blind he'd put up on the window of his bedroom at number 24 was so effective that in those first few seconds of swimming back into consciousness it was difficult to remember which world he was in. The disarray of drawings, books, models and wood carvings that were strewn throughout both dwellings didn't help clarify the situation. Neither did his hyper-realistic dreams, which always seemed to become more active in between commissions. He'd got used to it over time, this drifting between reality and creating. When Mike was working on a sculpture, his intensity was all-consuming. Hours could be lost in his warehouse studio when he was immersed in a project. When he would eventually rouse himself to check the clock and discover it was sometime in the small hours, he would more often than not crash out on the old but comfortably accommodating sofa for what remained of the night.

Now, as he reached from the warmth of his bed to pull the blind and let the first tentative fingers of light into the room, his attention was drawn to the sea, rather than the haphazard state of his living quarters. It was presently changing from slate to milky blue, as smudgy clouds scudded by above it, in an undecided sky. Dawn had held a fascination for Mike long before he realised he was an artist. As a child, it signalled the secret beginning of a day spent with his father on the occasions he was allowed accompany him on their working midlands farm. Cattle, sheep, and hens would be fed, water checked, manure shovelled, and hay loaded. The tractor would be warmed up, and as he and the dogs clambered aboard and chuntered along through the waking fields, constant surprises awaited him, from the sudden swoop of a sparrow hawk to the unexpected appearance of new baby lambs. For as long as he could remember, it was the best part of the day.

Now, though, it was time to swim.

He found he was the first one there when he jogged down the steps to Mariner's Cove – as still and promising as an emerging negative in the early light. The freezing cobbles of the pier stung his feet as he dived in – relishing the combined shock of cold and adrenaline slicing through him as he broke the surface gasping, pushing his hair back from his face before swimming out to the buoy, where he stopped to catch his breath. By the time he headed back to the cove, he saw Doctor Ed was in the water too. When he reached him, they treaded water for a bit.

'You're even earlier than usual,' Doctor Ed said.

'No point hanging about once I was awake.'

'Nothing like it, is there?' Doctor Ed looked up at the sky. 'When you have it to yourself. You must be looking forward to the sculpture going up – won't be long now.'

'Three weeks, and I'm not sure if *looking forward* is how

I'd put it. I'll be relieved though to have him up – at least then I'll know how he really looks.' Although Mike was intimately familiar with every millimetre of his work, no sculptor ever really knew how the piece would interact with the surrounding environment until it was actually in situ. Every piece generated its own unique energy, which people responded to differently.

'I'm sure he'll look great – and we'll wonder how we ever managed without him.' Doctor Ed gazed at the spot on the pier where the foundations were being laid.

Mike rubbed some water from his face with a hand. 'Hopefully it'll go better than last time.'

Mike's last sculpture had been put on hold after a small group of locals had decided the mythical Celtic shapeshifting figure that had been commissioned and approved by the council looked too raw and fierce – or as one local had put it: *demonic*. As a result, the divisive piece had been taken down, pending collaborations between the local council and parish.

'I think you were just unlucky,' Doctor Ed said as they got out. 'There's no pleasing all of the people all of the time. Happens with patients too.'

'That's for sure.'

They dried off and sat in their usual spot, watching the sun come up. Doctor Ed handed Mike a cup of hot tea from his flask. 'Any idea what you'll do next – or is it too soon to ask?'

Mike shook his head. 'I'm still a bit too buzzed. I'm just sketching and chilling for a bit. Oh, and I'm working on a wood sculpture with Freddy.' He grinned.

'Marvellous!' Doctor Ed laughed. 'What's this one?'

Mike made his wooden sculptures for fun. He had started them a few years ago when he did a piece for his then Italian girlfriend, who owned a flower shop and needed a focal piece for her Christmas window display. He had been studying in Florence at the time, and made a wonderful reindeer out of hundreds of wooden twigs and pellets, which increased her sales phenomenally. He had enjoyed the experience so much, he continued to make them for friends, and increasingly for himself when he needed to wind down and de-stress. He had just finished a stunning hare in full flight that would go in the garden, and had several others in various stages of development in his flat.

'A dinosaur. A raptor, to be precise – or *rapper*, as Freddy calls it. At least that's what it started out as, but the creative direction changes on a daily basis.' He lifted his eyebrows. 'It's displaying definite tyrannosaurus and brontosaurus vibes now.'

'I can't wait to see it. Freddy must be loving it.'

'It's fun – for both of us,' Mike said. 'He's such a great kid.'

'Isn't he? He seems to be taking Bruce's new girlfriend in his stride too, which is good.'

Mike nodded. 'She seems really nice.'

'Not sure how Stella's taking it, though.' Doctor Ed frowned. 'Morah seems to think she was rather . . . well . . . put out about the situation.'

'Life's complex, doc. I can't say I'd enjoy having my ex in the same house – but if it floats your boat . . .'

'Yes, well, it did seem to be working – but there are always unforeseen challenges in these situations. Life was a lot simpler when I was your age.'

'Was it, though? Really?'

'Yes, I think so.' The doctor was thoughtful. 'Or perhaps it was just that *we* were less complicated. We had our challenges of course, every generation does – but things were more straightforward. Fewer options, I suppose – I think that simplifies things.'

'You might have a point.'

'Evelyn and I discuss it quite often.'

'Does she think life was simpler back then?'

'Evelyn doesn't really think along those lines – she's more of an opportunist.' He looked at Mike. 'And I mean that as a compliment. She's not the type of person to let the confines of any contemporary thinking define what she does. I suspect Evelyn would have been pretty unstoppable in whatever century she was inhabiting. What did you think of Truth? Isn't she lovely?'

'Yeah, she's a striking-looking girl alright. I wasn't talking to her really – a few of us were just chatting at the barbecue last week.'

'Didn't I see her talking to you on the pier earlier that day?'

Mike was taken aback. 'Yeah – that was random. She was there when the guys were putting down the foundations and I was playing. She came over to ask about it.'

'Ah. She clearly finds you interesting.'

Mike wasn't so sure. He had been so taken aback to find Truth standing in the garden when he'd come out to the barbecue, and then discovering that she was Evelyn's granddaughter, that he'd been completely lost for words and clammed up. He wasn't usually so affected by meeting a woman but something about Truth had made him behave like an awkward teenager that day. Now he felt like an idiot.

'She was just wondering what the deal was.'

'And did you tell her?'

'Yeah, I said it's what I always do when a sculpture's going up.'

'Well, I'm sure you'll have lots of other opportunities to talk to each other now you're housemates.'

'What are you saying, doc?' Mike gave him an amused look.

'Just that it's good to talk.' He finished his tea and stood up. 'Why don't you ask her out to dinner? If I were forty years younger that's what *I'd* be doing. Is that even a "thing" anymore, having dinner?'

'Not sure – I'm kind of out of the loop on the dating scene.'

'Well, you should get back in the loop. It's not healthy to spend too much time alone, you know.' He reached for his swimming bag.

'I'm hardly alone in the house.'

'You know what I mean. You hardly saw daylight while you were working on *The Waiting Man*, and we hardly saw *you* at all.'

'Well, you'll see plenty of me for the next few weeks,' Mike said. 'I'm not going anywhere – not 'til the *Man* is up. I'm just going to crash and take things easy for a while.'

'Good. I'm glad to hear it. Look, here come the early

birds.' He waved at a few regulars making their way down the steps, Nessa and Rory among them.

'I can't believe you're here ahead of us!' Nessa sounded put out.

'What can I say? You're slacking,' Doctor Ed joked, tapping his watch. 'Rory, I'm impressed – haven't seen you here before at this time.'

'Yeah, well, I just hopped on the bike from Rathfarnham, you know, worked up a sweat.' He peeled off his cycling gear to reveal impressive shoulders and abs.

'Put those away, lad – you're putting us to shame!' one of the older men said as he tottered down holding the hand rail. 'How's Evelyn doing?' he called back to the others. 'Tell her it's not the same without her.' He disappeared under water and kicked off.

'No, it isn't,' Doctor Ed said, to no one in particular.

'Since when did you decide to join the early birds?' Mike asked Rory. 'You're usually at the gym at this time.'

'I decided it would work better if I got the swim in first, y'know?' Rory did some energetic arm rolls and stretches. But his gaze was following Nessa, who was wading gingerly into the water and winding her curls up into a headband.

'Of course you did.' Mike pulled on his shirt and grinned at him. 'Don't worry – your secret's safe with me.'

'I'm an athlete, Mike – focus is everything. I'm visualising the end goal.'

'I'm impressed.'

'I'm serious, man, never more so. Also,' Rory tapped his nose, 'I figured the water's way too cold for our visiting neighbour.' He grinned. 'You gotta seize your chance to streak ahead, right?'

'Hey, guys!' Nessa called from the water once she was in. 'Are you around for a coffee after?'

'Sure,' said Mike.

Rory's face fell. 'Bloody hell,' he muttered. 'I won't be able to make it – I have a client.'

'You can't win them all.' Mike shrugged.

As the water began to fill up with more of the regulars, and Nessa swam over to join a group of chatting women, Mike shook his head in amusement as she missed the perfectly executed jack-knife dive Rory performed especially in her honour.

Chapter Twenty

It was Morah's afternoon off and she was going to spend it well. She had been looking forward to the undertaking all week. The evidence was laid out neatly before her on the table. The letter – and, more importantly, the bank accounts. She'd had time to go through everything last week in Evelyn's flat, so she took what she needed and had the relevant pieces photocopied before placing the documents back exactly where she had found them. The letter from Robert Radcliffe to *My darling Evelyn* – which was dated just a couple of weeks after Evelyn had moved into her flat in Doctor Ed's house – had revealed something interesting, and that was that Robert – Morah's long ago former employer – was paying Evelyn's rent at number 24. Or at least he clearly thought that was what he was doing, although from the bank statement it was evident that Evelyn had lied about the amount due, because Robert's monthly deposit was twice what the other tenants were paying. But why was he subsidising Evelyn at all?

From reading the letter it appeared that Robert was paying this princely sum because he was very grateful to his former mistress for some unspecified reason – 'for keeping this to yourself', he said. Keeping what to herself? They were hardly still carrying on their affair? Robert didn't even live in the country anymore. The address and contents of the letter confirmed he had retired to Portugal fifteen years ago. So what was the secret Evelyn hadn't told? Was it to do with her, Morah, and what had happened that day? Had Robert been in on the nasty little plot – not caring that his fragile wife might be driven over the edge, as long as he could get her to fire Morah? Whatever the reason, Morah thought darkly, she was going to get to the bottom of it. And then, with a bit of luck . . . Evelyn Malone was going to get what was coming to her. The two of them deserved to pay for what had happened to Morah . . . Not only had he and Evelyn conducted a blatant affair all those years ago – Evelyn would have been about thirty-five or thirty-six then, Morah did the maths, and was already a married woman with a little girl of her own – but their illicit romance had resulted in Morah's *own* life being bitterly thrown off course. It had all been Evelyn's doing, of course – Morah realised that from the beginning – but the trouble was proving it. But surely that would be easier now she was in possession of some pertinent facts. Figuring out what to do with them would be her next move, and Morah would take her time. After all, she had waited forty years already – what was a few more weeks? She picked up the photo of her younger self with little Joey and Susan Radcliffe and looked at it wistfully. It had been her dream job, coming to work for a wealthy, glamorous family in Dublin as nanny to their two children. She had been happy, full of hope, and the children adored her. But then everything had started to go wrong, to unravel – until that fateful day when little Joey went missing. Just remembering it sent a shiver of horror down her spine.

She had been outspoken, back in those days, feisty – she'd always been known for it – but Sister Julia in the convent had said that it was a *good* trait, that people always knew where they stood with plain speaking. That was why Morah had thought over her options and had decided to confront her employer, Robert Radcliffe, face to face about the matter. To let him know she knew he was conducting an affair behind his depressed wife's back and that if he didn't address his behaviour then she would feel duty bound to do something about the matter herself. She had been quaking in her boots at the thought of saying it, but when the time came, she felt strangely empowered – as if all the years of witnessing her own poor mother being treated like dirt by her drunken father and brothers were somehow being avenged.

He had listened to her, very politely, as she said her piece, sitting behind the large antique desk in his study – that more closely resembled a library – Morah still remembered the rows upon rows of leather-bound books on the polished shelves behind him. She had concentrated on them, on a spot above his head, speaking quickly, before she could change her mind.

When she'd finished, he had burst out laughing, shaking his head at her as if she were an errant child. 'Evelyn Malone is the wife of one of my dearest friends, Morah. The idea that I would be conducting an affair with her is absolutely preposterous. I think you must have been reading too many romance novels, my dear! Evelyn has been a great help to Sarah and me, advising us on decorating the new extension, especially as Sarah hasn't been able to cope with much – it would be entirely normal for her to be dropping by the house from time to time with fabric samples and so on. Why don't you just concentrate on the children, hmm? After all, that's what I pay you for.' His easy smile didn't reach his eyes.

She had been ready for him to deny it all, of course. 'Then you won't mind me telling Mrs Radcliffe I saw you and Evelyn Malone together in the garden, kissing, when Mrs Radcliffe was away visiting her sister for the weekend.' She put the few snapshots on the table of him and Evelyn strolling in the garden hand in hand and sharing a passionate kiss that was anything but friendly – it was downright compromising. She had seen them from her room upstairs, and it wasn't the first time. They had been quite brazen, hadn't given a thought or a care to whether she, Peggy the housekeeper, or indeed the children might have seen them.

He hadn't laughed then.

'You took these?' He was incredulous.

'I did.'

'But why?' He seemed genuinely bewildered.

'Because I don't like to see a good, kind wife and mother taken advantage of by people pretending to care about her.'

He had had the grace to flush then. 'What's your game?' he asked crossly. 'What are you after?'

'I'm not after anything. But if you don't stop carrying on with this woman, I will tell Mrs Radcliffe – your wife, and the mother of your children. I feel it is my duty. She has been very kind to me since I came to live in your home.'

He had looked at her strangely then, warily, and adopted a confidential tone. 'Look, Morah.' He sighed. 'You're a young girl, up from the country. You can hardly be expected to be accustomed to how things sometimes appear in people's lives. Evelyn Malone is . . . fragile . . . and she's been having a difficult time. Her husband travels a lot. She was lonely, confused . . . she developed a silly crush on me, that's all. What you witnessed was my attempt to comfort her. Furthermore – not that it's any of your business – I have already told Sarah, I mean Mrs Radcliffe, all about it and she fully understands. There's no need to worry your head about any of this, Morah.'

She knew he was lying, but at least he knew now that *she* knew about the affair and she was pretty sure that that would be enough to make him break it off. 'Do I have your word?'

'You have my word that Evelyn Malone will not be in this house again or in my company, alone.'

'That's good enough for me. You can keep those,' she added. 'I have the negatives.'

'No, no, thank you.' He pushed the embarrassing evidence away from him. 'That won't be necessary.'

How naïve she had been then – just an innocent girl up from the country.

Robert Radcliffe had appeared to be as good as his word – there had been no further sightings of Evelyn Malone in the house. No more covert phone calls made by him – or imperious messages left for him to ring Evelyn, if Morah had, by chance, picked up the phone. For the few days that followed, life at the Radcliffe residence seemed to have returned to its reasonably predictable routine.

Then the unthinkable had happened. Morah had been leaving the Radcliffes' daughter Susan to a friend's house in the neighbourhood. She'd brought little Joey along in his pushchair, as she always did, for a stroll. On the way home, she'd stopped to get an ice cream for him at the local shop, where she'd picked up a weekly copy of her favourite magazine. The small newsagent's had been crowded that day, and she'd parked the Silver Cross pushchair outside, as she often did, along with the other prams and pushchairs that were regularly left there, telling Joey she would be back in a jiffy with the ice cream. It had only taken a minute – possibly three, for her to take her magazine, pay for it and the ice cream cone, and come back outside – to find an empty pushchair and no sign of Joey. She hadn't panicked, not immediately – he couldn't have gone far, he must have somehow undone the heavy straps and buckles and clambered out, and would appear any minute. People were strolling by as normal; there was no traffic on the quiet road at that time of the afternoon. But he didn't appear. Not even after she had frantically searched for him and, gibbering with fear, had to run back into the newsagent's and ask the woman behind the counter to phone the police.

Back at the Radcliffe residence pandemonium broke out. Mrs Radcliffe was hysterical. Police had called to the house and were taking statements from an increasingly unhinged Morah, who was repeating herself like a broken record. 'It was only a moment – I swear to you!' she said, wringing her hands. Over and over again. Then Mr Radcliffe – Robert – had been called home. His big Mercedes swung into the driveway in a spray of gravel, and he leapt from the car to stride grimly past police, onlooking neighbours, and – to Morah's further horror – a local reporter and photographer, who were, respectively, taking statements from people and snapping pictures. He swept by her – as she cringed in the background – and the look of cold anger he shot her could have pinned her to the wall.

A few hours later, at around five that evening – after Morah had been crying in her room – she heard shrieks from downstairs. For a long, horrible moment she feared the worst, hearing footsteps running up the stairs, until the housekeeper, Peggy, rushed in to give her the good news.

'It's alright, Morah, pet – Joey's been found, he's safely back home.' She patted her shoulder. Morah made to run downstairs to join the jubilant scenes of joy as Robert Radcliffe swung his son in the air and his wife Sarah clung to them both – but instinct made her hang back, watching the scene unfold instead from the landing above. For a moment she was taken aback to see Evelyn Malone there in the front hall with them, looking exultant – but listening to her mellifluous, familiar voice, everything became clear.

'It was just pure *chance* I came across the little chap,' she was saying. 'I couldn't believe my eyes when I saw him toddling along at the side of the road – he could have been *killed*. Of course I pulled over immediately and ran over to get him, poor little mite. He was quite lost and alone – and I think he was very happy to meet someone who knew his name, weren't you, Joey, dear?' She tickled him under his chin as Joey ducked his head and looked away.

'We can never, ever thank you enough, Evelyn,' Sarah Radcliffe said, tearfully. 'When I think what could have happened, my blood runs cold.'

'Well, it didn't, sweetie.' Evelyn hugged her. 'So all's well that ends well.'

'Thanks to your quick thinking, Evelyn,' Robert said, as they shared a warm glance. 'I won't forget this. I'd better let the police know, so they can call off the search.' He handed Joey to his mother and went into his study. 'They'll be relieved to hear he's been found safe and sound.'

Morah kept to her room for the rest of the evening, declining the offer of soup and sandwiches Peggy had kept for her in the kitchen. Later, when they were all in bed and the house was still, she slipped quietly into Joey's room, sitting on his bed, watching him sleep with his arms akimbo, his little blond head resting on his favourite Postman Pat pillowcase. How could she have let it happen? She would never forgive herself as long as she lived. What harm might have come to him – and all because she had been stupid enough to leave him alone, even for a second. Tears ran down her face and she swiped them away angrily. When she had been allowed to see him earlier, he had reached out his chubby little arms to her. Picking him up, she had begun to sob as she said, over and over again, 'I'm sorry, Joey, sweetheart, I'm so sorry.' Until Mrs Radcliffe had taken him gently from her. But not before Joey had murmured to her quite clearly, putting his little hands on either side of her face, 'Don't *cry*, Morah! Joey went with *Eblem* to play. I'm back now . . . I told her you'd be sad if I was away too long – so we came home.' He smiled happily.

At the time, with all the commotion in the house, and the hysterical relief that Joey was safely home, no one had heard what Joey said to her. Even then it didn't quite register with Morah either, until she had been in her room, afterwards, lying on her bed, going ever everything again and again. That was when it had dawned on her. Joey hadn't magically undone those complicated buckles and wandered off. He would never do that – he was only three – especially when there was an ice cream on the way. Having ice cream was their daily ritual on their walks home and Joey was fanatical about it. He hadn't gone anywhere on his own – he had been taken by Evelyn Malone. Morah knew with every fibre of her being that Evelyn Malone had manipulated the whole thing to get her, Morah, into trouble. The problem was, though – Morah would never in a month of Sundays be able to prove it. Joey wasn't old enough to tell a coherent story, or to be believed even if he could.

The following day Mrs Radcliffe – most unusually for her – took Joey and Susan to spend the day with her sister in the country, leaving Morah at rather a loose end. She was tidying out the toy box in the playroom when Peggy popped her head around the door and told her she was wanted downstairs in Mr Radcliffe's study. Morah took a deep breath and checked her reflection in the landing mirror before going down the stairs slowly, preparing herself for the telling off she was surely in for. Knocking gently before entering, she slipped into the room. This time Robert Radcliffe was walking up and down his study looking thoughtful. He indicated she should sit down, which she did, on the chair in front of his desk. He smiled at her then, as if she had suddenly been the inspiration for a solution he had been pondering over.

'I'm so sorry,' Morah began. But he held up his hand to silence her.

'Morah . . .' he said, walking around to his side of the huge desk. 'Good of you to come so promptly. There's no need for any more apologies or histrionics – God knows we've all had enough of those in the last day. Thank God Joey is home safe and sound, thanks to our good friend Evelyn Malone finding him in time.' He paused while he sat down opposite her. 'However . . . after the whole terrifying ordeal,' he leaned his elbows on the desk and steepled his fingers, 'Mrs Radcliffe and I cannot get past the indisputable fact that you lost our son.' Again he put his hand up to silence her. 'In light of this unfortunate development, Mrs Radcliffe has asked me to terminate your position in the household. I will pay you an additional month's salary, of course, as a gesture of gratitude for all you have done for Joey and Susan up until this unhappy episode. I'm sure you will see this as the generous offer it is and leave today, quietly and discreetly. I think that would be best for everyone involved. My wife's health, as you know, is fragile at best – this incident could very well have pushed her over the edge, indeed it may yet do so. If you try to cause any trouble . . .' he smiled kindly '. . . you will find yourself up against the full force of the law.'

Morah's mouth, frozen in disbelief up until this moment, now dropped open. 'It wasn't me who lost the child, it was Mrs Malone, she stole him from the pushchair and kept him away, Joey told me himself, he said—' The words came out in a rush.

'Morah,' Robert shook his head, 'I would advise you to

get over this very strange *obsession* you have with Mrs Malone. It's most unhealthy. Quite unhinged, really. I would like you to leave this house today, I will not be writing you a reference, and your parents will be told exactly why you have been dismissed – you may go to your room and pack now.'

'But the children!' she blurted. 'I have to say goodbye!'

'I'm afraid that will be out of the question. My wife has taken them for the day. And if you try to make any contact with them, or set foot in this house again, I will take this matter further, *a lot* further – to the courts, if necessary. Which reminds me . . .' He looked at her. 'Before you leave, I would like the copies of those photos and negatives you took without permission, while you were *spying* on me – your employer – and Mrs Malone. I hope you have them, Morah . . . because if you don't, I will have to explain to your parents myself just why it was necessary to hand you over to the police, and why you will end up in jail by the time I have finished with you.'

'At least let me say goodbye . . .' she murmured, rigid with disbelief. 'The children . . . they won't understand.'

'Run along now, Morah, and let me have those photos, please – there's a good girl. There's no need to make this any more unpleasant than it has to be, eh?'

She stood up then, slowly, holding onto the desk for support, afraid her legs were going to give way beneath her. At the door she turned to look back at him, as if to check that he really meant what he was saying, that she hadn't – by some strange quirk or misinterpretation – misunderstood him.

He was seated now, behind his desk. He looked at her,

his face a mask of concerned sympathy. 'You didn't *really* think you could come into this house – my own home – and *threaten* me, Morah, did you?' He smiled, shaking his head as if it were all a silly misunderstanding. 'Close the door behind you, please.'

And in this manner, she was dismissed.

Upstairs, she walked mechanically around her allocated room – whose generous wardrobes provided far more space than her meagre collection of clothes would ever require – then dragged her suitcase from the lower cupboard, put it on the bed, and began to fill it. It took her less than ten minutes. The clothes were followed by her few ornaments and other possessions, none more carefully stowed away than the photographs of her with her charges, Susan and Joey – their happy, laughing faces looking out at her from a technicolour summer's day that now seemed like a thousand years ago. She pulled the other incriminating photographs from their hiding place in the envelope in her good handbag – the ones she dearly wished now she had never taken. She wore her only winter coat – glad of it as a strange chill crept through her body. Her suitcase – bumping down the stairs and pulled along the wooden floor of the hallway – echoed strangely throughout the now completely still house. There was no sign of Peggy – who had clearly been given the rest of the day off – and without the children, the place was eerily empty. She knocked on the door of Robert Radcliffe's study again and went in, placing the envelope on his desk. 'They're all there,' she said, dully. 'You can check them.'

'Thank you, Morah.' He was brisk but didn't look at her. 'I'll take your word for it.'

She went back to the hall, fetched her suitcase, and took one last look at the house she had been happy in for such a short time. Then she pulled the heavy front door behind her and set off to find a passing cab that would take her to the train station. She had nowhere else to go but home – in disgrace.

Chapter Twenty-One

Truth was on her way back to the house after morning coffee at Nessa's café, when her attention was caught by shrieks of fun coming from a local park. She took a detour to stroll through, figuring if it wasn't a short cut, then at least it would be a scenic route, pausing to watch some little kids running around the playground and others by the pond feeding the ducks with their parents.

When she was little, she used to beg Pauline to take her to the park, where she would spend every minute on the climbing frame and in the tunnels. She stayed away from the swings, because that was where the other kids always seemed to have dads to push them. 'Why don't we have a dad?' she asked her mum one day on the way home.

'We do have a dad,' Pauline said. 'We have two, actually. My dad – your Grandpa Chris who you never got to meet – is in heaven.' She paused. 'Then there's *your* dad, Tony – who . . . had to go away.'

'Why did he have to go away? Where is he?'

'Honestly?' Pauline hunkered down and looked her in the eyes. 'I don't know where he is, honey. But he wasn't happy, and I think he wasn't very well, and he had to go away to find a way to get better.' She held Truth's face in her hands. 'But

I know he loves you more than anything. One day he'll tell you that himself.' She straightened up. 'Come on, we'll go get an ice cream.'

'Do you think he's on his own?'

'I don't know, honey, but it doesn't really matter.'

'I don't think he should be on his own.' She looked up at her mum. 'He might be sad.'

Pauline held her hand a little tighter then.

One of Truth's talents that stood to her as a lawyer, and made her a feared opponent in court, was her capacity to remember word for word almost any conversation. Depending on the circumstances, it was an ability she discovered could prove a curse or a blessing in her personal life.

She realised now – years later – how hard it must have been for Pauline as a young single mum and acknowledged all the sacrifices her mum had made for her. And to her credit, back then Pauline had never spoken a harsh word about Tony, her absent father.

It wasn't until much later – when as a rather truculent teenager Truth had painstakingly fitted all the various pieces of Pauline's accounts and explanations together, after working and reworking them like some particularly intricate jigsaw puzzle – that she had been able to confront the harsh facts. 'He just walked out on us, didn't he?' she had said to Pauline, startling her one day as she walked into the kitchen of their tiny flat.

Even then, her mum had tried to defend him. 'Things are never that simple, Truth. Hopefully you'll get a chance to hear his side of the story some day.'

'I don't want to hear it.' She was fourteen and angry.

'Don't be too hard on him, sweetheart.' Pauline gave her a rueful smile. 'He gave you his long eyelashes and your drop-dead gorgeous looks.'

'I don't want to be like *him*.'

'Just because you share the same DNA, Truth, doesn't mean you have to make the same choices.'

And she hadn't. Pauline had always encouraged her to be independent, to be responsible for her own decisions, to carve out her own future, and she had done that, admirably. But sometimes Truth wondered what it would be like – just once – to let someone special get close enough to help build her dream of the happy family unit she had missed out on, and secretly longed to be a part of one day.

She was so absorbed in her thoughts, it took a minute for her to realise that a man was jogging towards her and waving. She was about to look behind her – assuming it was someone else whose attention he was trying to attract – when she saw it was Ari.

'Truth!' He came to a stop, pulling up beside her. 'Hey, I thought it was you!' He seemed pleased to see her. 'I'm just getting my run in before I head into town to give a lecture.' He pushed back a lock of dark hair from his forehead with one hand, looking remarkably cool for someone who'd been running. 'What brings you to the park?'

Truth shrugged. 'I was just wandering through on my way back. I'm still getting my bearings.'

'Are you by any chance free this evening?' The question took her by surprise.

'Ah, I guess so – unless Evelyn might need me for anything.'

'Excellent! Then you can join me for dinner. Would 7 p.m. suit? I'm going to be working all day in the city centre – maybe you could meet me there? A very good French restaurant has been recommended to me – and I always think it's a shame to eat alone.'

If she hesitated for a fraction too long, Ari was undeterred. His expression was confidently expectant. Although she would have much preferred to spend the evening with her grandmother – she had been hoping to do a little more digging as regards the relationship between Evelyn and Pauline – the invitation had been so unexpected, Truth couldn't think of a reason to refuse.

'Sure, that sounds good, thank you.'

'Let me have your number, and I'll text you the restaurant details.' His happy grin was infectious. 'See you at seven then.'

'Great,' Truth said, as he waved back at her, already on his way.

✧

'I knew it!' Evelyn was triumphant when Truth mentioned her dinner date. 'I knew he'd ask you out. I love a man who doesn't pussyfoot around and goes after what he wants. It's so attractive. Foreign men are much more assertive than our lot when it comes to approaching women, don't you find? Of course you probably haven't experienced any Irish men, have you?' She didn't wait for an answer. 'What are you going to wear?'

'I have no idea.' Truth was mildly surprised at Evelyn's reaction.

'Well, you can't wear jeans. Gavotte is a double Michelin-starred restaurant – it'll be very stylish. You never know who might be there.'

'It's a casual after-work dinner, Evelyn – I'm not going to a cocktail party.'

'You don't know where you might end up afterwards.' Evelyn shot her a mischievous look. 'Better to be prepared. Feel free to raid my wardrobe.'

'In that case, I might have a quick look in some of the local boutiques. I haven't been shopping in ages.'

'Good idea. I wish I could come with you – but you can give me a fashion show when you get back. Wait 'til I tell everyone you're going out with the plastic surgeon!'

'Ah, I'd appreciate it if you kept this to yourself. It's only a dinner, and I need to let Nessa know,' Truth said hastily. 'I don't want her to think I'm going behind her back.'

Evelyn looked at her speculatively. 'It's none of her business who you have dinner with.'

'It was Nessa who met him first,' Truth reminded her. '*And* introduced him to everybody. He was talking to her quite a bit at the barbecue.'

'But it was *you* he was looking at. He couldn't take his eyes off you. Besides, you can't let other women's wishful thinking make you feel guilty for accepting an invitation. Nobody would ever get a date with an eligible man with that attitude.'

'I just don't want Nessa's feelings to be hurt,' Truth said. 'She's been so kind to me since I got here.'

'The only person hurting Nessa is Nessa.' Evelyn was brisk. 'She's too . . .' she paused, searching for the right word '. . . soppy.'

'She's not soppy! She's lovely! She's kind and sensitive – she's had a bad experience with a loser boyfriend. She just hasn't met the right guy yet.'

'Well, she's not going to while she's wasting time with all the wrong ones. Nessa doesn't have enough self-respect, that's her problem. She should never have allowed that ghastly sounding ex-boyfriend to treat her so appallingly.'

'She loved him. Nessa is gorgeous – any man would be lucky to get her.'

'I couldn't agree more with you, Truth. But the fact of the matter is that Nessa herself doesn't believe that any man would be lucky to get her. On the contrary, she feels *she* would be the lucky one to be chosen – and that's the kiss of death to any prospective romance. And it doesn't matter what you look like – it's all about attitude. A man needs to think he has a prize in his sights when he shows interest in and pursues a woman. It's a simple transaction. An illusion, perhaps – but one that's crucial to establish. Plenty of time to be disappointed in each other later on, when the real self rears its ugly head.' Evelyn gave her a wry look. 'But by then you should have a wedding ring on your finger.' She laughed.

Truth was feeling increasingly uncomfortable at the turn the conversation had taken, but she didn't want to get into an argument. Evelyn had a rather wicked side to her – in a fun way, she supposed. She meant well. She was clearly the kind of person who would be wonderful in a crisis, but maybe not so much fun to have as a mother. As for the rest of it – she was simply ludicrously out of touch. The world had moved on since Evelyn had been on the dating scene, and relationships were no longer defined by a ring on your finger.

In Truth's line of work, she knew just how much misery getting locked into the wrong relationship could inflict on a person. The thought of it made her shudder. All the same, she couldn't help but be more and more convinced that Evelyn's attitude had been responsible for making her own mother – Pauline – rebel the way she clearly had. Pauline's life had been a lot more difficult as a result. Truth wondered if it had all been worth it for her mum. But it wasn't the kind of question she felt she had any right to ask her.

Chapter Twenty-Two

After making Evelyn a light lunch and helping her down to the garden where she said she wanted to sit and read in the shade – or rather, Truth suspected, hold a book in her lap while she gossiped with Doctor Ed as he worked in the garden – Truth strolled into town. It was a warm afternoon, although cloudy, and Mariner's Cove was busy as she passed by. She fished out her phone, thinking the best way of telling Nessa about her prospective dinner with Ari was to ask her to come shopping with her, if she could. It went straight to voicemail, so Truth left a brief message, explaining what had happened, hoping Nessa wouldn't be too deflated by the news. She found the boutique she had in mind – Cave – without much trouble, remembering Nessa pointing it out to her on their way past the other evening. It proved to have exactly what Truth was looking for. It took a minute for her eyes to adjust to the dim interior, where discreet and artful lighting revealed rails of very cool gear, shoes, and other accessories, all set into mirrored alcoves along the walls. Despite her love of clothes and fashion, Truth was a decisive shopper and didn't like to dither. She picked up a silk khaki jumpsuit, which worked equally well with flats or heels, two wrap dresses, and a ridiculously feminine tiered shell-blue dress with a V-neck and enormous puffed sleeves to her elbows – which was really not her usual style at all but made her feel like an Edwardian heroine. Two pairs of sandals – rope wedge and leather flats – and some cool beads and earrings, and she was done.

Poppy, the proprietor, took her card and wrapped the clothes. 'They look amazing on you. Mind you, anything would, I guess.'

'Thanks. You have lovely stuff. I'll be back, I'm sure.'

'Are you new in the neighbourhood? Haven't seen you before.'

'I'm just here for a while, staying in Ulysses Crescent – Nessa from the café told me about this place.'

'Well, I hope you enjoy your stay. Any friend of Nessa's is a friend of ours. Right, Rambo?' She smiled at the large marmalade cat curled in a tub chair beside her.

'Thanks, that's really kind of you – see you around.'

The sun had come out while she was trying on her new gear in Cave and, lugging her bags back up the hill, Truth felt beads of sweat breaking out on her forehead. She stopped for a takeaway cold drink and decided to take some time out to sit on one of the benches along Mariner's Cove before going back to the flat. It was a relief to dump her bags for a bit. She read her messages: one from Pauline asking how she was getting on, a couple from girlfriends, one from a colleague – thankfully nothing from Josh. She sat back, closing her eyes, enjoying the feel of the sun on her face and the light breeze that lifted her hair.

'Looks like you've been busy.'

The voice startled her and she looked up to see Mike smiling down at her, indicating the bags.

'Yeah, well, I kinda came over here at short notice.' She squinted up at him. 'I didn't bring much with me. I needed a few things. Were you swimming?'

'Yeah. The hair's a bit of a giveaway. Mind if I join you?' He indicated the bench.

'Sure, be my guest.'

He sat down, stretching out his legs. 'I feel like we got off on the wrong foot at the barbecue. I must have seemed rude ignoring that we'd met earlier on the pier? I was kind of taken unawares, just seeing you standing there in the garden and hearing you were Evelyn's granddaughter. The cat got my tongue.'

'That's okay.' Truth grinned at his honesty. 'It must have seemed a bit weird alright, I felt it too. The weirdness, I mean.'

'Good. I mean, that's not good – but it's good you understand.' He thumped his head. 'Sometimes I think my sculptures have better conversational skills than I do. Bear with me, I get better . . . I'm just out of practice . . . been spending too much time with statues.'

Truth laughed. 'Well, I argue for a living, so I'm happy to take some time out. The floor is all yours.'

'Can we start again, then?'

'Sure. Let's stick with the sculpture theme . . . How are the foundations for your piece shaping up?'

'Yeah, they're looking good – everything's on track – so far . . .' He frowned.

'But . . .? You don't look very happy about it.'

'No, everything's fine. It's just that last time things took a bit of a turn for the worse – it came out of left field. It's made me a bit edgy.'

'What happened?'

'It's a long, boring story – I'll tell you another time.'

'I'd like to hear it – really.'

'Well, to put it in a nutshell – some locals decided they didn't like my last piece. There was a protest, the whole thing got a bit political – and the local councillors backed down and the entire project was cancelled, so to speak.'

'Can they do that?'

'Yeah, if there's enough of an objection they can do anything.'

'That's so unfair.' Truth shook her head. 'You must have been devastated.'

'It was my own fault. I didn't play for it.'

'Didn't . . .?' For a moment she was confused.

'I missed my train so I didn't get to play "The Swan". I won't be making that mistake again.'

'Oh, that's awful.'

'I was mostly pissed off at the time.' He shrugged. 'But actually they ended up doing me a favour. The publicity it generated did more for my career than I could have imagined.' He shook his head. 'Still – I could have done without it.'

'Where's the piece now?'

'In my studio.'

'I'd love to see it sometime.'

He looked surprised. 'That can be arranged.'

'I'll take you up on that, but for now I'd better be getting back.' She stood up. Mike did too, and before she could reach for them, he picked up her bags.

'Oh, thanks. You don't need to—'

'I insist.' He smiled. 'It's not like it's out of my way.'

'Well, thank you.'

They chatted easily the rest of the way until they reached number 24 and went up the steps, where Truth took out her key and opened the front door. Once inside, Mike said he'd be happy to take the bags up the rest of the way.

'I can take them from here, really – but thanks, I appreciate it.' She flashed him a grateful smile as he handed them over.

'Just a thought,' he said, as she was about to go up the stairs. She looked back at him. 'If you're not doing anything this evening – you could take a look at the sculpture and we could grab a bite to eat after, maybe?'

Her shoulders sagged at the unfortunate timing of the invitation. 'I'm really sorry' – she really was – 'but I already have plans for this evening.'

'No worries.' His face closed down and he shrugged. 'It was just a thought.'

'I'd really like to do that another time?'

'Sure. Have a great evening.' And he disappeared into his flat. As the door closed behind him, Truth felt sure the likelihood of any future invitations had shut down too. Why did he have to ask her to see the sculpture today, of all days?

✧

Ari was charming, there was no doubt about it. He was also an amusing and engaging dinner companion. He had been waiting for her at the restaurant and stood up immediately from the table to greet her when she arrived, kissing her on both cheeks, and was eager to hear her opinion on the bottle of red he suggested from the wine list.

'Looks great,' Truth said. So he ordered his current favourite – a very fine Château Lafite.

Over dinner, he appeared genuinely interested in her work, asking probing questions and making insightful observations, only telling her about his own career when she pleaded that she had been talking about herself for long enough. Truth was impressed by his genuine passion and dedication to operating on children in poorer parts of the world where facial deformity was not only a misfortune, he explained, but greatly increased a child's chances of aban-donment and even death as a result. Then he made her laugh with stories about some of his appearance-obsessed clients in LA.

'Don't you think it's unhealthy, though?' Truth asked. 'All this non-stop messing with your face?'

'Of course it's unhealthy – if it becomes an addiction. But an improved or refreshed appearance also brings people a lot of joy and gives them back lost confidence. I have to say it gives me real pleasure to see my patients' eyes light up when they feel a part of them that was lost has been restored. This is usually the case, I am happy to say, when they return to me after surgery. Also, you have to remember, it is these cases which are often considered superficial that allow me to provide the service I do in poverty-stricken communities.'

It was after an amusing story Ari told her – about an enraged ex-husband making death threats to him after he had performed a particularly successful facelift on the man's former wife – that Truth decided to tell him about her own online abuse and cancelling.

Ari listened to her account, shaking his head in disgust at her story. 'These people . . . one can only wonder about the horrible minds they have. So that's why you came here, to Dublin? To get away from it all?'

'Not exactly, although it was part of the reason, sure. But I also wanted to take the chance to get to know my grandmother.'

'Of course – and what a wonderful woman she is . . . such spirit! I could see that even from the brief time I spent chatting with her. But Truth . . .' He looked at her intently. 'You cannot let these people – these insane people – intimidate you. That is what they want. You cannot let them win.'

She lifted her chin a fraction. 'I don't intend to.'

'Then of course you will be returning to London to resume your career and the important work you do?'

It must have been the question – which was delivered as more of a statement – that triggered the reaction, but to her horror, Truth suddenly felt her eyes fill and her hands – which she hurriedly withdrew under the table – begin to tremble. Fortunately, Ari was looking to attract the attention of a passing waiter, so he didn't notice. She took the opportunity to grab her bag and say she was heading for the ladies' room. In the safety of the cubicle, Truth took out a tissue and dabbed her eyes, sat on the loo, and forced herself to breathe through her nose, which she had read somewhere was a calming technique, and waited for the trembling to subside. What was the matter with her? Why was she behaving like this? Of course she was going back to her career in

London – what else was she going to do? But the thought of it – which she had been managing admirably to keep at bay since she arrived in Dublin – suddenly filled her with profound unease. *I won't think about it now*, she decided. It was just stress, which was completely understandable given what she had been through recently – to be expected, even. But as she checked her make-up, and reapplied some lipstick before making her way back to the table, a small voice warned her that maybe she needed to pay more attention to the signals her body was sending her.

'Is something the matter?' Ari stopped mid-sentence a few minutes later over coffee. 'You seem . . . a little on edge . . . distracted?'

'No, not at all,' she lied. 'I'm just tired. I think I'd like to go home now, if you don't mind.'

'Of course.' He called for the bill, looking concerned. 'Are you ill? Was it something you ate?'

'No, it's nothing, really. Nothing a good night's sleep won't fix.' Truth reached for her wallet. 'Let's split this.'

'Absolutely not! I insist,' Ari said.

'I'd really prefer . . .'

'Please!' He smiled disarmingly. 'Allow me the pleasure of buying dinner for a beautiful and interesting dining companion, Truth. I may live in America, but I am a Greek man at heart. That is not a bad thing, I hope . . .' He made a wry face.

'Well, thank you, Ari – that was really lovely. I enjoyed it.'

'I hope we can do this again soon, Truth?' He locked eyes with her. 'You and I have been thrown together here in a new city for a while . . . we could have a lot of fun . . .' He lifted his eyebrows.

Despite herself, Truth smiled. At least he was upfront about it. 'I don't think so, Ari. But I'm sure you won't have any trouble finding many other willing dinner partners.'

As they stood up, Ari shrugged. 'You win some, you lose some – but I wouldn't be a true Greek man if I didn't at least try.'

'I know Nessa enjoys eating out,' Truth said innocently. 'It gives her a break from her own restaurant. That girl is so talented . . .'

'Really?' Ari sounded interested. 'She was very charming to invite me to your barbecue. Tell me more about her.'

'Well, she's very creative. She's a fantastic cook, obviously . . . she can also design and make her own clothes and . . . she's psychic. She reads tarot cards.'

'Is that so?' Ari nodded. 'I'm a very spiritual person.'

'Maybe you should ask her to give you a reading sometime?'

'Now that is an idea I shall follow through on!'

Ari hailed a taxi easily outside the restaurant, and the journey back to Abbottsville was relatively quick, despite the occasional glut of summer traffic. All along the seafront, people were still out walking, sailing, and swimming, enjoying the beautiful evening. At half past nine, it was still perfectly bright as they pulled up on Ulysses Crescent. 'I don't suppose I can persuade you to come in for coffee?' Ari said.

'No thanks, Ari.' Truth made to go up the steps of number 24.

'At least let me see you to your door. I promise I won't try to kiss you – although I would very much like to. But I am guilty of being irritatingly old-fashioned.' He lifted a shoulder and smiled. 'What can I say? A lot of money and tradition has gone into my education. Old habits die hard.'

'There's no need, but if you insist.' They walked up the steps, where Ari waited while Truth fished out her key. 'Goodnight, Ari,' she said. 'And thanks for dinner.'

'My pleasure.' He turned to go.

It was just as she was closing the door, waving Ari off, that she saw another figure had turned onto the Crescent and was running up the steps, taking them two at a time, passing Ari on his way down. The two men acknowledged each other.

When he reached the top of the steps, Truth stood back awkwardly to let Mike through – she could hardly shut the door in his face. 'Hi,' she said lamely.

'Hey,' he said, looking back at her before letting himself into his flat. 'Hope you had a good evening.'

It hadn't been a bad evening, Truth thought as she headed upstairs, but her timing these days definitely left a lot to be desired. She just hoped Mike wouldn't think she and Ari were an item . . . The thought brought her up short. Why would she care what he thought? She slowed on her way up the stairs, holding onto the rail. Was this some silly crush she was developing? That was the last thing she needed right now. It was ridiculous. Truth didn't do whimsical romance. Everything in her life had been carefully planned and worked around. She never allowed her heart to rule her head. Romance had only been considered whenever the timing and the person concerned could be carefully fitted in around her workload. Maybe that was it . . . she was off duty for the first time she could remember since her student days (even then she had worked through holidays) – maybe this was what a holiday romance felt like. She shook her head and grinned. Obviously Dublin was having a regressive effect on her psyche, which seemed to be telling her to lighten up, have a little fun for a change.

✧

It was later than usual for a week night when Doctor Ed noticed Mike wandering down to the garden. He had been about to go inside himself, but it was such a beautiful late June evening he had allowed himself an extra half an hour and had been enjoying night falling and the beginnings of shadows casting reflections on the small pond where a ladybird sat quietly under the shade of a leaf, probably waiting to lay her eggs. He'd also been mulling over the research he'd done earlier on the company Ari had suggested he might consider buying shares in. Doctor Ed had invited Ari to lunch in his club, which he kept on for mostly social purposes. His sailing days were long past, although he'd been quite a keen sailor when he was younger, but he maintained a pavilion membership in the yacht club which meant he had somewhere quiet to retreat to on a winter's day if he needed to escape the bunker, and the place provided a picturesque seafront location to invite guests in summer. It also meant he got to keep up with a modicum of what was actually going on in the lives of his former circle of friends, who were sadly diminishing year by year.

Lunch with Ari had proved very interesting. The man led a

fascinating life, coming as he did from a long line of both aris-
tocratic and wealthy families. But apart from his family
connections, Ari's own global connections in the field of science and pharmaceuticals were impressive, to say the least. The
man was a powerhouse of knowledge. Just talking to him about
the imminent advances coming down the line in medicine and
surgery made Doctor Ed wish he were back in the cut and
thrust of his hospital days. He had decided to take Ari's advice
and to research this one company that sounded of particular
interest. If Ari was right, it might prove a rather lucrative investment. If not, Doctor Ed would still have enough to live on from
his current arrangement to enjoy what years were left to him.
But at least it would add a little frisson of excitement back into
his business affairs – he'd been careful enough setting up his
house in flats, so he could afford a little speculation.

'Hey, doc,' Mike said, coming to sit opposite him by the
pond. 'How's it going?'

'Very well, I have to say.' Doctor Ed smiled. 'Can I interest you in a G&T? It's such a beautiful night, one of those
ones that never quite becomes fully dark . . . pity not to
appreciate it for a little while longer.'

'Sure, I'll have a nightcap.' Mike sounded weary.

Doctor Ed was discreet as he came out with the drinks.
He'd heard both from Ari himself, over lunch, and also
from Evelyn – who had been delighted to pass the news on,
in confidence of course – that Ari had asked Truth out to
dinner. Ed wondered if this was perhaps the reason Mike
was seeming a little out of sorts. He worried about Mike; he
thought of him as the son he'd never had, and the two shared
an easy rapport.

'Everything alright?'

'Yeah, fine – was just having a bit of trouble sleeping lately. I'm always a bit distracted between projects.'

'Mmm, yes, of course. Only to be expected. You need to get out a bit again. Did you think about what I said at all? About asking Truth out?'

'Pretty sure she's seeing Ari, the surgeon guy.' Mike looked up at the sky.

'In my day, an attractive woman was considered to be worth competing for, a reason to throw your hat into the ring, so to speak . . . not a reason to back off. Is that another thing that's become unacceptable nowadays?'

'Like I said, doc, you're asking the wrong guy. I'm out of the loop.'

Doctor Ed didn't push. They sat for a while watching the moon rise, chatting amiably. Doctor Ed retired first, going in to his bunker. Crawling in between fresh sheets – courtesy of Morah – he reflected not for the first time on how youth was indeed wasted on the young. But having Ari around was a bit of fun – even if he might prove to be something of a cat among the pigeons. In Doctor Ed's experience, a bit of male competition was a healthy thing. He was in agreement with Evelyn on that point.

Chapter Twenty-Three

'You never told me how dinner *really* went the other night.'

'Yes, I did.' Truth was helping Evelyn with her support stockings. 'I told you the food was excellent, that Ari was good company, the restaurant was busy, Ari insisted on paying, and that I was tired and wanted to have an early night.'

'Yes, but are you *seeing* him again?'

'No.'

'What?' Evelyn was horrified. 'Do you mean he didn't suggest another date? I'm sure he will . . .' She drummed her fingers on the arm of her chair. 'He's probably just keeping you in suspense for a bit – not wanting to come on too strong, you know. That's the type of thing I'd tell Bruce to do . . . but I'm surprised at Ari – I thought he'd be more upfront about it.' She frowned.

'Oh, he did suggest another date . . .'

'And?'

'I declined.'

'You turned him down?'

'I told him I wasn't interested. So . . . yes.'

'Are you playing hard to get? You need to be careful you

know . . .' Evelyn's eyes narrowed. 'Men's egos are very fragile – as a tactic it could backfire.'

'I am not playing hard to get.' Truth sighed. 'I don't believe in playing games with men or anyone else, Evelyn. I just don't want to see him again – I have zero interest in him.'

Evelyn's mouth was agape. 'Whyever not? Did he insult you? Was he rude, or unkind?'

'No.' Truth tried to be patient. 'I told you – he was a perfect gentleman. He's simply not for me. Besides, he's just passing through – so am I for that matter.' She emphasised the latter part of her statement, as much for her own benefit as Evelyn's.

'Yes, but you have to give things a *chance* . . . you don't know what it might lead to. Imagine the life you could have . . .' Evelyn looked wistful. 'Homes on every continent, yachts, glamour, oodles of money . . .' She lifted her eyebrows.

'I make plenty of money, thank you very much. All that I need anyhow.'

'And that's very admirable, darling, it really is. But it won't keep you warm at night.'

'I'll take that chance any day,' Truth murmured.

'What did you say?' Evelyn frowned.

'I said I'll take my chances.'

'You know, Truth, you must be a very intimidating prospect to most men. You shouldn't act as if you're invincible. Strength is all very well . . . but you don't want to scare people off. You should try showing a softer side . . . you know, try acting a little bit more vulnerable. Men love that.'

Truth turned around slowly to look at her grandmother. 'Are you for real?'

'What's that supposed to mean?' Evelyn was indignant.

'Evelyn, I work with women who are victims of sexual assault and harassment. I know exactly what men are capable of – even the timid ones – and if you think I'm going to adopt some ridiculous simpering, Victorian, man-worshipping act – you are in for a big disappointment.'

'I didn't mean at work, obviously.' Evelyn sniffed.

'That goes for out of work hours too. I'm interested in a *life* partner, Evelyn. Someone who is my equal, who shares the same ambitions and dreams as I do. Not someone whose pathetic ego I have to massage all the time.'

Evelyn smiled. 'So you *are* looking for someone, then. For a moment there you had me worried – I thought you wanted to be all on your own.' She looked triumphant. 'Well, I suppose that's something.'

Chapter Twenty-Four

'The furnishings are great,' the prospective tenant was saying, 'but I think I'd like to move some of my own pieces in. The space is perfect for them.' She gazed around the generous double reception rooms of the house in Dublin 4 that Stella was showing. 'D'you think that would be okay? Excuse me . . .?'

'Sorry?' Stella was distracted. Her client – an elegant American diplomat – was frowning. Stella forced herself to focus.

'I was asking if it would be okay to move in some of my own pieces.'

'Oh, yes, yes, I'm sure that wouldn't be a problem.'

'Okay, then.' She was looking at Stella strangely. 'I have a couple of other places to see – I'll get back to you.'

'Sure.' Stella showed her to the door of the newly refurbished Edwardian house. 'If you have any questions, just call me.' Then she watched the woman get into her car and drive away, and felt absurdly envious of her. Imagine your work taking you all around the world, and the finest houses and apartments being put at your disposal. Everything being organised for you – schools found for your children, invitations issued for your social life – you just had to show up and do what you were paid to do. She wandered back through the house making sure everything was as it should be, finishing up in the huge light-filled kitchen, with its pristine presses and beautifully empty fridge. Just being there in the clutter-free space made her feel better, clearer. She sat down at the marble counter and took some deep, slow breaths – trying to quell the awful sensation of overwhelm that had begun to course through her on a daily basis. It had all gone horribly wrong, her life. She had not been paying proper attention and now it was completely out of control – *her* control. Things were spiralling ever faster out of her grasp and she had no idea how to reclaim them. And it had all happened right under her nose. She took a nectarine from the nearby fruit bowl, rolling it mindlessly back and forth beneath her hand.

When it had just been the three of them – her, Bruce and Freddy – she could manage things. But now – since Annika had arrived on the scene – there was another person involved. She hadn't seen that one coming. And Annika – in her calm, untroubled, quietly confident manner – was trying to steal her son from her. Stella was utterly sure of this. She was quite clearly wooing Freddy away from her. It was *Annika this, Annika that*, and *When is it my turn to stay with Daddy and Annika again, Mummy?* It was driving Stella mad. Something would have to be done about it . . . but what? Stella put the nectarine down and, fishing her phone from her bag, began to text Bruce, rapidly. She would insist on a meeting with him this evening. Things couldn't continue like this. Standing up from her seat, she was mildly surprised to see that at some stage while she had been ruminating there, she had arranged the entire bowl of nec-tarines in a meticulously straight orange line along the centre of the white marble counter. She was about to gather them back up and return them to their bowl – then decided against it. She thought they looked perfectly fine just as they were.

Chapter Twenty-Five

'I'm beginning to get an inkling about why Mum found Evelyn so difficult to live with.' Truth was sitting in the kitchen of Nessa's café, having a quiet cappuccino before the lunchtime crowd arrived.

Nessa reappeared from her pantry holding two bags of gluten-free flour. 'What makes you say that?'

Truth chewed the inside of her mouth while she searched for the right word. 'There's something . . . remorseless about her . . . merciless, even.'

'Evelyn?' Nessa placed the bags on the counter and laughed. 'Are we talking about the same person?' She shook her head, bemused. 'I know she's a bit full-on at times, but she means well. She's just one of those kinds of people who won't accept defeat, I think. A real go-getter. I wish I could be more like her.' She took out a large bowl from a cupboard below. 'She's so . . . irrepressible.'

'Hmm.' Truth was thinking about what Evelyn had said about Nessa. About her being soppy and not having enough self-respect.

'So, what was it she said? Something about your mum?' Nessa poured some flour into the bowl.

'No . . . just more of an attitude. Perhaps you're right. Maybe I'm imagining it.'

'So, how was your date with Ari?' Nessa lifted her eyebrows.

'It was fine. The food was great—'

'I should think so! Not one, but two Michelin stars . . .'

'Ari was very nice and pleasant company but we both knew before the second course we had absolutely nothing in common.'

'I find that hard to believe!'

Truth shrugged. 'It's true.'

'So you're not seeing him again?'

'Nope. But he is – I can tell you this on good authority – on the lookout for dinner companions.'

'Really?'

'Yes. He told me he hates eating alone.'

'Of course he would.' Nessa shook her head in sympathy. 'There's something so joyless about eating alone.'

'He also told me he's very spiritual.'

'Seriously?'

'Yes. He was also asking me about you . . .'

'Me?'

'Yes. He sounded very interested. Particularly when I told him you did tarot readings . . .'

'What?' The sifting of ingredients paused. 'Do you think he'd like one?'

'I wouldn't be a bit surprised.'

'I don't think I'd be able to concentrate on the cards, looking into those gorgeous brown eyes of his. Then I could suggest he stays for a bite to eat afterwards – casually, I mean, couldn't I?'

'You could – but I bet he'll ask you out to dinner.'

'D'you really think I'd stand a chance?'

Truth finished her coffee. 'Just remember he's only passing through, though, Ness – he's only here for a couple of months.'

'*Anything* could happen in a couple of months!'

Truth shook her head. 'You sound just like Evelyn.'

'I do, don't I?' Nessa was delighted. 'That's the best thing anyone has said to me today!'

Chapter Twenty-Six

Bruce took a deep breath before ringing the bell of flat number 4, to where Stella had summoned him for a meeting. Despite feeling more confident and happier than he had ever before in his life, he still found his heart rate accelerating and he was well aware it wasn't for any of the right reasons. Even so, he preferred to put it down to the fact that he had been drinking way too much coffee and Diet Coke, rather than confront the possibility that he was still reasonably intimidated by his ex-wife. He hadn't had a chance to brief Evelyn on this latest development and he wasn't sure he wanted to. Stella's behaviour, and in particular her outburst to Annika at the barbecue, had both shocked and embarrassed him. It was time he handled things himself.

'Bruce, thanks so much for making time for this.' Stella was cool as she ushered him in to her immaculate and minimally furnished flat. 'I know how busy you are.'

'Where's Freddy?' Bruce looked around instinctively – he had expected a three-year-old bundle of compressed energy to hurtle towards him.

'Mum's taken him . . . so we can have some space. She's dropping him back to me later. Sit down, please.'

'Right.' Bruce had the distinct impression that this was

not going to be about the apology he imagined Stella would want to make. On the contrary, it felt more like a strange business meeting.

'Drink?' She pointed to a bottle on the counter. 'I have some white wine open . . .'

'Just water, thanks.' Bruce looked around while Stella poured some water for him and a glass of white for herself. She had lost weight, he noticed. Her more angular appearance, along with her outfit of crisp white shirt, black trousers and tightly pulled back hair (Bruce used to love her loose, glossy brunette mane) lent an additional severity to her already grave expression. The flat shared similar proportions to its neighbours', but although the evening sun was pouring through the windows, filtered through slats of metallic venetian blinds, the furnishings – sparse and clinically modern as they were – managed to counteract any feeling of warmth or comfort in the room. Looking at all the angles and sharp edges, Bruce wondered how Freddy avoided doing himself a serious injury. He gave an involuntary shudder.

'Are you cold?' Stella's eyebrows lifted.

'No, why?'

'Never mind.' She sat down opposite him, crossing her legs.

'So,' Bruce let out a breath, 'what was it you wanted to talk to me about?'

'Do you really have to ask?'

Bruce frowned. 'Sorry?'

Stella sighed. 'Fine, if you want to play dumb, I'll spell it out.'

'Spell out what?'

'I am not happy – actually, rewind . . . I am extremely

unhappy – with the fact that your girlfriend is under the impression that she can steal my son from me.'

Bruce looked at her incredulously. 'What are you talking about, Stella? No one is trying to steal Freddy from you.'

'Well, you would say that, wouldn't you? Of course you're going to back *her* up.'

'Hold on a minute, Stella – just back up there. What gives you the idea – no, wait – what gives you the *right* to make such a ridiculous accusation? Annika has been nothing but kind and attentive to Freddy when he's with us.'

Stella gave him a grim smile. 'I wouldn't expect *you* to see it.'

'See what?' Bruce was flummoxed.

'What she's trying to do.' Stella made an exasperated sound. 'Annika is clearly trying to steal Freddy from me – to turn my own son against me. She may be fooling you   but I can see exactly what she's at. And . . .' she leaned towards him, narrowing her eyes '. . . if she thinks she's going to get away with it – if either of you think you're going to get away with it – you are very much mistaken.'

Bruce sat back and shook his head. 'Stella I have no idea what you're talking about. You're not making sense.' He leaned forward and looked her straight in the eye. 'Let me remind you of a few things here . . . It was you who wanted *me* to move out. *You* who wanted to end our marriage and break up our family. *You* who wanted us to have separate lives but live here in Ulysses Crescent sharing the same house – all for Freddy's sake.' He stood up and began to pace across the room. 'That was how you sold me the whole idea of moving in to this place . . .' He paused to draw breath. 'This . . .' he spread his hands in disbelief '. . . was all *your* idea. I never wanted any of it. But you forced me into a new life, into new living quarters, new parenting arrangements . . . and now . . .' He turned to face her. 'Let me get this right. Now you are accusing Annika and *me* of stealing our son away from you?' He glared at her. 'Freddy is a three-year-old *child*. Are you for real? Have you *listened* to yourself?'

'There is no need to raise your voice, Bruce.' Stella was cold, but she was looking at him oddly, blinking rapidly – almost as if she was impressed.

'Why not? There's no one here, is there? I think it's perfectly reasonable of me to raise my voice.' Bruce couldn't remember ever being roused to this level of anger, but the injustice of Stella's accusations, coupled with the gigantic upheaval she had put him through over the last two and a half years, not to mention the downright misery he had endured trying to facilitate her wishes, had taken its toll and was now driving him to fury.

'You don't understand, Brucie.' Stella gave him a bright smile. 'Sit down . . . here.' She patted the space beside her on the unforgiving-looking sofa. 'We can make all this better . . . if you'll just listen to me.'

'Don't talk to me as if I'm Freddy's age! What do you think I am? Your bidding boy?'

Stella's eyes widened. 'You don't understand . . . you *have* to listen to me . . . it's all Annika's doing . . . she's trying to play happy families with you . . . she clearly has designs on you, and Freddy is just a pawn to her . . . she's trying to make him prefer her to me – so she can take everything from me . . .'

'No one is trying to take anything from you, Stella – least

of all Freddy. You are his mother! Why – in the name of God – would anyone be trying to take him from you? We've all been bending over backwards to accommodate you.'

'You're making me sound as if I was a difficult client.'

Bruce felt difficult clients paled in comparison, but now was clearly not the time to point this out. He sat down beside her and gave a deep sigh, putting his head briefly in his hands. 'Look,' he said, trying to compose himself, 'I don't know what you've got into your head, Stella . . . we've all been through a difficult adjustment period recently . . . but no one is trying to take Freddy or anything else away from you. Can you understand that?' He turned to face her, trying his best to be reasonable.

'No, I can't.' Stella's voice was almost a whisper. 'But I want *you* to understand this . . .' She leaned in to him and took his face in her hands. 'Brucie . . . this is all wrong. I made a horrible mistake . . . come home to us – to Freddy and me . . . just move back in . . . it would be so easy . . .' She leaned forward and kissed him, pulling him to her.

For a second, perhaps two – during which Stella intended to progress the kiss – Bruce was rigid with shock. Then he leapt to his feet as if electrocuted. 'What the hell, Stella? What d'you think you're playing at?' He looked down at her with disgust and wiped his mouth. 'You – you – what the hell has got into you?'

'I just need to make you understand . . .' She got up and tried to put her arms around him. 'It's all been a mistake . . . a terrible mistake . . . you need to come home, Brucie . . . to me and Freddy.'

Bruce shook his head in disbelief, prising her arms from

around his neck and stepping away from her. 'Okay, whoa, whoa, whoa!' He held his hands up. 'Stella, you need to calm down. I don't know what you've been telling yourself . . . but I am with Annika now. You and I are legally separated . . . we're waiting for a full divorce . . .' He made for the door. 'You and I are over. We're history . . . okay?' He paused. 'You know, when I agreed to meet you I thought it was because you wanted to apologise for your behaviour to Annika at the barbecue. But this . . .' He looked aghast. 'I don't know what's going on with you, Stella. But you need to accept the situation you went to a great deal of trouble to create all by yourself. This . . . all this, this misery and upheaval . . . for me and Freddy. This was you. No one else . . . just you! So now you need to move on – like you forced me to.'

Stella looked as if she'd been slapped. She turned away, and when she faced him again, the dazed look had been replaced by anger. 'Fine. That's absolutely fine by me. Just remember this: if Annika continues trying to take Freddy away from me, I'm going for full custody. So tell your scheming girlfriend that, why don't you?'

'I don't have to listen to this.' Bruce left, closing the door behind him, before he said something he really regretted. His heart was still racing – but this time about an entirely different and more worrying concern. He hoped Stella's threat of going for full custody had been her anger talking – but if she was serious, he could be about to face into a whole new level of stress.

Chapter Twenty-Seven

Morah had taken special trouble with her appearance. Although it was a formality, rather than an interview, she still wanted her prospective temporary employer to be clear that she was a woman with standards. It had been Doctor Ed who had run the idea by her earlier when she was mopping his kitchen floor. 'Morah . . . how would you feel about doing a couple of hours a week for our friend Ari next door? He needs someone to do a bit of light cleaning, keep everything ship-shape, you know? He's using very little of the house, he tells me . . . but he asked me if I knew of anyone who might be available. I know how busy you are, of course,' Doctor Ed was quick to add, 'but as he's only here for a couple of months I thought I'd ask you first if you could perhaps fit him in . . .'

Although Morah hadn't answered immediately – it didn't do to look too keen – the prospect of having another house to go through, and with such an esteemed cosmetic surgeon in residence, delighted her.

She had let Doctor Ed know that she would be amenable to taking on additional hours – but only as it was a temporary arrangement, and as Doctor Ed himself had asked her. Now here she was in her favourite multicoloured floral print summer dress, new red leather shoes with rope wedge soles, that were rather high for her – but she liked the extra inches they added to her five-foot-two-inch frame – and her still prettily shaped legs encased in summer tan tights. Morah was a firm believer that no woman over fifty should ever reveal bare legs – no matter how nice said legs were. How that Evelyn Malone bared all for everyone to gawk at every morning in a swimsuit, at *her* age, made Morah shudder with revulsion – but then, the woman always had been brazen. Reaching the top of the steps, Morah pressed the doorbell firmly. Ari opened the door himself and ushered her into a beautiful reception room on the right. 'Thank you so much for taking the time out of your busy schedule, Ms Finlay – I am most grateful – please . . . have a seat. Can I offer you any refreshment? Some tea or coffee?'

'Thank you, Doctor Christopoulos,' Morah was pleased he observed formalities, 'but no – I'm assuming this won't take long?'

'Not at all.' He sat down on an adjoining sofa and smiled.

'And you may call me Morah.' She inclined her head. 'It's the modern way, isn't it? Although I don't always approve of them.'

'And you must call me Ari.'

'I'll probably call you "doctor", out of habit, you understand . . . should we go ahead with the arrangement.'

'Of course,' Ari said. 'I feel very fortunate that someone with such a glowing reference will consider the position.'

'What, exactly, has Doctor Ed told you about me?' Although Morah trusted Doctor Ed with her life, she was wary of the medical community at large. Her experience in the small town mental health hospital all those years ago hadn't endeared them to her. Doctors, she supposed, gossiped to each other as much as any other profession.

'He said that he thanks his lucky stars for the day you came to live and work with him. He said you are as meticulous in your duties as you are honest in them, and that he couldn't manage at all without you in number 24.' Ari smiled. 'He would probably have continued singing your praises had I allowed him to – but I told him that was more than enough information for me.'

'Doctor Ed has been very kind to me also, over the years,' Morah acknowledged. 'What would you be expecting of me in the way of duties?'

'Well, I'm not here for much of the day – I leave early and come back to eat and sleep. I occupy one bedroom, use the ensuite bathroom, and grab something to eat at the kitchen counter.'

'So you'd need the usual tidying and cleaning done in those areas . . . and a quick whip around the rest of the house occasionally?'

'That's exactly what I am looking for.'

'And what about laundry? Ironing and so forth?'

'I usually avail of a collection and delivery service back home . . . if you could recommend one?'

'I'd be happy to include laundry in my duties seeing as it's just for yourself. If you have guests, I will send it out.'

'Allow me to show you around the house, Morah.'

The house, she saw – as soon as she had come through the front door – was decorated with great taste and with no expense spared. It could have taken its place in the pages of any glossy interiors magazine. The walls were painted in neutral shades in the common areas, the floor in the hallway and kitchen was of various shades and patterns of Italian stone, and the kitchen itself was bright and white – rather clinical, in Morah's opinion, but easy to maintain. The reception rooms were done in dark grey, which reminded her of Evelyn's flat – although she banished the thought immediately. The sweeping curtains were deep yellow silk and operated by remote control. Upstairs there was wall-to-wall velvet-soft carpet and beautifully decorated bedrooms all with spectacular bathrooms.

'What do you think?' Ari asked her as they made their way back downstairs.

'I think two hours twice a week should be sufficient,' Morah said. 'However, my work at number 24 will take precedence. So if it's alright with you, I would have to come in whenever I could – it wouldn't be regular days or timeslots. But I can promise I will keep the house immaculate.'

'That is music to my ears, Morah – I couldn't face having to interview a stream of people sent by an agency. I will give you a key, of course. Now tell me – what about salary? Name your price!'

'The going rate will do just fine, doctor.' She named it.

'Consider it a deal!' He held out his hand.

'There is just one other thing . . .' Morah tilted her head.

'What is that?'

'You told me at the barbecue that I had good skin.'

Ari was taken aback. 'And I meant it – you do!'

'Well, I would like to keep it that way for a little longer, if at all possible. I've been reading about certain new machines . . . techniques that women can avail of . . . would you know anything about those?'

'I can assure you I know all about them.'

'They'd probably be beyond my price range?'

'Allow me to have a word with my secretary in the hospital, Morah. I feel sure she will be able to arrange some appointments for you to avail of in that area – we can consider it a trial process for which you will have to pay very little. I will supervise the treatments myself. Would that be acceptable?'

'More than acceptable! You're very kind, doctor – that was precisely what I had in mind.' Morah beamed as Ari showed her out. 'I'll text you to let you know when I'll be coming in.'

'Goodbye, Morah.' He waved.

Morah sailed back up the steps to Doctor Ed's as if she was walking on air. Evelyn Malone didn't have a monopoly on glamour. She wasn't the only woman in the house with a trick or two up her sleeve. At the top of the third flight of stairs, she went in to her flat and changed into her work trousers and pulled on her overall. It was her day to clean for Bruce, and as she let herself into his flat she noticed how much tidier it was now that there was a new woman involved in his life – hardly any need for someone to come in and clean at all now, really, she thought as she began to dust the furniture and wipe down the kitchen. Morah was fond of Bruce, and she was worried about him. She didn't altogether approve of the current situation and the new girlfriend staying over as regularly as she now did, mostly because she felt it must be confusing for little Freddy. But Annika wasn't the problem here, Morah realised. Morah knew that she herself wasn't the sharpest tool in the box – God knows her own father and brother had told her as much at every possible opportunity they could get. But she knew, from her own painful experience of a breakdown, when someone was unravelling . . . when the wheels were beginning to come off. And Stella wasn't doing well at all in that respect. Not well at all. Morah had seen Bruce go into Stella's flat yesterday evening – she had been on her way downstairs just behind him and had paused outside after Bruce went in, to do a bit of light dusting on the landing. She had heard the raised voices, heard Stella's wild accusations and threats – and, more disturbingly, had heard her begging Bruce to come back to her, to move in with her again. It was clear that Stella had somehow thrown herself at Bruce – this had horrified Morah most of all. She had left at that stage . . . but she had seen Bruce coming downstairs to the hall minutes later looking downright shaken. Morah shook her head. It wasn't boding well, the situation. She would have to keep an eye on things, maybe have a discreet word with Stella later.

Chapter Twenty-Eight

Nessa was doing everything wrong. She was aware of this while at the same time being hopelessly unable to change her behaviour. It had started with the tarot reading. Having Ari suddenly arrive at her door asking for a reading, and then come straight into her small flat wearing his immaculate dark blue linen suit and trailing an expensive fragrance in his wake had been intimidating enough, but to have him sitting at such close proximity, with just a small table between them, as he removed his jacket and slung it on the back of the chair, had unnerved her even more. Her nervousness manifested in her being unnecessarily gushy and talking far too much, instead of maintaining the rather detached, mysterious manner she had intended to, as would befit someone who was aligned with things spiritual. Instead of appearing enigmatic, Nessa found herself hanging on Ari's every word rather than studying the cards he had come to consult.

'It has been a very stressful year,' he said, running a hand through his hair and exhaling. 'I'm hoping that isn't going to continue.' His dark eyes looked into hers.

'Let me just look at your career . . .' Nessa shuffled the

cards and laid them out again, forcing herself to tear her eyes away from his.

'Actually,' Ari said, with a wry smile, 'it is not my career that is the source of my stress. My ex-wife is very neurotic . . . demanding . . . no matter what I do for her it's never enough.' He shook his head. 'And there's an ex-girlfriend, who is also becoming unreasonable.' He sighed. 'I would love to know if there was any end in sight to this cycle. All I want,' he said, shrugging helplessly, 'is to meet someone nice, normal, and down to earth . . . who isn't going to expect that I can make the world bend to her needs. I am a surgeon,' his eyes were looking into hers again, 'not a miracle worker. My work with the less fortunate must take precedence over more . . . frivolous activities.'

'Of course,' Nessa breathed. 'What you do is so . . . amazing.'

'You are very kind.' Ari smiled at the compliment. 'But I consider it a privilege to be able to do what I do.' His gaze fell on the cards again. 'What I would love to know is whether there is any hope of me meeting a kind, understanding woman who will love me simply for who I am – ever?'

Nessa swallowed. She looked at the cards which were now glazing over before her. 'I see several women here,' she cleared her throat, 'who would all be very happy to get to know you.'

'What about a relationship . . . is that on the cards?'

'Um, yes, I see a very committed relationship, in the near future – one that will bring you a lot of happiness.'

'And children?' He looked eager. 'I would love more children.'

'Yes, this relationship will bring a lot of good things into your life.' Nessa looked up. 'It will be the universe's way of repaying you for the good work you have done.'

Ari looked intrigued. 'And how will I know this woman? Where and when will we meet?'

'I can't tell you that exactly, but I feel it will be before Christmas, before the year is out.'

'So . . . that could be any time from now?'

'Yes . . . it could.'

'Then I will take extra care to look out for this woman, this . . . soulmate.' He sat back and crossed his legs.

The rest of the reading included advice that Ari should look after his own health, which could become compromised if he succumbed to too much stress.

He nodded in agreement with this. 'I need to take more time to unwind, to go out more, the theatre, music scene . . .'

And that an opportunity would arise where he would very likely become involved in a lucrative investment scheme which would lead to a position as an ambassador for this project, or possibly setting up his own global non-profit. 'It's definitely on the world stage.' Nessa met his eyes. 'This isn't smalltown stuff. It could be to do with working in famine-affected parts of the world.'

'Something I am very committed to,' Ari said as Nessa finished the reading. 'But now, I am wondering' – he checked his watch – 'if by chance you don't have any plans, would you consider having dinner with me? I'm sure you are a very busy woman, and forgive me if you are already committed.' His glance lingered on her hands, which were adorned with rings. 'But a guy can hope . . .?'

'I'm not.' She shook her head and smiled. 'And I don't have any plans for this evening.'

'It's my lucky day!' Ari spread his hands.

'But I have a better idea.' Nessa stood up eagerly. 'I have a couple of steaks in the fridge and a dessert in the freezer I've been dying to have an excuse to defrost and share with someone. 'If you don't mind waiting a little – we could eat here?'

Ari shook his head in disbelief. 'Really? What a wonderful and generous offer!'

Nessa beamed.

'Well, in that case,' he said, reaching for his jacket, 'you must allow me to go and pick up some champagne!'

'That sounds like a good plan,' said Nessa.

Ari was as good as his word and arrived back with champagne and red wine. The time had flown by. Busying herself preparing dinner had allowed Nessa to relax, and Ari was a thoughtful and easy conversationalist. He complimented her on her cooking and her interesting and artistic decorating style. Before realising it, Nessa heard herself saying, 'But your place . . . it looks spectacular! I'd love to see it sometime.'

'I would love to show it to you.' Ari's smile was warm. 'If I may say so . . . I'm not a bad cook myself. Although I don't often get the chance, or indeed have a reason, to cook, unless the kids are around. I hope you'll have dinner with me next week? Perhaps we could have a drink at the house first – then I'll give you the guided tour. How about Tuesday? I have to be in Kildare this weekend – there are some horses I have to look at.'

'That sounds perfect,' Nessa said.

'Why don't you choose the restaurant?' he suggested. 'Otherwise I will only be guided by tourist recommendations.'

Afterwards they had gone for a stroll along the harbour front, and when Ari accompanied Nessa back to the front door of number 24, he bowed over her hand in a chivalrous, old-fashioned manner that almost made her swoon. 'Thank you, Nessa,' he said, 'for a wonderful dinner and a very interesting reading.' His eyes creased when he smiled. 'I'll be looking forward to Tuesday evening all weekend.'

Nessa undressed and slipped into bed, happy that, for once in her romantic life, doing everything wrong seemed to be producing the right effect.

Chapter Twenty-Nine

It was mid-afternoon when Truth went out to the garden in search of Doctor Ed. She had the beginnings of a headache pulling at her temples, Evelyn was at the hairdresser's, and there didn't seem to be any painkillers in the flat. She thought he would probably keep a few to hand. Before she reached the bottom of the garden, she could see Doctor Ed was sitting in the shade reading a medical journal. He looked up as she approached. 'Truth, how nice to see you – have you come on an errand for Evelyn?'

'Hey, doc. No, I'm here on purely selfish grounds. I was wondering if you had any painkillers? I can't find any in the flat. I just feel a headache coming on. It'd be good to catch it before it gets a hold.'

'Hang on a sec, yes, I'll get you some now.' He got up slowly. 'How about a cup of tea? I'm going to make one for myself.'

'Thanks, I could do with one. I've been drinking far too much coffee.'

Truth sat down on the bench in front of the small pond, where a trio of water lilies were flowering. Tilting her face to the sun, she closed her eyes, enjoying the relaxing sound of water rippling from the small fountain in the pond and strenuous birdsong coming from the old oak tree. After a few minutes, she became aware of a movement. Assuming it was Doctor Ed coming back, she opened her eyes and straightened up. But there was no sign of the doctor – the sound she had heard was the muffled thud of a shovel hitting its mark. To her right, beside the rewilding area at the back of the garden that grew amok, Mike was digging compost with his back to her, unaware of her presence. She took a moment to watch him – the worn grey T-shirt straining across his shoulders, the muscles of his arms – bulkier than she had imagined – his dark hair, damp and messy as he pushed it from his forehead. It was only later she would admit to herself that she went on watching him because she enjoyed it; there was something reassuring about the way he worked – his utter concentration. She could have waved and said hi, but that would have spoiled the moment – and the moment lingered with her for quite a while.

Doctor Ed's voice made her start. 'Here we are.' He put a tray on the table with three mugs, a pot of tea, and a pack of painkillers. 'Mike!' he called. 'That's more than enough you've done for me, there – time for a tea break!' He filled the mugs.

'Oh, thanks,' Truth said, taking a couple of pills.

Doctor Ed sat down. 'So, how are you getting on with Evelyn?' he asked, regarding her, as Mike joined them.

'Very well, I think.'

'She's a forceful personality, you know.'

Truth laughed. 'I'm beginning to see that. Although I was warned.' She bit her lip, realising too late what she had said.

'By whom?' Doctor Ed stirred his tea.

'My mum. They've been estranged for years, ever since I can remember, really.'

'That's a pity,' he said. 'I gathered there was some degree of separation alright. Evelyn has mentioned they didn't get along. She never said any more than that and I never probed.' He was thoughtful. 'Must have been hard for you, though.'

She shrugged. 'It was all I knew. It was always just Mum and me. It was only later I began to realise how hard it must have been for Mum after Dad left. She brought me up on her own, totally.'

'Well, she's done a very fine job.' Doctor Ed smiled, while Mike listened, frowning.

'When did your dad leave?' Mike asked.

'When I was a baby – eighteen months – I don't remember that. It was a pretty messed-up scene back then, I think. They were both punks, they'd lived in a squat – when I came along they tried to get straightened out, Dad couldn't hack it, and he left. But we're good now – I got in contact with him a few years back. I have a much younger half-brother and -sister. They live in Germany. And there's my mum's younger half-brother, Uncle Tristan – he lives in New York, he's an artist.'

'Yes, Evelyn talks about him quite a bit.'

'So Evelyn was married twice?' Mike was interested.

'Yeah, I think she was pretty young when she had Mum with her first husband, like nineteen or twenty, maybe. Then he died and she married Leonard, and Tristan came along a lot later, so he's, like, fourteen or fifteen years younger than my mum – which makes him kind of like an older brother to me rather than an uncle – which was also good. I guess he's always been the bridge between Mum and Evelyn too. Either way . . . it's good that I'm getting this chance to spend time with her. She's still my grandmother whatever happened before.'

'How interesting,' Doctor Ed said. 'And how fortunate for Evelyn to have the chance to get to know you, too.'

'Families.' Mike shook his head. 'Right,' he swallowed the rest of his tea, 'I think I'm about ready for a swim. See you later.'

'He's an interesting guy,' Doctor Ed said, after Mike had left. 'Have you had a chance to talk to him at all?'

Truth realised she was blushing and shifted uncomfortably at Doctor Ed's question. Why was the mere mention of anything to do with Mike making her lose her usually iron-clad composure and behave like an awkward teenager? 'Ah, not much, no. We had a bit of a chat the other day – he was telling me about his last sculpture being objected to by some locals and taken down. I couldn't believe that . . .'

'Yes, that was unfortunate.' The doctor nodded. 'Art is so subjective. I think he's feeling more apprehensive than usual about this one now. He seems pretty tense lately. But I'm sure it'll be wonderful. Mike's incredibly talented. But putting your work on view to the world at large has to be intimidating. I'm not sure I'd be able for it.'

Truth shook her head. 'Me neither.'

'He'd probably enjoy a bit of distraction,' Doctor Ed said amiably.

'What do you mean?'

'Why don't you drag him out for a drink . . . or to dinner, or something?'

'Me?'

'Why not you?'

'I, uh, well, I suppose I could, but I'm not sure that—'

'I think it would do him good.' Doctor Ed waved a curious bee away. 'Sometimes we men need a little encouragement to – you know – get out and about again. Creative types especially tend to become too immersed in their work if they don't watch it. Mike's been through a gruelling stint for the last few months, and he needs to have some fun. I also think you'd find him interesting company.' He smiled. 'Just a suggestion . . .'

'Sure, well – maybe . . . I'll see what I can do about that.'

Doctor Ed had a point, Truth decided. Maybe she should ask Mike out for a drink or something. After all, he'd already asked her to see his studio and she'd had to turn him down. It made sense. If nothing else, at least going out for a quiet drink or bite to eat with the guy, having a proper conversation and getting to know him a bit, might put a stop to this weirdly over-sensitive vibe she was feeling whenever they bumped into each other.

Chapter Thirty

The swim was good. So was the hot shower afterwards. But neither helped Mike shake the sense of foreboding that stalked him. He told himself he was being silly – he always felt uneasy before a piece of sculpture was going to be unveiled, but there was something different about this time . . . something he couldn't put his finger on. For an hour or so earlier, while he was helping Doctor Ed in the garden, he'd been distracted, happy to get stuck into some manual work – or *proper work*, as his late father would have called it. Then afterwards, having tea with Doctor Ed and listening to Truth talk about her family and childhood had got him thinking. Growing up knowing your dad had walked out on you and your mum when you were just a baby would lead you to have some issues with men, he'd guess. He wondered how much her obvious career success had been driven by those same issues – wondered if it was why she was still single . . . She was beautiful, for sure, but for all people commented on the likeness between her and her grandmother, Evelyn, Truth's beauty had an edge to it that was more arresting, far more unusual. Mike didn't need to see the photos of Evelyn as a younger woman that Nessa and Doctor Ed often referred to. As part of his training he had studied anatomy in its most miniscule details for several years in Florence under the expert tutelage of dedicated professors. He could tell just by looking at any person fully dressed exactly what they would look like naked. It was the sculptor's superpower. He'd noticed her that day on the pier when she had stopped to listen to him playing his euphonium. He'd been struck then by her beauty – had felt the urge to trace her bone structure, see emotions cast fleeting shadows of expression on her face, watch fierceness give way to vulnerability. She could have been a model – or a warrior queen. He'd been more disappointed than he admitted when she had turned down his offer to see his work, and grab something to eat afterwards, after she had expressed such an interest in doing just that only minutes earlier. Then he had realised why – later that evening when he had seen Ari from next door leaving Truth home, Mike knew that Ari had clearly been thinking along the same lines and had got there first. Somehow Mike wouldn't have put Truth and Ari together, but what did he know. And Ari, as he had subsequently learned from Rory, was a fast mover. Rory had grabbed Mike for a coffee – or in Rory's case a protein drink – to relate his latest woes. 'Nessa's dating Ari,' he had said miserably.

'How do you know?'

'Theresa told me, in the café. He went for a reading . . . can you believe that?' Rory shook his head. 'Sly or what? And now they're a thing. She's been in the house and everything.'

'I thought Truth and him—'

'Nah, that was just a one-off – didn't go that well, apparently. Nessa told me that herself. Now she's all *Ari this* and

Ari that – she even wants to start training with me to lose weight!' Rory was disbelieving. 'Her exact words were, *Rory, I want to get lean.*' He sounded horrified. 'She doesn't need to change a thing – she's perfect. What am I going to do?'

'Hmm. Awkward, ' Mike agreed. 'But – as you say yourself – stay strong.' He put a consoling hand on Rory's shoulder. 'He's only here for a couple of months.'

Rory scowled. 'Anything could happen by then – and I don't mean in a good way.'

There wasn't a lot Mike could say to raise Rory's hopes, but he knew Rory wouldn't stay down for long.

Looking around his own flat now – as he pulled on his jeans – which was in its usual state of disarray, Mike thought briefly about making a start on tidying it – and just as quickly abandoned the idea when there was a knock on the door. He grabbed a hoodie and pulled it over his head, then reached to open the door to find Truth standing there. Instinctively, he stepped forward and pulled the door almost closed behind him to conceal the state of untidiness. 'Truth,' he said, running a hand through his hair.

Chapter Thirty-One

S he knew it would be a mistake – just calling to his door like that. It was later than she had realised. Mike was clearly a private person, and, if she was honest, she wouldn't have liked anyone to do the same to her – just turning up on her doorstep like that – not without warning. A text would have been better, but she didn't have his number. Now he was standing in front of her, one arm on the doorframe, looking extremely uncomfortable – guilty, even. She must have walked in on something, caught him at an awkward moment – he might even have a woman in there.

'Hi,' she said. 'I, ah, just thought we could maybe go and look at your work . . . grab that bite to eat afterwards, maybe, like you suggested . . . but if this is a bad time . . .' She already wanted to back away. Why had she listened to Doctor Ed? This was excruciatingly embarrassing. 'It really doesn't matter,' she added hastily. 'I just thought—'

He rubbed his jaw distractedly. 'You'd better come in.' He stepped back, opening the door.

It took a minute for her eyes to adjust, but in the dim light as Truth followed Mike into the main room, she felt as though she was walking onto an obscure movie set. Everywhere she looked there was something extraordinary.

Wooden sculptures, made up of hundreds of tiny pieces and slats of wood, stood in various parts of the room. A hare in full flight seemed ready to leap out the window. A fox crouched beside the couch, his gleaming eyes appearing to follow her. A life-size reindeer tossed its antlers in the far corner and something that looked like the beginnings of a large dinosaur took up the middle of the room. The floor was strewn with anatomy studies, drawings of skeletons and cadavers whose limbs were draped at freakish angles. What looked like a human skull sat on a table in the alcove.

'It's a bit of a mess, sorry,' Mike said, shoving some papers aside so Truth could sit down. 'I wasn't expecting company.'

'I've never seen anything like it.' Truth looked around her, astonished.

'Well, I hope you won't have to again – it's not usually this bad – I just haven't had the time or inclination to sort it since I finished my last piece.'

'What's that?' She pointed to the part-dinosaur.

'It's one I'm doing with Freddy,' Mike said. 'It's a dinosaur, a raptor – Freddy calls it the rapper.' He grinned. 'But I think it's going to be a bit alternative.'

'They're incredible.' She shook her head.

'Thanks. Can I get you a drink? I can probably find the fridge – or we could just go to the studio now . . .'

'Yeah, let's go now – I'm even more curious to see it after this display.'

'Actually,' he said, 'my studio is a lot more organised.'

✧

They took the DART into town, racing to catch a train that was just about to leave the station, Truth laughing as she ran to take the hand Mike reached behind him to help her make it through the closing doors.

Away from number 24, the reminders of family responsibilities faded and the torment of her recent trolling receded, surrounded as she was by other happy commuters, all intent on maxing out the generous stretch of a summer evening. Truth felt a weight gently lift – a weight that had become so familiar she had almost ceased to be aware of it – and the knot between her shoulder blades relax. As they trundled along the curve of Dublin Bay, coves and inlets were dotted with swimmers, flurries of sailboats clustered around the yacht clubs, and a ferry made its stately way out to sea towards Wales. Mike pointed out various landmarks, and when he suggested places he thought she should see while she was here, he made it sound as if it was something they would do together. The prospect, she realised with surprise, filled her with delight. Something about their togetherness on the train felt entirely natural and right. That, and the occasional brush of his bare arm against hers in the seat, sent shivers of happy expectation rippling through her. She noticed too the casual glances of interest other women cast in Mike's direction that he seemed completely unaware of. She glanced at him now. Since he had been spending more time outdoors, his former pallor had been replaced by a deepening tan. He'd gained a little weight which his tall frame could carry easily – and it suited him, filling out the angles of his face and making his expression more relaxed. When he smiled, which he was doing quite a bit of now, a dimple she had never noticed creased his cheek and his eyes seemed even greener against the white of his T-shirt. 'This is us,' he said, getting up as the train slowed to a stop near Trinity College.

Mike's studio was in a renovated stone tower close to the river and the entire building was given over to artists' workshops of one kind or another. To the left of Mike's studio was a designer of leather goods, and on his other side, a modern jeweller. 'It's good to have fellow artists around,' he said, 'it makes for a creative atmosphere. Here we go.' Mike let her into the long, narrow room and turned on the lights. Truth was surprised at how spacious the place was, where sculptures in clay, wax and bronze of men, women and animals sat on various surrounding shelves and plinths. Along the far wall a comfy-looking sofa leant an air of cosiness. What surprised her more were the beautiful paintings hung on the whitewashed brick walls. 'These are fantastic.' She was blown away.

'Thanks,' Mike said, pushing aside some post.

'I'm guessing this has to be it?' Truth made her way to an arresting piece of sculpture at the end of the room, representing the body of a human man with a large horse's head. 'The piece that caused the controversy?' The mouth of the horse was wide open, appearing to be either laughing or grimacing. She ran a hand along it, marvelling at the intricate detail. 'It does look quite . . . fierce,' she said, standing back to consider it, 'scary, even.'

'I prefer visceral,' said Mike, grinning. 'Although I can assure you he's harmless.'

'What is it?'

'He's a púca. A shapeshifting figure from Celtic folklore. They mostly took the shape of animals – horses, goats, cats, dogs – although they could assume human forms as well, usually with animal features. They were considered good or bad luck in rural communities, depending . . . but mostly noted for causing mischief and havoc. In this fella's case, he didn't disappoint. Within days of him being put up, a group of locals decided they didn't like the sculpture and complained to the council. So he was taken down. They're still arguing about him, last I heard.'

'That's such a shame. They should have given him a chance.' She flicked a glance at Mike. 'First impressions can be so misleading . . .'

'Can't they just.'

'It's such a great location, here.' She looked out the large window at the end of the room that overlooked the river.

'It is, yeah. I'll be sorry to leave it in many ways. My work has really developed while I've been here.'

'You're leaving?'

'Not right away.' He replaced a book on a high shelf. 'But I'm building a house as part of a site I'm developing back home – where I grew up – a studio will be part of that. A mate of mine is an architect, and he's drawn up some really interesting plans. I haven't had the chance to give the project my proper attention until this sculpture is up – then I'll need to get cracking on it.'

Truth felt somehow deflated at hearing this news, although she reminded herself quickly that her life was in

London. Wherever and whenever Mike was moving was none of her business. It wasn't as if she was in the market for a short summer fling. It would be silly and completely irrational to allow the thought to spoil her good mood and high spirits.

'Which material do you prefer working with?' Truth stroked a life-size clay greyhound.

'All my bronzes start out in clay,' Mike said. 'But I work with the "lost wax" method. It's quite a process.'

'Explain to me how it works.' Truth was curious; she leaned against the wall.

'It's pretty labour-intensive,' he said. 'There are roughly five stages to a finished bronze.' He reached for a book and opened it, showing her illustrations of the process. 'Positive, negative, positive, negative, and positive. The original sculpture, like Luna here,' he indicated the greyhound, 'is modelled by the artist in clay. That's the first positive.' He went on to describe the complex process.

'It's strange,' Truth said. 'The term "lost wax" sounds so romantic, but it's pretty hardcore.'

'The guys at the foundry would agree with you,' Mike said, grinning. 'There'll probably be a few of them around there later, if you fancy dropping by? They work all hours when they have to . . . The final stage is patination, or colouring,' he went on. 'Chemicals are applied to the heated metal to obtain the desired colour or patina. And that's it, really.'

Truth was impressed. 'You weren't kidding when you said it's labour-intensive.'

'It's part of the attraction. Nothing worthwhile is easy – is it?' He gave her a searching look. 'Let's go and eat,' he said. 'Looking at all this work is making me hungry.'

✧

In the small Italian tucked away down the cobbled lane, over pizzas that were works of art in their own right, Mike told Truth about his years studying in Florence, and how his dad had never really forgiven him for not taking over the family farm.

'That must have been difficult.'

'Mum supported me, though,' Mike said. 'That made it easier – but really I didn't have a choice. I couldn't have been a farmer any more than I could have been an accountant. It was art or nothing for me. I'm just sorry he didn't live to see how things turned out for me. He was killed six years ago in a tractor accident.'

'I'm so sorry.'

'Thanks. But I've made my peace with it. Parents and their offspring aren't always cut from the same cloth. My career choice was the only thing we really clashed over.'

'The girl in Florence you mentioned – what happened?' She was curious after hearing about the wooden sculptures he had done for her.

'She was pregnant.' He paused, frowning. 'It wasn't planned. We lost the baby at almost three months . . . I knew she hadn't been happy about discovering she was pregnant, but as soon as she was over the miscarriage, she broke up with me.' He shrugged. 'Initially I thought maybe it was a reaction to all she'd been through, but it turned out the unplanned pregnancy clarified her feelings about us as a couple. It was a shock, I had no idea she wasn't happy until she told me, but I'd have hated to know she was staying with me because of the baby.' He toyed with his wine glass. 'Isabella was great, but she was much more extrovert than me – more of a party animal – I could never really have managed the social life she wanted and needed. We had some great times, but . . .'

'I'm so sorry . . . that must have been really hard.'

He nodded. 'Yeah, it was at the time, I probably channelled it into my work – I tend to do that. I came back to Ireland later that year – and that's when things really started to take off for me workwise.' He smiled. 'I hear from Isabella occasionally. We stayed in touch a bit – you know, Christmas cards, birthday greetings, that sort of thing. Funny thing is . . . she's married now with four kids in the space of as many years.'

Truth began to laugh at his wry expression.

'Guess when a girl knows, she knows, right?' He laughed. C'mon.' He called for the bill. 'Let's go see *The Waiting Man* – we don't want to keep him waiting.'

The foundry was about a fifteen-minute walk away. They strolled through town, and when Mike casually put his arm around her shoulders, Truth slid hers around his waist – it felt good. They walked up Dame Street, past Dublin Castle, then ducked under an archway leading to another square where people sat outside, eating, talking, and laughing – it reminded Truth of the TV ad she'd seen when she had spent the weekend with Pauline in the country house spa – that seemed like another lifetime now. Further up, into the

Liberties, the older part of the city, Mike turned in through a large open gate and stopped outside what looked like the entrance to a garage. A couple of steel pull-down doors glinted in the evening sun.

'This is it?' Truth asked, surprised. 'This looks more like a building site than somewhere sculpture is being made.'

'Yup, this is where it all happens. You'll see.' He pressed a buzzer and a side door opened.

'Howya, Mike.' A small man pulled down his work mask and nodded at Truth as he showed them in. 'He's all ready for you, Mike. He's in the wax room. I'll leave you to it, shout if you need anything.'

'Will do, thanks, Brenny.'

Inside – although it wasn't yet dark – the place was ghostly and full of shadows, resembling for all the world a big grimy warehouse. Ignoring the visitors, and intent on their work, half a dozen men roamed from section to section, attending to the task at hand. Truth followed Mike as they made their way through the various areas, each one revealing different works of sculpture at different stages. Tools that looked like builders' implements lay on dusty worktops, and from down the way hammering and drilling could be heard.

Mike went into a small room and switched on the light. Truth followed him as he turned into another open space, then she stopped and gave an involuntary gasp. There, standing one and half times taller than his maker, in all his finished glory, was Mike's sculpture, *The Waiting Man* – and she had never seen anything so beautiful or awe-inspiring in her life.

The statue was staggeringly lifelike – not just because of its flawless lines, but the poignancy of expression Mike had captured. In his arms, the man held a child, about the same age as Freddy, Truth guessed. The child rested his head against his father's shoulder, while the father looked ahead, one hand cradling the child's head. But it was the man's bereft expression that was extraordinary – it managed to combine both strength and unbearable pain. The acute sense of loss was palpable.

'It – it's just beautiful . . . breathtaking,' she said, as Mike stood back, then opened the bottle of champagne that stood on a small table with two glasses. Then he moved around the sculpture, assessing his work.

'I wasn't expecting the child,' Truth said, curious. 'Tell me the story about this man.'

'In 1807, there was a terrible storm,' Mike said, handing her a glass of champagne. 'It hit Abbottsville particularly hard. Two ships came a cropper that night, four hundred lives were lost, most of them military men, but civilians too. Legend has it that this local man's wife was one of them. Our man not only lost his wife, but their other child along with her. According to the legend, though, he couldn't accept that his wife wasn't coming back to him. Every night, without fail, he'd go and stand with his remaining child at the end of the pier, scanning the bay for any sign of her, convinced she was coming home.'

Truth bit her lip. 'That's so sad.'

'According to the legend, his ghost still stands and waits. He's been seen the odd time on the pier, according to locals. Usually it's to warn of an impending tragedy.' Mike lifted a shoulder. 'That's the legend anyway. But when I came across his story when doing research on the local area – well, I could kind of relate to his loss. That's why the legend grabbed me.'

'What you've done . . .' Truth tried to put it into words. 'It's . . . just . . . completely . . . amazing.' She shook her head in awe. 'You have such a gift . . . he looks like he could turn around right now and just walk away.'

Mike smiled. 'Well, I hope he doesn't. He's due to be installed on the pier in a few weeks' time. It'd be pretty awkward if he went AWOL. Anyway' – he raised his glass to her – 'we need to toast him.'

'What shall we drink to?' Truth was still overawed.

'How about to finding what you're searching for . . .?' He held her gaze.

'I'll drink to that,' she said softly.

Afterwards, while Mike was taking some shots on his phone, Truth noticed the instrument case she had seen on the pier leaning against the wall. 'Is that what I think it is?' she said, indicating the case.

'Yeah.' Mike walked over to it and took the instrument out. 'One last tune for luck.'

'Where did you learn to play?'

'Mum was a primary school teacher – but she played in a jazz band before she met my da. She passed her love of music on to me, I guess. I played a few of the brasses, but the euphonium just clicked with me.' He picked it up. 'I usually give the sculpture one last tune . . . when I'm here on my own.'

'And when you're not . . .?' She held her breath.

He lifted the instrument to his mouth without breaking eye contact. And when the beautiful notes of a familiar love song swelled and filled the room, Truth knew this time he was playing just for her.

Chapter Thirty-Two

Evelyn and Truth were in a taxi on their way back from an appointment with Evelyn's surgeon, who had been very pleased with her progress. 'It's marvellous I'm down to only one crutch now!' she said. 'It'll give me so much more mobility – I won't know myself.'

'You'll still have to be careful,' Truth warned her.

'Yes, yes, I know that . . . but I felt like a complete *invalid* on two crutches. Psychologically, apart from physically, one is much more liberating. Soon I won't need any! And I'll be able to swim again.'

The driver had taken the coast road, and as they approached Abbottsville, the foundations for Mike's sculpture on the pier were visible from the car – they seemed to be almost finished. 'Mike's sculpture will be going up soon,' Truth said. 'Did you know his last piece of sculpture was taken down because some locals in the town decided they didn't like it and objected?'

'Hmm. I remember Doctor Ed saying something about that – vaguely.'

'He seems like a really interesting guy.'

'What makes you think that?' Evelyn was dismissive. 'He disappears for months at a time to the studio he has, or some warehouse place, when he's working . . . only gets about one commission a year, and makes peanuts as far as I can tell. What's interesting about that?' She looked at Truth. 'Now Ari, on the other hand . . .'

'He's not my type, alright?'

'Couldn't you just give him another teeny chance . . .?' Evelyn pleaded. 'I'm sure if you just—'

Truth cut her off. 'Ari went to Nessa for a tarot reading, and now he's taking her out to dinner. And that's what I suggested he should do – in a manner of speaking.'

'Nessa . . .? Why did you—?'

'Because she's a gorgeous person who needs cheering up and she needs to be around a man who's not afraid to make her feel like the fabulous woman she is . . . and I think Ari will do exactly that.'

'I didn't mean *that*!' Evelyn retorted. 'I meant why did you hand him to her on a plate like that?' She was clearly annoyed.

'I'm not handing anyone to anyone on a plate, Evelyn.' Truth rolled her eyes. 'I just think Ari would be good for Nessa . . . I think he'd give her a much-needed confidence boost and show her a good time. He's looking for someone to have a bit of fun with while he's here. That's exactly what Nessa needs after that loser ex-boyfriend. She told me she'd love to go out with a man like Ari.'

'I bet she would . . .' Evelyn muttered.

'Sorry?'

'I said that's very thoughtful of you, Truth.'

'Everyone deserves to grab some happiness while they can – unless it's at someone else's expense, of course.'

'Of course,' Evelyn agreed.

Chapter Thirty-Three

At twelve fifteen The Friendly Plate was relatively empty as Rory made his way in and sat down gingerly at a table with a good view of the counter. Theresa had a phone tucked under her chin and was making notes, and smiled a greeting in his direction – there was no sign of Nessa. As he shifted self-consciously in his seat at the small table for two, Rory fervently hoped it wasn't Nessa's day off – he had a rare window between clients at the gym, which he would usually spend training, but since he had finally worked up the courage to ask Nessa on a date, he was hoping for a chance to initiate a casual conversation with her. The prospect had kept him awake for most of the night. Despite his formidable bulk and intimidating countenance, Rory was a gentle soul, and his easy manner and banter around guys deserted him woefully when in the company of women – particularly one that he fancied – when despite his best efforts, his shyness was often mistaken for aloofness, or worse, a glowering ferocity. He ordered the house salad from Theresa when she came by, and hoped he wouldn't be wasting time that could be spent fine-tuning his squat lift technique. Ten minutes later, when was he was halfway through his salad, Nessa breezed in. 'Hey, Rory!' She wandered over to him when she had put her bag behind the counter. 'How're you doing? Haven't seen you for a few days, how's tricks?'.

'Good, good.' He swallowed.

Nessa was wearing a white clingy top with cutaway shoulders and wide-legged blue linen trousers. The glimpse of soft golden skin against the white material made him immediately imagine caressing it. He inhaled sharply and began to choke as a food particle went down the wrong way.

Nessa patted him on the back, which only made him cough more.

He grabbed his water and took a gulp, giving her the thumbs-up sign with his free hand.

'Are you sure you're okay?' She sat down across from him, looking concerned, as Rory tried to breathe normally and nodded.

'Thank God for that!' Her eyes widened. 'I wouldn't like to have to try giving you the Heimlich manoeuvre.'

The mental image of Nessa clasping him from behind was enough to trigger another fit of coughing, but Rory managed to remain calm – instead he grabbed the nearest napkin to mop his flushed face and perspiring forehead. 'I'm grand now, thanks,' he said. 'Went down the wrong way.'

'Happens all the time.' She made a sympathetic face. 'Coffee?' She waved Theresa over. 'Make that two coffees, Theresa,' Nessa said. 'I'll join you for a quick one.' She glanced at her watch. 'Then I have to call a whole lot of suppliers for the fair day.'

'I was wondering . . .' Rory began, hoping to finally ask Nessa the question – when he realised Nessa was distracted by Theresa talking to someone at the counter and pointing in Nessa's direction. Following her gaze, Rory saw Ari had just come in and was now making his way towards their table.

'Nessa! Rory!'

Rory was gutted to see a girlish blush creep over Nessa's cheeks as she looked up. 'Ari! Hello!'

'I was hoping I'd catch you before my surgeries this afternoon,' he said, smiling. 'I so enjoyed our tarot reading,' he rolled the r, in a continental accent, making the word sound almost indecent, 'and I just wanted to double check you're still free for dinner on Tuesday?'

'Sure, of course.' Nessa got up to join him, looking flustered. She guided him back to the counter. 'See,' she showed him her diary, 'I'm all yours!'

'Fantastic!' he said, with a flash of perfect teeth, as he turned to leave. 'I'm looking forward to it already!' Nessa followed Ari outside while Rory watched them miserably through the window as they stood chatting.

By the time Theresa brought Rory's solitary coffee to the table – 'Nessa says sorry, but she's had to take a call from the IT people' – Rory's previously buoyant mood was thoroughly deflated. He settled up, then trudged wearily back towards number 24 and his basement gym – psyching himself up for his next, particularly neurotic client.

✧

Mariner's Cove looked particularly beautiful this morning, Truth thought, as she wandered down to join the early swimmers, humming a happy tune. From the top of the steps, the small cove below was picture-postcard pretty in the early light, and the sea, dotted with swimmers, shone calm and blue. She wasn't yet quite as early getting down as the first early birds, but she was catching up on them day by day, beginning to realise how essential the practice was to her general well-being. Evelyn was pleased with her. 'I told you you'd become a convert,' she'd said. 'You're looking better every day. Not that you didn't look well when you arrived, of course,' she'd clarified. 'But you're less uptight looking, more . . . relaxed . . . radiant, even. If I didn't know firsthand what wonders sea swimming worked on a woman I'd say you might be in love.' She'd tilted her head, assessing Truth. 'But the sea works its own magic . . . and it's much less trouble and turbulence than a love affair.' She seemed wistful. 'Although I wouldn't have believed that either when I was your age.'

Leaving her swimming bag now on the stone ledge, Truth slipped off her jeans and sweatshirt and twisted her hair into a topknot, waving back at Nessa, who had spotted her from the sea. She was making her way towards the slipway when Mike – whom she hadn't seen – hauled himself out from the water behind her and called her name. 'Hey, Truth!'

She turned, watching him as he jogged over to grab a towel and sling it around his waist, then pushed his hair back and walked over to her.

'Hey,' she said, feeling a little exposed, super aware, and hyper-appreciative of what good shape he was in, droplets of water highlighting his broad shoulders and defined abs.

'I was wondering,' he said, 'if you fancied going for a

drive to the country this afternoon? I have to meet Tom, my architect mate, to go over some stuff – you could come along, take a look at the site? It's a nice day for it . . .'

'Sure.' She didn't have to think twice. 'I'd love to.'

'Great.' His eyes were warm when he smiled. 'I was planning to leave around two thirty – I'll text you when I'm downstairs.'

'I'll see you later, then.'

Minutes after, Truth slipped into the water, blissfully unaware of the bracing shock to her body temperature. The two days that had passed since the evening she'd spent with Mike viewing the sculpture in the foundry had dragged like weeks, and try as she might, she'd been thinking of nothing else since. Evelyn's observations had been more on the mark than her grandmother could have possibly known, Truth realised. She would have to be careful . . . swimming wasn't the only addictive pastime she was feeling hopelessly drawn to. Longing to be in Mike's company was proving to be a far more powerful attraction.

✧

'Where did you say you were going?' Evelyn asked her later as Truth read the text on her phone saying Mike was downstairs in the hall.

'Oh, nowhere in particular.' She was vague. 'Just thought I'd have a wander around town, visit a couple of museums, maybe.' Since their conversation in the taxi, Truth didn't feel like sharing with Evelyn that she was meeting Mike. Her grandmother had been less than complimentary about him – and besides, who Truth spent time with was no business of Evelyn's. She also felt surprisingly protective of Mike – Evelyn, she realised, just wouldn't get him. She simply wasn't someone who would ever appreciate a man for who he was – she was more interested, Truth had learned, in what they could provide.

'Museums?' Evelyn raised her eyebrows. 'On a day like today? I don't know how on earth you could bear to be inside . . .' She looked at her speculatively.

'Just boning up on my heritage.' Truth smiled. 'There's such a lot I don't know about Ireland.'

'Well, if you wanted I could—'

'See you later . . .' She blew Evelyn a kiss as she went out.

In Mike's car – which was more of a truck, really – Truth sat back and watched as the city receded surprisingly quickly. Once they made their way along the motorway, the countryside began to reveal itself – slowly at first, then, as the miles went by, unfolding its full summer beauty. Lusciously green fields spread out on either side, dotted with crops or home to peacefully grazing cattle and sheep. They chatted easily as the miles sped by, while a country music station played on the sound system, and Truth – usually attentive to dialogue as a lawyer – found herself dreamily wondering how she had never before appreciated the lyrics of these plaintive tunes, so capable of capturing the collective yearning, hopes, and downright craziness of love.

After about an hour and a half, they arrived at Ormondbarry, Mike's hometown, where the ruins of an ancient medieval walled castle looked out over the sleepy town, which in recent years had become popular as a tourist destination. Driving past multicoloured houses, shops, and pubs on the main street, and admiring the pretty thatched whitewashed cottages beyond, Truth was struck more than ever by the different pace of life in this place compared to the franticness of London. Here, the most strenuous activity on view seemed to be the vigorous casting of lines by the fishermen intent on securing their catch from the grassy banks of the large river. They met Mike's mate Tom at a local coffee shop, where he took them through the latest plans. Then together they walked the prospective site. 'If we get planning through,' Tom was saying, 'you could be looking at a finished house this time next year, guys.' The comment, although innocent, brought a flush to Truth's cheeks. 'We'll make that the priority. The studio will follow after.'

'Sounds good,' said Mike, nodding. 'I really like what you've done, Tom. You can go ahead and submit these – the sooner I get going with this build, the better.'

'Great,' Tom replied. 'Good to see you, mate – and great to meet you, Truth.' He climbed into his car. 'Good luck! Got to run to another meeting – I'll leave you to it.'

They walked for a while then, hand in hand, as Mike took her to the river and showed her where he used to fish with his dad and muck about with the dogs. After that, they dropped by his mum's house, where Mike let himself in, seeing her car was gone. 'She's probably out with the horses,' he said. 'I didn't tell her we'd be coming by.'

Truth was relieved. She hadn't anticipated meeting Mike's mum, and she would have liked a bit of warning. Looking around the room while Mike made tea, she saw photos of a glamorous blonde woman, mostly on a horse. Then others of her with a darkly handsome man – clearly Mike's dad. 'This is your dad?' She indicated a photo of the three of them, featuring Mike as a young boy.

Mike smiled and nodded. 'Yeah, that was at the county fair.'

'You're a dead ringer for him.' She marvelled at the likeness.

'I've been told that alright.'

'It must have been hard for your mum, losing him so suddenly.'

'It was.' He placed the mugs on the table. 'She was great, really. Never let herself get down when I was around anyway. She's always been mad about her horses, it helped that she could throw herself into that . . . then she met Richard. She's made a new life for herself now and I'm happy for her. You'll meet her when the sculpture goes up.'

During the hour and a half journey back to Dublin, they were comfortably quiet together, but Mike's hand rested easily on her knee, covered by her own hand, while Truth tried to still the stealthily increasing rhythm of her heart. How was it, she wondered, that someone she had met so recently could feel so easy and familiar? As if he'd been in her life all along . . .

It was after seven o'clock when they pulled up in Ulysses Crescent. Number 24 was quiet when they went in the front door, until it became evident, from the sound of laughter drifting up through the open back door, that a few of the tenants were sitting outside in the garden.

'Do you want to go out and join them?' Mike looked uncertain.

Truth shook her head.

'Good.' He grinned. 'Me neither. We could get a take-away?' He let them into his flat.

'That's a great idea. Hey, you've clearly been busy.' She noted the flat had undergone a major tidy-up.

'Yes, well, it was a bit overdue. Me and the sculptures aren't used to having visitors. Do you need to check on Evelyn?' He handed her a local takeaway menu.

'No. I said I might be late, and she's pretty much able to look after herself again now. I think Doctor Ed's dropping in for a game of chess this evening. They seem to have a pretty regular schedule.'

'I get the impression he's very fond of her,' Mike said. He went to the kitchen to open some wine.

'What makes you say that?' Truth was curious as she sat down on the sofa and took the glass.

'Just the way he talks about her – he brings her up in conversation quite a bit. I think he has a soft spot for her.'

'Well, they're of a similar vintage. I guess they have a lot in common.'

When their takeout order was ready, they strolled to the seafront to pick it up, then, instead of going back to the flat, went to sit by the foundations for *The Waiting Man* on the pier.

'Not long 'til he's up, right?'

Mike nodded. 'Sooner the better. After the last episode, I can't say I feel relaxed about it. I just hope he gets a good reception.'

'Of course he will. It's a stunning sculpture. Everyone's going to love it. But I know what you mean about public opinion – it can be fickle at the best of times. I've had my own run-in with it recently, and it wasn't pretty.' She told him about her online abuse. 'I know all about what being cancelled feels like, trust me.'

Mike listened and let out a breath. 'That's so screwed up . . .' He shook his head. 'What's the matter with these trolls? I mean, I can understand people not liking a piece of art – they have every right to their opinion, even to request it being removed – but for some group to start a hate campaign against someone over an innocent remark about accidentally falling over in high heels? Jeez . . . I can't even imagine what that must have been like . . .'

'Pretty unreal in the beginning,' Truth said quietly. 'Then it began to take its toll. These people know what they're doing . . . they don't mess around. Sadly it's not that uncommon, either. Christina Lamb of *The Sunday Times* suffered something similar. But when the death threats started coming in . . . well, it was just too much. That was part of the reason I came over here. Of course I was glad to help out, and it was a good chance to get to know my grandmother.' She looked at him. 'But I won't lie . . . I needed to get away.'

'I can believe it. What a bloody horrible thing to have to go through. You poor thing.' He put his arm around her and she leaned her head on his shoulder. 'So . . . is it still going on, this trolling thing?'

'My firm have people on it. I had to shut down all my social media accounts, obviously, and last time I checked in with them, things were calming down. These people always find some other victim to target. They'll lose interest in me eventually. In the meantime, well, I try not to think about it.

That's been easier over here, thankfully – I've hardly thought about it at all.'

'Well, that's good. Let's keep it that way.' He dropped a kiss on her head. 'Did you know it's the summer solstice today?'

'No, I've pretty much lost all track of time since I've got here,' Truth said.

'So, it's the longest day of the year,' Mike said. 'Which is good,' he squeezed her hand, 'because it means I get more time to spend with you.'

'We should probably start by walking off some of this food.' She took his outstretched hand as he pulled her to her feet.

'Good idea, but first there's something else I want to do.' He took her in his arms and kissed her, slowly, while gulls wheeled and cried above them, and passers-by smiled fondly. But Truth was blissfully unaware of either. 'That was what I was thinking about doing the first time I saw you,' he said, finally pulling away. 'Which may go some way to explaining why I was completely lost for words at the barbecue . . .'

Chapter Thirty-Four

Evelyn was trying on her favourite swimsuit, and was delighted to find that, if anything, it was a little bit looser. Truth had gone out with Nessa to do a supermarket shop and Evelyn had the flat to herself. It was a beautiful July day and the weather, combined with the flurry of activity she could see from her window onto Mariner's Cove, was making her itch to get back in the water. Her surgeon had been happy with her progress and had given permission for her to get into the sea on the condition that she was at all times accompanied by a strong swimmer, that her physiotherapist was agreeable, and most important of all, that no unnecessary exertion or stress would be applied to her new hip. Now Evelyn regarded herself in the full-length mirror, with her finger traced her impressive eight-inch scar that ran along the middle of her hip, and assessed that no irreparable damage had been done to her marvellous physique – at least nothing that a little sea swimming wouldn't cure.

She was contemplating how the iodine in the water worked wonders to maintain her skin elasticity – when a distinct series of raps on her apartment door caught her by surprise. She wasn't expecting anyone. Truth had a key, and none of the other residents would have knocked on the door in that almost jaunty fashion – they would have used the bell or more likely texted her first. Despite her rather awkward state of semi-undress, curiosity overcame Evelyn. She quickly reached for the embroidered silk kimono that hung on her bedroom door, pulled it on over her one-piece swimsuit and tied it, fluffed up her hair, and, grabbing her crutch, walked as fast as she could to open the door – expecting maybe a surprise parcel or delivery of some kind. Instead, a handsome young man with dark blond, swept-back hair, piercing blue eyes, and a distinctly amused expression stood at her door, partially obscured by a large bouquet of colourful and flamboyant flowers.

'Hello!' he said, taking in Evelyn's outfit. 'I'm looking for Truth Malone . . . but you've *got* to be her infamous and – if I may say so – extremely beautiful grandmother. Would that be correct?'

Evelyn threw back her head and laughed. 'I have no idea who *you* are, but you've got a good line in opening gambits and that's good enough for me.' She ushered him in. 'Come along in, Truth's gone out for a while, but yes, this is the right place to catch her . . . and yes, I am the invalid grandmother.' She waved her crutch and then held out her free hand to shake his. 'I don't normally allow strange men into my apartment, despite my apparent state of *déshabillé* . . . I was trying on my swimsuit to see if it still fitted me, and had to grab this old robe to make myself decent . . .' She made a wry face. 'You caught me on the hop, so to speak. Come in and sit down, then you can introduce yourself. Oh, and pop those beautiful flowers in the sink until Truth gets back.' She indicated the small kitchen. 'Would you like a cup of tea . . . or something stronger? If so, you'll have to make it yourself.' Evelyn sat down in her armchair.

'I'm Josh.' He bowed over her hand. 'And I'd love a glass of water. Let me grab one and then I'll explain everything. And by the way, these flowers are for you. I brought something else for Truth.'

When he came back into the room and put down his glass of water on the small table beside him, Josh sat on the sofa opposite Evelyn, leaned his elbows on his knees, steepled his fingers, and looked her in the eye. 'I take it she hasn't told you about me, then . . .'

Evelyn shook her head, looking puzzled, and then realisation dawned on her. 'Wait a minute . . . are you the barrister chap? The ex-boyfriend?'

He nodded. 'One and the same. Although I'd dispute the "ex" description. Truth and I have been together for almost two years. I'm madly in love with her, and I know she loves me too. We'd been planning our future together when this bloody awful online business exploded – and since then . . . well . . .' He spread his hands. 'It pains me to say it . . . but Truth just hasn't been thinking straight.'

'What online business?' Evelyn was mystified. 'What on earth are you talking about?'

'Ah.' Josh leaned back. 'So she hasn't told you about that?'

'I haven't a clue what you're on about.'

'When is Truth likely to be back?'

'In an hour or so, I'd imagine . . . possibly sooner.'

'Right, well, I'll try to explain as quickly as I can, then.' Josh did his best to educate Evelyn, in simple terms, about the nature of online abuse. He told her that Truth was a high-profile lawyer, considered a glamorous career icon in fashion circles, and described as succinctly as possible what had transpired after the deliberate twist had been manipulated on an innocent comment that Truth gave in an interview to a fashion magazine. When he had finished, Evelyn looked equally exhausted and outraged.

'Are you telling me . . .?' She was furious. 'That some nasty, spiteful, bitch of a journalist deliberately twisted a comment my granddaughter made, and that somehow . . . as a result of that and the ensuing article . . . that a – a mob of – of unhinged people have – have attacked and tried to . . . how was it you put it . . . cancel her?'

'That's exactly it, Evelyn.' Josh sighed. 'I'm afraid it's a hazard of contemporary life – you have no idea how powerful and vindictive these people can be. Truth even had death threats. That's why I suspect – although of course she was anxious to come over and help to look after you – well . . . she needed an escape of sorts herself too. Which is all perfectly understandable, but I'm extremely worried about her. I don't want these people to win, you see. Truth is amazing . . . she's an amazing lawyer, she does amazing work for abused women . . . and I can't bear the thought that she may be considering abandoning all that just because – as you so correctly say – a group of unhinged, spiteful people have targeted her and want to take her down. And that's before my own, very personal interests, of course.'

'Which are?' Evelyn was quick to pin him down.

'Well . . .' Josh fished in a pocket of his linen suit jacket and produced a small square box which he proceeded to open and proffer to Evelyn, who leaned forward to inspect it. 'This.' He revealed a solitaire diamond of generous proportions.

'Oh, my!' Evelyn breathed. 'What a beautiful stone . . . may I?' She reached for it.

'Of course.' He handed it to her.

She took the box from Josh, where the ring sparkled from its black velvet mound, and reverently extracted it, slipping it as far as it would go onto the ring finger of her left hand – it stopped at her knuckle. 'I must say you have very good taste . . .'

'Let's hope Truth is of the same opinion' Josh said, grinning.

Evelyn returned the ring to him. 'So, you're planning to propose to Truth.'

'Yes, yes I am. Unless you think that wouldn't be a good idea right now?' He looked at her questioningly.

'On the contrary.' Evelyn was pensive. 'I think it's a terrific idea – and the sooner the better. Strike while the iron's hot and all that.' She tilted her head. 'Do you make a lot of money?'

Josh grinned. 'Yes, I'm doing very well, as a matter of fact. I'm the youngest full partner in my firm, which is a rival to the one Truth works for – and the future is looking very profitable. Not that money is everything, of course.' He lifted his eyebrows.

'Of course not,' Evelyn agreed. 'But it does make life a lot easier if you have enough of it.' She frowned, suddenly realising something. 'What about Truth's mother, Pauline – have you met her?'

'Yes, of course I've met Pauline – she's great. Although . . . she's very different to you. Truth is pretty reticent to let anyone into her family circle, I've noticed. But Pauline and I got along well, on the few occasions we all went out together. I didn't tell her I was coming over, though . . . it was a kind of spur of the moment thing.'

'Well, she won't be hearing it from me. Truth's mother and I are estranged.' Evelyn was matter of fact.

'Yes, I was given to understand that – and I'm sorry.'

'Don't be sorry.' Evelyn sighed. 'Pauline was a law unto herself from the very start. I couldn't cope with her – I'm not sure anyone could. I simply hoped that at some stage she'd outgrow her demons and find some kind of peace to make with whatever life she insisted on carving out for herself.'

'I think she's happy now,' Josh said. 'If that's any consolation. Truth seems to think so.'

'Well, that's good. I'm glad to hear that. I don't like to ask Truth too much, you understand. It would feel like prying. We're only just getting to know each other. I'm sure she'll approach the matter of her mother and me when she's ready.'

'Of course.'

'So . . . back to more pressing matters . . . how are you going to go about this?'

'Well, I just thought I'd take Truth out to dinner somewhere nice tonight . . . take it from there. I'd rather be on home turf doing this, obviously – ideally I could have arranged something pretty spectacular – but events have spiralled out of control a bit since then.' He frowned.

'I can think of something much more romantic than that,' Evelyn said. 'When Truth comes back, which could be any minute now . . . I'll suggest she takes you out to show you around a bit. There's a lovely old ruin – Abbottsville

Castle – nearby, overlooking the sea. You could ask to see it. It would be a perfect location to propose . . .'

✧

Truth let herself in to Evelyn's apartment. She was slightly breathless from hauling supermarket bags up the two flights of stairs in the heat. 'Hello!' she called out. 'It's me . . . I come laden with goodies.' She went into the tiny kitchen and deposited the bags on the countertop, where she began to unpack them. It was only then, as she heard Evelyn call to her, 'Oh, you are a dear . . . come in and help me up . . . I seem to have got stuck in this old chair since you went out!' that Truth became aware of a familiar scent that she couldn't quite place. She put this down to the large bouquet of flowers she suddenly noticed sitting in the sink, and was about to enquire as to their origins. Opening a bag of crisps mindlessly, she put a handful in her mouth, then wandered in to the sitting room expecting to find her discommoded grandmother. Instead Evelyn was sitting up straight in her chair, looking – if anything – gleeful.

'What?' Truth didn't get any further. As she looked at Evelyn, another figure rose from the sofa. 'Hello, Truth. I just *had* to see you . . .' Josh said.

As Truth's hands flew to her face, Josh leapt forward to pick her up and swing her around, before putting her down. He was laughing. 'It's so good to see you!'

'Wait a minute,' Truth said, wide-eyed, when she caught her breath and looked at Evelyn. 'Were you in on this . . .?'

'Absolutely not! He caught me not only by surprise – but

in a state of near undress!' Evelyn was delighted. 'You never told me you had such a good-looking, not to mention *charming*, suitor.' She glanced at Josh appreciatively.

'So when – how –?' Truth looked from one to the other.

'I just got in . . .' Josh explained. 'I did some juggling between cases and moved a considerable slice of heaven and earth and . . . well . . . here I am – just for one night. Your grandmother was—'

'Evelyn.' Evelyn corrected him.

'Evelyn . . . was kind enough to let me in and wait here for you to get back.'

'I don't know what to say.' Truth shook her head; she felt partly cross with Josh, but she couldn't help laughing. Apart from anything else, it was good to see his friendly, familiar face.

'Well, I do!' Evelyn took charge. 'You two need to catch up and go out and have some fun! I'll deal with the groceries, and Truth – why don't you take Josh out and show him around our lovely part of the world? It's such a lovely day it would be a shame to waste even a minute of it inside.'

'But I've only just got back . . .' she protested. 'Are you sure?'

'I'm positive! I'm fine here. Go on! Out with you!'

'Okay.' Truth looked at Josh. 'Well, let's go.'

'Why don't you go up to the castle?' Evelyn suggested. 'The views will be fabulous today.'

'There's a castle?' Josh was curious.

'Oh, yes,' Truth said. 'That's a good idea. Yes, we have a lovely castle . . . all our very own.' She was eager to show off Abbottsville. 'Come on, then. I'll give you the guided tour and you can bring me up to date with all the news. You can buy me a drink while you're at it – the least you can do after springing this shock on me.'

'I'd be only too happy to.' Josh glanced back at Evelyn warmly. 'Thank you, Evelyn – for your very undeserved welcome and hospitality under such unforeseen circumstances. I intend to repay that as soon as I can.'

'No need at all, Josh.' Evelyn returned the warm exchange. 'Unforeseen circumstances tend to be the most enjoyable ones!' She gave him a thumbs-up and a wink while Truth's back was turned. 'Have fun! Might see you guys later if I don't get a better offer!'

✧

Mike had worked all night on the sculpture made up of teeny, tiny slats of wood. The finished work portrayed a small child, who appeared lost, holding out its hands in confusion and bewilderment. Connected to it, by a fragile link, on one side, was another figure – adult, male – who was looking back at the child while walking away from it. The male figure seemed stooped, desolate . . . his face covered by his hands. On the other side, connected to the child by a stronger link, was a female figure, larger than the other two, holding out her arms to the child, although her own torn apart, broken heart was clearly visible in delicately fractured pieces. He called the piece *Abandonment*. He didn't usually work on such emotional interpretations with his wooden pieces, but after talking to Truth that night, listening to her story, and sharing his own difficult experiences with his late father, something prompted him to create it – and once the muse got hold of him like that, sleep would have been impossible. So he had worked through what remained of the night and all through the morning, until the piece was finished. It took more out of him than he had expected, not just because it required meticulous detail, and concentration, but because the theme – although meant to reflect Truth's childhood parental experience – also brought up memories of issues with his own father, how he had metaphorically turned away from Mike once he had become serious about pursuing a career in art, rather than taking on the family farm.

He made himself another cup of coffee and looked around him blearily. The flat was still reasonably tidy since he'd cleared it up in anticipation of Truth coming back to it – but something else about it felt different. He became aware of an absence. Little clues to it were all around – from the imprint of her lips on an unwashed tumbler, or the gentle dent on the sofa where she had sat, to the lingering trace of fragrance that he caught from time to time unexpectedly in the air around him. It was a long time since he had felt this connection with someone, or opened up to anyone about his dad and what had happened to him – and it bothered him. Truth was only here for a few weeks, after all. Once her stint helping to look after Evelyn was up, she'd be going back to her big career and her life in London. *London's only a fifty-minute flight away*, a small voice whispered to him. In spite of that, he felt they had shared something special in these few days together, and he wanted to give her the wooden sculpture so she would remember it, irrespective of what direction their lives took in the future. He lowered the sculpture carefully into a box, and made his way upstairs to Evelyn's flat and knocked on the door. It was a while before anyone answered, which confirmed his suspicion that Truth was out – but in a way that was better. He wasn't sure he wanted to be there when she looked at the sculpture for the first time. It would be too . . . revealing. This way she would have time to study it before they spoke again. The footsteps making their way towards the door eventually stopped, and the door opened. 'Mike!' Evelyn seemed surprised. 'How nice to see you! To what do I owe this unexpected visit?' Her eyebrows lifted.

'Hey, Evelyn . . . sorry for disturbing you . . . I just have something for Truth, something I wanted to, uh, run by her.'

'Oh, I'm afraid she's not here, Mike – she just went out.'

'No problem, I can leave it here—'

Evelyn interjected. 'It's been very exciting . . .' She adopted a conspiratorial tone. 'Truth's fiancé, Josh, arrived over to surprise her, only about an hour ago, and she's taken him out to show him around. They're going out to dinner later – it's all terribly romantic!'

A fractional pause. 'Her fiancé? Are you sure?' Mike kicked himself for asking, but the words slipped out before he could stop them.

'Didn't she mention him? He's very handsome . . . a lawyer, very successful, apparently.'

'No reason why she should – it's her business . . . I just – well, she wasn't wearing a ring or anything.'

'You should see it . . .' Evelyn breathed. 'The ring . . . oh.'

She put her hand to her heart. 'It's exquisite . . . the most enormous diamond . . . just glorious. If it was mine I'd never take it off!'

'Well, like I said, I'm really sorry for disturbing you, Evelyn.'

'You're not disturbing me at all – always lovely to see you, Mike. I'd ask you in for a cuppa only things are a bit chaotic in here now what with Josh and—'

'Thanks, but I've got to run myself.'

'Did you say you wanted to leave something . . .?'

He began to back away, holding up his free hand. 'No, nope, nothing at all – just wanted an opinion on something . . . no need to bother Truth with it, it's nothing important at all.'

'Well, if you're sure . . .'

'Thanks, Evelyn . . . in fact, probably better not to mention I was here at all. Easier all around.'

'Whatever you say. It'll be our little secret! Goodbye, Mike!' She gave a little wave, and the door closed behind him.

Mike was so intent on getting down the stairs and out of there, he almost tripped on the flex of Morah's hoover, which trailed down to the landing below. Morah herself was crouched polishing the bannisters as he passed her on the stairs outside Evelyn's flat. 'Careful, Mike! What's the mad rush? We don't want any more broken bones . . .' She looked after him, shaking her head. He waved a hand in the air in response but didn't look back.

✧

Evelyn was so pleased she had availed of that random opportunity while Truth was out that she made herself a celebratory
gin and tonic (she kept her crutch tucked under her armpit –
she was able to do more and more without it, if she was
careful) and sat down to savour it before the return of the
soon-to-be happy couple. Mike's timing couldn't have been
better. Truth was becoming far too interested in him for
Evelyn's liking. Although Truth tried to hide it, it was as
plain to Evelyn as the nose on her face that she was becoming infatuated with the sculptor. To be fair, Evelyn could see
his obvious attractions to a girl. She freely admitted Mike
was terribly attractive in a smouldering, rather aloof sort of
way – he just wasn't suitable for Truth *at all*. Certainly not
when Evelyn saw what other men were on offer . . . Ari was
handsome *and* wealthy! And Josh too was gorgeous, and
clearly mad about Truth. Mike, on the other hand, was just
an unpredictable and (she suspected) temperamental, rather
tortured artist, with not a lot to show for it. Just because he'd
got one reasonably important local commission didn't mean
he had any sort of successful career prospects ahead. And
besides – clearly he didn't even own his own home. Ari had
property all over the place, and she had learned during her
talk with Josh that he owned at least one house. No, Evelyn
was very glad she had nipped that tentative relationship in
the bud. If Evelyn knew men at all (and she had read them
perfectly all her life), after their little conversation at the
door, Mike would never trust Truth again. He was also
extremely unlikely to explain himself to her since his pride
would have been wounded, so Truth would be none the
wiser for any distance between them. Not that it would

matter, of course – unless her granddaughter was stark raving mad, the next time she walked back in the door Truth would be sporting that divine ring on the third finger of her left hand. Either way, Evelyn felt she had taken the right course of action. Truth could do far better for herself than take up with an artist with dubious, if any, prospects. It was all very well to be a hard-working career woman now . . . but no one knew better than Evelyn what it was like when money ran out and your back was up against the wall. Truth might want to take life easy later on. It would be nice to have that option. Of course you couldn't persuade young people they would *ever* be old and tired, but those years sneaked up on one all the same – Evelyn was living proof of it, and she had more energy than most.

✧

At three thirty in the afternoon, Truth and Josh easily got a table outside The Monk, the quaint local pub on the way to the castle. Locals and tourists alike were strolling around, water or ice creams in hand. Parents took photos on phones of small children who grew fractious and tearful in the increasing heat of the day. Without the benefit of the seaside breeze at Mariner's Cove or the harbour, a heavy stillness had settled in the town.

'So, how are you doing, really?' Josh asked. He took a sip of his beer, while Truth played with the stem of her wine glass.

'I'm doing fine. It's like I've stepped into another universe, in some ways – but that's exactly what I needed. And it's been great getting to know Evelyn.'

'She's certainly a character . . . there's a very strong resemblance, looks-wise,' Josh said. 'I noticed it straight away. She seems very independent, though – and pretty well able to get about now. How long more are you planning to stay?'

'Who wants to know?'

Josh shrugged. He seemed subdued. 'Just wondering . . . I bumped into Frank in court the other day – he was saying how much harder they're having to work without you. They're missing you.'

'My six weeks aren't up yet.' Truth folded her arms. 'I'm enjoying this sabbatical. I didn't realise how much I needed it.'

'I talked to someone, you know, a colleague who was very highly recommended . . . he specialises in taking on these online trolls, and—'

'I don't want to talk about it, Josh. I haven't thought about it for weeks and I don't need to start now.'

'Of course, and we don't need to talk about it now either – but sooner or later you're going to have to tackle it, Truth. Frank agreed with me . . .'

'You've discussed this with Frank?' Her voice rose.

'We're both concerned about you – about the effect this is having on you. Truth, please, be reasonable . . . these people may be targeting *you* . . . but it affects everyone who cares about you. Don't shut us out.' He spread his hands. 'That's all I'm asking.'

She sighed. 'Why are you here, Josh?'

'I wanted to see you – to see for myself that you're alright. You . . . haven't been yourself of late – and that's perfectly understandable . . . but I'm concerned about you, Truth – you know how I feel about you . . . there's a big, gaping hole in my life without you . . . I'm trying to understand, to be supportive of you – but I'm allowed to have feelings too, you know.' He frowned.

'Of course you are.' Truth bit her lip. 'I'm sorry, and you're right . . . I have been very self-obsessed for the last few months . . . but I just don't want to think about any of that stuff now. I'm not in the right headspace.'

'Point taken.' Josh sat back. 'You have my word I won't mention it again. Why don't you show me this wonderful castle now?'

They strolled through the town, Truth pointing out Nessa's café, and the art gallery, and stopping to point to Mariner's Cove, the sea just visible at the end of a narrow side street. 'That's where we all swim every day. I'll take you there later.'

'Did you say swim?' Josh looked at her as if she had taken leave of her senses.

'Yes. It's fantastic having the sea on your doorstep. I didn't believe I'd do it either, but now I'm addicted to my morning swim.' They were almost at the entrance to the castle, from where Paddy – ever on guard – regarded them with interest as they approached.

'How much is it?' Josh asked Truth, fishing in his pocket. He looked around for a sign.

'It's more of a token than a fee,' Truth explained quietly. 'This is a self-appointed business undertaking – he's been here forever, apparently.'

'Ah, I see.'

'Howya, Truth,' said Paddy, smiling broadly.

'Thank you indeed, sir.' He eyed the generous amount Josh dropped in his jar. 'Although I generally make a rule of not charging locals.'

'Well, I'm not a local – so you're not breaking any rules.'

'Ah, but any friend of Evelyn's is a friend of mine . . . so if you're a friend of Truth's here . . .' He nodded in her direction.

'I appreciate your generosity, but I must insist on making a donation.'

'Fair enough – you're a hard man.'

'How does he know your name?' Josh was puzzled as they moved on.

'Paddy knows everyone. But I've been up here quite a bit with Nessa, the girl who runs the restaurant – she has a flat in the house. We've become friends. She sets up the local fair day they have here every year – I've just been helping her out with a few bits and bobs.'

'Right . . . I see.' Josh followed Truth along the path that led to the ruined remains. 'There's not much of it left, is there – as castles go?' He seemed unimpressed, looking around.

'It's more of a ruined abbey, really – it's the location that's beautiful.' She pressed on ahead. 'You'll see what I mean in a few minutes.'

After a little while, they reached the top of the hill, where Truth stopped and waved her hand. 'See what I mean?'

'Yes, I do.' Josh looked down over the harbour and the bay spread out beneath them. 'It's a very beautiful spot.' He was uncharacteristically quiet for a minute.

'I'm glad I could show it to you,' she said. 'And I'm glad to see you, glad you took the trouble to come over, despite everything.' She smiled. 'I'm really glad we can be friends, Josh – you mean an awful lot to me.'

'I can't be friends, Truth.' He turned to her then, serious. 'That's what I came over to tell you.'

She frowned, confused. 'Why not?' Realising, as she asked, what was about to unfold.

Josh had taken something from his pocket, was opening a small box, and getting down on one knee. 'Truth Malone,' he offered her the diamond ring, 'I've been madly in love with you since the first evening we spent together. I'd planned to do this over Christmas in New York – but the path of true love never runs smooth . . . and events have since taken a very unexpected turn. Which is why I have to seize the moment and ask you, please . . . will you do me the honour of marrying me?'

'Josh,' she shook her head, exasperated, 'please . . . get up.'

'Is that a yes?' He stood up.

'No, it's not.' She turned to look back out to sea, trying to keep calm. She was aware of a tremor in her voice, and wasn't sure if it was completely due to anger, although she felt angry, but there were other conflicting emotions too. She turned back to face him. 'Josh, we broke up. I made myself perfectly clear. And don't look at me like that – as if I've hurt your feelings. I know you from the courtroom, remember? This isn't some – some – game. I'm not some difficult witness you have to work your way around and crack. You of all people should know me by now.'

'I do know you, Truth! And that's why I want to marry you! And why you should marry me! Trust me! *Please!* You are not thinking clearly right now! We're great together! We would have such a fantastic life together. Everyone says we're made for each other. We were happy! *You* were happy . . . everything was *perfect* until this bloody awful online trolling shit started.' He ran his hands through his hair in exasperation. 'And it – it's changed you, Truth! You've let it change who you are!'

And there it was. The accusation had finally been articulated and levelled at her.

✧

'Truth? Is that you . . .? Evelyn called from her bedroom. 'I didn't expect to see you for ages, Evelyn appeared fully made-up, in her wide-legged green linen trousers and a colourful silk top, as she came in to the sitting room on her crutch. 'Did you forget something?' She looked around her. 'Where's Josh?'

'I don't know – back at his hotel, I guess.' Truth sat down wearily and rubbed her face.

'What's the matter?' Evelyn was perplexed. 'Is something wrong?'

'I don't really want to talk about it, if you don't mind.'

'Talk about what? What's going on?'

'Nothing. Nothing's going on, Evelyn.' Truth looked at her. 'Josh asked me to marry him and I said no. It didn't go down well, so I assume he's probably heading back to the airport as we speak.'

'What?' Evelyn was aghast. 'You mean you sent him packing with that magnificent ring when he came over especially to—?'

'You saw the ring?' Truth's head snapped up. 'Wait a minute . . . You mean you knew he was going to propose and you didn't give me a heads-up?'

'Well, how could I without spoiling things? I thought you'd be thrilled . . . I mean, what girl wouldn't be – Josh is lovely . . . he's—'

'I know exactly what and who Josh is, Evelyn – we were together for almost two years. He's very good at making a first impression and even better at going after what he wants. What I don't understand is why you would—'

'Never mind me! Is this about these thugs who are hounding you on the computer? These . . . these . . . what was it he called them . . .? Troll people?'

'He told you about that?' Truth's voice rose. 'I don't believe this . . .'

'Well, I'm very glad he did! He's very worried about you, Truth . . . he says it's had a terrible effect on you – that you're not yourself at all since it started. Does your mother know about these people harassing you?'

Truth gave Evelyn a look that pinned most people to the walls. 'You are not, do you hear me, under any circumstances, to tell my mother about this . . . Do you understand me?'

But Evelyn was undeterred. 'I must say I do think you're being a bit unreasonable about all this. I mean, Josh has a point . . . and he doesn't even know about Ari – you sent him packing too! What's the *matter* with you, Truth? Men like that don't grow on trees, you know. I don't blame Josh for being concerned and confused. After all, he only has your best interests at heart.'

'What are you talking about?' Truth was incredulous. 'I broke up with Josh for a reason – none of which is any of your business, by the way. And how would you know what his interests are?'

'There's no need to take it out on *me*.' Evelyn looked pained. 'If he came over here and spent thousands of pounds on that magnificent diamond solitaire . . . well, it's hardly rocket science to work out he has your best interests at heart. Why else would he go to the trouble? I bet he has women chasing him from every direction!'

Truth looked at her curiously. 'You just don't get it, do you?'

'I get that you're turning down rich, handsome men left, right and centre as if they were infectious!' Evelyn was warming to her theme. 'One of whom has purchased a hugely expensive ring and flown over here to surprise you with it, and been thoughtful enough to bring *me* some flowers while he was at it . . . and you don't even seem in the slightest bit—' She stopped mid-sentence. 'Wait a minute . . .' Her eyes widened. 'Are you . . .?'

'What?' Truth looked at her frankly. 'A lesbian?'

'Well, yes.' Evelyn shifted in her chair.

'Is that really the only reason you can come up with for me choosing not to go out with either Ari or Josh?'

'Well, you must admit it's peculiar – even with all this computer business.'

Truth stood up slowly. 'I'm not gay, Evelyn. But I'm not

going to discuss this any further with you. It's my life we're talking about here – not yours, and certainly not Josh's. What I *am* going to do is go for a swim. I need to clear my head.'

'Suit yourself.'

'Oh, and Evelyn?'

'What *now*?'

'I expect you to keep what happened today strictly between ourselves. If you breathe a word of any of what Josh told you – which he had no right to, by the way – I won't be responsible for what I do.'

'Fine by me.' Evelyn shrugged. 'You know, Truth, it may seem as if I've led a rather dull existence since you've been here – seeing as I've been confined by my recent injury, although I'm regaining my strength and mobility every day. But for your information, I never have been – and never intend to be – one of those awful bores who only talk about their children, or worse, grandchildren.' She shuddered. 'So you can relax. Your secrets are safe with me.'

Chapter Thirty-Five

Morah was lost in thought, sitting at the small table in front of the picture window in her room through which the late afternoon sun now slanted. Although it was only four o'clock, she had poured herself a small sherry to mark the occasion – and maybe for a bit of Dutch courage as well. It sat beside the old portable typewriter she had held on to, but rarely used, since its purchase in the charity shop when she still had ambitions of writing a memoir. She could still type, though; she had done well in the community school course her mam had insisted she take after leaving school – even though Morah already knew back then she only wanted to work with children. Her mother said it would always stand to her. Now she was glad of it. She had attempted a few early handwritten drafts in the notebook which sat on the other side of the table, but she hadn't been happy with them. The undertaking was proving trickier than she had anticipated. Her intention was simply to write to Robert Radcliffe, pretending to be Evelyn, and get him to stop paying her rent. But she had to make sure Robert didn't contact Evelyn, or it wouldn't work – she'd talk her way around it. Whatever secret Evelyn was keeping for him could hardly be that important at this stage of their lives? Robert must be nearly eighty by now, Morah did the maths. She had never liked the man, although as her employer he'd had little to do with her – being out of the house for most of the day. Her dealings had been with Mrs Radcliffe, a lovely woman of whom Morah had been extremely fond. Robert had been under Evelyn's spell back then, and clearly still was. It was time to do something about that. It was when she noticed a minibus pull up across the street, and two young men getting out and opening up the rear of the bus from where they lowered the passengers out one by one in their wheelchairs, for a seaside outing, that inspiration struck. She swiftly fed a sheet of writing paper into the typewriter, before she lost her nerve, then typed the made-up address of a nursing home, Journey's End Residential Care Home, on the centre top of the page, dated it, took a sip of her sherry and began.

Dear Mr Radcliffe,

I am writing to you at the request of Mrs Evelyn Malone, a resident of this nursing care facility. As secretary to the manager (who is carrying out Mrs Malone's wishes at this sensitive time), it has fallen to me to transcribe this request, which was made known to us by Mrs Malone's day nurse. I am sorry to inform you that Mrs Malone has suffered a stroke. She dictated her wishes to her nurse with great difficulty, as she is now permanently disabled. She wants you to stop paying her rent as she is not long for this world and will spend her remaining days here, in the care of our community. Mrs Malone's exact words were as follows.

'My Dear Bob, I am dying. Please cancel all payments to my account. I don't want my children to find them. I am in a nursing

*home and paralysed from a fatal stroke. I am dictating this letter
to my trusted nurse. Please don't attempt to find me. Remember
me as I was. Our secret will die with me. Goodbye.
Your affectionate friend Evelyn. X
PS. I still feel guilty about our affair and hope you do too.'*

Morah read her handiwork back several times until she was
happy it was perfect, then folded the sheet carefully and put
it into the matching envelope, onto which she had typed
Robert Radcliffe's Portuguese address, and marked it 'strictly
personal'. Then she finished her sherry and got ready to set
off for the local post office before it closed. She wouldn't post
the letter from there – but she needed to make sure the correct postage was on it. Then she would take the DART to
Bray, which was full of nursing homes, and pop it in a post
box there.

✧

Truth welcomed the bracing shock as she waded into the sea
at Mariner's Cove. It was quiet at this time of the evening,
and she didn't recognise any regulars among the few people
drying off, or sitting chatting in the last of the evening rays.
She dived under quickly, grateful that the cold took her
mind off her still-simmering anger. Josh's behaviour was not
such a surprise, even if his showing up with a ring and an
impromptu proposal was unexpected. The guy just didn't
know when to back off. Up until today she had given him
the benefit of the doubt, making allowances for the fact that
he still had feelings for her and realising how used he was to

getting his own way. But none of this excused what he had told Evelyn. He had betrayed her trust. That was what was making her blood boil. Now she knew her earlier instincts about him had been right on the button. Josh didn't care how he got what he wanted – he just cared that he got it. Any pretence of caring about Truth's feelings had been just that – pretence. She pulled through the water in a strong front crawl, pushing the earlier scenes between them further behind her with every stroke.

But Evelyn . . . Truth had been genuinely taken aback at how one-dimensional her grandmother's attitudes were towards men. All that seemed to matter to her was money – with looks coming a very poor second. Nothing else seemed to register with her. And asking Truth if she was gay? It would have been amusing if it hadn't been so inappropriate. Truth had found it quite unnerving how close she had come to having a full-on row with Evelyn. Now on top of everything else . . . Evelyn knew about the online abuse too. Truth turned on her back to float for a bit. That had been unforgivable of Josh, to tell her that. He knew very well how hard she had worked to keep any mention of it from her own mother, Pauline. Truth had suspended all her social media accounts, and if the lawyers in her firm had done their stuff, then any other references would or should have been removed by now – she hadn't had the heart to look herself. But just because the trail of threats and horrific online remarks had been taken down, it didn't mean the experience itself could be erased. Coming to Dublin had put some much-needed distance between her and the threats she had left behind – she didn't need to be reminded of them again. The only real worry now was if Evelyn were to tell Pauline about it . . . but that was extremely unlikely since they didn't talk unless absolutely necessary. And she had warned Evelyn in no uncertain manner.

Truth was fiercely protective of her mum. She was also aware that Pauline was only too familiar with the effects of violence and threats on the women she worked with at the shelter. She would know very well how her only daughter could become a victim of some unhinged perpetrator . . . and Pauline would make herself ill with worry. That was what Truth was determined to avoid above all else. She spoke to her mum every couple of days, just to check in. Truth worried that Pauline worked too hard. Her mum, she felt, had a tendency to become too involved in some of the issues going on in the lives of the women who passed through the shelter. She certainly had no intention of adding to her worries and concerns.

She swam back at a more leisurely pace, feeling marginally calmer about things. No real damage had been done, she reasoned. She had made herself clear to Josh, and left him with no illusions that they had any kind of a future together. She was sorry they couldn't remain friends, but she was pretty sure he'd get over it. He'd just be an even more aggressive opponent in court than ever now – but that, she could handle. *But is that what you want?* The thought sent a shiver through her, although her body temperature had already acclimatised to the water. She batted it away. Of course it was what she wanted, she had spent her entire working life building up her career, but lately the thought of going back to it didn't fill her with any sense of anticipation – on the contrary, a cold, hard, dread had begun to knot in her stomach at the prospect. But she couldn't think about that now. She couldn't think about it because that might mean her life – everything she had worked so hard for, had been so single-minded about, had sacrificed so much for – was wrong. And she couldn't even begin to contemplate that.

After she dried off and changed, she made her way back slowly to Ulysses Crescent, psyching herself up to face Evelyn again. She considered buying her a small bunch of flowers from the kiosk on the way back as a peace offering, and then remembered Josh's magnificent arrangement was already in place of honour on the table beneath the window – and also that she – Truth – had absolutely nothing to apologise for.

She let herself in to the house and was checking the post laid out on the table when she heard the door of Mike's flat open behind her – seeing him made her feel like smiling for the first time in hours. 'Hey,' she said, turning to catch him as he made for the front door. 'Fancy grabbing a beer later?'

'Uh . . . sorry, no.' He looked at her oddly, she thought, as he pulled open the door. 'Tomorrow?' she called after him.

He looked back at her for a second on his way out. His expression was closed and his manner definitely cool. He shook his head. 'I've got a lot on just now. See you.' Then the door closed behind him.

For a moment she was puzzled, but then put it down to him having a bad day – artists were always being tempera-mental about stuff. She'd catch him again when he was in a better mood. Upstairs, she took a deep breath and let herself in to Evelyn's flat, expecting another frosty reception. Instead, Evelyn seemed to be in ebullient form, and had a visitor. Doctor Ed and she were having a drink and sharing a joke. 'Truth! You're just in time . . .' Evelyn beamed at her. 'Ed, pour her a drink . . . you'll join us, won't you?'

'Sure.' Truth sat down, feeling not a little disoriented. Clearly Evelyn was as eager to put their previous spat behind her as she was. Truth wasn't one for holding a grudge and decided a drink and a good laugh was just what she needed to forget what had so far been a pretty rotten day. She accepted the G&T Doctor Ed handed her, and took a sip. They chatted about Evelyn's new hip and how Doctor Ed and a few of her other friends were going to take her swimming next week.

'No wonder you're looking so happy,' Truth said.

'I can't wait to get back in the sea.'

'How are things looking for the castle fair day?' Doctor Ed asked.

'Nessa's got everything under control – she seems to do it with her eyes closed.'

'She told me you've been a great help to her.'

'I really haven't,' Truth said. 'I've just run a few errands for her and looked over a couple of contracts that needed checking.'

'Ed,' Evelyn leaned forward in her chair, 'tell Truth what you told me earlier.'

'Evelyn!' He gave her a look.

'No, you must! She needs to hear it.'

'Hear what?' Truth looked from one to the other.

'Well, I was just telling Evelyn, before you came in, that going through any kind of online abuse – never mind something as serious and vicious as you have been subjected to – would be classified as trauma. That means that you may very well be suffering from post-traumatic stress, Truth – and that's not something to take lightly. I wanted to—'

'You told him!' Truth glared at Evelyn, who was looking unperturbed. 'I expressly—'

'Evelyn didn't tell me anything, Truth,' Doctor Ed said gently. 'It was Ari who mentioned it to me in passing.'

'Ari . . .' Truth felt a rush of heat to her face. For a second she was speechless, then had to swallow the rage that threatened to erupt. 'He had no right to—'

'Oh, relax, Truth,' Evelyn said, glancing at her and waving a dismissive hand. 'This is exactly why I'm concerned about her, Ed.' Evelyn turned back to Doctor Ed, as if discussing a wayward teen.

'In all honesty, Truth,' Doctor Ed tried to explain, 'Ari and I were just having lunch at my club, in town – we were discussing how computers are transforming how surgeons work and he mentioned he'd been out to dinner with you and that you'd been having a horrible time with this cancelling business.'

'I suppose he told you I made a complete idiot of myself and had to run and hide in the loo, too – did he?'

'Did you?' Evelyn's eyes widened.

'No, he didn't,' Doctor Ed said.

Doctor Ed was trying to be kind, she knew, but she still wanted to scream.

'He did say though that he thought what had happened had taken its toll on you, Truth – that you were very shaken by it. We're none of us invincible, you know. Ari's a doctor, remember . . .'

So Ari *had* noticed her panic that evening at dinner – he just hadn't said anything to her at the time.

'I just wanted to say—' Doctor Ed didn't get any further, because to her horror, Truth suddenly felt tears begin to roll down her cheeks. She brushed them away roughly. What was it with everyone here? Did everyone always stick their noses in other people's business? Offer their opinions without being asked? They had no right. But try as she might, she couldn't stop the tears, which seemed to be streaming of their own accord. She was angry, she was confused, and she was very, very tired. 'I'm sorry,' she said, 'I'm just . . . not used to . . .'

'I think Ari is right,' Doctor Ed said sympathetically, handing her a tissue. 'And I just wanted to offer my services if you felt like talking about it. Or I could find someone else for you to talk to – it might help to discuss it . . .'

Chapter Thirty-Six

'What's the matter?' Annika asked. They were halfway through a lovely dinner she had cooked earlier, then heated up when she arrived at his flat.

'Nothing,' Bruce said, toying with his food. 'I'm just tired.'

'Stressed, more like.' Annika was concerned. 'Is it Stella?'

The mention of her name made Bruce visibly tense. He put his hands over his face and decided to tell Annika what had happened. 'I don't know what to do,' he said, peering out through his fingers. 'I really don't.'

'What's going on?'

'She's just becoming more and more unreasonable . . . paranoid, even.'

'About what? Us?'

'She's convinced that you're trying to steal Freddy from her – that you're . . . trying to turn him against her, I think her exact words were.'

'She really said that?' Annika frowned.

'That wasn't all she said.' Bruce took a swig of his wine.

'But I've only been trying to help . . . I'd never try to turn Freddy against her! The very thought! He's a three-year-old child! You don't believe her, do you?'

'Of course I don't!'

'When did this happen?'

Bruce let out a breath. 'She asked me to drop by a couple of days ago – she said she had something she wanted to discuss with me. I thought maybe she wanted to apologise for her behaviour at the barbecue. So I went.'

'And what did she want to discuss?'

'Basically, she wanted to spell out that I was too stupid to see what you were trying to do.'

Annika shook her head. 'And what did you say to that?'

'I'm afraid I lost it. I reminded her in no uncertain terms that this whole arrangement had come about because she had wanted it. It was all her doing.' Bruce sighed. 'But that's when it got really weird.'

'What do you mean?' Annika leaned her chin on her hand.

'Well . . .' Bruce looked uncomfortable. 'She started saying that the whole thing had been a big mistake and she wanted me to just move back in.' He spread his hands in bewilderment. 'As if nothing had ever happened.'

Annika went very still.

'And then . . .' Colour flooded Bruce's face. 'Then she tried to kiss me.'

Annika bit her lip.

'I didn't – of course – I pushed her away immediately and asked what the hell she thought she was doing . . . that I was with you now . . . and that's when she lost it. She said she was going to go for full custody of Freddy and that was the end of it.'

'Do you believe her?'

'I don't know, Annika. Stella's always been controlling, I guess. I just didn't really notice it before – when we were together, I accepted it was just the way she was. But now . . . I don't recognise her anymore. It doesn't really matter what I believe – what matters is what *she* believes . . . whatever she's persuaded herself is going on in that head of hers.'

'Perhaps she was just angry, feeling foolish, and wanted to scare you . . .' Annika paused.

'Well, she's done that alright. And not for the first time.' Bruce looked at her. 'I know I'm weak, but—'

'You are not weak, Bruce – it takes a lot of strength and generosity of spirit to have handled things the way you have with Stella for this long. I don't know any other man who would have been as patient, as selfless, as you have been. She turned your whole life upside down – Freddy's too.'

'I know – I know, believe me. The thing is,' he looked at her despairingly, 'I couldn't bear to lose him, Annika – I just couldn't. Freddy's my whole life . . . I can't lose him.'

'You won't, Bruce . . . it won't come to that – how could it? You've been a wonderful father, the best.'

'The mother always wins in a custody case.'

'Not always . . . not if . . .'

'Not if what?'

'Not if you can prove she's unstable.'

'Sometimes I think *I'm* the one who's unstable.'

'What are you talking about?'

'My life . . . it's just . . . it's turned into something I don't understand anymore. I don't know how I got here. I don't understand how the wheels came off. We used to be so happy.'

Bruce stared at his plate morosely, hardly noticing Annika looking concerned.

'We are happy, Bruce – aren't we? You know, you and me . . .?' Annika said quietly. 'I thought we were, anyway.'

'I didn't mean that.'

'Then what *did* you mean exactly, Bruce? What are you saying?'

'I don't know . . . all I know is if it comes to losing Freddy . . . well, if moving back in with Stella is the only way I can get to keep my son in my life . . . then I might have to consider doing just that.'

Annika pressed her lips together. She didn't say anything for a minute – she just got up and quietly took the plates to the sink.

Bruce's misery increased dramatically. He hadn't meant to say that. He just wanted someone, anyone, to understand how tortured he was feeling. The misery was too much for him – he wanted to disperse it. He was a coward and he hated himself for it. But he was a coward who had assumed that Annika would strenuously argue with his last state-ment. She didn't.

'If that's how you feel . . . then that's what you must do.'

His head snapped up. 'I don't. I really don't – I just don't know what to do.'

'When you told me about your argument with Stella, Bruce, you referred to your life just now – to your current state of affairs – as an "arrangement" . . .' Annika was calm. 'Is that how you see our relationship? As an arrangement?' She bent to load the dishwasher. 'Something that has come about only because of how the chips have fallen? Because I do not think of you and Freddy as an "arrangement".' She straightened up and turned to look at him, folding her arms. 'On the contrary, you have become a very important part of my life . . . perhaps the most important part – but that remains to be seen. I fell in love with you quickly, you know that. I don't like to play games. But now I love Freddy very much too. If you are not as invested in our relationship as I appear to be – then it would be kinder of you to make that clear to me. There won't be any drama,' she waved a hand, 'I think we've all had enough of that lately – but I need to know where I stand, Bruce. Because I do not want to be part of any *arrangement* – I want to be part of a loving family unit. We all have a right to aspire to that.'

Bruce was momentarily blindsided – not just by Annika's calm, measured assessment of what he had said to her, but by her reply, which amounted to a solid, steadfast declaration of love and loyalty to him and little Freddy. For a moment he just looked at her. Then he got up and went over, putting his hands on her waist. 'I'm totally in love with you, Annika, and I'm one hundred per cent invested in our relationship. It's just taken a bit of getting used to – that's all – having someone in my life who actually cares about what I think.' He smiled. 'I don't want to lose you now.'

She leaned her head on his shoulder. 'Good. That was the right answer.' She looked up at him as he turned her to face him and pulled her close. 'You can't let her mess us around like this, Bruce. You need to stand up to her. This isn't just about what Stella wants anymore.'

Bruce was filled with a sudden confidence – a wave of

certainty swept over him. 'I'll get on to my family law solicitor in the morning – get her to send Stella a letter.'

'I think that's a good idea,' said Annika. 'We need to start drawing some boundaries around acceptable and unacceptable behaviour.' Stella may be trying it on . . . or perhaps she really is struggling . . . in which case perhaps she needs to see someone – talk to a therapist or something. But you need to take charge of this, Bruce.'

Chapter Thirty-Seven

Pauline was on her lunch hour when her phone rang, showing Tristan's number. She was sitting on a bench in the park enjoying a sandwich in the sunshine after a particularly draining meeting with a member of the local council about a grant. Privately cursing Tristan for interrupting her peace, she forced a cheery hello.

'Good news,' he said. 'I sold two of my big paintings so I'm in funds. I thought I'd go over and see Mum for a few days, maybe even a week. I'll book an Airbnb. It's time one of us went over.'

'One of us did,' Pauline said. 'Truth is there, in case it had slipped your memory.'

'I know that.' Tristan made an exasperated sound. 'You know what I mean, Pauline – I meant one of *us*.'

There was a pause as Pauline took a bite of her sandwich and chewed – digesting this latest piece of information.

'You still there?'

'Yup.' She swallowed. 'Funny you should say that – I was thinking of going over myself.'

'Seriously?'

'Mmhmm.' This was true. Pauline was becoming concerned about Truth. Truth had told her about Josh turning up out of the blue and uninvited – but hadn't gone into details of the visit except to say it hadn't gone well. Since then she'd sounded down on the phone when Pauline spoke to her, when prior to that she had been particularly upbeat, full of chat about the upcoming fair day at the castle and some sculpture that was going up. She seemed to have made friends, particularly with a nice-sounding girl called Nessa who also lived in the house. Pauline knew her daughter well enough to know she would never find out if something was bothering her over the phone – she would have to sit down with her face to face, and even then it would probably take a couple of days. She was also feeling guilty herself for letting Truth go over on her own, even though it had been her own choice. But if Tristan was going over . . . then that would be the perfect excuse to join him. Pauline couldn't quite contemplate meeting her mother again on her own – not because she was intimidated by her, more because she knew how exhausting it would be trying to be pleasant. But if Tristan was there as well, that would lessen the prospective tension considerably.

'When were you thinking of going?' she asked him now.

'Friday next – could you do that?'

'I'll just have to clear it at work, let me get back to you – oh, and can you book a two-bed Airbnb? I'll split it with you.'

'Sure. Hey, that's great, really great – it'll be like old times.'

Since her half-brother was almost fifteen years her junior, Pauline stopped herself from pointing out that there had been no 'old times' with the three of them. But she didn't want to be negative – the trip would be daunting enough as it was.

'I'm going to ring Mom to tell her this evening . . .' He paused. 'I don't think I'll mention about you coming – that would be better coming from you, right?'

Pauline grinned. Of course Tristan wouldn't want to be the bearer of less than upbeat news. He knew perfectly well that Evelyn wouldn't be thrilled to hear that Pauline was arriving over – that was partly why she enjoyed the thought of the impending visit.

'Don't worry,' she said. 'I'll let Truth know first – she can tell her grandmother. We'll take it from there.'

'Great.' Tristan sounded relieved. 'Let me know when you've booked your flights, I'll email you mine – I'm really looking forward to seeing you guys.'

'Yeah, me too – it'll be fun.'

✧

Truth was feeling unusually vulnerable since Doctor Ed's suggestion that she talk to somebody about the online abuse. She understood it made sense, but she didn't want to discuss it with a professional – she wanted to talk to Mike, again, but he didn't seem to want to give her the time of day, never mind engage her in conversation. The realisation hurt more than it ought to have. She'd been hoping to bump into him again in the house – but Nessa had mentioned casually that he had gone away for a few days.

'Gone where?' Truth asked her.

Nessa shrugged. 'Didn't say. Why? Do you need to talk to him?' She was curious.

'No, not at all,' Truth said. 'We just had a really nice time together recently, he brought me to his studio, and to the foundry to see the sculpture – and then – well, it's all sort of come to nothing.'

'You never said!'

'There wasn't anything to tell, as such.'

'Are you kidding? He showed you the sculpture . . . that's a really big deal.' Nessa was clearly surprised. 'I bet it's amazing, is it?'

'Yes, it is. And now it appears he doesn't want anything to do with me. Artist's prerogative, I guess.'

'Did he tell you the legend behind it, about the ghost?'

'Yes, he did. I thought it was lovely . . . really poignant. Didn't realise it was an omen, though.'

'Of what?'

'Well, clearly that's what Mike's doing.' Truth made herself sound more upbeat than she felt. 'Guess he's ghosted *me*.'

Nessa shook her head. 'Mike's not like that. I hope there isn't a problem with his mother . . .' she said, speculating. 'She's a widow, and Mike's an only child, maybe that's what's going on. But he didn't mention that, and I think he would have – to me, anyway.'

Now, two days later, Truth was at the castle, having walked back up to the spot overlooking the bay where Josh had ambushed her with his proposal.

With the bay spread out beneath her, all appeared restored

to its usual peaceful ambience. Josh's performance and presence here seemed unreal, swallowed up like one more ripple in the tide. But now she was confused and upset for an entirely different reason – and the only person who could clarify the situation didn't appear to want to talk to her. She thought about texting Mike, asking what was going on with him, but the thought of a brusque reply – or worse, none – was enough to still her itching fingers. After all, she knew close to nothing about him, really – it was hardly as if she had a right to any explanation, but all the same, thinking of the last time they had been together . . . the complete turnaround seemed unexpected and hurtful – unless he had some urgent business to take care of. Either way, she felt the loss of some small, hopeful beginning that had unfurled, that now filled her with unexpected dismay. When her phone buzzed in her pocket, she allowed herself a brief second of hopeful anticipation, but fishing it out she saw it was her mum. Truth took a deep breath, forcing herself to sound cheerful.

'Hey, Mum.'

'I'm only on for a minute.' Pauline sounded harassed. 'We've a situation here.' Truth could hear shouting in the background, no doubt her mother's workplace, which would not be unusual. 'I'm coming over on Friday . . .'

'What? Here?'

'Of course there – where else would I be going? I want to see you. Anyway, I just wanted to let you know – and maybe ask you to tell your grandmother. You know – let her get used to the idea. I think it would be better coming from you. Then I can take it from there.'

'Well, sure, yeah.' Truth ran a hand through her hair. 'Wow, well, that's great.'

'I can't talk now. I'll ring you this evening with all the details. Tristan is coming over too – I just wanted to let you know . . . gotta run, sweetheart, love you!'

'Love you too.'

Truth was slightly dazed when she finished the call. Pauline was coming over, this Friday . . . That was . . . great – but unexpected. And she needed to tell Evelyn. Doing the maths, Truth remembered the last time her mother and grandmother had been in the same room had been for her First Holy Communion – which was about twenty-five years ago – at best a hazy memory. This was a real opportunity . . . a chance for them to begin again, to put the past behind them. It was exciting! With a spring in her step, thoughts of her own situation receded as Truth made her way back to the house to find Evelyn.

The house was quiet when she got there, and through the open back door the sounds of laughter floated up from the garden. Following the voices, Truth found Doctor Ed, Evelyn, Nessa, Bruce and little Freddy, sitting around the pond. Evelyn was holding court, looking radiant as she relived the delights of her first sea swim since her surgery, facilitated by Doctor Ed and Bruce holding firmly onto her as they helped her into the water. 'I can't tell you how wonderful it was – I really can't! I felt as if I was finally fully alive again,' she was saying. 'I will never forget the feel of the water on my skin, never. I thought the day couldn't possibly get any better, and then—' She stopped, spotting Truth coming over. 'Hello, darling! Come and sit down, I was just telling everyone about my swim.'

'Actually, Evelyn, I have something to tell you too – some news . . .'

'Oh, so do I, Truth – you won't believe it! What a day this is turning out to be! What's your news?'

'You go first!'

'Well, it was just after my swim, and my phone rang and who was it but Tristan! He's sold two of his big paintings at his latest exhibition, and he's coming over to see me! This Friday! Imagine that! It was such a wonderful surprise, I still can't quite take it in . . .' She looked around, beaming. 'Just when I thought things couldn't get any better! It's going to be so wonderful to see him. Now, tell me your news, Truth . . .'

Truth hesitated, unsure for a moment how to proceed. 'Is that all he said? That he was coming over on Friday . . .?'

'Well, isn't that enough?' Evelyn laughed. 'It's the loveliest surprise.' She looked mystified. 'Well, go on, don't keep me in suspense . . . tell me your news.'

'Well, that's just it,' Truth said. 'I thought Tristan would have mentioned it to you.'

'Mentioned what? How could he possibly know *your* news?'

'Because Mum's coming over too, on Friday. She called just now to tell me – Tristan and she are coming over together.'

'Pauline's coming over?' Evelyn's face fell. 'I don't understand.'

There was a beat of uncomfortable silence. 'Well,' Truth went on, 'she's coming over to see me . . . and you, of course. It'll be a reunion of sorts.'

'Well, I don't know what to say . . .' Evelyn recovered herself quickly. 'There's just one surprise after another today!'

'I think this calls for a group gin and tonic,' said Doctor Ed, to no one in particular. 'Don't you?' He patted Evelyn's shoulder as he brushed past.

✦

'Was this your idea?' Evelyn was smiling as Truth made sure her grandmother had everything she needed beside her as she settled in her chair back in the apartment, but her mild tone failed to disguise the steeliness behind the question. 'Your mother coming over?'

'No.' Truth was equally mild, but her lawyer's instincts were on full alert. 'Not at all. I'm as surprised as you are.' She busied herself topping up Evelyn's glass of sparkling water. 'I assumed she'd come over at some stage – but I've had as much warning as you have. Odd that Tristan didn't mention it when he rang to tell you about the visit, don't you think?'

If Evelyn did, she didn't reply.

'How *do* you feel about it?'

'I don't know.' Evelyn was curt. 'How would you feel about it if your only daughter, who behaved like a delinquent and habitually shamed you in front of all your contemporaries, despite your best efforts, left her comfortable family home in Dublin to live in a squat in London, and do God knows what with whom, and then as good as turned her back on you for thirty-odd years . . . decided to rock up and visit you because her brother was coming over and probably had made her feel guilty – and she was too cowardly to come on her own?' Evelyn leafed through a magazine.

'That's a little harsh, don't you think?' Truth was careful to keep her tone light.

'I don't know what to think.' Evelyn looked her in the eye. 'And I don't need you to be telling me how I should be thinking either.'

'I wouldn't dream of it. My guess – if it makes you feel any better – is that she's mostly coming over to check up on me.'

'Why? You're perfectly alright here, aren't you?' Evelyn was indignant.

'Of course I am.'

'Perhaps Josh told her you turned him down and she's worried about that.' Evelyn threw her a slanted look.

'I warned Josh on no account to contact Mum about any of what happened. And I'd prefer if you didn't enlighten her, either. Mum has enough on her plate as it is – I don't want her worrying about me.'

'You have nothing to worry about on that count, Truth. I'll be extremely and pleasantly surprised if your mother can bring herself to be civil to me for any length of time. That's what I'm concerned about – if you must know.'

'How do you mean?'

'Well, you're not the only one with a reputation to protect in the family. I did everything in my power to help and understand your mother when she was younger, but it was met with downright aggression. Pauline was never quite . . . normal. I might as well tell you that now. I always felt she had some sort of mental, or personality, problem – but of course she refused point blank to visit any specialist. I did my best for her. To be quite frank, I don't need her turning up now and making some kind of awful scene in public.' The magazine snapped shut. 'Which she is more than capable of doing. I've worked very hard to build a nice life for myself since Lenny died and left me bankrupt.' Evelyn dabbed her eyes with a tissue, before going on. 'I have a nice circle of good friends and a certain standing in the community, if you like. I don't need your mother bowling in and wrecking all that for me. That's what I'm afraid of. Is that good enough for you? You of all people should understand . . . having been through this computer stalking business.'

Truth recognised deflection and manipulation when she heard it – but even she was taken aback that Evelyn could make the leap to comparing the online abuse she had suffered at the hands of trolls to her own mother's youthful and clearly misunderstood rebellion. She decided on this occasion not to challenge her – there had been a subtle change in Evelyn's mood this evening since she'd heard that Pauline was coming over. Her tone was veering on petulant and something brittle glittered in her eyes.

'I can safely promise you that Mum will not make any scenes that might affect your standing in the community, Evelyn. She's a respected social worker – she's eminently qualified to defuse tension, not exacerbate it.'

'Hmmm.' Evelyn didn't sound convinced. 'You won't understand until you have your own children – no one does.'

'I can't argue with that, but I can promise you I won't let anything get out of hand – not that I think it might – but if it makes you feel better about Mum's arrival I'll have a quiet word with her myself. I think we should all approach this as a chance to begin afresh – get over whatever happened in the past.'

'Nothing happened in the past – nothing bar your mother going off the rails and causing total havoc, that is.'

'Let's just take this as it comes, hmm? I'm really looking forward to seeing Tristan, it's been a few years.'

'Speaking of seeing things . . .' Evelyn was regarding her keenly. 'Have you been going through my drawers, by any chance?'

Truth's head whipped around. 'I beg your pardon?'

'You heard me. Have you been going through my things – snooping, if you prefer? I'd much rather you were up front about it . . .'

Truth made a small sound of disbelief. 'No, I have not!' She was careful not to allow herself respond in anger. 'Whatever gives you that idea?'

'Some of my papers have been moved around – I'm sure of it. I always keep my nail file and some mementos in a certain place in my bedside drawer and they've definitely been moved. It's probably that Morah woman – I knew I should never have allowed her unsupervised access to my apartment – she probably had a good root through everything. I've never understood why Ed would choose someone like her as caretaker – but he seems to be very loyal to her, God knows why.' Evelyn shuddered. 'She gives me the creeps.'

'I'm sure she was just trying to help out,' Truth said carefully. 'Everyone in the house seems to have been very concerned about you after the accident – in a good way.'

'Yes, well.' Evelyn lifted her chin. 'That's all very well. But I'm back now – and I'm perfectly well able to look after myself again – although I'm very grateful of course for having you here.' She flashed Truth a smile. 'I don't like to think of how I might have coped without you. By the way, are you doing anything this evening?'

'No, I've no plans.'

'Well, why don't we get a takeaway and watch a nice movie?'

'That sounds like a good idea, have you anything in mind?'

'I'd love a Chinese, I've had a hankering for one since I came out of hospital, and let's watch a nice *glamorous* movie, nothing depressing . . .'

'I should be able to arrange that,' Truth said cheerfully. At least if there was a movie to watch, it would take Evelyn's mind off the impending visit. Truth found her grandmother's sudden change of mood unsettling. Evelyn had reverted to being charming again, pretty smartly . . . but Truth wondered how long it would last. She would talk to her mum tomorrow – warn her that Evelyn might be unpredictable. Twenty-five years was a long time not to see each other . . . they would all need to tread carefully.

Chapter Thirty-Eight

Robert Radcliffe wandered out to a secluded table at the outdoor restaurant area of his exclusive Portuguese golf club, and sat down with his morning paper. At seventy-eight years of age he was still a fine-looking man, although the vestiges of his former rugby-playing physique, and handsome profile, had rather succumbed, not just to the accumulation of years, but to the excesses and spoils his luxurious lifestyle afforded him. Nevertheless, he was careful to maintain a certain level of well-maintained appearance, not least because his excessively fitness-obsessed second wife Alannah – thirty years his junior – expected it. Now, at 11.15 in the morning, he had the place pretty much to himself. As he'd hoped, his contemporaries were practising their swings, and the morning coffee crew had mostly dispersed to pursue beach-related activities. These days the golf course was not alone the venue for his preferred form of exercise – but a welcome respite from both the demands of home and what he referred to as his state of 'semi-retired' business interests. Men like Robert Radcliffe didn't retire – they simply made other people work harder for them.

When he was reasonably sure he was unobserved, Robert put down his newspaper and nonchalantly withdrew the envelope with the Irish stamps from his shirt breast pocket. It was addressed to him by hand, which in itself was unusual, but it was also marked *strictly personal* – the words underlined for emphasis. Robert was used to being on the receiving end of crank calls and begging letters over the years, and mostly his PA deflected any mail of dubious origins – but this one had slipped through the net, and something about its rather forlorn appearance had prompted him to pick it up and save it for when he had some quiet time. Despite his millions and an enviable collection of homes in various countries, Robert found that the older he became, the more he fell prey to a certain type of homesickness when he least expected it. It wasn't as if he couldn't get back to Dublin often enough – if he wanted to – but the longer he lived away, the fewer reasons there seemed to be to return. His children and grandchildren were long grown up and brought their own families when they came to visit – and he saw more of friends here than he ever did in Ireland. Also, Alannah wasn't keen on going back to Dublin – she preferred trips to London or New York. She maintained he was melancholy for days after a trip home – and that it made him depressing to be around.

So now in a rare moment of solitude, and to the accompaniment of some cheerful birdsong, Robert adjusted his glasses, opened the letter, and began to read.

He wasn't sure how much time elapsed while he sat there – memories flooding his mind – scene after scene unspooling like some extended trailer to a well-loved movie . . . Evelyn when he had first met her . . . at a dinner party they had both attended with their respective spouses.

Hearing of Lenny Malone's gorgeous new wife, and not believing the gossip until he had sat across a table from her himself and experienced her thrillingly forceful personality, and the powerful attraction that had sprung up between them . . . Evelyn diving off a boat in the south of France, swimming like a mermaid . . . their discreet trysts snatched at perilous risk at home – even though the guilt of his wife Sarah's fragile temperament clung to him like smoke. But he had been unable to resist Evelyn, and had almost been ready to give up everything for her . . . until the strange incident involving that very peculiar girl Sarah had hired as nanny to Joey and Susan . . . Robert hadn't thought about that for years . . . funny how life had a way of intervening when one least expected it. If it hadn't been for the very odd country girl nanny and her obsession with spying on him and Evelyn, eventually threatening him – he still shook his head in disbelief remembering this – he and Evelyn might have spent these last forty years together as man and wife. He had been besotted enough by her certainly, and they had both been ready to leave their respective spouses and begin a new life together, but the intervention of the nanny – he couldn't recall her name now – had had the effect of bringing him sharply to his senses. Made him truly consider the huge implications involved. This hadn't been modern Ireland as they knew it now. The shockwaves in the circles they moved in would have been seismic – and although Robert didn't like to admit it at the time, he had felt not a little relief that their romantic escapades had been brought to a necessary halt before serious – perhaps irreparable – damage to his own reputation had been inflicted. Evelyn, however, had not taken their break-up lying down, so to speak. She had been furious. They had had an almighty row and she had told him never to contact her again as long as he lived. He couldn't say he blamed her. And so they had gone their separate ways and back to their respective spouses, who, if either knew of their affair, had the presence of mind to pretend otherwise. And bit by bit, life returned to its former predictability. Robert worked even harder, made even more money, and when Sarah succumbed to cancer fifteen years later, he eventually met and married Alannah. But although Evelyn had been out of sight since he had moved to Portugal full time, she had never been out of mind. And not infrequently, as the demands of keeping up with a much younger wife took their toll, Robert considered how different his life might have been if he'd had the courage to see it through with Evelyn and wondered *what if* . . .

But this . . . he looked at the offending piece of correspondence in front of him, as he struggled to make sense of it. This was unthinkable . . . Evelyn had suffered a debilitating stroke . . . was in a nursing home . . . wanted him to cease the payment to her account he had been so readily agreeable to make when she had contacted him out of the blue after Lenny had died and told him about the secret she had kept to herself all these years – loyal to the end. It was . . . he just couldn't take it in . . . any of it . . .

As he leaned his elbows on the table, with his head in his hands, the contents of the strange letter still swimming before him, Robert was unaware of the curious glances he attracted from more than one passerby, as the restaurant began to slowly fill with the early lunch brigade, one of whom would later remark to his wife that he could have sworn Robert Radcliffe was crying.

But the letter had been merely the first part of what was becoming an increasingly bizarre situation. Later that day, Robert set out to track down the manager of this residential care home – to find that no home of that name existed (he had thought Journey's End sounded a little twee, but . . .), not in Bray, from where the letter had been posted, nor anywhere else in the country. He had then phoned the last number he had for Evelyn, and a young female voice had answered saying, 'Evelyn's phone . . .' so he hung up before probing any further. It may have been a nurse . . . or not. Robert became increasingly worried that something dreadful had happened to Evelyn and that possibly the people responsible were trying to take control of her bank account, and worse. It was time to find out just what exactly was going on. Scrolling through his phone contacts, Robert dialled the number of the discreet and trusted detective service he used when circumstances required, and vowed to get to the bottom of this upsetting, perplexing, and very possibly sinister state of affairs.

✧

There was an air of discreet excitement in number 24 at the prospect of not one but *two* of Evelyn's offspring arriving to see her so unexpectedly. Truth had been aware of it building since the news had been announced – publicly – to Evelyn's displeasure. Whereas Doctor Ed might have been counted on to keep the prospective visit to himself, once Bruce and

Nessa had been party to Evelyn's obvious shock at hearing Truth's mother was coming to see her, the news had spread through the house and beyond. No one had mentioned it to Evelyn since – of course – but all the same, the house was vibrating with quiet expectation. If Evelyn was aware of it, she wasn't saying as much to Truth.

Once it had been established that Pauline and Tristan's flight got in at around twelve thirty, it was decided that, with Truth's help, Evelyn would put on a light lunch at the apartment and, depending on how the general prevailing mood turned out to be, that Truth would then take Pauline out for a walk to catch up – and leave Tristan with Evelyn to do the same. 'That way none of us will feel trapped,' Evelyn said. 'You and your mum will be dying to catch up, of course, and it will give Tristan and me a chance to do the same.' She was matter of fact. But despite her practicality, Truth knew Evelyn was rattled at the prospect of reuniting with her own daughter after all these years. Truth couldn't help feeling sorry for her, or perhaps she was just sad at the general situation between the two women. How awful to feel such antipathy towards your own daughter or mother – she couldn't imagine it, despite it playing out in front of her own eyes. Growing up she had been consumed with the absence of a father figure in her life – so much so, she had hardly noticed the lack of grandparents. It had always just been Pauline and her – and for Truth, that was just what home and family meant.

Now, the fateful hour had arrived. Nessa had prepared a lovely selection of salads and pastas and fresh crusty breads which Truth had picked up earlier. The small table which sat with its leaves folded underneath the rear-view window had been extended to its full length and moved out to accommodate the four places it was set for. In its centre was Doctor Ed's contribution – a very simple arrangement of fresh flowers from the garden. The guests were due to arrive any minute. Evelyn, who was sitting in her armchair looking elegant in black linen trousers and a black silk shirt, with matching black leather flats, her crutch by the side of her chair, glanced her watch again.

'Where did you say they were staying?' She frowned.

'At an Airbnb just around the corner,' Truth said, straightening a glass. 'In Clarinda Avenue. It's perfect, they'll be just a short stroll away.'

Evelyn fidgeted in her chair and patted her hair, which she wore up for the occasion arranged in an artful pleat. A heavy gold torc neckpiece was at her throat, and matching chunky earrings gave the otherwise sedate outfit a modern edge.

As the buzzer rang on the intercom, Truth went to release the door. 'Well,' she said, turning to Evelyn, 'they're here . . .'

'I'd better get up, I suppose.' Evelyn stood up and positioned herself behind the armchair, holding on to it with her free hand to steady herself, with her crutch under her other arm. She took a breath and lifted her chin.

Then everyone, it seemed, was in the room at once. Pauline was hugging Truth, and Tristan went to fold Evelyn in a bear hug, until she gasped, laughing, and said, 'You'll have to let me go, you idiot! I can't breathe.' But her face had lit up when he held her at arm's length to really look at her, shaking his head. 'I can't get over how well you look, Mum.'

'Well, I can put that down in large measure to Truth here – who has been taking very good care of me.' She looked at Pauline, who was smiling, Truth's arm still draped over her mother's shoulder. 'Hello, Pauline.' Evelyn smiled. 'It's very good to see you.'

'It's good to see you too, Mum.' Pauline stepped forward to give her mother a rather awkward kiss on the cheek before retreating back. 'Tristan's right – you're looking really, really well.'

'Thank you.' Evelyn seemed relieved. 'I can return the compliment – you're both looking very well yourselves. Well, now that we've got the compliments out of the way, let's all sit down and have something to eat . . . you must be hungry, I hope?'

'I have a better idea,' said Tristan, pulling out a bottle of champagne and popping it.

After that, lunch proceeded very amicably. Truth was so happy to see Pauline – she hadn't realised how much she had missed her mum. Pauline, too, seemed happy and relaxed. Evelyn showed polite interest in Pauline's work at the shelter and Tristan kept them all entertained with stories from his recent exhibition and his creative friends in New York. Evelyn, Truth noted, once she had sensed there was no immediate tension to be negotiated, had slipped into what was clearly a familiar role to her as a delightful and considerate hostess. After coffee had been made and lingered over, Evelyn smiled meaningfully at Truth. 'Why don't you show your mum around, Truth? I know you both must be dying to have a proper catch-up. Tristan will help me clear away and we'll have a chinwag too . . .'

'That's a good idea,' Pauline agreed, pushing back her seat and standing up. 'I could do with stretching my legs.'

Truth grabbed her bag, noticing out of the corner of her vision how Evelyn's eyes flicked over Pauline astutely as she stood up, assessing her daughter in what Truth instinctively understood was an unflattering light. She immediately banished the unpleasant observation from her mind, putting it down to her over-sensitive disposition regarding her mother. Evelyn hadn't seen Pauline in over twenty-five years – it was perfectly natural to look her daughter over from head to toe. After all, Pauline had pretty much devoured Truth with her own eyes when she saw her – but that had been accompanied by a joyous expression and a giant and unrelenting hug.

Chapter Thirty-Nine

'So . . .' Truth looked at Pauline as they strolled around the town, linking arms. 'How was it, finally seeing your mother after all these years?'

Pauline considered the question. 'It still feels very unreal, to be honest. Everything about this does . . . being back in Dublin, seeing Tristan, and of course Mum – it all came together so quickly.'

'It's so funny to hear you calling someone mum,' Truth said, giving Pauline's arm a squeeze.

'I've been thinking about that a lot lately.' She turned to look at Truth.

'What? Calling Evelyn mum?' Truth was amused.

'No. Thinking that you lost out so much on the grand-parent front – I deprived you. And as for your dad and me . . . well . . . I have a lot of remorse about that . . . what it must have been like for you.'

'You were always enough for me, Mum – I loved our little world together – it was always you and me. I knew we were unshakeable. That's all that mattered to me, really. And Dad and I have made our peace with things, so it's all come good, really, hasn't it?'

'That's very generous of you to look at it like that, Truth – I don't know what I did to deserve you.'

'You were you.'

They were coming up to The Friendly Plate, and Truth turned down into the narrow street. 'Nessa's dying to meet you – she insisted I bring you in,' Truth said. 'Then we can go for a stroll down to the seafront.'

'Sounds lovely.'

Inside, the café was quiet, with just a few tables occupied. Nessa was delighted to meet Pauline and had reserved a corner table, insisting they all had a glass of wine to mark the occasion. 'I'll be squiffy if I don't watch it,' Pauline said, as Nessa toasted her visit. 'And thank you for the lovely lunch selection – I believe that was all your doing.'

'I'm really glad you enjoyed it.' Nessa smiled. 'It was a pleasure to help out Evelyn – she's such a mainstay of our community here,' Nessa said.

'I'm sure she is,' Pauline said.

'I'm just off to the loo – back in a mo'.' Truth slipped from the table.

'It's so good to finally meet you,' Nessa said to Pauline. 'We've heard so much about you! Truth talks about you all the time – she's been dying to see you.'

'I've heard a lot about you too.' Pauline smiled. 'It's been lovely for Truth to make a good friend here. I was worried about her coming over on her own . . .' She trailed off.

'Well, the whole thing's been a real success,' Nessa said. 'Evelyn is delighted with her, and the rest of us love her too – she's such a lovely addition to our family – and we really are like a family of sorts in the house. The wrong person there would really have affected the vibe.'

'That's the impression Truth has given me herself . . . she really appreciates how welcome she's been made feel. It's just . . .' Pauline frowned.

'What?'

'Well, I get the impression she's a bit down at the minute . . . and I was wondering why. Nothing's happened between her and her grandmother, has it?'

Nessa shook her head. 'No . . . not that I know of. But . . .'

'What?'

'Well, there is this guy I think she might have liked . . .' Nessa saw Truth approaching the table.

'Too late . . .' she whispered. Here she comes . . . I'm sure she'll tell you herself.' Nessa changed the subject quickly.

After leaving the café, Truth took Pauline down to the seafront, where they bought an ice cream and strolled along the pier. 'I'd forgotten how good the air is here,' Pauline said, inhaling.

'I do love being by the sea,' Truth said. 'There's something soothing about it.'

'I'm glad you're getting a break from the legal world . . . you were working far too hard. I was worried about you.'

'You worry about me whatever I'm doing,' Truth said.

'True – that goes with the territory.'

'Well, you don't have to – I'm fine, really.' They were coming up to the slipway now, and the foundations for Mike's statue were ready and waiting for the bronze sculpture to take its place. Pauline sat down on the ledge. 'What's this for, anyway?'

'There's a sculpture going up . . .'

'Oh, right. Nice spot for it.' Pauline finished her ice cream and wiped her hands on a tissue. 'You don't seem yourself,' she said, looking at Truth. 'What's bothering you? Was it Josh coming over?'

'What? Oh . . . no.'

'I didn't think he'd take the break-up lying down.' Pauline frowned. 'Are you sure about it? I mean he *was* mad about you.'

'No, I'm sure.' Truth looked out to sea.

'Is there someone else?' Pauline asked gently.

'I thought there might be . . .'

'Who?'

'Oh, just this artist guy who lives in the house. We had a couple of really nice times together. I thought we really had a connection . . . but for some reason he just stopped talking to me. I thought initially he was just having a bad day, you know, artistic temperament, maybe . . . but it looks like he's had second thoughts.'

'Well, if he's that unreliable' – Pauline shrugged – 'you don't need him, do you? Men who blow hot and cold are such a pain . . .' She shook her head.

'At least Evelyn's happy about it.'

'How d'you mean?' Pauline frowned.

'Oh, you know what she's like! She thought I was insane looking at a penniless artist. She had me married off first to the surgeon guy Nessa's seeing – and of course she *loved* Josh when she met him.' Truth made a wry face.

'I can just imagine.' Pauline was thoughtful. 'Shall we head back now?'

'Sure,' said Truth, pulling herself up.

Truth had just let them in the front door when Pauline noticed an attractive guy coming up through the back of the house. He was looking at something on his phone, but when he looked up and saw Truth his expression became closed. 'Hi, Mike.' Truth was casual, and Pauline realised immediately who it was.

'Hello,' she said, smiling. 'I'm Pauline, Truth's mum.'

But Mike only nodded in greeting without introducing himself and went back to his phone, headed for the door to his flat. Truth, clearly embarrassed, ran ahead up the stairs.

✧

Morah had not been idle. She had planned her day – to dust and hoover the landings – for just such an opportunity as was being presented to her now. It was the only hope she had of catching Truth's mother alone. Doctor Ed had warned everyone to give Evelyn privacy and space when her children were visiting – but Morah knew perfectly well he was referring in particular to her. 'I have better things to be doing, frankly, doctor,' she had retorted. 'I'll probably be in Doctor Ari's house for most of the weekend,' she'd added for good measure.

Now, she had witnessed Truth run into Evelyn's flat, ahead of her mother – who was looking rather bemused at Mike's reaction in the hall as she began her ascent up the stairs. Morah took her time to assess the woman on her way up. In the strange lottery that makes up genetic inheritance, Pauline was as unlike Evelyn as it was possible to be. She was smaller, for starters, with features that were reassuringly nondescript. Her hair, which had clearly been dark, was now pepper and salt, flecked generously with grey, and cut in a short, no-nonsense style. But it was the warmth of the smile she greeted her with that took Morah most by surprise. 'Hello!' she said. 'You must be Morah. I'm Pauline, Truth's mum. She's told me all about you, and how helpful you've been to my mother. It's lovely to finally meet you.'

'Likewise,' Morah said, shaking the hand she offered. 'Look,' Morah took a furtive glance around her, 'there's not much time . . . I need to be frank with you, if I may?'

Pauline looked taken aback. 'Of course, go ahead.'

'The fellow you just met downstairs, Mike . . .' Morah nodded in the direction of the hall where the terse exchange had taken place. 'He's very disappointed about Truth, you know.'

'Why?' Pauline was mystified.

'Ever since your mother told him Truth was engaged to the lawyer fellow who came over – Josh, his name was.'

'Truth isn't engaged to anybody!' Pauline was indignant.

'That's what I thought.' Morah looked at her meaningfully. 'But you can understand how Mike would be upset at Truth keeping something like that from him – if it were true, that is – when they were beginning to get to know each other, if you get my drift. I think he's quite cut up about it, to be honest. That's all I wanted to say to you. I hope you don't mind but I thought it was my duty. Now I must be getting on,' Morah said. 'I hope you enjoy your visit.'

'Thank you,' said Pauline, taking her arm. 'I mean that – I'm very grateful to you, it explains a lot.'

'You're very welcome, I'm sure.'

✦

Back in the flat, the remains of lunch had been cleared. Evelyn and Tristan were deep in conversation and Truth had disappeared into her room.

'Did you have a nice stroll and catch-up?' Evelyn asked. She was relaxed and looking cheerful in her armchair.

'Yes, it was very interesting, actually.'

'There's some more wine there if you'd care to help yourself – will you have some more, Tristan? It's in the kitchen, on the counter – be a dear and go and get it.'

Pauline followed him in to the small room, and took him by the arm. 'Forget the wine. You need to go out now. Tell Truth you want to see the castle, or somewhere, anywhere . . . to paint it . . . make any excuse – I don't care what you say – just take Truth out and leave me and Mum alone. I need to talk to her.'

'What's brought this on?' Tristan was suspicious. 'Are you going to make some sort of scene? Because things are going so well . . .'

'No, I'm not. Look, this is probably the only chance I'm going to get to say some things to her – things I really need to say, mother/daughter stuff.'

'But you'll have lots of chances . . . why now?'

'Because I'm in just the right frame of mind. Look, I can't explain it – but this sort of thing really freaks me out, Tris, and it's been so long . . . maybe it was lunch or the wine . . . I don't know – but I just know this is the right time – please, just indulge me, will you? I'll tell Truth – she'll understand.'

He sighed. 'Fine. Just let me top up Mum's glass – do you want some?'

'No, thanks, you're fine.'

'What are you doing in there, Tristan?' Evelyn called from the sitting room. 'Can't you see it?'

'Here we are.' He brought out the bottle while Pauline went to find Truth.

'I need you to do something for me,' she said to her daughter, when she found her about to come back and join them.

'What?'

Pauline repeated what she'd just said to Tristan. 'I really need to do this now, Truth. I can't explain why, exactly. But I've never asked you to do anything for me before – have I?'

'Well, no . . .' Truth looked at her searchingly. 'It's just – well – I guess if it means you and Evelyn finally putting things behind you . . .'

'Oh, it will. I'm sure of it.'

'Well, then . . . sure. I might go for a swim, the tide's right – Tristan can come with me and look around or whatever.'

'Perfect.'

'I wouldn't mind some fresh air,' Tristan said, stretching.

'I was just thinking of going for a swim – why don't you come down to Mariner's Cove with me?' Truth emerged, followed by Pauline.

'God bless your energy,' Pauline said. 'She must take after you, Mum.'

'Yes, she does, in many ways,' Evelyn said. But her expression was wary. 'Won't you get some fresh air when you walk home, Tristan?' The implication was clear. 'Why rush out now?'

'It's the light. It's perfect,' he said, averting his gaze from Pauline, who stifled a smile. 'I can get some shots on my phone and keep them to paint when I get back to New York – do a Dublin collection. See you very soon, Mum.' He dropped a kiss on Evelyn's head, who smiled on cue but sat up a little straighter.

When Truth and Tristan had left, Pauline sat down on the sofa, opposite Evelyn, and looked her in the eye.

'You know . . . I really had hoped . . . as much for Truth's sake as my own, that perhaps it was true, and you maybe *had* changed, or developed more of a conscience during these intervening years, but clearly that was wishful thinking.'

Evelyn gave a laboured sigh. 'I knew it was too good to be true. I knew you'd insist on making some sort of scene when you got here. And I was right. At least neither of us disappoint. So let's have it. You have my full attention, and as you can see,' she indicated her crutch, 'I'm still in a semi-incapacitated state, so you'll have a captive audience . . . but I warn you, Pauline – I really won't stand for any histrionics. I'm just too old. There's nothing to be gained from dragging the past up again – nothing whatsoever. Why don't you join Tristan and Truth and go for another walk. It'll save you having to breathe the same air as me, which you clearly find so objectionable.'

'Not until I've said what I need to say. And I won't be dragging up the past either – at least not the one you're thinking of. The past I want to address is a good deal more recent.'

'What do you mean?'

'I mean . . . that you had no right – none whatsoever – to interfere in Truth's friendship with Mike, downstairs.' Pauline's eyes flashed. 'How bloody dare you!'

Evelyn looked at her as if she had taken leave of her senses and she made a small sound of disbelief. 'Pauline, I have no idea what on earth you're talking about!'

'Oh, I think you do. I think you know exactly what I'm talking about, but if you need your memory jogged . . . according to Morah – who overheard the whole exchange – I believe you told Mike that Truth was engaged to Josh. That was an out-and-out lie, and you know it.'

'I didn't know any such thing!' Evelyn was indignant. 'The man had come over with an engagement ring! He showed it to me! And Morah – for your information – is a very strange woman who Doctor Ed employs out of the kindness of his heart. You can't believe a word she says. She's a complete fantasist – among other things.'

Pauline refused to be distracted. 'Josh tried a last-ditch attempt to get Truth back after she had broken up with him. I heard all about it, after the event. But I'm guessing you didn't like the idea of Truth and Mike getting together and saw your chance to put your spoke in as usual – and instead of waiting to see, or should I say, *care*, what Truth wanted or was going through, you seized your chance to make what *you* wanted happen. It's always about you . . . isn't it?'

'That is an outrageous accusation! I was only ever acting

in Truth's best interests . . . something I'm not sure you're capable of doing!'

'I've devoted my whole life to acting in Truth's best interests . . . not that you'd know anything about it.'

'And what a life it's been, Pauline . . . drugs . . . squats . . . council flats . . . a marvellous start for any child, I'm sure . . . no wonder her father left you . . .'

Pauline forced herself to breathe. 'That was the past, Mum. I've worked very hard to make good on that, and I have no regrets whatsoever about how I brought Truth up. She's a credit to both Tony and me, but most of all, to herself. And yes, I kept her away from you, and I'm glad I did. If you'd had your way she'd be as vain and manipulative as you are. I wasn't going to have that. Truth is her own woman. She's strong and kind and confident and we don't play games with each other.'

'Is that so?' Evelyn gave a little smile. 'You might be surprised to discover you don't know all you think you do about her.'

'What's that supposed to mean?'

'Well, were you aware she's being harassed by a group of thugs on the computer?'

'What are you talking about?'

'I didn't think you were . . .' Evelyn said, failing to hide her triumph. 'Josh told me all about it . . . apparently Truth also confided in our neighbour next door – another very eligible man who clearly found her attractive, a surgeon. But the point is, these awful people – whoever they are – have been hounding her, threatening her, all sorts of dreadful carry-on. It was part of the reason she came over here – to get away from it all, I suppose – but she won't discuss it with anyone. Something needs to be done about it.'

Pauline was momentarily speechless. She shook her head as if to clear it. She felt her stomach clench uncomfortably. She should have known Evelyn would have a low blow up her sleeve – and this one hurt. But she couldn't let it weaken her resolve to make her mother undo her latest destructive interfering. 'Fine, I'll ask her about it. I'm sure she has her reasons . . . But right now I want you to ring Mike or go downstairs and tell him you got it wrong about Truth being engaged. I mean it, Mum, if you don't . . .'

'I don't have his number.' Evelyn looked stubborn.

'Truth mentioned there's a WhatsApp group for the house – you'll have it on your phone, won't you? Give it to me – I'll find Mike's number. If you don't . . . I'll tell Truth what you've done.'

Evelyn weighed up her options. 'I've done you a favour telling you about this computer business. If I agree to ring Mike, tell him I got things mixed up, confused . . . whatever . . . you have to promise not to tell her.' Evelyn shifted in her chair. 'I don't want her to hate me like you do.'

'You mean you don't want to get found out. I don't hate you, Mum.' Pauline gave a long sigh. 'We just weren't cut out to be mother and daughter. It happens sometimes. You made it very clear I was a disappointment to you from as far back as I can remember. You had zero interest in me – you left me alone or with nannies at every possible opportunity.'

'Oh, for heaven's sakes! I was a young woman . . . I had a life! You were always an awkward child . . .'

'Look. Just make the phone call. Do it now.'

'And you promise you won't tell Truth?'

'Not if you stay out of her business and behave. I think we can both be civilised about things at this stage of our lives.' Pauline handed Evelyn her phone. 'Don't you?'

Evelyn pressed the dial button, took a breath, and fixed a bright smile on her face. 'Hello, is that Mike? Yes, yes, I know it must be a surprise to get a call from me, but you needn't worry, this won't take a minute . . . the thing is, I wanted to apologise to you . . . Oh, yes there is . . . you see I sort of got the wrong end of the stick the other day when you dropped by for Truth . . . she isn't engaged at all to that law-yer chap. Never was, ever, apparently. He was just a rather impulsive work colleague who's had an enormous crush on her . . . and she ordered him to go home on the same day . . . Yes . . . you see he spun a real yarn to me and I'm afraid I fell for it, old idiot that I am. Oh, no I *am* . . . I'm not myself at all since the operation, usually I'd be very on the ball . . . but the thing is, I'm always *scrupulous* about put-ting my hand up when I'm wrong about something . . . *mea culpa*, and all that . . . and I'm afraid this time I've been *very* wrong. And . . . although it pains me to say it . . . Truth has been very upset about the whole thing. She doesn't know, obviously, about our little exchange. I kept it to myself, as you asked me to . . . but I think she's terribly disappointed not to have, eh, heard from you . . . I understand you two were becoming great friends . . . I'd so hate to think I'd done anything at all to upset that . . . Might you have a word with her, sometime . . .? Put things . . . right? Oh, and while we're on the subject . . . I would be so appreciative if you kept this to yourself . . . Truth would be horrified if she thought I'd given you the wrong impression . . . You do understand, don't you, Mike . . .?'

Evelyn finished the call and looked Pauline in the eye. 'Well, I've kept my end of the bargain,' she said. 'Are you going to keep yours?'

'Yes, I am.' Pauline frowned. 'But only because I don't think Truth needs to know she has a grandmother who would wilfully lie to someone she was clearly interested in getting to know. What you did was wrong, Mum. The only reason I'm not telling Truth is because soon she'll be back in London and safely away from any further attempts at manipulation. But if you ever pull a stunt like that again – all bets are off.'

'Fine by me,' Evelyn said.

Chapter Forty

'Sorry?' Stella was roused from her stupor. 'I was miles away, there.' She was sitting in the garden with Morah and Doctor Ed, while Freddy played with a toy boat. At six in the evening it was still a reassuringly warm July day, and although they were mostly in the shade, Morah was wearing a wide-brimmed floppy sun hat she had taken to producing any time she was in the garden. 'Doctor Ari told me it's very important that I protect my complexion,' she said. 'It's very delicate.'

'I was just wondering had the place on the avenue sold yet?' Doctor Ed was asking Stella.

She had to focus. It was becoming increasingly difficult. She was suffering from acute insomnia, and when she did drop off fitfully, she had terrifying nightmares. The most recent – just last night – had been so real she'd been convinced she was awake. In the dream she had been paralysed in her bed, unable to move a muscle, while sinister unseen intruders had broken into her flat and stolen Freddy – right before her eyes. She had tried to scream and couldn't manage that either. When she'd finally woken in a lather of terror – she'd been so convinced she would find Freddy gone when she ran into his room that she had collapsed by his bed and sobbed. She knew she needed to see her doctor, to talk to someone about the escalating panic and overwhelm she was experiencing – but the thought that Bruce might use the knowledge against her in a prospective custody case frightened her more. So she bought more natural medicines at the health shop and availed of some Valium a friend of her mother's, recently back from a trip to Thailand, had procured.

'Um, it's still under offer as far as I know. They haven't completed yet, anyway.'

'It'll be interesting to see what it goes for eventually.'

'I'll enquire when I'm back in the office tomorrow.'

'Oh, no need . . . I was just curious. How are you getting on in Ari's place, Morah?' Doctor Ed asked her. 'I bet it makes number 24 look a bit shabby by comparison . . .?'

'They're very different properties, doctor – different decorating styles entirely, as Nessa I'm sure has told you.' Morah didn't altogether approve of the burgeoning relationship between the two neighbours. 'However, for my own part I would choose number 24 every time. A house is so much more than its interior decoration – it's the general ambience that's important, and I have always felt that number 24 is a particularly happy house in that respect.'

'Well, I'm very glad you feel that way, Morah. Number 24 certainly owes a great deal to the care you take of it.'

Stella was tuning out again. She wasn't entirely sure when she became aware of Bruce and Annika's voices carrying down the garden, but when she turned around to look, Freddy had taken off and was running to Annika, throwing himself against her with abandon. But then everything turned black . . . and she was paralysed again, just like she had been in the nightmare last night. She was trying to scream . . . trying to breathe . . . something was immobilising her . . . pinning her to the chair . . . and Freddy was being taken away . . .

And then Doctor Ed's voice . . .'Stella, Stella . . . are you alright? Can I get you anything?' He was looking concerned as his face swam into view. 'Morah, fetch Stella a glass of water from the bunker, please.'

When her vision cleared, Bruce and Annika were nowhere to be seen, and Freddy was standing in front of her looking worried. When Morah came rushing back with the water, Stella took a gulp and then got up, clutching Freddy to her.

'Take it easy, Stella, you took a bit of a funny turn there – must be the heat, I suppose,' said Doctor Ed. 'Why don't you just catch your breath for a minute? You almost fainted . . .'

'It's nothing. I'm fine,' she said tersely. 'C'mon, Freddy, it's time to go inside.'

✧

Morah sat down in Stella's vacated chair and looked after her as Stella dragged Freddy, all but running into the house. She shook her head. 'She's not well, that one . . . mark my words . . .'

'How do you mean, Morah?' Doctor Ed frowned.

Morah tapped her temple. 'I may not be the sharpest tool in the box, Doctor Ed, but I know when someone's beginning to unravel. When you've gone through it yourself . . . the warning signs are unmistakable.'

Doctor Ed looked thoughtfully up at the window of Stella's room. He hadn't noticed anything out of the ordinary about Stella up until the episode just now, which he had put down to a fainting spell at best, and a possible mini-stroke at worst. But the thought of mental illness hadn't crossed his mind. All the same, he knew better than to dismiss Morah's remark. She had been through some pretty rough mental health issues herself over the years. And there wasn't much that went on in the house that she missed. 'Thank you for drawing my attention to that, Morah. I'll make sure to keep an eye on Stella, try and have a friendly word with her, see if I can help at all.'

'I think that would be very wise, doctor.'

✧

It was Nessa's day off and she was having a leisurely afternoon swim with Truth. The good weather and summer holidays combined meant Mariner's Cove was particularly popular at this time, and the place was thronged with parents bringing little kids on a family outing, and a lot of bored-looking, fake-tanned young teenage girls standing chatting in waist-high water, tossing their hair. Their male counterparts larked about nearby, splashing and shouting, engaging in the age-old ritual of male attention-seeking. It was quite a struggle for Nessa and Truth to make their way to the water.

When they were out of earshot of the other bathers,

Nessa decided to seek Truth's advice. 'I need to ask you something . . . about Ari and me.'

'I was just going to ask you how things are going,' Truth said. 'If the way you're looking these days is any indication, clearly he's agreeing with you. You're positively glowing. Everyone's saying so.'

'Are they?' Nessa was pleased. 'Everyone except Morah, I'll bet. You know she looks after his house now too? I think she disapproves heartily of me being there at all. Not that I've stayed overnight or anything but . . . we've overlapped a few times when I've let myself in, and she either ignores me or is frostily polite.'

'You have a key? Well, that's good.'

'It's just easier . . . he's so busy with work it means I can get in before him and do some cooking or make things nice for him when he gets in.'

'I hope you're not doing too much for him, Nessa?' Truth said. '*He's* supposed to be showing *you* a good time, remember?'

'Oh, and he is . . . really. We've been to some amazing places – he's really thoughtful like that.'

'I'm glad to hear it. I bet he can't believe his luck at finding someone like you.'

'Well, that's the thing . . .'

'What?'

'He's being really thoughtful and charming and entertaining and everything . . . but we're not moving things on . . . otherwise, if you get my drift.'

'You mean he hasn't asked you to bring your toothbrush with you?'

'Exactly . . . and I'm wondering how to . . . nudge things along a little. Don't get me wrong, everything between us is great in that respect – really good chemistry – but a few romantic kissing sessions are as far as we've got. I'm just feeling a bit confused, that's all – what do you think I should do?'

'Talk to him,' Truth said. 'It's always the best thing. You need to ask him.'

'But what if he doesn't find me attractive that way?'

'Oh, Nessa, don't be ridiculous, of course he finds you attractive – you said yourself the chemistry was there.'

'Well, *I* think so . . . but maybe he doesn't. And what if it's like some old Greek or Argentinian tradition? He's from a really posh family . . .'

'You mean like he's protecting your honour?' Truth was amused.

'That's just it – I don't know what he's doing – I haven't a clue what's going on. And I really don't want to ask him – it'll ruin the lovely romantic vibe we have. It's kind of old-fashioned and courtly . . . he's such a gentleman – and so appreciative of every little thing I do for him.'

'You still need to ask him.' Truth was firm. 'It's the only way you're going to find out what's going on.'

'I might try something first . . .'

'What?'

'Well, just setting the scene a bit more – you know . . . making it a bit more obvious where I'd like things to be going . . . a romantic dinner . . . suggest staying over, just see what happens . . .'

'I still think you should talk to him first.'

'But that will spoil the mood – I'd much rather be spontaneous.' Nessa was warming to her theme. 'That's if I can manage to set up a nice seduction scene with Morah around – but I don't think she's coming in this Friday, now that I think of it. It would be perfect!'

'Well, good luck,' Truth said. 'I'll be dying to hear how it goes. Just be careful, Ness . . .'

'Of what?'

'Of you.'

'Oh, Truth . . .' said Nessa, kicking her feet up as she turned on her front to swim for home. 'You don't have to worry. I've never been happier.'

✧

It had taken some ingenuity – and a lot of hard work – because Morah seemed to have an uncanny sixth sense that Nessa was trying to plan something special, and seemed intent on thwarting her at every opportunity. Nessa had decided to go all out. She was making a special lamb tagine she knew Ari loved. That was the easy part. Champagne was chilling in the wine fridge, but it was the other, more intimate details she was itching to implement that were posing a problem. The specially procured rose petals she wanted to trail up the back stairs and into the bedroom. The mosquito net she had borrowed from a set-designer friend which would turn the already luxurious bed into a seductive, safari-like cocoon. The massage oils she wanted to leave by the bed . . . all of these were impossible to arrange while Morah was prowling around the house radiating suspicion. Just when Nessa thought she had finished, having mopped the already immaculate floor, Morah took out a pile of ironing and set up the board where she had blocked access to the kitchen exit and therefore the back stairs. It was driving Nessa slowly insane. Ari was due back in under half an hour – the whole day's preparations would go to waste if she couldn't set the stage now. Then inspiration struck – Nessa texted Truth to ask Doctor Ed to invent an excuse to request Morah's presence back at number 24 immediately. She never knew what the invented pretext was, but ten minutes later Morah answered her phone, shook her head, and said, 'Isn't that just typical,' and put away the ironing board reluctantly. 'I'm needed at number 24,' she said to Nessa. 'Tell Doctor Ari I'll make up the time tomorrow – I can come in early.' She slanted her a look. 'Very early. He won't even know I'm here,' she said.

Nessa almost wept with relief.

So the rose petals were strewn, the mosquito net hung, the massage oils left beside the bed. By the time Ari got home, the tagine was perfect, the champagne was ready to pour, and Nessa was wearing her favourite silky lingerie underneath her summer dress.

'How pretty you look!' Ari said, as he came through the hall and discovered Nessa in the kitchen. 'And what is that wonderful smell?'

'Lamb tagine – just the way you like it,' Nessa said as they embraced. 'And we have time for a glass of champagne first.' She handed him a flute. 'To the weekend.'

'I'll drink to that.' He took a sip and put the glass down.

'I think I'll just run upstairs and take a quick shower, then I'll join you—'

'Oh, no, don't . . . you can do that later,' Nessa said. 'Stay and talk to me – I've been looking forward to seeing you all day.'

Ari shook his head. 'What did I ever do to deserve such a wonderful woman coming into my life?'

Over dinner, Ari told her about his day, and Nessa listened, prompting him occasionally. After the tagine, there was a feather-light orange soufflé, and while they lingered over coffee Ari looked at her, puzzled. 'Is there something you're not telling me?' he said. 'You're being . . . different this evening.'

'That's because I feel differently.'

'About what?'

'Us?'

'How do you mean?' He sat back in his chair.

'I think it's time we . . . moved things on a bit.' Nessa stood up and held out her hand. 'Don't you?'

Ari took her hand and followed her, as she led him through the kitchen and to the back stairs, where the trail of rose petals began. 'Nessa? What is this?'

'Do you really have to ask?' she said, smiling as they reached the landing and she pulled him into the bedroom.

'Nessa . . .' Ari took in the rose petals, the oils, the net draped over the bed. 'This is . . . it's amazing . . . you're amazing . . . but I have to stop you – it's just not the right time . . .'

'What do you mean?' Nessa felt the first chill of the day.

'Come back downstairs with me – please. I have something I need to explain to you.'

She followed him, hollow-hearted now, back to the kitchen, as he filled their glasses with what remained in the bottle and sat down, pulling her gently to sit down too. 'There is something I had totally forgotten about – you know what a scatterbrain I am . . . when I become involved in my work everything else goes out the window.'

'I don't understand what difference—'

'I was going to tell you after dinner, but then, well, I hadn't anticipated . . .' He rubbed his forehead. 'What I had forgotten is that tomorrow my ex-wife and my two children are arriving for a week. It had completely slipped my mind until my secretary reminded me – you must believe me. I didn't even remember to ask Morah to prepare the bedrooms . . .'

Nessa was perplexed. 'But what does that matter, why should—?'

'I'm trying to explain, as gently as I can, that while the thought of being intimate with you is more than wonderful . . . tonight is just not the right time. Believe me, you have no idea how sorry I am, but you . . . us . . . taking this to the next level is not something I would wish to rush, under any circumstances – especially when my ex-wife is due to arrive . . .'

'Why is she coming here at all?' Nessa hated her petulant tone.

'She always travels with the children, it's just how she is . . . I think she likes to check up on me from time to time.'

'Will I meet her?'

'I think not.' Ari was looking at her kindly. 'I'm not sure it would be a pleasant experience for you. Elena can be . . . let's say cold, at best.'

A knot of bitter disappointment settled in Nessa's stomach. 'So I was just someone to fill in the time for you?'

'Nessa, nothing could be further from the truth.' Ari took the hand she had pulled away. 'But I go back to Boston in three weeks' time . . . I thought you understood that.'

'I did. I do . . .'

'Well, in my experience, long-distance relationships simply don't work. On top of that, I am married to my work. I hoped that you—'

'That I what? That I'd go quietly? That I wouldn't make a fuss? Make a scene like all the others . . .?'

He shook his head sadly. 'That you would understand. That's why I was . . . well, I was being careful not to take advantage of you.'

'What I understand is that I've made a complete idiot of myself again.'

'Nessa, that's not true. You are a wonderful, beautiful, sexy, generous woman – one who has become a dear friend, very dear to my heart. I just don't want to take advantage of your incredibly giving nature. It's what I most love about you . . . but a relationship between us just isn't going to work. I have to go back to my life in Boston and you must stay here . . . in your beautiful part of Dublin. I think you know that's the only outcome here. Anything else I promised you would be dishonest of me.'

'Well, we can't have that, can we?' Nessa began to load the dishwasher.

'Please, Nessa. Leave that – you don't need to—'

'While I'm at it, I may as well get the stupid mosquito net from the bedroom. You can keep the rest of it. Share it with your ex-wife, maybe. Oh, and before I forget, Morah is planning to come in tomorrow morning, early. She'll also be very happy not to find me here.'

'Nessa, please. Don't leave things like this . . .'

But Nessa had disappeared upstairs. When she returned, with her overnight bag, she paused. 'I know you never promised me anything, Ari . . . but you told me I was special, and wonderful, and a woman in a million. You were also very generous and affectionate with me when we were together. Is it any wonder I might have hoped there would be something more serious between us? After all . . . if a woman is all of those things to a man, geographical distance should hardly be an obstacle. Maybe you should think about that before you tell the next woman in your life how wonderful she is.'

And with that, Nessa let herself out, leaving Ari sitting forlornly behind her. For an instant she allowed herself to savour the satisfaction of leaving him with a suitably chastening remark that he might reflect upon – but that was only because she was desperate to get back to her flat in number 24 before the full misery, defeat, and prospective loneliness of her latest romantic let-down struck home with full force.

Chapter Forty-One

Since the incident in Stella's flat, Bruce had been careful never to have a conversation with her alone, except over the phone. He was meeting her now in the front hall of number 24 to hand Freddy back to her after an afternoon spent at the beach, just the two of them, Bruce and Freddy – Annika had been at work, and although Bruce would never have allowed Stella's outburst to prevent Annika joining them, all the same he was relieved to be able to suggest the outing and confirm it was just father and son. As they came through the front door, Freddy brandishing a bucket and spade and Bruce a deepening tan, Stella was standing by the hall table looking pointedly at her watch.

'Mummy, we made huge castles and dug rivers so the sea came right up to them!' Freddy said.

'That's nice, sweetie. I hope Daddy remembered your sunblock.'

'Daddy always does, doesn't he, champ?'

'Icky,' said Freddy, sitting down on the floor and banging the upturned bucket.

'I wanted to remind you about the fair day,' Bruce said.

'What about it?'

'Well, it's my weekend. I'll be taking Freddy, Annika's

helping set up some of the art stands for a bit, I said I'd go along and help her. There'll be plenty for Freddy to do there – it means you're free for the day.'

'No.'

'Sorry?'

'You heard me. I said no.' Stella's voice was flat and cold. 'You're not taking him to the fair and you're not having him anywhere near that woman.'

For a moment Bruce just looked at her.

'What's the matter with you, Stella – really?' Bruce was genuinely concerned. 'What will it take for you to accept that Annika has no interest or incentive to take Freddy from you? She's simply my partner and you have to get used to her being around when I have Freddy.' Bruce sighed.

'Nothing is the matter with me. I have simply decided that I will not allow my son to be anywhere near someone who is deliberately scheming to take him away from me. I offered you a chance to come home to us. You've made your choice, so now you can deal with the consequences.'

'I think you'll find you are not the one in control of any consequences here,' Bruce said.

'What's that supposed to mean?'

'That I've contacted my lawyer about this. You should be hearing from her any day now. I've had enough, Stella. I gave in to you at every juncture, I bent over backwards to make you happy, to accommodate your wishes – mostly so I could be sure of Freddy's happiness and well-being – but you've pushed me too far. This nonsense isn't going to go on for a second longer. There'll be no more Mr Nice Guy, Stella – you've got a full-blown fight on your hands. I hope you're ready for it.'

'Bring it on!' Stella shouted.

Bruce just looked at her and shook his head. Then he turned on his heel and went out to the garden, mostly so he didn't have to listen to the heart-breaking sound of his son beginning to cry.

✧

Doctor Ed wasn't just concerned about Stella. He was now concerned about Bruce, and most of all about Freddy and what Stella's escalating aggravation was doing to him. He found Bruce sitting with his head in his hands by the garden pond and asked him what on earth was wrong.

Bruce had to take a few breaths before he could speak. He was close to tears, Doctor Ed realised. 'I can't take any more of this – I really can't.'

'What is it, Bruce?' Doctor Ed sat down beside him on the bench. 'What's going on? You can talk to me – you know you can.'

'It's Stella,' Bruce said. 'I think she's losing the plot. I really do. She's objecting to Annika being anywhere near Freddy and says that Annika is plotting to steal him from her. The worst part is I really think she believes that.'

'Well, these situations can be very stressful for a couple.'

'But everything was so amicable before . . . now we're facing a full-scale custody battle, and the mother usually wins, doesn't she?' Bruce fought to keep his emotions under control. 'I couldn't bear to lose my son, Doctor Ed. I won't let that happen. I won't.'

'I'm quite sure it won't come to that, Bruce. You're a

wonderful parent – everyone here can testify to that. But I am concerned about Stella . . . I do think – with your permission of course – that it might be an idea for me to have a word with her. It might make her feel more supported, if she's feeling threatened.'

Bruce looked at him gratefully. 'Oh, would you, Doctor Ed? That would be brilliant – just to know you were keeping a friendly eye on things would reassure me hugely.'

'Well, that's all it will be, Bruce. I certainly won't be acting in any medical capacity – but I'm more than happy to have a word with her – to reassure her in any way I can.'

✧

It was the end of the week, but Stella's day was not going well. When she had dropped Freddy off at her mother's for the day, her mum, Maureen, had said that Freddy had told her the day before that his mummy was cross all the time and that Daddy and Annika's flat was much more fun. 'Who's Annika?' Maureen asked.

'Bruce's girlfriend.' Stella was terse.

Maureen shook her head. 'I warned you. I saw him last week, did I tell you? In Tesco Dundrum. I was looking at the tall, attractive man across the aisle and I couldn't believe it was Bruce.' Maureen was wide-eyed. 'He didn't see me,' she added. 'But I'm not surprised he's been snapped up. He was always very good-natured. Are you sure you're happy about him seeing someone else? Do you not think it might be an idea to have him round for a friendly dinner or something? You know, before this one gets her claws into him too much . . .'

'It won't last. Trust me.'

Maureen didn't look convinced as she stood at the door with Freddy, waving Stella off.

Stella had gripped the steering wheel so tightly on her way to work her knuckles ached all morning.

Now her boss, Simon, had called her into his office for a quick chat. She was already behind on her emails and had a viewing in under forty-five minutes to show a house in the next suburb. 'I'm very busy, Simon, can we—?'

'This won't take long, Stella, have a seat.' He indicated the chair in front of his desk.

She tried not to look impatient as she sat down, remembering just then the promotion at work Nessa had predicted in her tarot card reading.

'We've been having some feedback from clients, Stella.'

She smiled and nodded.

'Rather worrying feedback.' Simon's eyebrows lifted.

'What do you mean?' She was indignant.

'Well,' Simon proceeded carefully, 'reports have reached us of some . . . erratic behaviour, on your part.'

'I beg your pardon?'

'Bear with me here if you would, Stella. This is . . . delicate,' Simon went on. 'We've had two reports of you being . . . shall we say . . . distracted – at properties you were showing. To be, uh, specific you appeared to be talking to yourself . . . or to someone no one else could see . . .'

Stella's clasped hands dug into her thigh.

'There have also been reports of things being . . . rearranged . . . at properties you have shown, including the entire contents of a wine cellar – which caused great distress to the vendor concerned.' Simon looked at her. 'Stella, is everything alright at home?'

'It's fine. Everything's fine.'

'I see. You know you can take some time if you—'

'I don't. I don't need any time – I just need to get to my next viewing, which I'll be late for if I don't get a move on.'

'Ah, I was just coming to that, Stella,' Simon said. 'I think in light of whatever stress you seem to be experiencing, it would be better for everyone concerned if you stuck to admin duties for the moment. Karen and Laura will be taking over all your viewings for the short term. After that, well, we'll see how things go, shall we? In the meantime, it is my duty as your supervisor and managing director to advise you to seek professional help in this matter. I'm sure your GP could recommend someone.' He made a sympathetic face.

'I am not suffering from any stress!' Stella shouted – banging the door on her way out.

That evening, she picked Freddy up, tight-lipped.

'He's been dying to see you, love,' Maureen said, handing him over. 'Haven't you, sweetheart? And he's been the best boy for me, we had great fun.'

'Thanks, Mum,' Stella said, not meeting her mother's eyes.

'What's the matter, Stella?'

'Nothing,' she said, fastening Freddy into his car seat. 'Everything's fine.'

'You don't look fine . . .' Maureen was concerned. She waved at Freddy in his seat as he looked out the window at her. 'Have you anything nice planned for the weekend, love?'

'What do you think?' said Stella, getting into the car and driving off.

✧

Nessa was not relishing the prospect of yet another looming, lonely weekend. She was too mortified to ring Truth and tell her what had transpired with Ari, and besides, Truth had her family visiting. Nessa still had a few bottles of wine in her flat that Ari had left there, and though it pained her to think of anything at all to do with him, she felt the least she could do was drink one. It was that or give them away, and they were too good a vintage to waste. The worst of it was, though, that she knew that this was only the beginning. As the days and weeks went by she would feel increasingly worse, ever more hopeless. That's how the pattern unfolded. Nessa wasn't prone to depression, but she'd had a brush with something that felt very like it once or twice – and it was always after a man she had mistakenly thought she might have a future with who subsequently left her that the abject misery would creep up on her. Now, though, she was still in the righteous anger stage, and she wanted to prolong it for as long as she could. She'd been short with everyone in the café, which was most unlike her. Then up at the castle, when she had been going over the plan for the stalls, she had barely passed the time of day with Paddy, or even raised a laugh at his latest joke. Poor Paddy had been wounded. She was on her way back to her flat now, with two bags of shopping she had picked up, and she felt irritation flare again as a small group of cheering onlookers appeared to be gathered outside number 24.

'Excuse me!' She attempted to barge through the few young fellas and old ladies blocking her way. 'I need to get through here, please . . . do you *mind*? I *live* here.'

And that was when she saw him. Ryan, her ex, seemed to be putting on some kind of bizarre show with – of all people – Rory. As far as Nessa could make out, through her confusion, this display consisted of Ryan trying to dodge past Rory and get to the open front door of number 24. But as sure as Ryan hurled himself towards the entrance of the house, Rory would block him and push him back, effortlessly . . . almost playfully . . . although the expression on Rory's face was anything but. The onlookers, unaware of Nessa's bewilderment, were shouting encouragement and the odds. 'Nice one, man!' a young fella said as Rory blocked an increasingly infuriated Ryan yet again. This was followed by Ryan pausing to catch his breath then charging at Rory with a headbutt – but Rory's abs might as well have been a brick wall.

'Ryan!' Nessa said, horrified. 'What the hell is going on?'

'Nessa!' Ryan looked relieved. 'Finally!' He made his way over to her. 'This fucker wouldn't let me in when I rang the bell – I told him who I was and how you were expecting me, but he wouldn't budge. Tell him!' Ryan was panting with the exertion of it all. He pointed an accusing finger at Rory.

'Don't know who this guy is, Nessa.' Rory's eyes narrowed. 'Never seen you before, mate – don't like your attitude, either. No one gets into Nessa's flat unless she expressly lets them in herself.'

'Who is this guy? Some mad security head?' Ryan was angry. 'Tell him, Ness!'

'Nice to see you too, Ryan.' Nessa put down the bags wearily.

'Aw, c'mere, honey!' Ryan changed tack and lunged at her for a hug and a kiss. 'It's good to see you, Ness' – he squeezed her, winking – 'even if there's a bit more of you since I saw you last, eh? Guess that's the problem when you work in a café, yeah? Too much temptation . . .' He laughed. 'C'mon, let's go upstairs . . . I'm starving!'

Suddenly Nessa found herself unable to move. It was as if there was nothing left, no fight, no anger, no strength. Her legs were beginning to quiver and she just wanted to make it to the front steps and collapse. It was a minute before she realised she was crying.

But she didn't need to stand up, because Rory had lifted her up in his arms and stood glowering at Ryan. 'Sling your hook, mate – or I'll do it for you. Nessa doesn't need the likes of you around.'

A cheer went up from the onlookers.

'What the f—?' Ryan wasn't following. 'Nessa, tell him!'

'You heard me. Take yourself and your suitcase some-place else, pal. No vacancies here. Show's over, folks.' And with that Rory carried Nessa over the threshold of number 24 and kicked the door shut behind him.

When he put her down gently outside flat 2, she tried lamely to protest and go back for her shopping. 'I'll get it, Nessa. It'll wait. There's something I need to say to you.' Rory wasn't going to be deflected now – he'd missed way too many opportunities already. 'I love you, Nessa. I've loved you since the first minute I set eyes on you. You're the only girl in the world for me.' He wiped the tears from her face with a thumb. 'I'm not good enough for you – no one's good enough for you! You're, you're . . . a . . . a . . . goddess! But if you'll let me, I'll spend the rest of my life making you as happy as I possibly can. I promise I'll devote every minute, of every hour, of every day – except when I'm training, but even then I'll be thinking about it – to making your life as good as it can be. Will you let me try, Nessa? Will you, please?'

And Nessa began to cry all over again. 'You'd better come in.' She half sobbed and half laughed.

✧

Back in her flat upstairs, things hadn't improved for Stella. She had fed and changed Freddy and put him in front of the TV to watch a favourite cartoon until it was bedtime. Now she was pacing up and down her living room with a glass of wine in hand when her door buzzer sounded. Putting the glass on the counter, she went to answer it, hoping it might be Bruce, come to make peace. But it was Doctor Ed. Stella's face dropped.

'Stella, may I come in for a moment? I've brought you some flowers . . . the dahlias are being particularly bountiful this year and I've been distributing a few to my tenants. I thought you might like some.'

Stella stood back to allow him in, reluctantly. 'That's very kind of you, Doctor Ed.'

'Not at all, not at all,' he said, handing them over. 'I must say I do like how you've arranged the flat so cleverly – I'd never have thought of this sort of furniture – you have very good taste.' He looked around the room. 'Hello, Fred!' Freddy waved at him and turned back to the TV. Doctor Ed caught sight of the glass of wine on the counter. 'Well, I mustn't disturb you – I can see you're a busy woman!' he said.

'Would you like to join me in a glass of wine, doctor?' The invitation was half-hearted.

'What a kind offer! How could I possibly refuse?'

Stella listened to Doctor Ed's chatter about Evelyn, Morah, and Nessa, and tried to look interested, but her foot was swinging back and forth with exasperation. She saw the doctor glance at it and willed herself to keep still.

'The fair day will be upon us before we know it . . .' he was saying. 'And of course Mike's statue will be going up – that'll be something to behold. Will you be going to the fair, Stella? I'm sure Freddy is looking forward to it. Are you, Freddy?'

'Oh, we have other things to do, doctor. I doubt we'll make the fair day. It's always a bit of a bunfight, isn't it?'

'I must say I think it's wonderful how you and Bruce make things work so smoothly for little Freddy here. I have to admit I had my doubts initially about a newly separated couple moving in to the same house – but I discovered any reservations I had were completely groundless once I saw how both you and Bruce are such dedicated and devoted parents. It's such a great way of doing things. You're both an example to us all. Everyone thinks so.'

'You should try telling Bruce that.'

'I'm sure Bruce is well aware of the fact. He's always saying what a wonderful mother you are.'

'Is that so? Funny then that he's going to fight me for full custody of Freddy. I got a letter this morning threatening as much. Of course, it's all Annika's doing. She's trying to take Freddy away from me.' Stella gave a mirthless laugh. 'Steal my family. Destroy my life, make out I'm an unfit mother . . . Well, they can bring it on.'

'Destroy your life? Stella, I don't think—'

'She thinks I don't know it's her behind everything – but I'm not stupid. Do you know she's even lodged invented complaints about me at work?' Stella shook her head. 'My boss called me in today, said there had been complaints about properties I had shown – of course I knew immediately who was behind it. I've always been meticulous in my work. I'm very good at what I do, you know.'

'I'm sure you are, Stella, but—'

'That was a low blow,' she shook her head, 'but no more than I'd expect from her.'

'I really don't think—'

'No one ever does, Doctor Ed . . . do they? Not until something bad happens – then people say, *Oh, now that I think of it . . . I did notice such and such . . . but I thought nothing of it at the time . . .* Well, I'm on to her. That's all I'm saying.'

'Stella, you do know how highly I think of you and I want you to know you have my full support at all times . . . but if things are difficult at work and you need to talk to someone . . . I can recommend several marvellous—'

Stella interjected. 'You don't believe me, do you?'

'Of course I believe you, I'm just saying that sometimes it helps to talk these things over with a professional . . . there's no—'

'They put you up to this, didn't they?' Stella was cold. 'So that Bruce can prove I'm an unfit mother! God, I'm so stupid!' She stood up. 'I think you'd better go now, *doctor*.'

'Stella, please don't upset yourself – nothing could be further from the truth. I just want you to know I'm here for you . . . that's all.'

'I don't need your help, thank you, Doctor Ed – I don't need any help – Freddy and me will be perfectly alright on our own. Won't we Freddy?' But Freddy was totally immersed in his cartoon.

'Well, look after yourself, Stella – and my heartfelt apologies if I've upset you . . .' Doctor Ed was downcast as he left. 'It was certainly never my intention.'

Stella put Freddy to bed. Then she poured herself another glass of wine and sat staring ahead at the muted TV screen, until the flickering images cast kaleidoscopes of light in the growing darkness of the room.

Chapter Forty-Two

'Would you not talk to him?' Pauline looked at her daughter as Truth sat behind the wheel of Nessa's car, driving them to Glendalough. They had planned a nice walk and lunch afterwards.

'No, why should I?' Truth was tight-lipped. 'I'm not the one who stopped talking – he is.'

'But perhaps there's been some misunderstanding.'

'Such as?' Truth glanced at her.

'I don't know, but with Josh coming over and everything . . . who knows, he might have got the wrong end of the stick.'

'Josh was nowhere near him – and even if he was, don't you think he should at least ask for my side of the story?'

'He might not feel it's any of his business.'

'Why are you suddenly interested in Mike anyway?'

Pauline shrugged. 'He looked interesting . . . and I didn't buy the disinterested act in the hallway – he was rattled when he saw you. I just think it's worth finding out what's on his mind. Whatever's happened between you is clearly bothering *you*.'

'What's bothering me is that I thought he was different . . . clearly my judgement leaves a lot to be desired.'

'Or maybe you're right . . . and if you are, don't you think it's worth finding out?'

'Here we are.' Truth pulled off the road and into the car park of the beautiful setting of the medieval monastery.

They set off around the lower trail, pausing to look at the famous round tower and ruined church, surrounded by graves mottled by lichen and time. 'I think the last time I was here must have been a school trip.' Pauline paused to take a photo.

'Which school was that?'

'The posh one.'

'Was it awful?'

'Actually, no. It was very nice. It was a small boarding school, in a lovely old house, it had its own farm and the nuns were kind. It was me who was awful.'

'I've never heard you say that before!' Truth looked at her. 'Don't you think you're being a bit hard on yourself?'

'I was making them pay the price for my mother not wanting me around – it wasn't their fault.' Pauline kept walking. 'I didn't realise that then, of course. Every time I could get expelled from a school it would make life a bit harder for Evelyn. That was all I was interested in. I never stopped to think about the damage I might be causing to the other girls, or the teachers who actually cared about me and tried to help me. If I couldn't make my mother love me, I was going to make her pay for it.'

'Do you really believe that?' Truth said. 'That she doesn't love you?'

Pauline was quiet for a bit while she thought about the question. To their right the lake glinted in the sunlight, its depths reflecting ancient images. 'Yes. I do.' She looked at Truth. 'I know she was young when she had me – there's only twenty years between us – and I have an idea that was behind her wedding to my late father. Whether I was an unfortunate accident, or whether Evelyn deliberately trapped him by getting pregnant, I have no idea – but either way, she simply didn't have a maternal bone in her body as regards me. She literally couldn't bear to be around me. All my early memories are either with a variety of nannies, or my dad. I don't think I can remember one outing with her alone – ever. Children know, you know – when they're not wanted – they're not stupid, and Evelyn made it abundantly clear she didn't want me anywhere near her.'

'But . . .' Truth was struggling to make sense of what her mum was saying. 'She seems to get along well with Tristan.'

'Yes, you're right, she does. I thought I'd resent that, but I never did – probably because I was thrilled at the prospect of having a brother or sister after such a long time on my own. Although by then my dad had died and Evelyn was married to Lenny – Tristan's father. He was always kind to me, Lenny,' Pauline said, smiling. 'I think even that irritated Evelyn. But Tristan was her golden boy. He was a beautiful child – unlike me – maybe that mattered to her, or maybe age had mellowed her as regards him. Perhaps she was happier with Lenny than with my father? Who knows? But whatever it was . . . she never warmed to me, and like I said, even though I didn't understand it at the time, I was hurt, confused, and angry, and the only way I could get her to notice me at all was by causing as much trouble as I knew how – and I got quite good at that.' She looked at Truth.

'But it's no way to live and I wouldn't recommend it. Luckily it never seemed to affect my relationship with Tristan, either. We were always close, despite the age gap – although I know for a fact Evelyn tried to put her spoke in there too.'

'What? You mean she tried to come between you?'

'Oh yes, Tristan used to tell me what she'd said to him about me. She did her best to turn him against me, but happily she didn't succeed. If anything, it made us closer.'

'But why?' Truth was bewildered. 'Why would she do that? Why would any mother do that? It doesn't make sense.'

'I'm not sure she knows the answer to that, Truth. Self-awareness isn't part of Evelyn's repertoire. In my opinion she has narcissistic personality disorder. I've researched it quite a bit. That's the problem . . . they're very complex people. A therapist explained it to me once. Not everyone who's narcissistic has the personality disorder. There's a spectrum . . . like all of these things. Usually they're very charming and charismatic people. They tend not to show negative behaviour in the beginning, particularly in relationships. And they like to surround themselves with people who feed their ego. They build relationships to reinforce their ideas about themselves, even if those relationships are superficial. But *everything* is about them – and anything that isn't part of their agenda, or gets in the way of them getting what they want, is pretty rudely dismissed. Basically, what I keep coming back to is simply that having a daughter like me – who wasn't pretty or engaging – just didn't fit with her agenda, and so I was dismissed. It's as simple as that.'

'Well, I think you're beautiful *and* engaging.' Truth hugged Pauline.

'Thank you, sweetheart. That's sweet of you. But I gave up worrying about how I looked years ago. Tristan lucked out on the looks front, which is a large part, I suspect, of why Evelyn was able to bond with him in as much as she has . . . but I'm pretty sure if he was proving a problem to her in any other way, she'd be pretty quick to dump on him too. It's just who she is. Arguably, she can't help it. She's an extremely manipulative person.'

'I think I do know what you mean, though,' Truth said. 'In the beginning I didn't believe it, really. I just thought she was a bit of fun – a bit mad and old-fashioned in her ideas . . . but then she was pretty mean about Nessa, who you've met. And Nessa's the loveliest person you could ever come across. There isn't a bad bone in her body. And some of Evelyn's advice . . . well, let's just say it leaves a lot to be desired.'

Pauline laughed. 'I can only imagine. I knew she'd love having you around, though. You make her look good, you see. I bet she just loves introducing you as her granddaughter. My worry was that she'd try and manipulate you.' Pauline hesitated.

'I think I'm a bit long in the tooth for that kind of game,' Truth said. 'Particularly given what I do for a living.'

'That's true.' Pauline was thoughtful. 'But when we do let our guard down, it's usually with family members who press our buttons.'

'What do you mean?'

'Well, you said something the other day when we were coming back from our walk, by the foundations for Mike's sculpture . . . you said at least Grandma's happy – she thought you were mad looking at an impoverished artist . . .'

'So?'

'Well, that's exactly the kind of thing Evelyn *would* say to subtly dissuade you – to put you off someone.'

'Oh, I don't think so. I mean, she knows that nothing she said would hold any sway if I really liked someone. I mean, I didn't go for the guys she *did* like . . . Josh and herself had a real mutual admiration society going on.'

'But it's Mike that you're refusing to sound out.'

'Only because he blanked me!'

'As you would say yourself: (a) you don't know that, it's supposition, and (b) there's no hard evidence to indicate what, exactly, is behind his recent behaviour,' Pauline said.

'Whatever the reason or reasons are – I don't care.'

'Well, that's good. Because, as you so rightly pointed out, Evelyn must be delighted. But the main thing I'm pleased about is that you clearly have not inherited any shred of my stubborn or self-destructive tendencies as regards relationships. Now let's go and get some lunch. I'm starving.'

Chapter Forty-Three

Mike had been walking for an hour now, but it wasn't helping the way it usually did. There was no walking this one off, it seemed. He'd left his mum's house, gone through the village, then towards the sea, and was heading – he realised – to the old cemetery overlooking the bay, where his father was buried. He was angry, and had been since that unfortunate day when Evelyn had told him about Josh. Apart from anything else, he felt like a prize fool, and imagined Evelyn had pitied him, clearly so infatuated with her granddaughter – who unbeknown to him was engaged to another man. He still felt the flare of anger when he thought about it, but mostly all he felt was sadness. Then there was the bizarre phone call from Evelyn, just days later, telling him she had made a mistake . . . got the wrong end of the stick . . . that Truth wasn't engaged at all. The whole thing reeked of Evelyn being in trouble and presumably being put under pressure by Truth to try and rectify the situation. None of it made sense – but either way, he was through being taken for a fool. That was what hurt the most. That he really had thought Truth was something special . . . the girl he'd been holding out for.

He'd been open with her, revealed himself to her in a way

he had never done with any other woman. That day when she'd called at his flat, and he'd brought her in to show her his sculpture at the foundry, had been so special . . . so intimate. When the guys at the foundry had discreetly left them alone with his work, *The Waiting Man*, the energy in the musty room had been charged, had taken on a totally new dimension. He had felt it instantly, and thought Truth had too. Every piece he worked on developed its own energy as it came to fruition. In many ways, sculpting a figure was a process of getting to know that energy . . . sensing it evolving as the piece progressed and developed a personality all its own. It had been a very special moment for him – choosing to share that with her. Now, he realised, clearly it had meant nothing to her. And when they had spent the afternoon walking the site he was developing, and Tom, his mate, had assumed Truth and he were a couple, he had thought it had pleased her as much as it did him. And when they'd kissed later that evening on the pier, tentatively at first, Mike had felt an energy he had never felt before, with any other woman. Now, he realised, it had been nothing more than a game to Truth. She had just been playing with him. She didn't even seem to care or notice that he couldn't be anywhere near her since. He could barely speak to her . . . could hardly meet her eyes. She must think him such an idiot. And yet . . . he couldn't get her out of his mind.

Before he knew it, he found himself standing at his father's grave, where fresh wild flowers had been placed, presumably by his mother. A photograph of his parents, arms wrapped around each other, looked out at him from its marble casing on the headstone. They had been devoted to each other, although Mike had always found his father a difficult taskmaster. 'He's only hard on you because he wants to protect you,' his mum used to say to Mike. 'Farming can be a hard life.' But Mike had grown up with a distinct sense of being a disappointment to his father, along with a nagging conviction that he had no desire whatsoever to take over the family farm. It had been his final decision to become an artist that his father couldn't fathom or bring himself to forgive Mike for. Then he had been killed in the tractor accident before he had seen how commercially successful a sculptor his only son was becoming. Mike knew *The Waiting Man* was generating quite a buzz in art circles even before its unveiling. The guys at the foundry reckoned it was his best work yet. He had been excited by the finished sculpture himself, but now all he felt was a hollow sense of disenchantment and a growing unease at the prospect of the piece going up next week. He hoped Truth wouldn't come to the small ceremony – it would be hard enough to get through it as it was. Heading back towards home, he took the shortcut through the fields and lanes that led to his own piece of land. After his father's death the working farm had been sold. His mother had built a smaller house on the land she had kept, and Mike had inherited the plot he chose himself. That's where his future house and studio would be. He had three acres to work with, in a sheltered valley, through which a small river ran. It was a spot where he had always loved to fish and muck about with the dogs when he was younger. He had been so consumed with work of late that he had put the project on the back burner. Now, more than ever, he needed to press ahead with it. He needed somewhere to call his own and put down roots – and after what had transpired, he wanted to get as far away from Abbottsville and all he associated with number 24 as soon as possible. Once the sculpture was up, he would tell Doctor Ed he'd be moving on.

Back at his mum's house, he had a cup of tea with her before setting off. Marie was sixty-three, active in her local community, and kept fit riding and looking after her two beloved horses. She'd developed a close friendship with a vet Mike liked a lot, and by the looks of it things had progressed into something more serious. He was happy for her. She was too young to be on her own.

'You're looking tired,' she said to him now, sitting down across from him. 'You've been working too hard, Mike, you should have a good rest now the sculpture's finished. Why don't you go away somewhere nice?'

'Yeah, I might. I need to get going on the house plans. It won't build itself.'

'It'll be good to have you down the road.' She smiled. 'But you know there's no pressure – you can always sell up here and move wherever you want to, you know.'

He shook his head. 'No. It's the right place for me. I just need to get on with it.'

'He'd be very proud of you, you know, your dad.'

'I'd better make tracks.' He stood up. 'I'll see you on Friday?'

'Of course, Richard and I will both be there – we wouldn't miss it.'

✦

Back at number 24, Nessa was having one of her feelings. She told herself the growing sense of unease was simply due to the fact that she was unable to take in that she was now – and clearly had been for some time previously, although unbeknown to her – Rory's object of undying devotion and adoration. Since the night when he had so magnificently intervened and dispatched Ryan, and declared his true feelings for her, the pair had been inseparable. This came as a surprise to no one as much as Nessa herself. Ever since, he had been spending more nights at her flat, from where he would descend to his basement gym in the early morning radiating an infectious happiness to anyone he came in contact with. Even his most unenthusiastic clients couldn't help but be affected by his deliriously buoyant mood.

So Nessa too had been existing in a kind of daze of happiness, which was why she initially put her uneasy feeling down to her being so unused to such a forthright and strenuous declaration of love – of which Rory meant every word.

Now, sitting by the pond with Doctor Ed, she decided to risk sharing her thoughts. 'Is everything alright . . . you know . . . in the house?'

'How do you mean?' Doctor Ed looked up from his tablet, on which he was perusing a gardening site.

'Well, I'm having one of my feelings . . . a peculiar one. I feel very . . . uneasy about something – and I don't know what. Something to do with the house . . .'

Although Doctor Ed was a medic, he was not a man to dismiss an intuitive hunch, quite apart from Nessa's obvious gift of a sixth sense, or whatever it was called these days. He had come across the phenomenon more than once in his own career. 'Well,' he chose his words carefully, 'there is a certain amount of, shall we say, tension in the air.' He looked at Nessa meaningfully. 'Evelyn has family visiting, as you know, and it's been a very long time since she and her daughter Pauline have seen each other. Although it's lovely for Truth to have her mother in town, I can't imagine it's without its rather stressful aspect for Evelyn. Then there's Mike's sculpture about to go up – we're all excited about that – but Mike is obviously unnerved about it. And, well, there's the whole Bruce and Stella situation which is rather upsetting, to say the least.' Doctor Ed frowned. 'I must say I feel for Bruce. I told him I'd do anything I could to help, but I'm afraid Stella is feeling very threatened about the whole situation . . . she seems convinced Bruce and Annika are plotting to take Freddy away from her . . .' He sounded concerned. 'So I'd say you're not the only one feeling uneasy at the moment . . . if that's any help – probably impossible *not* to pick up on it if you're in any way empathetic to these things.'

'Yes, I suppose so.' Nessa wasn't altogether convinced.

'Anyhow, never mind those feelings,' Doctor Ed said. 'What about the positive ones? Rory is certainly looking like the cat who's got the cream, these days.'

Nessa felt herself blushing. 'It's all happened so suddenly, I had no idea that—'

'That Rory was madly in love with you? It must have been the worst-kept secret in Abbottsville.' He laughed. 'But whatever the case, I'm very glad you've put him out of his misery. Rory's a good man and I think you'll make a lovely couple. I hope you'll be terribly happy together.'

'Here comes Mike,' Nessa said, getting up. 'I'd better get back to the café. There's still a few loose ends that need tying up with the food stalls for the fair day. See you later!' She waved at Mike as they passed.

'How was your visit home?' Doctor Ed said, as Mike sat down on the bench.

'Good, yeah, it was good to catch up with Mum and have a look at the place again. Ah, that reminds me . . .' Mike said. 'I'll probably be moving on at the end of the month.'

'Really?' Doctor Ed took off his glasses and looked at him keenly.

'Yeah, it's time I got on with building my own place. A pal of mine is working on the plans I told you about. I really need to get a handle on it.'

'But can't you do that from here? At least until it's ready to move in to?'

'Be better if I was nearby, to be on site, you know. Besides, Mum's got plenty of space – I can stay there while the build is going on.'

'Of course,' Doctor Ed said. 'We'll be very sorry to lose you, you know that, don't you? It won't be the same without you, Mike – but of course I understand completely. None of us stay around forever. Although I must say I do think the last three or four years here have been a wonderful mix of characters. I've grown very fond of you all – I think of you all as family, you know.'

'I feel the same way about you, doc.' Mike looked into the distance.

'What about you and Truth?' he risked asking. 'I thought you two were finally getting somewhere . . .'

Mike's expression closed. 'Yeah, so did I – but turns out she had other plans.'

'What kind of other plans?'

'There was another guy in the wings. It's serious, apparently – he came over to see her a couple of weeks back.'

'I had no idea.'

'You and me both. It was Evelyn who put me in the picture. I'm grateful to her for that. Just wish her granddaughter had thought to do the same. But no real harm's been done. Just lucky I found out when I did. Women, eh?' Mike got up. 'Anyway, I just wanted to let you know about the flat. I'd better be getting on. See you later, doc.'

When Mike had gone, Doctor Ed went in to his flat and made himself a stiff gin and tonic to bring outside with him. At four in the afternoon it was earlier than his usual time, but he felt the developing situation warranted it. Mike deciding to move out from number 24 so abruptly . . . and Truth covertly involved with another man clearly being the cause of this move . . . it was too extraordinary. That kind of deception just didn't fit with the girl he had come to know and become so fond of. As he sat thoughtfully sipping his drink in the shade, Doctor Ed began to understand Nessa's feeling of general unease. There was something going on that just didn't add up. Something seriously out of kilter. You didn't have to be a clairvoyant to figure that one out.

✧

Truth could see the small crowd gathered below from the castle walls. Since the statue had been brought to the site by lorry-mounted crane last week, and lifted and slotted on to the waiting plinth, it had been kept hidden behind hoarding from prying eyes while curiosity and excitement built in the community. The hoarding had now been removed, she saw – probably early that morning – and the statue was covered in sheets, waiting for its final unveiling. Nessa would be there with Rory, so would Doctor Ed and Morah – and of course Mike. Truth should have been there too, but she wasn't. What was the point? She had told Nessa she would cover for her at the castle, being on hand for stallholders to go through any last-minute queries or problems. It was only for an hour or so. Just while they cut the ribbon, unveiled *The Waiting Man*, and the local councillor and Mike said the appropriate few words and photographs were taken and congratulations shared. She didn't need to watch from here, torturing herself, so she turned and walked away. She'd seen the statue already. That night was indelibly printed on her mind. And she didn't want to think about that either.

Chapter Forty-Four

Dawn broke on the day of the castle fair, reaching rosy fingers through a lightening sky. Mike hadn't been sleeping, despite the relief of his sculpture being so well received. Getting up for a swim was a welcome distraction from the restlessness which seemed to be stalking him. The house was still as he made his way out, although Rory would shortly be in the gym and others possibly swimming soon – but for now he was alone, which was what he needed. Just one more week and it would all be over. He would be leaving number 24 and building a new home outside Dublin – and Truth would be going home to London. Life could begin again, yet he felt only a sense of quiet desolation at the prospect. He told himself it was always this way after a piece of work was completed and erected, that certain sense of loss that invariably accompanied it. The artist's abyss, he called it. That indefinable space between one piece of work ending and the next endeavour yet to begin, even as a glimmer of an idea in his mind. The bleak no-man's land every artist had to walk through. Only this time he thought he'd have a loving relationship to focus on. He'd been prepared to give it everything he had – he'd thought Truth was the girl he'd been waiting for, prepared to hold out for.

Clearly – as Doctor Ed had pointed out – he'd been spending too much time alone. He couldn't believe he'd got it so wrong. What a fool she must think him.

By the time he reached the steps to Mariner's Cove, he spotted Doctor Ed already preparing to get into the water. The good weather always attracted more people, even at this early hour; the water temperature had stabilised and new faces were showing up every day alongside the regular swimmers.

They swam out a bit together in companionable silence. Doctor Ed spoke first. 'Will you be going to the fair today?'

'Wasn't planning to. You?'

'Oh, I'll probably go for a wander – have a look at the food stalls. Give Nessa a wave. It's lovely about her and Rory, isn't it?'

'Yeah. Finally. Couldn't happen to a nicer pair.'

They turned and headed back. 'Have you talked to Truth yet?'

'No. I don't intend to either.'

'Ah.'

'What's that supposed to mean?'

'Don't think it's worth at least a conversation?'

'So she can make me feel even more of a fool?'

'The only foolish thing I can think of is not finding out exactly what she's thinking – what's really going on. If you don't ask her . . . how will you ever know? Could you live with that? I know I couldn't. It would drive me mad not knowing all the facts.'

'I know all I need to know, doc. Believe me.'

'If you say so. But hearing things second hand is never a reliable indicator of a situation. Evelyn might have meant well – but she may have got the wrong end of the stick. People often get things confused post-surgery.'

'Oh she did ring me, Evelyn, a couple of days after to say that she'd got it wrong, that there'd been some kind of mix-up – but you know I'm glad she told me what she did. It's given me time to think – and what I've discovered is that Truth just isn't the person I thought she was. I think Evelyn was just trying to mark my card – that's all – and ended up getting into trouble for it.'

'Well, if you're happy with her account of things.'

'Look, doc, I know you mean well, but can we change the subject, please?'

'Of course, consider it closed. Plenty more fish in the sea, eh?'

Chapter Forty-Five

Nessa woke up to sunlight streaming through her gauzy curtains and Rory leaning up on one elbow, gently stroking her face. 'I could look at you forever,' he said.

She checked to see if the uneasy feeling was still there – she was pretty sure it was – but there were other, far nicer feelings to concentrate on, so she pushed it to the back of her mind.

'I can think of even nicer things you could do,' she said, taking the palm of his hand and kissing it. 'Starting right now.'

Chapter Forty-Six

Morah wasn't a fan of fair days – at the castle or anywhere else. In her opinion they usually attracted far too many undesirable people and noisy, boisterous children. They were, quite simply, a complete waste of time. Besides, there were far more interesting opportunities to be gained from remaining indoors. Pauline and Tristan were visiting Evelyn today and Morah as yet hadn't worked out whether Pauline had acted on the information she had given her regarding Truth and Mike, and the part Evelyn had played in coming between them. She would like to be a fly on the wall – or in the more likely case, up against the door – to listen to the conversation that might ensue after all that came to light.

Chapter Forty-Seven

Evelyn wasn't going to the fair, although she would have quite liked to be. Pauline and Tristan were calling to the flat and that meant she had to be on good behaviour – which was an awful bore for her. Pleased though she was to see Tristan, having Pauline around was a whole other kettle of fish, and it was becoming a strain. It was clear that Truth adored Pauline, and one wrong move on Evelyn's part would cause Pauline to drop her in it and that would be the end of any relationship she might have with her granddaughter. But soon they would be going back to London and Tristan to New York, and Evelyn – now that she was almost back to full mobility – would be able to resume her normal life, such as it was. Never, she vowed, would she take her carefree existence for granted again. She would also take good care never to wear flip-flops going up or down stairs.

Chapter Forty-Eight

Bruce was allowing himself to feel hopeful. It was a beautiful summer's day and he was helping Annika keep an eye on all the stalls she was in charge of at the castle fair and making sure everyone had what they needed. Stella had handed Freddy over to him the evening before, albeit sullenly, but without any unnecessary drama (the solicitor's letter had obviously had the desired effect), and the little fellow was having the time of his life on the bouncy castle along with a lot of other over-excited children. Watching him, Bruce couldn't help laughing. After the escalating stress of the last few weeks, and Stella's irrational behaviour, it was a welcome relief to see things return to some sort of normality. He was now deeply in love with Annika and hopeful that their future together was something they could plan in earnest. Life was looking good again. Which was possibly why, in the midst of such dreamy good humour, Bruce took a step backwards not noticing the artist's stool that caught his foot – and sent him tumbling to the ground, wrenching his ankle resoundingly in the process.

Chapter Forty-Nine

Freddy was having far too good a time to notice his daddy fall over. When he did look to check that he was watching his last terrific jump, where Freddy flew in the air before landing and bouncing up again, he was nowhere to be seen. But that didn't matter, because suddenly Mummy was there, waving at him, beckoning for him to come over to her. She came right up to the bouncy castle and caught him as he threw himself into her arms.

'Freddy,' she said, taking him by the hand. 'Come with Mummy, we're going to play a little game of hide and seek.'

Freddy loved hide and seek – it was his favourite game to play. Grown-ups didn't usually like playing it, so it was an added bonus that Mummy was even suggesting it. He was light-headed and dizzy from the bouncy castle and rather glad to have his feet on firm ground again. Mummy moved away from the crowds, taking them to where a low, crumbling wall marked the outer boundary of the castle. She sat him down.

'Mummy has to go away for just a few minutes to find someone, and you are to sit right here, okay?'

Freddy nodded. He liked the sound of this game.

'You are not to move from this spot until Mummy comes back, alright?'

He nodded again.

'I won't be long, I promise, just a few minutes. Then I'll come back and we'll go for ice cream, okay?'

''Kay, Mummy.'

'Good boy. As much ice cream as you want.' Mummy smiled. 'Just stay right there. Back in a jiffy.'

Then Mummy disappeared back through the bushes.

Chapter Fifty

It took a minute before people realised what had happened. Bruce yelled in pain, someone alerted Annika, and suddenly she was by his side, while two guys who had seen what happened helped him onto his good foot and held him up. Bruce couldn't put any weight at all on his ankle and was helped to a chair, where he sat down, gingerly stretching out his injured foot in front of him.

'It's fine,' he said, wincing. 'It's only a sprain – stupid of me . . .'

'We need to get you to a doctor.' Annika was concerned. 'You'll need to get it seen to.'

Someone went to fetch a golf cart from the golf stall, which could take Bruce down to street level, from where they could then get a lift. In all the commotion, it took a moment before either Bruce or Annika deciphered Stella's face peering at them – until her shrill voice cut through the chatter.

'Where's Freddy?' she demanded. 'Where is he?'

Chapter Fifty-One

Morah was perplexed when she heard the front-door buzzer. Pauline and Tristan had already arrived and were now in Evelyn's apartment, along with Truth. Morah was hovering on the landing below, duster to hand, in the hope of some kind of drama erupting. She was annoyed to be distracted. She put down the can of polish and duster and smoothed her overall to go and see who could be calling at this hour – probably yet another online delivery for one of the tenants.

That was when she got the second shock of her life upon opening the door to someone in number 24.

'Hello.' The expensively dressed, familiar-looking older man turned to face her, removing his summer trilby. 'Please forgive this intrusion . . . but I'm hoping you may be able to help me. My name is Robert Radcliffe . . . You see, I'm trying to find Mrs Evelyn Malone . . .'

'Well . . .' said Morah, realisation dawning. 'In that case, you've come to exactly the right place.' She stood back to invite him in with a gleeful smile. 'Please, follow me . . .'

Chapter Fifty-Two

There are events which remain deeply embedded in a family's collective consciousness despite the relentless passage of years and circumstances, and the scene that was about to unfold in Evelyn's flat would indeed become one such indelible memory. For now, though, Truth – until the bell to Evelyn's flat sounded – had been enjoying the determined, if rather tenuous, bonhomie that was playing out between her mother and grandmother. It was as if some secret truce had been agreed between the two, and Tristan seemed as relieved by it as Truth was. The earlier tension that had accompanied their gatherings had now dissipated – and had been replaced by a general sense of good fun. And Evelyn could be very entertaining and charming company when she was of a mind. Even Pauline, who leaned towards being overly earnest a lot of the time, had livened up and was relating humorous accounts of incidents at the shelter where she worked.

Which was why, when Tristan said, 'I'll get it', and went to answer the door, there was a bemused silence . . . as a strange man, ushered in by Morah, walked into the room where they were all sitting, looked at Evelyn, shook his head as if in disbelief, then with tears streaming down his face went to embrace her as she stood up – transfixed at the sight of him – while he said in a muffled voice, 'Evelyn! Oh, *my darling* Evelyn! I thought I might be too late! I thought you might be dead!'

Chapter Fifty-Three

Despite the unusual nature of the unexpected – and as yet to be introduced – guest's appearance, Truth – amid the disruption – became acutely aware of two things, both of which lent a rather surreal dimension to the drama. One was the look of horror which replaced the initial surprise on her grandmother's face, as Evelyn appeared to recognise the stranger. The other was the look of what could only be described as gleeful triumph on the part of Morah, who stood back, surveying the unfolding scene with ill-disguised relish.

'Bobby!' Evelyn eventually said, when she had disentangled herself from his emotive embrace. 'What on *earth* are you doing here?'

Chapter Fifty-Four

Robert Radcliffe was overcome. An intense week of detective work on the part of the agency he had hired had led him to the address he had originally started out with, which was the place he had believed Evelyn to be living – and that indeed he was paying for – until the terribly upsetting letter he had received from the bogus retirement home led him to suspect otherwise. Despite the growing irritation and disinterest his younger-by-thirty-years wife Alannah clearly felt towards him, he had become completely obsessed with finding out what had happened to the woman he fondly remembered as the love of his life – even though at the time his conviction to run away with Evelyn and spend an idyllic life with her had faltered somewhat under the pressure of the cultural and financial expectations as regards marriage and family in 1980s Ireland. Divorce hadn't been an option at that time and such marital separations that had existed – never mind those with possibly millions at stake – had been, to say the least, unsat-isfactory. Robert had chickened out. Pure and simple. He had let Evelyn down when it counted, and now – even though it was forty years later – whatever the cost, whatever was going down, he was determined to prove his undying devotion. Age, if nothing else, had given him perspective. And Evelyn, despite the passage of years, appeared more beautiful to him than ever. Her beauty was luminous . . . incandescent . . . her obvious shock and delight at seeing him after all these years had been betrayed by her trembling in his embrace, from which she pulled away, as ashen, shaken, and breathless as himself. All this, and thoughts of the wasted years that had languished between them, lent Robert a bravado he had thought long lost.

He turned now to address the gathering at large. There was a young woman, dark and beautiful, a replica of Evelyn as he remembered her, who had to be a relation. An older, sensible-looking woman he couldn't place . . . and then . . . sitting beside Evelyn, sharing her easy gracefulness, but with fairer colouring, a handsome young man. A young man who clearly had to be their son . . . their closely guarded secret, which Evelyn had held to herself and her heart at such great personal cost for all these long, lonely years.

'Son . . .' Robert was openly sobbing now, as he turned to embrace a horrified Tristan. 'I know I've let you down . . . but that's all behind us now . . . I'm going to make it up to you . . . whatever it takes. You're my own flesh and blood . . . and that's all that matters . . . that and how much I've always loved your mother,' Robert sank into an empty chair as he inhaled and exhaled a shuddering breath. 'Evelyn . . . I think it's time we explained things to our respective families . . . don't you? Son . . .' He was looking at Tristan again, who replied curtly, 'My name is Tristan. And I have no idea in hell who you are! Mum?' Tristan looked at Evelyn.

But there was no stopping Robert now, who was in full

flow. 'I'm Robert Radcliffe, Tristan. And I realise this may come as something of a shock . . . but I am your father . . . and you are my son. Tell him, Evelyn . . .'

There was a beat of excruciating silence before Evelyn, who was listening in growing anger to Robert's declarations, replied coldly, 'I will do no such thing.' She glared at Robert. 'I have no idea how you found me, or what you are doing here . . . or, more to the point, who let you in without permission.' Her eyes flicked towards Morah, who was hovering near the door hanging on every word. 'But I would like you to leave my apartment this instant. I haven't set eyes on you in forty-odd years and I can only assume you've taken leave of your senses. That, or you are in the grip of some kind of advanced delusion.'

Her face was white with fury. 'Tristan . . . I'm so sorry . . . pay no attention to these insane ramblings – Robert had a ridiculous crush on me many years ago when I was married to your father, Lenny. I didn't return his feelings then, and I certainly don't appreciate this ridiculously inappropriate intrusion on my home and family now. Tristan . . . you only have to look at that photo,' she pointed to a framed photograph on the wall of Lenny, 'to know who your father is.'

'Robert,' Evelyn continued, as Robert sat with his mouth open in disbelief, 'I must insist that you leave my home this minute.'

'She's lying.' The accusation rang across the room, as all heads swivelled towards Morah. 'She was always a liar!' She stood leaning against the wall, arms folded. 'Oh, Tristan may or may not be your son,' she said to Robert. 'I don't know about that . . .' She glanced back around the room. 'But I do know that Robert and Evelyn here had an illicit affair while they were both married to their respective spouses. And I know that for a fact, because I worked in the house where it took place – all those years ago. Remember? Evelyn was a liar then, and she's still a liar.' Morah turned to face Robert, whose mouth was now opening and closing wordlessly. 'She stole your *actual* son, little Joey . . . that day he went missing from outside the shop. It was her. She took him. With the sole intention of getting me – the children's nanny – into trouble. And it almost worked – didn't it, Evelyn?'

'You . . .?' Robert was incredulous. 'You're the nanny?' He shook his head as if to try and clear it.

'Yes, that's exactly who I am. Morah Finlay. It's been quite a while, hasn't it, Mr Radcliffe? Evelyn . . .?'

And then no one said anything at all, not even Evelyn, as a commotion was heard from downstairs, doors banged, and footsteps came running upstairs, and through the door of Evelyn's flat, which Morah had left open, came shouts of panic and calls for everyone to come and help . . . that little Freddy had gone missing and was nowhere to be found.

Chapter Fifty-Five

'Well,' said Evelyn, sitting down after the others had left to join the search party, 'you've really gone and done it now, haven't you?' She looked at Robert, who sat opposite her, looking for all the world as if he'd been punched. They were finally alone.

Evelyn ran her fingers back and forth along the triple strand of pearls she was wearing.

'That woman . . . Morah . . .' Robert was trying to make sense of what had just transpired. 'Did you know . . . did you know that's who she was?'

'Of course I didn't,' Evelyn snapped. 'How could I possibly have known? I hardly ever laid eyes on her back then . . . I certainly didn't know her name. I would never have taken any notice of her at all until you told me she had threatened to tell Sarah about us.'

'So . . . is it true? Was it you who took Joey that day?'

Evelyn made a dismissive sound. 'Of course it was me. I was doing you a favour. The girl had left him alone outside the shop, anything might have happened to him.'

'Only for a minute. People did that sort of thing all the time in those days.'

'Not people who are paid specifically to look after children.

It was a dereliction of duty, plain and simple. I was protecting your son and teaching her a lesson in the process.'

'That's how you see it, is it? While we were going out of our minds with terror, much as these poor parents of the other little chap must be now,' Robert sounded dazed, 'you sat back and let an innocent girl be blamed for allowing a child to go missing . . . when you could have alerted us at any time to tell us he was safe . . .' Robert went on talking, as if explaining the event to himself.

'What does it matter?' Evelyn was withering. 'He *was* safe. Safer with me than with her. She was an interfering bitch. You said so yourself. She still is – clearly. The woman's quite mad . . . she should be locked up. Wait until Doctor Ed hears about this – he'll have to send her packing immediately.'

'But why, Evelyn?' Robert was increasingly bewildered. 'Why did you do it?'

'What do you mean why did I do it?' She looked at Robert as if he was stupid. 'I did it for us . . . if you'd had half the guts I thought you had, you would have fired the girl and left Sarah like you'd always promised to. But you turned out to be just like all the others – completely bloody spineless when it came down to it.'

'Sarah was fragile . . . I couldn't leave her – it would have—'

'What? Killed her? Don't flatter yourself! The only thing you were afraid of losing were your millions . . . and perhaps getting a bit of flack on the reputational front which would have been history in a couple of months. Instead you almost ruined my life.' She looked at him. 'You never did say . . . why *did* you come here now? Why . . . after all these years?'

'I thought you were dying.'

'I beg your pardon?'

'I thought you were dying. Someone wrote me a very odd letter – saying you were in a nursing home and hadn't long to live . . .'

'Ah, I see. No prizes for guessing who'd like *that* to be the case.'

'Naturally I was concerned – more than concerned. I got my security people to check it out – the letter turned out to be bogus . . . then I wanted to make sure for myself you were alright . . .'

'How touching. Well, as you can see, I'm perfectly alright – or at least I will be when my hip has fully healed. I have my final check-up this week.'

'It was a mistake to come . . . I can see that now.'

'No, Robert, I don't think you can. I don't think you have any idea how much of a mistake it has been. Quite a colossal one – as far as I'm concerned, at any rate. But too late to do anything about that now . . .' Evelyn sighed. 'Why in the name of God couldn't you just have left well enough alone?'

'I've told you why! I thought you were dying – or that something awful had happened you and people might be trying to take advantage . . . to steal money from you . . . anything could have been going on. Speaking of money . . .' Robert cleared his throat.

'Yes?'

'Did you really need it? I mean, when you got in touch with me that time after—'

'Yes, Robert. I did really need it. Lenny died with huge

debts. He left me pretty much with nothing once the house was repossessed. I was on my uppers. I needed every penny.'

'But the boy . . . Tristan . . . he's not mine, is he?' He looked at the photo of his late friend and business partner on the wall. 'He could be a young Lenny. That's just how I remember Lenny when we were kids.'

'No, Tristan isn't yours. That was . . . an embellishment.'

'But why?' Robert looked pained. 'Why did you tell me that? I would have given you the money anyway – it wouldn't have mattered.'

Evelyn shrugged. 'I couldn't be sure of that, Bobby. And maybe I wanted you to feel bad, to feel some sense of responsibility for the way you let me down so spectacularly. It was touch and go for a while with Lenny after you left me. I never knew if he knew about us – I suspect he did. But Lenny was too much in love with me to confront it, if he did know. We got over it eventually.' She looked at Robert. 'But I could have lost everything. And you didn't give a damn – just ran off to play happy families and hide behind Sarah's skirts.' She gave a bitter laugh.

'That's a bit harsh,' Robert said.

'Life is harsh, don't you find? Speaking of which . . . how is your latest marriage working out?'

'Alannah and I don't spend much time together. I irritate her. Sometimes I think she can hardly bear to be in the same room as me. I'm pretty sure she's having an affair with her tennis coach. Before that it was the personal trainer.'

Evelyn shook her head. 'How terribly predictable. That gives me no pleasure to hear, Bobby.'

'I'm sorry, Evelyn . . . I know you probably don't believe

me . . . but I know I screwed up. I should have had the nerve to leave Sarah and be with you – but I just panicked – it was all too much. I can tell you I've lived to regret it. Not a day goes by that I don't think of you and how our life together might have been.' He looked as if he might cry again. 'I never had feelings for any other woman that came close to the way I felt about you, Evelyn. Never.'

'Yes, well, what's done is done – no use dwelling on what might have been.'

'The thing is . . .'

'What?'

'Well, I've had a tip-off from a good friend that Alannah is likely to spring divorce proceedings on me at any minute.'

'Surely that can't come as a complete surprise?'

'No . . . not entirely. But it does pose a few problems. That was the other reason I came over.' He cleared his throat. 'After the letter, well, I was led to believe that you didn't want any loose ends lying around that might have led your family to our little . . . arrangement.'

'Bit late for that now.'

'Well, that's just it. You see, I can't afford to have any – shall we say – inappropriate financial arrangements in place either, especially to another woman . . . The lawyers will go through everything with a fine-tooth comb, you know what they're like. I'm afraid I'll have to wrap up any further trans- actions to your, ah, account. You do understand, Evelyn . . . don't you?'

'Yes, Bobby, of course I understand.'

'Will you be alright? I could leave you a few thousand in cash if you need it?'

'That won't be necessary, thank you.'

'If there was any other way . . .'

'There is *always* another way, Bobby . . . and I will find it. Don't worry about me – I can take care of myself. I don't know about you, but I could use a drink. I hate histrionics at the best of times. Be a dear and make me a G&T, would you? The kitchen's just there, behind you – you'll find the glasses in the top cupboard.'

And that – despite everything that had just transpired – was how Pauline and Tristan found them when they returned to the apartment an hour and a half later, exhausted and dispirited from their fruitless search for Freddy. Evelyn and Robert, sipping their drinks, and reminiscing over times gone by, for all the world like a pair of sentimental old friends, which of course, underneath everything else, is exactly what they were.

Chapter Fifty-Six

'I want a DNA test!'

'Oh, for God's sake, Tristan, listen to yourself!' Evelyn said. 'Don't be so completely ridiculous! You're forty years of age – not fourteen. Lenny is your father and always was.' She pointed to the photograph that hung on the wall. 'The resemblance is clear to anyone with eyes in their head.'

This was true, arguably, but nonetheless Pauline couldn't help deriving a huge sense of amusement watching Tristan wrestle for the first time in impotent fury with their mother's steely personality when the matter under discussion was not to her liking.

He shook his head, pacing across the room. 'I don't know how you can just *sit* there, both of you – as if nothing has happened.' He looked from an unrepentant Evelyn to a shamefaced Robert. 'You had an affair . . . an *affair*, behind my father's back! With his friend! How could you? How could either of you betray him like that? I thought you were happy together, Mum.'

'We were happy together, Tristan. I like to think I made your father very happy. He told me so often enough. So I don't think you have to worry on that account.'

'You're unbelievable, you are!' This was directed at Evelyn. 'I never saw it until now . . . but . . . you just don't give a damn – do you?'

Evelyn rolled her eyes. 'These events took place years ago, Tristan, before you were even born. Quite frankly, they are none of your business.'

'Are you for real? A strange man comes into my mother's apartment, calls me "son" and announces he's my father . . . and it's none of my business?'

'That was all a silly misunderstanding. Wasn't it, Bobby?'

'Yes, yes, I, ah, may have been a little hasty . . . got the wrong end of the stick, you know . . . I'm almost eighty now . . . memory isn't what it used to be.'

'I still want a DNA test.' Tristan glared at him. 'In fact, I insist on it.'

'Well, son – I mean Tristan,' Robert said, 'I'm more than happy to oblige. I'm here for another day or two, just tell me what you need from me.' He handed him a card. 'You can reach me on any of these numbers.' He got up awkwardly. 'I think I'll be getting along now. I'd like to have a word with Morah before I go, to, ah, well, to try and explain . . . things were different back in those days. I can see I was hasty with the girl . . .'

He turned to Evelyn. 'It's good to see you looking so well . . . perhaps we might see each other again before I leave?' He looked hopeful. 'You might have dinner with me tomorrow?'

'I think not, Bobby.' Evelyn smiled. 'But it was good to see you too – even under such unforeseen circumstances.' Her face softened momentarily. 'I'll take care to make sure that someone of authority contacts you – my solicitor, probably – to inform you of my *eventual* demise, should I predecease you.'

'Evelyn—' Robert looked stricken.

'That was a joke, Bobby. Now be a good sport and go home. We've had quite enough excitement here for one day,' she said. 'I'd see you out myself, only it would involve using my crutch, and I'd rather – as they say in the movies – you remembered me as I was. Besides, I'm too old for all this drama and I'm exhausted.

'Tristan, show Robert out, would you? You can make any arrangements you need to then. Morah resides in flat number 6, Robert. She's the caretaker here. I don't think you'll have to look too far to find her – I'm quite sure she hasn't finished with her bizarre undertaking to wreak as much havoc in my life as humanly possible – she'll be delighted to talk to you. But I have no doubt whatsoever she was behind that unconscionable letter that was sent to you and I shall be taking legal advice as to how to seek redress. You can tell her from me this isn't over. Not as far as I'm concerned.'

Chapter Fifty-Seven

'So . . .' Pauline said, when Tristan and Robert had left. 'Do you want to tell me what all that was about?'

Evelyn looked suddenly tired. 'Oh . . . God.' She shook her head. 'It was all so long ago . . . as you've probably gathered, Bobby and I had an affair. I know it was wrong of me . . . of us . . . but it was one of those lethal attraction things. There was just no other way to describe it. I know you think I'm a dreadful mother already . . . but you were at boarding school at the time and that's just what happened. There's no point in dressing it up.'

'But the Morah thing . . . is that true?'

'It would appear so, unfortunately,' Evelyn said, running a hand down her face. 'What were the chances?' She shook her head. 'I don't think I even laid eyes on her, back then. I mean, I may have *seen* her, in some respect, when I was at the house . . . but she was just the children's nanny,' Evelyn was mystified. 'I would never have taken any *notice* of her . . .'

'But apparently she took quite a bit of notice of you?'

'It was the strangest thing. I remember thinking Bobby was making it up, at the time, when he told me. Imagine . . . the nanny . . . threatening him! Robert Radcliffe, one of Dublin's wealthiest businessmen of the time . . . she was threatening to tell his wife about us. I didn't believe it at first.'

'And that's when you . . . what – took the child? That's the bit I don't get.'

'It wasn't like that,' Evelyn said. 'I was driving around, trying to get my head together . . . to think what to do . . . how to make sense of it all . . . when she suddenly materialised in front of me . . . I recognised the child, Joey, immediately. I watched her, then . . . and she left the little fellow outside – alone in his pushchair – while she went into the shop. I acted on pure instinct. That was my chance – and I took it.'

'You kidnapped a child.' Pauline lifted her eyebrows.

'Of course I didn't kidnap him. The child was safer with me than with her. I was just teaching her a lesson . . . anything could have happened to him. Then, after a suitable amount of time – only a matter of hours – I brought him home to his parents.'

'And took the credit for finding him,' Pauline said. 'That bit makes sense.'

'I don't expect you to understand. You've always hated me.'

'I don't hate you, Mum,' Pauline said. 'I'm just trying to understand you. I'm not sure I ever will. I'm not judging you, either, by the way. I gave up judging people long ago, since I began working in the shelter. There's nothing anyone could tell me anymore that could possibly shock me. Except maybe learning that Truth had kept the online abuse from me. That hurt – still does.'

'Perhaps I shouldn't have told you that. But she only wants to protect you. She thinks the world of you, you know – adores you. I'm quite envious of the relationship you have with each other. She's a credit to you, Pauline. I take my hat off to you. You've raised a wonderful daughter and clearly overcome some very difficult circumstances in your own life. I'm only sorry I couldn't have been more of a support to you during that time. I'm paying the price now, if it's any consolation.'

'So what are you going to do now? Are you going to talk to Morah about this?'

Evelyn made a wry face. 'Morah is the least of my problems, right now.'

'How do you mean?'

'Bobby and I had an arrangement, you might say. Lenny died with huge debts, he left me penniless, really. The house was repossessed – our investments were gone – I had nothing. By chance I met Doctor Ed, found this apartment – and I just knew I had to have it. My living surroundings have always been important to me. I didn't need much space, but I needed to love where I was – I always have. And I knew immediately the outlook here – the location, everything about it, really – was perfect. I knew I could begin again here. The only problem was I couldn't possibly afford it. I had enough for about three months' rent, that was it. That's when I thought of Bobby. After he let me down . . . ended our affair . . . I told him never to contact me again. I knew he was devastated, but men are selfish creatures – they'll always think of themselves, put themselves first. Bobby owed me, in a manner of speaking. His life had been successful, he was richer than ever – I knew he could easily afford to help me out with the rent here.'

'So you got him to pay your rent by telling him Tristan was his son?'

'Yes. He probably would have paid for it anyway . . . but I couldn't be sure of that. I needed to make him feel responsible in some way. I know it seems wrong now – but at the time I didn't think it could do any harm. We're old, for heaven's sake. Bobby is married to a younger woman. He lives in Portugal. He was happy to hear from me – thrilled, even. And more than happy to assuage his conscience by helping me out. It was all working perfectly well until today. Until that stupid, interfering – *mental case* of a woman went and ruined it all.' Evelyn was grim. 'Now he's stopping the monthly payments, so I won't be able to afford the rent.'

'I had no idea you had money problems when Lenny died.'

'Why would you? I was hardly going to ring you and tell you – was I? Tristan wouldn't have been any help – he was usually looking to me for a handout. I doubt he'll ever make a living from his painting – but that's not my problem either.'

'What will you do?'

'I don't know yet. But I'll think of something. This is just an unexpected obstacle . . . a fly in the ointment. Don't worry,' she smiled briefly, 'I won't be arriving on your doorstep expecting you to put me up.'

Pauline sighed. 'Even if I had the space, I don't think you'd like where I live, much.'

'Of course I wouldn't. I have every intention of staying here. I love Abbottsville. It's my home. If I can't stay on in number 24, well, I'll find somewhere else. It's as simple as that. Because I have no intention of moving to somewhere

I hate and where I'll be miserable. I envy modern women with their careers and their independent finances – all I had to work with was my looks and the men I attracted. Both of which generally run out on you when you need them most. I like to think that if I had the chance to do it all again, I might become a barrister, like Truth . . . But there you are. That's life . . . you play with the cards you're dealt.'

Chapter Fifty-Eight

So far, the search had turned up nothing – and for Stella, the unfolding nightmare was becoming all too real. What had started out as a harmless ploy to show up Bruce and Annika's lack of proper supervision of Freddy at the fair day – Stella had planned to bring him back immediately having put the wind up them – had turned into an official missing child case. The gardaí were taking it seriously, and a co-ordinated search was being orchestrated. Stella had been interviewed, white-faced, with Nessa at her side – helping her, prompting her, as details were taken of Freddy's age, height, colouring and what he was wearing. Both the kindness with which she was being treated and the gravity of the female garda's expression reinforced with growing desperation that Freddy, her little boy, really *had* disappeared – and much worse, it was all her fault. None of what had *actually* happened had been told to the police, of course. Stella may have been in shock, but she wasn't stupid. Instead, she repeated, trance-like, that she had decided at the last minute that she *would* go up to the castle to check out the fair, and when looking out for her son, who was under the supervision of her ex-husband and his partner, had been unable to find him. When she'd finally located her ex-husband, it was to discover that he was nursing a sprained ankle – and neither he nor his girlfriend seemed to have any idea where Freddy had got to. That was the first inkling anyone had that something was amiss, and the alarm was duly raised.

Now, two hours later, she was sitting alone in her flat while others searched for her child. She had refused the offer of a professional counsellor who would have waited with her, saying instead that her mother was on her way. Nessa and Doctor Ed had also offered to sit with her, but Stella couldn't bear the thought of seeing anyone – not even her mother. But at least pretending her mother was on the way got the others off her back. She couldn't get Bruce's white and bewildered face out of her head, or Annika's wild panic. The images floated in front of her ceaselessly. She sat now, staring at the phone in her hand, willing herself to call her mother but unable to do so. She couldn't bring herself to utter the words . . . that Freddy was gone . . . had disappeared . . . and it was all her fault. She willed the phone to ring with good news, to be the bearer of blessed relief – some disembodied voice telling her that this was all a horrible dream she would wake up from – but it remained silent. All she felt was the trembling, first in her hand and then her whole body, as she began to shake uncontrollably. The phone fell to the floor, and she clutched her head in her hands. Wracked by guilt, she sobbed uncontrollably.

She was unfit. Unfit as a mother, a bad, *terrible* person. She had lost her husband, her marriage, and now her little boy. Her career was in jeopardy. They were on to her. There was no hiding from any of it anymore.

Photos of happy days carefully arranged on shelves mocked her. The walls began to close in on her. On the floor, the phone rang, accusing her, shrilly, relentlessly. She couldn't take any more. Couldn't pick it up and listen to some hideous, harrowing account of what had happened to her little boy. She had to get out . . . she would find him herself. Intuition would lead her to him and then everything would be alright. But first there was something she had to get . . . She rushed to his bedroom and grabbed the soft toy dinosaur he wouldn't sleep without. That way she would feel him with her. She would find him and take him away – just the two of them – away from Bruce and Annika, away from anyone who tried to take him from her. Then everything would be alright, and they could begin again . . .

Chapter Fifty-Nine

Despite her reluctance to miss a moment of the drama unfolding in Evelyn's apartment, Morah raced to the scene as soon as she heard the news that Freddy was missing. She was talking to Nessa, still at the castle grounds, trying to piece together what exactly had happened. Bruce and Annika had been taken to the hospital to have Bruce's ankle seen to, which had turned out to be a nasty fracture, and were now, like Stella, waiting at home in their flat for any news. A search party was combing the surrounding area, locals were offering help where they could, and – following procedure, if discreetly – back at garda headquarters detectives were tracking the whereabouts and reports of any known traffickers or paedophiles in the area. That was the aspect no one wanted to think about just yet.

'Tell me again what happened, exactly,' Morah said to Nessa, who was sitting behind a food stall, pale-faced, chewing her lip.

'The last time anyone saw him was on the bouncy castle,' she said, her lip beginning to tremble. 'Then Bruce fell over and hurt his ankle, Annika rushed over to see what had happened, there were a few other people helping him up – and next thing Stella was there, demanding to know where

Freddy was . . . *Where is he?* she kept saying. That's when we realised he wasn't on the bouncy castle anymore . . .' Nessa began to cry. 'Oh, God, if anything has happened to him . . . poor little Freddy . . .'

'Don't assume the worst, Nessa.' Morah was grim. 'Children get themselves into all sorts of scrapes all the time and come out of them just fine.' She patted Nessa's shoulder. 'But something about this isn't adding up.'

'How do you mean?'

'I don't know . . . it's just a feeling.' She was thoughtful. 'Speaking of feelings . . .' She looked at Nessa. 'Are you getting anything?'

Nessa shook her head. 'Not really. Although I've been uneasy for weeks now. Couldn't shake it. I should have said something – done something.'

'Sure what could you have done? You didn't know what was going to happen, did you?'

'No, but I knew something wasn't right.'

'Even by your standards that's a bit vague.' Morah tried to make light of the comment. She didn't altogether hold with Nessa's so-called talent for having a sixth sense – but she didn't entirely dismiss it either. But when push came to shove, in Morah's experience the practical approach was usually best where small children were concerned.

Nessa shook her head. 'I keep seeing an image of a dinosaur . . . but it doesn't make any sense.'

'A dinosaur? Hmm. Wasn't Mike making a wooden one for Freddy back in the house? I remember Doctor Ed saying something about that. Maybe we should check there . . .'

'You think he could be back at the house? But how could—?'

'I don't know . . . but you did say a dinosaur.'

'I'll call Mike now – but I doubt Freddy's back at the house.'

Morah left Nessa on the phone and went to find the other person she wanted to talk to. On the fair day, Paddy generally didn't operate in his official capacity as gatekeeper, seeing as he couldn't really expect people to pay at the gate when they were already contributing to a local enterprise, but nonetheless he was relaxing at his table and chair, debating the chances of a runner in the two thirty at the Curragh with an equally grizzled-looking contemporary.

'Mind if I join you for a minute?' Morah said, eyeing the soon-to-be-vacated chair.

'Be my guest.' Paddy waved off his pal, who was getting up to go.

'Have you spoken to the guards?'

'Now, why would they be interested in talking to me?'

'Just answer the question.'

'No, I have not.'

'You know a child's gone missing?'

'I heard something about it alright, but sure kids go missing all the time on a day like this – the child will turn up.'

'It's not just any child,' Morah said, frowning. 'It's Freddy, Stella and Bruce's little fella from our house.'

'Ah, no!' Paddy was taken aback. 'But sure he can't have gone far. I saw him earlier, with his ma.'

'With Bruce's girlfriend, you mean?'

Paddy shook his head. 'No, with his ma, Stella. I know

Stella. She got me this new table and chairs from the sale of an old house a while back – she's decent like that.'

'And Freddy was with her? You're sure of that?'

'Of course I'm sure – I have eyes in my head, don't I?'

'What time would that have been?'

Paddy shrugged. 'Couple of hours ago . . . three at the outset – why?'

'Never mind.' She got up to go.

'But he wasn't with her when I saw him after that.'

Morah wheeled around. 'Where was he?'

'Come to think of it, he wasn't with anyone . . . not that I noticed . . . he was running after one of the stall fellas, chasing his dog. The one who had the *Jurassic Park* display at the toy section. There were a few kids running along – he was one of them. I remember that.'

'That makes sense, alright.' Morah turned to go. 'Thanks, Paddy, you've been a big help.'

'Let me know if there's any news.'

'I'll keep you posted.'

Chapter Sixty

There were hardly any cars on the road when Stella set off. Bruce and Annika had nearly won – but not now – not any more. Now it was just her and Freddy. No one would ever be able to take him away from her again. 'It's okay, little guy,' she whispered. 'It's just us from now on – just Freddy and Mummy – no one will ever hurt us again . . .'

The harbour came into view, just around the next corner, golden in the late afternoon sun, beams of light dancing on water. Stella drove slowly, methodically, down towards the water, unnoticed. *The Waiting Man* stood now, a poignant reminder of the 1807 tragedy when so many lives had been lost in the storm. He looked out over the harbour, still waiting for his lost wife and child . . . Stella wondered would anyone stand and wait for her and Freddy . . . her mother maybe . . . Would Bruce look out . . . would he miss them? She didn't care . . . she and Freddy were safe now . . .

The benzodiazepines were kicking in, making her drowsy. There was no one around. She left the driver and passenger windows open. She just had to stay awake long enough to cut the engine, leave off the handbrake . . . then it would all be over . . .

Chapter Sixty-One

The unusual aspect of the partly submerged car was that, afterwards, no one could pinpoint exactly how it had been discovered. There were conflicting reports: one said that a Laser sailing from the yacht club had spotted what it thought was a capsized boat floating in the water. Another swore that a power boat had passed by and alerted police. Neither party could be traced for comment. Others said it had been local swimmers in the area who had spotted something amiss. While more spoke of an unusual beam of light flashing across the harbour . . .

However it transpired, emergency services on hand for Fair Day had been alerted, lifeguards and paramedics had raced to the area on RIBs and Jet Skis, the car door had been prised open, and Stella, unconscious, had been pulled from the water. But although divers searched the area relentlessly . . . there was no sign of a three-year-old missing boy. No recovered body. Just a poignantly empty car seat and a floating toy dinosaur.

Chapter Sixty-Two

It was seven o'clock that evening when Frank O'Byrne, after a long day on the road, was told by his wife that there was a strange woman at the door demanding to see him. When he went to investigate, the woman, who introduced herself as a friend of the distraught family concerned, insisted that he should take her directly to his warehouse, or wherever he kept the van that had been used that day to transport goods on behalf of a maker of felt dinosaurs, among other animals. The matter, she said, was of vital importance, and concerned the disappearance of a small child. It would be easier for everyone concerned, she added, if he would agree to this – rather than involve the police, which might give the wrong impression.

'What are you implying?' He glared at her. 'Is this some kind of drugs business? Because I can assure you I have an impeccable record of integrity as regards any cargo my company is involved in.'

'Nothing at all just yet,' the woman said. 'But if you would be so kind as to take us to the van concerned, I think we may resolve this matter without additional upset.'

Grudgingly he rang his foreman to unlock the garage, and drove the woman and her grizzly looking partner to the car park, where he accompanied them to the van. 'I'm going to film this on my phone – my solicitor will be kept informed of every move you make,' he said.

'I think that's a very good idea,' said Morah.

Initially it was difficult to make out the dim interior of the van. The space was reasonably empty, a selection of folded tables rested along the sides, and at the back was a pile of boxes, some tablecloths – next to that a jumble of dustcovers. 'Well,' Frank said, 'this is it. What exactly was it you were expecting to find?'

'Freddy?' Morah called out gently. 'Freddy?' A little louder this time.

Paddy's eyes darted nervously in her direction. 'Maybe we should go,' he said. 'I think—'

And then the pile of covers moved. A small, confused, tousled blond head appeared and blinked. Then Freddy took his thumb out of his mouth and began to bawl.

Chapter Sixty-Three

Truth had to get out of number 24. She had to be alone. Walking mindlessly along the seafront, she forced herself to consider her immediate plans, despite her heavy heart. It was the end of July, and she was due back in the office the following Monday. Even though her trip to Dublin had thrown up some surprising revelations, she was glad she had come. She had made new and lasting friends, had got to know her grandmother – although right now she couldn't be in the same room as her – and she had almost fallen in love – if only Mike had worked out. But she wouldn't think about that now. If Evelyn was right about one thing – Truth always tried to give credit where it was due – it was not wasting your time or emotions on ill-fated affairs of the heart. Truth discovered with surprise that she felt stronger in herself. She was ready to get back to work, more fully committed than ever to representing abused women since her own ordeal. Her revenge on her abusers would be to continue growing as a person – she wasn't going to let anyone get in the way of that. Following the by now habitual route, she found herself at Mike's sculpture, which, as everyone had predicted, had been received with such awed admiration by the council and locals alike. *The Waiting Man* looked as if he had always been there, yet generated a completely new energy, causing people to stop as they passed by and smile as they read the story of his legend on the plaque. Now, in the quiet of the early evening, she sat down and leaned against it, looking out to sea.

The place was so peaceful now, it was difficult to believe that just days before it had been the cause of such frenetic activity when Stella's car had been spotted and the alarm raised. Stella was being monitored closely in hospital, and the last Truth had heard was that it was still unclear how much damage had been done and how – or if – she would be affected once she was fully conscious. Freddy had been found unharmed, thanks to Morah's quick thinking. It turned out the little fellow had followed the owner of the dinosaur stall into the back of his van to play with the toys he had found there – and unseen by the man, Freddy had accidentally been locked inside. He was now reunited with a frantically relieved Bruce – who vowed never to let him out of his sight again. The feeling of relief and joy was palpable all around the house – but for Truth, the recent revelations concerning her grandmother had dealt an unexpected blow that felt like yet another betrayal. Hearing Morah's account of what had transpired all those years ago, and the devious methods Evelyn had employed to get the young nanny into serious trouble, instilled in Truth a feeling of growing anger towards Evelyn. She couldn't remain in the same space as her, and had fortunately been able to move in to Doctor Ed's spare room until she left for London. 'How can you seem so unperturbed by it all?' she'd asked Pauline earlier when they were discussing the whole incident. 'I can hardly bear to look at her!'

'Probably because I can't say it surprises me all that much.' Pauline had made a wry face. 'I know your grandmother – remember?'

Truth had shaken her head. 'I should have believed you. I thought—'

'You were right to come and find out for yourself. Everyone has a right to properly get to know someone they haven't met – especially family. If it's any consolation, Truth, she thinks very highly of you. I stayed with her for a while after Robert and Tristan left, and I think it was the first time in her life she was actually honest with me. I wanted to be angry with her, but in the end I just pitied her. If life at the shelter has taught me anything, it's that we are all capable of falling by the wayside – of doing bad, sometimes terrible things. For Evelyn, they've finally caught up with her, and she's going to have to face the consequences. I don't think Tristan will get over it in a hurry – even though the DNA test did bear out her version of events.'

'It was pretty surreal, that part of it.' Truth had shaken her head, remembering.

She was still finding it hard to get her head around it all. But it would soon be time to go home. Pauline and Tristan were leaving tomorrow, and now that Evelyn was perfectly able to manage in her apartment, there was no reason for Truth to remain on either. But going back to London didn't feel like going home anymore. She wondered if anywhere ever would . . . Everywhere she went, these days, people were either not what they seemed, or perhaps she had just been too naïve and wrapped up in her work to see their true colours. Before she came to Dublin she had felt confident in her choices, in her decision to walk away from Josh – none of which she regretted. It was just that the new, totally unexpected, and hopeful beginnings that she had felt tentatively opening up for her were proving to be nothing but a letdown too. It was beyond depressing. Maybe when she was back at work the routine would kick in and she would shake this horrible sense of melancholy. But try as she might, she could muster up no enthusiasm for returning to London – any more than she could face the thought of staying on in Abbottsville with Evelyn.

It was a minute before she became aware that the figure walking towards her was Mike. Another person who had let her down. She didn't want to talk to him – much as he had made it clear he wanted nothing to do with her. She was done trying to please people – and that included avoiding the trolls who had been targeting her. She was ready to do battle with anyone now – they could bring it on. She didn't care. He was obviously coming to check on his precious sculpture – well, the bronze man might be stuck waiting, but she wasn't going to. She got up and began to walk away.

'Truth! Wait a sec, please!' he called out. 'I need to talk to you.'

She turned. 'Oh, so now it's alright to talk to me as opposed to, say, blank me?'

'I wasn't blanking you – I—'

'Really? You could have fooled me.'

'Well, that's just it – if you'd listen for a moment. I thought you were fooling with me.'

'What's that supposed to mean?'

'I discovered you were engaged. At least, that was what I was led to believe.'

'Led to believe?' She raised her eyebrows. 'Not that it makes any difference now – but why didn't you try asking me?'

'I could say the same to you! Why wouldn't you have told me? Or at least mentioned it to me?'

'Uh, because I *wasn't* engaged . . .? Still not, last time I checked.'

'But I didn't know that – Evelyn told me you *were* engaged . . . when I called to her flat that day with . . . something for you.'

'Evelyn told you I was engaged?'

'Yes, she was quite specific. Said the guy concerned had come over with a ring and that you'd been together for two years or something. Josh – I think she said his name was.'

'I know who Josh is.' Her eyes narrowed. 'I broke up with him three months ago.'

'Yes . . . well . . . I wasn't to know that, was I? I thought you were – well, playing me. I felt like a fool.'

'Nice to know you hold me in such high esteem.'

'Look, I get that you're angry. I should have talked to you, but I felt like an idiot. I realised that when Evelyn rang me to say she'd got it wrong – she asked me not to tell you – so . . . now it doesn't seem like it matters . . . but I was torn between coming between you and your grandmother and, well,' he ran a hand through his hair, 'like I said, I guess it doesn't really matter now – but I didn't want to leave things like this. I was angry because—' He let out a breath. 'Because I thought we had something really special going on. I know we didn't get to spend that much time together – but

I – well, I know the difference. I didn't want to get hurt, that's all. I should have said something sooner, but – this is the best I can do.'

'You have a lousy sense of timing.'

'Does that mean you're still talking to me?'

'Well, I'm listening to you, that's a start.'

'Look, I know you're going back soon – but can we just wipe the slate and pick up where we left off?'

She tilted her head. 'Remind me – where did we leave off?'

'If I'm not mistaken,' he stepped forward and took her face in his hands, 'it was somewhere about here.' He kissed her, slowly and thoroughly. Then for quite a while, neither of them said anything at all.

Chapter Sixty-Four

The lunch in the garden was to celebrate the news that little Freddy was safe, unharmed, and returned home. Stella was recovering and making progress in hospital. It was also a chance to say goodbye to Pauline and Tristan, who were going back to London and New York, respectively, later that day.

Truth had helped Nessa to set things up. Now they all – Doctor Ed, Nessa and Rory, Truth and Mike, Pauline and Tristan – sat in the shade of the big oak tree under the balmy afternoon sun and raised a glass to family and friends. Bruce and Annika were having a much-needed getaway in the country with Freddy. Evelyn was still keeping to her apartment, refusing to engage since Morah's dramatic revelation. The events of that fateful day were quite naturally being discussed.

'So is it true?' Nessa asked, still unwilling to believe the news. 'Did Evelyn really kidnap a young child to get Morah into trouble?'

'It would appear so,' Truth said. 'She admitted as much to Mum – didn't she?' She looked to Pauline.

'Yes. I'm afraid so.' Pauline nodded. 'She justified her

actions, of course, but at the end of the day, that's exactly what she did.'

Nessa let out a breath. 'I just can't believe it.'

'There *has* been a sort of quiet karma at work, though.' Doctor Ed smiled. 'As a result of discovering what really happened that day – all those years ago – and to make up for his mistaken accusations towards Morah at the time . . . Robert Radcliffe, Evelyn's old friend, has offered Morah a position as nanny to his two great-grandchildren, who now live for a large part of the year on his estate in Portugal. Morah will have her own apartment in the complex as part of the contract. She will be able to spend her free time as she wishes, and to avail of all amenities onsite. He has also offered her a retirement pension deal to go with the position. Morah is considering his offer as we speak – although she asked me to keep it to myself. But I feel sure she would be happy to have present company hear her news. But please don't mention it to anyone outside this group – especially Evelyn – until Morah has made her decision. I just thought you would all be happy to hear that a good opportunity has finally come her way after all this time. Morah's life has not been an easy one.'

'And what's the latest on Stella?' Truth asked.

'There's been progress,' Doctor Ed said. 'Although I blame myself for not spotting the warning signs earlier.' He shook his head. 'It was Morah who alerted me to the fact that things were far from happy in that situation. Stella has been evaluated by a psychiatric team and has agreed to accept help and therapy. It won't be quick or easy, but thank

God she survived the suicide attempt. She's suffering from an extreme and complex form of obsessive compulsive disorder.'

'What, like washing your hands over and over, and not skipping cracks in the pavement?' Rory asked, looking puzzled.

'That's a basic form of the condition. But there are also more insidious versions, concerning obsessive thoughts. Many sufferers believe they are about to, or indeed have already committed, some dreadful, hideous crime – even though they have not. In Stella's case, she became convinced over time that she would harm her son . . . rather than risk Bruce and Annika taking Freddy from her. She truly believed she was capable of drowning him. The tragedy was that it drove her to almost killing herself – and believing that she had taken Freddy with her.' Doctor Ed paused. 'Poor Stella. I don't think anyone has any idea what she's been suffering through. But at least her doctors have explained the situation now to her mother and to Bruce and Annika and everyone has agreed to help in any way they can. She's going to need a lot of support.'

'But at least Freddy is safe . . . and Stella is getting the help she needs. That's the main thing,' Truth said.

'It certainly is.' Doctor Ed looked around the table. 'Well, it's going to be all change here in the next few weeks. Mike's moving out . . . Morah will more than likely be moving on . . . and others undecided. Rory, I hear you're moving in.' He smiled at the lovebirds. 'It'll be nice to have a familiar face around while we play musical chairs. I'm going to miss all of you who are leaving . . . but I have a feeling we'll all stay in touch – at least I hope we do – and remain the very best of friends.' He raised a glass.

Far too soon, it seemed, Pauline and Tristan had to say their goodbyes. Hugs and phone numbers were exchanged. Plans to catch up soon put in place. 'We have to go up to say goodbye to Evelyn,' Pauline said. 'We'll call a taxi from there.'

'Please give her my very best regards,' Doctor Ed said. 'Whatever has happened or may have happened – between her and Morah – it's all in the past as far as I'm concerned. None of my business. Tell her to give me a call when she's feeling up to it.'

'I'll be sure to pass that on,' Pauline said.

'You're a good friend to our mother, Doctor Ed,' Tristan said. 'She's lucky to have you. It's been a pleasure meeting you all,' he said to the others. 'If at any time you find yourselves in New York, please look me up.'

✧

'It's good of you to come and see me before you set off. But please don't feel you have to put on an act – I know exactly what you all think of me.'

Evelyn sat down as Pauline and Tristan joined her in the sitting room. They were due to leave for the airport, but Pauline had persuaded Tristan not to leave Evelyn on bad terms. 'There's no point,' she'd said to him earlier. 'You'll only torture yourself if something does happen to her and you don't get a chance to make up. You've had such a good relationship with her it'd be silly to spoil it now, to let this one episode define it.'

'Only because I didn't know what she was capable of!' Tristan had said. 'Passing off your own flesh and blood as some convenient ex-lover's son, just to extort money from the guy, is hardly on the same scale as a family tiff – is it?'

'But you're not his son – the test was negative – and Evelyn has always adored you.' Pauline was soothing. 'It's not easy being a mother – trust me – just be nice and part on good terms – you'll be glad you did.'

Tristan had agreed grudgingly. They sat now having a glass of wine in Evelyn's flat, while they waited for the cab to pick them up.

'Have you thought about what you'll do, Mum – about the flat, I mean?' Pauline asked.

'Not yet.' Evelyn was vague. 'But I'll think of something. Don't worry about me, I've always been able to take care of myself.' If Evelyn was shaken by recent events, she wasn't letting on. She was a little pale, but defiantly upbeat.

'Well, it's been an interesting visit,' Tristan said. 'And it's good to see your new hip has settled down so well. I guess you'll be back swimming without support any day now?'

'Oh, yes, I've already been in on my own. I've had the all clear from my surgeon – it was absolutely fabulous.'

'Truth and Mike have got together,' Pauline said. 'I thought you should know.'

'So I heard.' Evelyn gave a thin smile. 'Doctor Ed told me. I believe she's moved into his spare room – hardly a surprise. Once she found out I'd told Mike she was engaged to Josh, I knew she'd never feel the same way about me.'

'I didn't tell her anything,' Pauline said. 'It wasn't me.'

'Oh, I know you didn't. And thank you for that,' Evelyn said. 'It was Mike. He told her what had happened – I should have known he would. She told me when she came to get the rest of her things. You can always rely on men to screw things up – that's one thing I've learned over the years. No offence.' She smiled at Tristan. 'It's a pity, but there you are.'

'Truth will come around, just give her a bit of time. She'll laugh about it all one day.'

'I'll miss having her around the apartment. It was fun while she was here – it was like being young all over again.'

'That's our cab.' Tristan looked at his phone. 'It's outside. We'd better get going.' He went over and kissed the cheek Evelyn proffered.

'I'm not really as terrible as you think, Tristan. I just made a mistake. You'll make a few of your own before it's all over. We all do.'

'It's okay, Mum . . . I'm over it. I'll call you when I get back to New York.'

'Thank you for allowing Truth to come over.' Evelyn took Pauline's hand and squeezed it. 'And thank you for not try-ing to turn her against me. That was good of you.'

'You did that all by yourself, Mum.'

'Yes, yes, I know. *Mea culpa*.' Evelyn rolled her eyes. 'But nonetheless I'm glad you came over, Pauline – I'm glad we got to . . . talk a bit. I don't mind telling you I'm quite in awe of you now, and what you've achieved with your life.' She tilted her head. 'Makes me feel I must have got something right, after all.'

'Don't push it, Mum.' Pauline grinned. 'But it was good to see you too. Look after yourself.'

'She's unbelievable, isn't she?' Tristan said when they were safely out of number 24 and settled in the back of the cab. 'Both remorseless and relentless.' He shook his head. 'No wonder Dad had a heart attack!'

'That's Evelyn,' said Pauline, amused at her brother's bewildered expression. 'That's our mother.'

And the cab pulled away, leaving number 24, and the elegant curve of houses on Ulysses Crescent, bathed in the late afternoon sun.

✧

'It's like this,' Evelyn said, ten days later, as she topped up Doctor Ed's wine glass. They were enjoying a bottle of Château Latour over dinner and a game of chess. Ari had left a case as a farewell gift to the doctor, knowing how fond he was of it. 'I'm in a bit of a pickle.'

'What kind of a pickle?'

'One only you can help me out of.'

'I'm flattered.'

'Don't be facetious! This is serious. I'm not going to beat about the bush.'

'Well,' Doctor Ed steepled his fingers and appeared serious, 'I will do my best to listen to your pickle, and help you out of it, of course I will.'

'I'm in a tight spot financially.' She looked him in the eye. 'A very tight spot. So much so that after this month . . . I will no longer be able to afford to stay on in my apartment – or rather *your* apartment.'

'I see.' The doctor lifted his eyebrows. 'Well, that does come as a surprise. I'm very sorry to hear that, Evelyn. How can I help? Would Mike's old flat perhaps be more—?'

'No.' She was brisk. 'I can't afford that either.'

'Well, in that case, I'm afraid, I don't see how I can—'

'You have a spare room.' She leaned her chin on her hands and regarded him across the small table. 'You know how well we get along . . . I was going to suggest that I move in with you. Think what fun we could have. I'll keep the place perfectly, I'm a good cook and, as you know, a very good . . . conversationalist.'

Doctor Ed laughed softly. 'You are indeed all of those things, and more, Evelyn. But interesting as I find your, ah, suggestion,' he returned her frank gaze, 'and much as I empathise with your current predicament . . . I'm afraid I don't think I would be able to risk jeopardising the wonderful friendship we enjoy by inviting you to move in to my all too modest abode.'

'You're turning me down?'

'I'm turning your suggestion down, yes.'

'Bugger!' She glared at him. 'Then I shall have to move out.'

'Where will you go?'

'I have no idea, but I'll think of something. It's just that I do so love living here, and I'll miss my swimming friends terribly.'

'Hmm.' Doctor Ed was thoughtful. 'Now that I come to

think of it . . . there will be another vacancy . . . something that just might work.'

'What do you mean?'

'Morah is moving out.'

'Morah?' Evelyn was surprised. 'That's the best news I've heard in weeks. Did you finally come to your senses and get rid of her?'

'On the contrary.' Doctor Ed was mild. 'A mutual friend of yours has offered her a position as nanny to his great-grandchildren . . . in Portugal. I believe Morah leaves at the end of the month.'

'Not soon enough for me.'

'Well, that's where you might be wrong . . .'

'What are you talking about?'

'Well, you see, when Morah leaves . . . there'll be a vacancy that needs filling. One I really would much rather *not* have to advertise and interview for.' He played with the stem of his wine glass. 'It may have slipped your mind, Evelyn . . . but Morah's small studio flat goes with the position of caretaker.' He sat back in his chair and smiled. 'It may be a rather unexpected solution to your predicament, but it would be a solution all the same – wouldn't it? I get a caretaker I know and trust. And you get a rent-free flat.' He watched her wrestle with the idea as realisation dawned. 'What do you say?'

Evelyn narrowed her eyes. 'You crafty old fox, you.'

'*Thank you* will do nicely. Will you take up the position, then?'

'I don't see as I have much choice in the matter, do I? Of course I'll take it. Silly not to.'

'That's the spirit.'

'You haven't told me how much I'll be paid yet.' She lifted her chin.

'I'm sure we can come to a mutually acceptable arrangement regarding your remuneration,' said Doctor Ed. 'Here's to new beginnings, dear Evelyn.'

Epilogue

Two months later . . .

Evelyn was heading out for her early-morning swim. She pulled on her red one-piece, tied up her shoulder-length hair with her favourite headband, belted her white towelling robe and paused to consider herself in the full-length mirror of her studio apartment before heading out. 'Evelyn Malone,' she said, tilting her head coquettishly at her reflection, 'you are some woman for one woman!'

As Evelyn descended the steps to Mariner's Cove, a group of regulars were already in the water or enjoying an after-swim chat and a cup of something warm. It was September now, and soon the days would be drawing in, but for now the vestiges of a warm summer were being prolonged and enjoyed, and people greeted each other warmly in the early morning.

'Hello, Peter!' Evelyn shrugged off her robe and smiled at an elderly retired judge as she passed him tottering out of the water, holding on to the hand rail. 'You're looking well! I was so sorry to hear about Dorothy . . .' She was sympathetic.

Peter straightened up slowly. 'Ah, thank you, Evelyn. It was a merciful release in many ways. She had no idea where she was or who she was for the last couple of years.'

'So difficult.' She patted his arm consolingly. 'You poor old thing! She was so lucky to have you.' She flashed a brilliant smile. 'You must find it lonely now, rattling around in that big old place of yours – I know I did when Lenny died.'

'It is very . . . disconcerting. The children are very good, but they have their own lives and families to deal with. I know they'd like me to sell the house and move into an apartment – and they're probably right, but, well . . .'

'Don't let them rush you into anything, Peter! That's the mistake I made. You know what? Why don't I make us a nice shepherd's pie this week? I can bring it over and we can have a good old chinwag – and I can give you all the advice I wish someone had told me when I was left all alone . . .'

Peter spluttered a bit and wheezed. 'That's awfully kind of you, Evelyn. I'd appreciate that very much. I still have a few excellent bottles tucked away in the wine cellar – I've been trying to come up with a reason to open them, but I've never been able to think of anyone to share one with.' His jowly face lit up.

'What a happy coincidence!' Evelyn smiled. 'How about this Friday? Would that suit?'

Peter assured her it would.

'Terrific! Let's say seven o'clock. I'm no good at late nights these days, and I'll be wanting my swim in the morning as usual.'

'Oh, me too, Evelyn. I won't be keeping you up, you can

be sure of that. But I would very much enjoy a bit of company. I'll look forward to that!'

✧

From his spot in the shade, hidden behind his newspaper, Doctor Ed witnessed the exchange and grinned to himself. Poor old Peter Robbins wouldn't stand a chance!

He knew, of course, that Evelyn was performing for his benefit. Just to let him see she wasn't *totally* reliant on the current state of play in number 24. In fairness, he could understand why. Evelyn was putting on a game show of being caretaker – but it wasn't going to last for long. He had to hand it to her – the woman had chutzpah. There was no keeping her down. He was glad to see her relationship with Truth seemed to have avoided becoming a casualty of recent events. Truth, he knew, had visited her grandmother on one of her recent trips back to see Mike – and they were still talking. He would keep Evelyn on tenterhooks for a while more, though. Two could play at this game. And they were both old pros. But the thing was, the doctor reminded himself, time was running out. They didn't have forever, however long was left. And women like Evelyn Malone rarely came around more than once in a generation. Life – whatever remained of it – would be awfully dull without her. But he would eke out the current arrangement for perhaps just a couple more months, or until things looked as if they might be becoming precarious. Then he would ask her to move in with him, and surprise her by suggesting that they share her old flat, which he had kept vacant, just as she had left it, minus the contents. He thought she might appreciate that.

Ed wasn't entirely sure when he had begun to love Evelyn, warts and all. He suspected it was from the first week she had moved in to number 24 and livened the place up – and his life – with her irrepressible attitude and energy. But that was the thing about life – as long as you were willing to grasp it with both hands, it continued to surprise you with the most unexpected developments – both good and bad. If he had learned anything at all in his seventy-eight years, it was to enjoy the good stuff for as long as it lasted. And with Evelyn in his life, the bad stuff could be faced too, with an indomitable adversary by his side.

He lowered his paper now, watching Evelyn tread water for a moment as she chatted with the regulars close to shore, then strike out to sea in her elegant backstroke.

Ed attempted to return to the headlines – whose dispiriting content failed to capture his attention, or indeed lower his buoyant mood. Instead he gave himself up to savouring the light breeze that rustled the pages, the sight of Dublin Bay stretching to the blue horizon, the thought of an evening gin and tonic in his beloved garden. He was grateful for his health, for the exchange of warm greetings as good friends passed him by . . . and most of all, for the prospect of the new day that lay ahead, brimming with possibility.

Acknowledgements

Grateful thanks as always to the wonderful team at Hachette Ireland, in particular to Editorial Director Ciara Doorley, and Marketing Director Joanna Smyth. hanks also to Donna Hillyer, to Aonghus Meaney for copy editing and to Emma Dunne for proofreading. And grateful thanks to my agent Megan Carroll (@MeganACarroll).

Research is one of the aspects I most enjoy when undertaking a new book. Both Elizabeth O'Kane (@okaneliz) and Aidan Harte (@aidanhartesculptor) gave generously of their time and expertise in this respect. Any mistakes in this area are my own.

For those interested in learning more about the Lost Wax method of casting bronze, I suggest following the link here to Elizabeth O'Kane's website where this fascinating process is explained in detail: https://elizabethokane. com/bronze-casting-process/

Thanks to the usual suspects who said a prayer or lit a candle (you know who you are!).

And grateful thanks to you, dear reader, you make the long, sometimes challenging hours at the laptop worthwhile. I really hope you enjoy *The Houseshare*, do let me know – and if you would be kind enough to post a review on Amazon or Goodreads, or post a comment on social media #thehouseshare that would be truly appreciated.

'The perfect holiday read'
IRISH EXAMINER

the
summer
we were friends

Summer has arrived in Derrybeggs and the biggest event of the year, the annual film festival, is less than a month away. But as the days pass, it becomes clear that nothing will go as planned . . .

Dot came to the seaside town for a fresh start and so far her B&B is proving popular. But fitting in isn't quite as easy. Dot thought joining the troubled festival committee would help, but she's really starting to wonder if moving to Derrybeggs was a mistake.

Marine biologist Merry spends her days working at her parents' café and trying not to think about the happiness she could have had. Everyone whispers about the tragic accident that destroyed her dream life in Florida. But Merry is the only one who knows the truth.

When an intriguing American visitor arrives at the café with no memory of who he is or why he's in Derrybeggs, Dot and Merry set aside their own problems and rally the community to help him find his way home. As the search gets underway and the countdown to the festival begins in earnest, everyone is about to discover what it really means to belong.

When handsome American Daniel O'Connell arrives in Ballyanna to research an old cable station for a documentary he is making, he's hoping that a stay in a sleepy Irish seaside town will help him and his traumatised son move on from a terrible accident. But Daniel soon finds that summer in Ballyanna is anything but quiet . . .

Meanwhile Annie Sullivan, daughter of the local hotel owner, has moved back home to mend her broken heart, telling everyone that she's there to figure out her next career move.

But as a secret threatens Annie's dysfunctional family, Daniel's past is about to catch up with him. Will the two be able to grasp the new future that lies ahead before summer ends?